The Cucu

Cousin Hilda opened the door, and Henry re-entered
her house with a deep sense of nostalgic gloom marbled
with affection. To walk across her dark, cold hall was to
embark upon a voyage of nasal nostalgia that made
Proust's madeleines seem insignificant by comparison.
Henry was met by the mingled smells of cabbage and
linoleum, of the dankness of darkness and the acridity
of burning coke, the whole pot-pourri warmed by the
succulent nourishing aroma of giant bloomers being
aired, and spiced with the only slightly less nourishing
imminence of toad-in-the-hole and sponge pudding
with chocolate sauce. Faithful readers will deduce that
it was a Wednesday.

David Nobbs was born in Orpington, the only son of a
schoolmaster. He has written many successful novels,
several of which he has adapted for television (*The Fall
and Rise of Reginald Perrin, A Bit of a Do* and *The Life and
Times of Henry Pratt*). He has also written the television
series *Rich Tea and Sympathy, The Glamour Girls* and
Fairly Secret Army, and the television plays *Cupid's
Darts, Our Young Mr Wignall* and *Stalag Luft*. He lives in
North Yorkshire.

The Cucumber Man

David Nobbs

Mandarin

A Mandarin Paperback
THE CUCUMBER MAN

First published in Great Britain 1994
by Methuen London
This edition published 1995
by Mandarin Paperbacks
an imprint of Reed International Books Ltd
Michelin House, 81 Fulham Road, London SW3 6RB
and Auckland, Melbourne, Singapore and Toronto

Reprinted 1995 (twice), 1996 (twice)

Copyright © 1994 by David Nobbs
The author has asserted his moral rights

A CIP catalogue record for this title
is available from the British Library
ISBN 0 7493 2267 5

Printed and bound in Great Britain
by Cox & Wyman Ltd, Reading, Berkshire

Contents

1 An Interesting Appointment

There was full employment in 1957, but there is an exception to every rule. The exception to this particular rule turned to his wife Hilary and said, 'Do you think I'll ever get another job?'

Henry Pratt was sitting on the lower end of a sadly subsiding settee in a rented ground floor flat in Stickleback Rise. He was twenty-two years old, pale, five foot seven tall, on the podgy side, and wearing reading glasses. It was Monday, September 30th. There were 11.72½ marks to the pound, winter fares for flying small cars across the English Channel had been reduced to £3 10s, paratroopers were on guard as black pupils attended the High School in Little Rock, Alabama, and it was raining in Thurmarsh.

That morning, a letter had arrived from the BBC, informing Henry that he had not got the researcher's job for which he had applied. In the last week he had also failed to become a public relations officer for ICI, and a reserves manager with the Royal Society for the Protection of Birds. Nevertheless, Hilary still had faith in him. 'Of course you'll get a job,' she said. She kissed him, and the springs went 'boing'. The settee, like Henry's career, was proving a disappointment.

An occasional car whooshed along the wet road, a tram rattled past on its way to Thurmarsh Lane Bottom, and, on the mantelpiece, above the hissing gas fire, the elegant art deco clock struck eight soft chimes. A wedding present from Lampo Davey and Denzil Ackerman, it provided the only touch of style in the unremittingly brown, bulkily furnished flat.

To add to Henry's feeling of inadequacy, Hilary had got the first job for which she had applied. From January she would be teaching English at Thurmarsh Grammar School for Girls, where she had been a repressed and depressed pupil less than five years ago.

She snuggled closer to Henry and kissed him again. 'Boing', went the springs. 'You're still my lovely lover,' said Hilary.

Henry smiled. He was a lucky man to have won the love of this pale, serene, beautiful woman.

8.00 became 8.07. Tick of clock. Hiss of fire. Whoosh of tyre. Boing!

It was impossible to imagine that, on that very evening, a world which didn't seem to care would send not one but two visitors, both of them with kind intentions, to Flat 1, 33, Stickleback Rise, Thurmarsh.

The first visitor was Howard Lewthwaite, Hilary's father. He was pale and looked all of his fifty years. The lines on his face were etched deep. He sat in the only armchair, accepted a cup of coffee, and gulped it eagerly, as if he feared that without its stimulus he might gently expire.

'I hope I haven't interrupted anything,' he said. 'You've had your tea, have you?' The Lewthwaites ate dinner, but he called it tea, because he was deputy leader of the majority Labour group on Thurmarsh Borough Council, and couldn't afford to be thought a snob.

'Yes, we've had our tea,' said Hilary.

They'd had sausages and mash, with two cups of tea each. They hadn't enough money to be sophisticated.

'I'm the sole cause of your unemployment, Henry,' said Howard Lewthwaite.

'That's ridiculous,' said Henry.

'Ridiculous,' echoed Hilary.

'No, no. No, no. You had a great scoop. It would have launched you on your journalistic career. You couldn't write it up, because my disgrace would have broken Hilary's heart. The sole cause.'

Neither Henry nor Hilary spoke. If a person is determined to take all the blame, there is nothing you can do. Besides, they had never discussed her father's misdeeds. Henry hadn't even wanted her to know about them, but Howard had insisted on 'wiping the slate clean'.

'I want to help you,' said Howard Lewthwaite. 'I'd like to pay your rent, but I can't. The golden age of drapery is over. One day, not this year, maybe not even next year, but soon, Lewthwaite's will fail. A hundred and seventeen years of family trading will cease. The proud tradition will crumble in my hands.'

'It's kind of you to come round to cheer us up,' said Henry, and Hilary gave him a warning look. He put his right hand on her left knee and felt a stirring of desire. It was, albeit by a narrow margin, his favourite of her knees.

'Naddy needs constant care.' Howard Lewthwaite's Yugoslavian wife Nadežda was crippled by polio. 'We hope Sam will go to university. He'll need a certain level of support for many years.'

'It's all right,' said Henry. 'I don't need money. I'll get a job.'

'Of course he will,' said Hilary staunchly.

'Of course you will,' said Howard Lewthwaite. 'After all . . .'

He hesitated. Henry, hoping that a ringing endorsement of his qualities as man, husband and potential employee would follow, composed his face into a suitably modest expression.

'After all, everybody gets a job in the end,' said Howard Lewthwaite.

'I'll be working from January,' said Hilary.

'Couldn't you get work as a teacher, Henry?' asked Howard Lewthwaite.

Henry shook his head. 'I went to too many schools as a child. I couldn't face any more.'

'I suppose they're looking for people with degrees, anyway,' said Howard Lewthwaite. He smiled warmly at Henry. Henry's answering smile was just a trifle strained. 'Anyway, Naddy and I don't think that your modest savings should be frittered away in rent, and we'd like to offer you a room in our house until you're both working and can afford a mortgage.'

He beamed, confident that his offer was irresistible. Slowly, his smile foundered on the long silence that ensued.

Henry looked at Hilary and realised that for the first time in their brief marriage he didn't know what she was thinking. He stroked her knee and felt an aching longing and an unaccustomed bleakness.

He knew what *he* was thinking. He was thinking that he didn't want to share his wife with her family. He didn't want to compare her slender loveliness with her mother's crippled body. He didn't want her obnoxious fifteen-year-old brother Sam banging on their bedroom door and shouting, 'Are you two having it off in there or can I come in?' He didn't want Howard Lewthwaite's guilt with their dinner that was called tea every night. He dreaded the faint amusement which he knew would greet the discovery that they had both started to write novels. He couldn't bear the thought of making love to Hilary in the room in which she had suffered her childhood depressions. Above all, he hated the thought of having to express any of these reservations to Hilary.

He caught her eye and wondered if *she* knew what *he* was thinking.

Hiss. Whoosh. Tick. It was becoming imperative for somebody to say something.

'That's very kind of you, Howard,' he said. 'Incredibly kind.'

'Amazingly kind,' agreed Hilary.

'I see,' said Howard Lewthwaite flatly. 'You don't want to come. The institution of the extended family in advanced Western societies has broken down irretrievably. I was a fool not to realise it.'

Henry 'You have a lively mind but it is our feeling that you are too creative a person to function well as a member of a team' Pratt looked to his wife for support. She didn't fail him.

'That's absurd, Daddy,' she said. 'It's an incredibly kind offer, but we need to think about it. We need to consider its implications for our sense of independence and our mutual self-fulfilment.'

Howard Lewthwaite nodded. 'That's fair enough,' he said. 'You're speaking my language there.' He stood up somewhat stiffly. His back was giving him gyp, and his temper hadn't been improved by his doctor's explanation that we were designed to walk on all fours, not on two legs, thereby implying that our endless pain is entirely the result of the hubris of the species and is in no way caused by the incompetence of the medical profession.

'Thank you for the coffee,' he said. 'It's love and support that

4

we're offering you. I can't pretend you'd be independent, but I hope we could do it in a way that isn't incompatible with your mutual self-fulfilment. Anyway, the offer's still on the table.'

Henry went to the door with him, shook his hand warmly, and came back into a room that suddenly seemed far too small. He felt awful. He didn't know what to say. He stroked Hilary's knee again, but the gesture was mechanical and he felt no stirrings.

'I agree with you,' said Hilary.

'Agree with what?'

'What you were thinking. Sam being impossible, Mummy crippled, Daddy guilty, our both writing novels seeming faintly amusing.'

Henry felt a surge of love and admiration and relief, but also a cold wind of unease. He was beginning to feel that Hilary was very much cleverer than he was. His novel wasn't coming on well. She said that hers wasn't either, but he wasn't sure that he believed her. He felt a twinge of jealousy, and didn't like the feeling.

'So what do we do?' he asked. 'Turn it down?'

'It's not easy to do that, is it?' said Hilary. 'It'll hurt them deeply, and it does make financial sense.'

Henry 'After careful consideration, although we believe you have a great deal to offer, we do not think public relations is necessarily the right field for you' Pratt nodded glumly. He felt awful.

He was still feeling awful twenty minutes later, when Cousin Hilda called.

Cousin Hilda refused even the limited comfort offered by the armchair. Hard chairs are more suited to life on earth, her rigid pose asserted. She sat with her legs slightly apart, as women do who have no thought of sex and its attendant dangers, and with stockings as thick as hers, and pale pink bloomers as voluminous as hers, she had never been exposed to its dangers.

'I'm sorry to call so late,' she said. She made it sound as if she was being unbelievably bold in calling at eleven minutes past nine. 'But I had my gentlemen to see to.'

'It's very kind of you to come at all,' said Hilary.

'Well, we haven't got much on tonight after Tony Hancock, to say we pay for a licence,' said Cousin Hilda. 'There's *Panorama*, and that's depressing, and so's the news, and *Picture Parade*'s no use to me because when can I get to the pictures, with my gentlemen to see to, and then there's ballroom dancing, and I've never been right bothered about dancing, it only leads to things, and anyroad it includes that rock and roll. On the BBC! Can you believe it?'

'How *are* your gentlemen?' enquired Henry.

'Mr O'Reilly doesn't change,' said Cousin Hilda. 'Mr Pettifer's never had quite the same spring in his step since he were taken off the cheese counter. I've lost Mr Peters. I've a Mr Ironside instead, but only through the week. He has family in Norfolk.' Cousin Hilda paused and went slightly pink. 'I've had a chapter of disasters with my fourth room.'

'Disasters?' said Hilary gently.

'Drink,' whispered Cousin Hilda, as if the gas fire might disapprove if it heard. 'And worse.'

'Worse!' said Henry. 'The mind boggles.'

'Well it might,' said Cousin Hilda, luckily missing the irony. 'Well it might. That's how I lost Mr Peters.' There was silence. Cousin Hilda was clearly torn between the need to unburden herself and the enormous difficulty of broaching a painful subject.

'Tell us what happened,' said Hilary gently.

'This man came recommended,' said Cousin Hilda. 'He were a regional under-manager with Timothy White's. Timothy White's, I ask you, a respectable firm! He made . . . he made . . .'

'Certain suggestions to Mr Peters?' prompted Henry.

Cousin Hilda nodded her gratitude, and sniffed violently.

'Times are changing,' said Hilary.

'You're right, Hilary,' said Cousin Hilda fervently. 'You are so right. You have a very sensible wife, Henry.'

Henry was thrilled by this unparalleled high praise from Cousin Hilda, albeit slightly hurt by the surprise in her tone.

Cousin Hilda leant forward, and Henry realised that she was winding herself up for something momentous.

'We had fun at number 66, didn't we, in the old days?' she said.

Henry tried to hide his astonishment.

'Oh yes,' he said. 'Lots of fun.'

'Plenty of good chin-wags.'

'Yes indeed. Very good chin-wags.'

'I've never been a great one for talk at table, and there were moments when I disapproved. I regret that now. Those meals, Henry, when you lived with me, they were the happiest times of my life.'

Henry could feel his heart thudding.

'It's different now,' said Cousin Hilda. 'Mr O'Reilly's never exactly been a live wire, Mr Pettifer's a shadow of his former self, at weekends when Mr Ironside's gone it's like a morgue. I have a little nest egg. I don't live particularly extravagantly. I don't need the rent from my fourth room, and you'll not want to be paying out rent every week when you're not working.'

Henry felt that he was drowning. He couldn't bear the thought of married life under Cousin Hilda's roof, in the little room which had been home to him from the time he had left Dalton College until he had bravely moved out into a flat early last year. He clutched Hilary's hand.

'I'm too old to cope with any more under-managers from Timothy White's or Macfisheries with their ideas.' Cousin Hilda, who must have been into her fifties by now, sniffed. 'I'd like it very much if you made my home your home.'

To Henry's horror, Hilary burst into tears.

'I'm sorry,' she said, 'but that is so kind of you.'

Cousin Hilda looked at Hilary as if regretting her use of the word 'sensible'. She sniffed disapprovingly.

Hilary blew her nose violently. 'I'm sorry,' she said.

Cousin Hilda's mouth was working with tension, and she had gone pink again.

'There is one other matter,' she said.

She pressed her legs together and Henry realised to his horror that she was going to talk about sex. Sweat was running down his back.

'I don't doubt that I strike you as odd and old-fashioned,' continued Cousin Hilda.

Even Hilary's famous tact was unequal to the task of denying this.

'However.' Cousin Hilda was remorseless. 'Even I am aware that there is a side to marriage in which folk . . . do things.' She had begun to sweat as well. Henry had never seen her sweat before. 'I know that it's the duty of married folk to do these things, otherwise there'd be no procreation of the human race.' Cousin Hilda was clinging rigidly to her chair. Her knuckles had gone white. 'I want you to know that you'd be welcome to . . . er . . . do your duty in my house whenever tha wants. Except mealtimes. Also, the normal bathtime restrictions would not apply. You could bath as often as you wished, provided that you didn't clash with my gentlemen.'

Cousin Hilda stopped at last and tried to smile.

Tick. Hiss. Whoosh.

Henry didn't dare look at Hilary. 'Thank you very much, Cousin Hilda,' he said in a stilted voice. 'That's a very kind offer, and well worth thinking about. Isn't it, Hilary?'

'It certainly is,' said Hilary. 'Very kind.'

'The thing is,' said Henry. 'The thing is . . . Hilary's father has offered us a room in their house.'

Cousin Hilda's lips began to work again.

'I see,' she said. 'I see. And you'd rather go there. More of a home. More fun than an ageing spinster and her gentlemen. I understand.'

'We haven't decided anything,' said Hilary with just a hint of asperity. 'These are very important suggestions, for which we're extremely grateful, but they'd change our lives considerably, and we really do have to think carefully about them.'

'Of course,' said Cousin Hilda. 'Of course. It were foolish of me to think you'd jump at my offer.'

And she sniffed twice, once in disgust at her own emotions and once in disapproval of her inability to hide them.

Henry and Hilary agonised after Cousin Hilda had gone. Hiss, tick, whoosh, and barely a boing. Who would they least offend if they accepted the other's offer? Which prospect filled them with the lesser dread? Wouldn't it be easier just to stay put? But why should they continue to pay rent when they didn't need to? And if they stayed, would they not simply offend both parties? They couldn't make up their minds, so they went to bed and did their bit for the procreation of the human race instead.

In the morning, as every morning, Hilary worked on her novel, and Henry pretended to work on his. Then, over their frugal lunch of Wensleydale cheese and digestive biscuits with plum chutney, they went back over the arguments of the night before, and reached a decision. Their solution was a good old British compromise, which would please nobody. They would spend half the time before Hilary began working with her family, and half at Cousin Hilda's, and then they would rent another flat, whether Henry had a job or not. They decided to go to Cousin Hilda's first, so that they wouldn't have to spend Christmas there. Henry couldn't bear the thought of another Christmas with Mrs Wedderburn and ginger cordial and Mr O'Reilly in a paper hat and the heady excitement of post-prandial Snap.

And so, just over a week later, Henry 'While we are impressed by your personality and enthusiasm we do not consider that you have the experience or physique needed to run a bird reserve' Pratt and his lovely wife Hilary caught a tram and a bus, because to travel by taxi would have been to incur an enormous sniff of disapproval right at the outset, and arrived at Cousin Hilda's stone, semi-detached house in Park View Road just twenty minutes after the hired van that had brought their worldly possessions in three suitcases and two packing cases.

Cousin Hilda opened the door, and Henry re-entered her house with a deep sense of nostalgic gloom marbled with affection. To walk across her dark, cold hall was to embark upon a voyage of nasal nostalgia that made Proust's madeleines seem insignificant by comparison. Henry was met by the mingled smells of cabbage and linoleum, of the dankness of darkness and the acridity of burning

9

coke, the whole pot-pourri warmed by the succulent nourishing aroma of giant bloomers being aired, and spiced with the only slightly less nourishing imminence of toad-in-the-hole and sponge pudding with chocolate sauce. Faithful readers will deduce that it was a Wednesday.

And so, that late Wednesday afternoon, as the sun sank with Henry's and Hilary's hearts, they arranged their relatively meagre possessions around the tiny little second storey fourth bedroom of number 66, Park View Road. The art deco clock went on the tiny mantelpiece. They didn't dare, in these stern surroundings, to unpack the bookends given them by Auntie Doris and Geoffrey Porringer. These had a naked man at one end and a naked woman at the other, and if the naked man was meant to be thinking about a book, it must have been *Lady Chatterley's Lover*. Their books remained in the packing cases with the bookends.

The room's furniture consisted of a severely sagging sofa which converted into a severely sagging three-quarter size bed at night, one hard chair, two small bedside tables with circles where Cousin Hilda's gentlemen had rested mugs of cocoa, and a rickety and wholly inadequate wardrobe cum chest of drawers. There were two pictures, the depressed monarch of a wet and misty glen, and a portrait of John Wesley in an unusually gloomy mood even for him.

'Ah well,' said Henry bravely. 'Our toad-in-the-hole awaits. I could do with a good chin-wag.'

And indeed at first the atmosphere round the little table in the blue basement room was quite lively. Mr O'Reilly rose to heights of eloquence unknown in his quiet life. 'It's very good to have you back, Mr Henry,' he said. 'Oh yes indeed. Very good. Oh, we had some fun in the old days, didn't we? Yes indeed. And now your lovely lady too. Yes yes,' and then he went very red and subsided into shiny silence.

'Welcome back,' said Norman Pettifer. 'Any novelty is welcome when one spends one's life putting tins on shelves.'

'Brian Ironside,' announced Brian Ironside.

'I believe you have family in Norfolk,' said Hilary.

'Yes,' said Brian Ironside.

'Which part of Norfolk?' persisted Hilary bravely.

'Swaffham,' admitted Brian Ironside reluctantly.

'It must be a difficult journey,' quipped Henry wittily.

'It is,' countered Brian Ironside thoughtfully.

'What line are you in, Brian?' asked Henry.

'Communications,' said Brian Ironside.

'Do you go to the theatre much, Hilary?' asked Norman Pettifer.

'Not as much as we'd like to,' said Hilary.

'I once saw Johnny Gielgud,' said Norman Pettifer.

'Really?' said Hilary. 'What in?'

'Regent Street,' said Norman Pettifer. 'He was coming out of Austin Reed's.'

Liam O'Reilly, who had never been to London, sighed, and there was a brief silence.

'Well come on, Henry, Hilary,' said Cousin Hilda. 'Tell us about your plans.'

'We're both writing novels,' said Henry.

Cousin Hilda sniffed twice, once for each novel, and gave Hilary a disappointed glance, as if to say, 'Nothing surprises me about Henry, but I thought you were sensible.'

Novels having fallen so flat, Henry felt a desperate need to change the subject. 'Is young Adrian still making a mess of the cheese counter, Norman?' he asked.

'Mess is not the word,' said Norman Pettifer through clamped lips. 'Farce, fiasco and cock-up are three other examples of total linguistic inadequacy. There isn't a word in the dictionary to do justice to what Adrian has done to the cheese counter.'

Norman Pettifer's bitterness, allied to Brian Ironside's reticence and Liam O'Reilly's exhaustion, cast rather a damper on the proceedings, and the sponge pudding with chocolate sauce was taken in silence.

Nevertheless, when her gentlemen had gone, Cousin Hilda smiled and said, 'Well, that were right nice. It's been so cheerless recently, as if I've been doing it all too long. You've given me a new lease of life.'

'It really is extremely kind of you to have us,' said Hilary.

'Nonsense,' said Cousin Hilda. 'What are families for? Incidentally,' she added, dashing their hopes of an early escape to the pub, 'please don't feel obliged to leave when my gentlemen do. Treat this room as your home.'

'Actually we were thinking of popping down to the park before the light faded,' lied Henry.

'It closes at six thirty,' said Cousin Hilda. 'You'll be too late.' She leant forward, to take them further into her confidence. 'I've had to make sacrifices for my gentlemen,' she admitted. 'I've never really been able to say that this house is my home.'

Henry and Hilary were astounded.

'Not your home?' echoed Henry emptily.

'Not as such. Not in the sense that Mrs Wedderburn's house is her home.'

'But your house is full of people and hers is so lifeless.'

'She has a parlour.'

'But she never uses it.'

'Of course she doesn't. That's the point of a parlour,' explained Cousin Hilda. 'It's a place for your best things.'

'But then you never use your best things,' said Henry.

'Of course not. Then they don't spoil,' said Cousin Hilda.

'Well what's the use of having them, then?' asked Henry.

'You know they're there,' said Hilary.

'Exactly,' said Cousin Hilda, and Hilary felt that she had regained some of the approval she had lost over the novel.

Little did Cousin Hilda know that, if ever Hilary had any best things, she would use them regularly.

But would she ever have any best things? It didn't seem likely that night, as they turned their sagging sofa into a sagging bed, clambered into it, realised how much it creaked, and attempted to do their duty towards the procreation of the human race.

'It's no use,' said Henry at last. 'It's not just Cousin Hilda. I don't want to make Mr O'Reilly envious and Norman Pettifer even more bitter. It's the thought of them all, down there, listening, wondering.'

'Well never mind,' said Hilary. 'Seven weeks isn't long, and you're still my lovely man.'

The next morning, Hilary and her lovely man walked over to the Alderman Chandler Memorial Park, where Henry, when he had thought he was a homosexual, had followed a fair-haired boy from the grammar school, and later, once he had realised that he wasn't a homosexual, had asked Stefan Prziborski about precautions. Now, twenty-two years old, married, with a beautiful wife whose small, shapely breasts and trim bottom he adored – how could he ever have thought her scrawny, even in Siena? – he ought to be feeling happy in the warm October sunshine. But he wasn't. For one thing, the park was failing him. It was very much as he had remembered – there were still very few animals in the cages, one of the swings was still broken, most of the glass in the Old Men's Shelter was still missing, and there weren't nearly as many varieties of duck on the pond as on the board which showed pictures of all the ducks that were supposed to be on the pond. But none of that had ever mattered, because the park had been a huge expanse, redolent of adventure and discovery. Now it had shrunk. It was small and neat.

Were their lives going to be small and neat? No! They were fighters. They wouldn't allow themselves to be dispirited by their surroundings.

Henry led Hilary home boldly. On the gravel drive they met Cousin Hilda with her shopping bag. 'Don't worry. I'll only be gone while half eleven,' she told them.

The gentlemen were all at work, and Cousin Hilda would be at the shops till half past eleven! Barely, if ever, can a sofa bed have creaked so much at 66, Park View Road, Thurmarsh.

Bravely, in the days to come, Henry and Hilary sat, one on the hard chair, the other on the converted sofa, with their manuscripts on the bedside tables. Bravely, Henry pretended to write his novel, but he already knew, in his heart, that he wasn't a novelist.

Bravely, Henry applied for further jobs. Bravely, he went for interviews. Bravely, he shrugged off the fact that his managerial genius was not recognised by British Railways, Blue Arrow or Thurmarsh Bottling Limited. Let the nation suffer late trains, unsuitable appointments and bottle shortages. See if he cared.

Bravely, Henry and Hilary adjusted the pattern of their love-making to the rhythms of Cousin Hilda's shopping. Four times a week was well above the national average, anyway, and if Monday (bread and household goods) and Tuesday (meat and vegetables) were rather rushed affairs, Thursday (meat, bread and groceries) and Friday (fish, meat, vegetables and sundries) were really quite leisurely.

Bravely, every afternoon, come rain or shine, they set off, across Cousin Hilda's dark, cold hall, past the barometer which, being slightly wrongly adjusted, took almost as pessimistic a view of the prospects as did its owner, and plunged into the knotted streets of Thurmarsh for an hour's brisk walk. Once or twice, nostalgia tempted Henry towards the dingy back-to-back terraces of Paradise Lane, where he had been born, and they gazed into the murky waters of the River Rundle, into which he had been pushed eighteen years ago, and into the marginally less poisonous waters of the Rundle and Gadd Navigation, into which he had been thrown eleven years ago, and he hoped, over-optimistically, as it turned out, that he would never be deposited in either of them again.

Bravely, they sat with Liam O'Reilly, who interspersed his silences with the occasional burst of gratitude for their return and regret at its impermanence; with Norman Pettifer, who grew gradually more disillusioned by their lack of knowledge of the theatrical greats; and with Brian Ironside, who unbent so dramatically under Hilary's gentle probing that in less than a month she had learnt the names and ages of his three children.

Bravely, they ate their toad-in-the-hole and sponge pudding with chocolate sauce on six more Wednesdays, their roast pork and tinned pears on seven Thursdays, their battered cod and jam roly-poly on seven Fridays, their roast beef preceded by Yorkshire pudding on seven Sundays, their liver and bacon and rhubarb crumble on seven Mondays, and their roast lamb and spotted dick on seven Tuesdays. How wrong Henry had been last January, when he had thought that he was eating his last spotted dick ever.

But what of Saturday, the careful reader cries.

Showing reserves of courage that can only be marvelled at, Henry and Hilary informed Cousin Hilda that they would be having a night out every Saturday.

'*Every* Saturday?' she exclaimed.

'Well, that's only once a week,' said Hilary. 'And we thought if we did it on a regular basis you'd know where you were.'

If they expected gratitude for this consideration, they were to be disappointed.

On the first of their seven Saturdays out, Henry and Hilary went to Troutwick, Gateway to Upper Mitherdale, to visit his Auntie Doris, who ran the two-star White Hart Hotel with her second husband, the slimy Geoffrey Porringer.

Auntie Doris could not be described as happy. She still loved her first husband, Henry's Uncle Teddy, whom she believed to have died in a fire at his night club, the Cap Ferrat in Thurmarsh. The fact that he was living in the South of France, and bigamously married to a girl who had been Hilary's best friend at school, had the effect of drawing Hilary into the circle of deceit and misapprehension, and making her feel thoroughly at ease with Auntie Doris. But then everyone felt thoroughly at ease with Auntie Doris. She was a splendid landlady. She had found her niche, and had suddenly grown huge without ceasing to look glamorous and attractive. She was fighting the effects of age and the enormous spirits that she now drank with enormous spirit, and if she spent more on herself than on redecorating the pub, that was part of its charm. Not for nothing had it become known throughout the Yorkshire Dales not as 'The White Hart' but as 'Doris's'.

Nobody, on the other hand, felt at ease with Geoffrey Porringer, because he didn't feel at ease with himself. And this, to Henry, was his saving grace, which was why Henry now called him Uncle Geoffrey, which Geoffrey Porringer liked, even though Geoffrey Porringer still referred to him as 'young sir', which Henry hated.

And so, as the young farmers bought pink gins for pink Doris in the antiques-stuffed lounge, Henry and Hilary sipped quietly with Geoffrey Porringer, who said, 'A novel, eh, young sir? Whatever next?' And when Henry told him that Hilary was also writing a novel, he said, 'Both of you, eh? Well well. Clever stuff.' And then he added, 'I read a novel once. Not my cup of tea. Still, more power to your elbows,' and when Hilary suggested that maybe he should try another novel, because novels did vary enormously, he said, 'No, no. It was rubbish, it's true, but it was the fact that it didn't happen that I couldn't cope with. Didn't seem any point to it. Still, I'll try your stuff. You're family. That's different.'

'Speaking of family,' said Auntie Doris, leaving the serving momentarily to her three stressed barmen, 'can you really live with the Sniffer?'

'She's very kind,' said Hilary.

'Oh yes,' said Auntie Doris. 'She's very kind, granted, but. . . ,' she lowered her voice, 'can you make love in a place like that?'

'Oh yes,' said Henry. 'She goes shopping four times a week.'

Auntie Doris's chins wobbled on her face, and her gins wobbled in her glass, and her breasts wobbled in their outsize bra, and farmers and vets and blacksmiths smiled and said, 'There goes Doris. Off again. Wonder what's tickled her this time,' and Auntie Doris said, 'I'll tell you what's tickled me this time,' and she told the story of Henry and Hilary's love-making; and Hilary went pale and smiled and hated it, and Henry went red and grinned and found to his surprise that he loved it, and Geoffrey Porringer slid into the shadow of his wife's personality and slipped a whisky into his beer when she wasn't looking.

And on the seventh of their Saturdays out, when they visited Auntie Doris and Geoffrey Porringer again, Henry and Hilary found that the joke was rumbling on. 'You look well, young sir, young madam. Hilda's obviously been shopping a lot,' said Geoffrey Porringer, whose blackheads seemed worse than ever.

They had extra staff on, so Henry and Hilary were able to have dinner with Auntie Doris and Geoffrey Porringer, in the small cosy restaurant with its low-beamed ceiling, fine Welsh dresser and moderate English food.

They were handed their menus by a very pregnant Lorna Lugg, née Arrow. Henry had to stop himself flinching visibly at the sight of his childhood sweetheart so enormous with child by Eric Lugg, his childhood tormentor. Her face, once so pert and lovely, was plump and almost bovine now.

He felt an unworthy desire to say something incredibly clever and witty, to show Lorna how much more there was to life than Eric Lugg could provide. It was easy to fight off this desire, since he couldn't think of anything clever or witty.

'Hello, Lorna, how long till the big event?' he said.

'Three weeks,' said his former sweetheart. 'This is me last neet.' How broad her accent was. How Henry hated that and how he hated himself for hating it.

'This is my wife, Hilary,' he said. 'Hilary, this is Lorna.'

'Hello, Hilary,' said Lorna Lugg. 'Nice to meet you. The soup of the day is vegetable, and the fish of the day is haddock.'

'It's nice to meet you too,' said Hilary. 'I've heard a lot about you. Can you tell me, is the pâté rough or smooth?'

When Lorna had taken their orders, the thing for which Henry had been longing occurred, but in the wrong context. He was offered a job at last.

'Come and be my restaurant manager,' said Auntie Doris.

'I can't,' said Henry. 'Hilary's got a job at Thurmarsh Grammar in January.'

'You can work here too, Hilary,' said Auntie Doris. 'A family hotel. A family business. Think what pleasure that'll give my poor Teddy, if he finds out.'

Henry's blood ran cold. Could Auntie Doris know that Uncle Teddy was still alive?

'How could he?' he said, trying to sound casual.

'No,' said Auntie Doris. 'He couldn't. Not from down there.'

Did she mean Cap Ferrat? Did she know it all? Henry couldn't trust himself to speak.

'Down there?' said Hilary. 'Down where?'

'Hell, of course,' said Auntie Doris. 'I loved my darling Teddy, but I can't pretend there was a chance of his getting into the other place.'

And she roared her new 'landlady with big personality' laugh.

Geoffrey Porringer frowned and looked sulky, either at Auntie Doris's reference to her darling Teddy or at the prospect of Henry and Hilary joining the staff of the White Hart.

'Thank you for the offer,' said Henry, 'but it's the wrong trade for me. I like my drink too much.'

'It does take some people that way,' said Auntie Doris, 'but it won't if you've got anything to you.'

On Tuesday, November 26th, 1957, President Eisenhower suffered a mild stroke, two RAF Canberras were destroyed by sabotage in Cyprus, an acoustics engineer in a restaurant in Chicago 'proved' that women were the noiser sex, and Henry Pratt ate what he hoped would be his last spotted dick ever.

The atmosphere round the little table in the basement room with the roaring blue-tiled stove was tense and stifling. Cousin Hilda could barely eat, and Henry had a lump in his throat, which is not a good idea when you're eating spotted dick.

'We'll miss you, Mr Henry,' said Mr O'Reilly. 'And you, of course, Miss Hilary. Oh yes.'

'It's been very nice to meet you both,' said Brian Ironside, to general astonishment.

'All good things come to an end,' said Cousin Hilda.

It was Hilary who found it difficult to make love in her family's pleasant brick house in Perkin Warbeck Drive. Her brother Sam, sixteen now, had become marginally more sophisticated and marginally less obnoxious. Instead of the crude, 'Are you two having it off in there?' that Henry had feared, he banged on their door and yelled, 'Are you two having coitus interruptus in there?' 'We don't have coitus interruptus, dope,' Hilary replied. 'You do when I'm around,' gloated Sam, and he burst in to find them

18

rearranging their clothes in the ample chest of drawers. As there were no locks on the doors, Hilary lived in constant fear that Sam would enter, so they could only make love during school hours. Henry, on the other hand, wanted Howard Lewthwaite to know that his daughter's husband wasn't falling down on the job, so he wanted to make love when Howard Lewthwaite was in. But the only time when Howard Lewthwaite was in and Sam was out was early closing day. Wednesday afternoon was therefore reserved for their main bout of the week. Every Wednesday afternoon, Hilary would say, 'We've got work to do,' and, as they left the room, Henry would turn and wink at Howard Lewthwaite, without Hilary knowing, as she would have been horrified, and without Nadežda seeing, as she would have been upset. Hilary feared that the knowledge that they were making love would upset her mother by bringing home to her what she was missing due to her crippled state.

'She must know we make love,' Henry pointed out. 'She must hope we make love, because she loves you.'

'Yes, theoretically she must. But at this particular moment of this particular afternoon, I doubt if she would want to know.'

'You feel guilty because she's crippled and you aren't.'

Henry regretted this remark as soon as he had made it. It wasn't kind, he felt, and he was aware that there were stirrings inside himself over which he had no control, under whose influence he could conceivably find pleasure in hurting the one he loved, and this disturbed him.

To his surprise, however, Hilary was not at all upset. 'Of course I feel guilty,' she said. 'I love her so very much.'

And so, Hilary attempted to make love very quietly, without rattling the bedhead, and eschewing the sharp cries of gasping passion that had occasionally surprised the neighbours in Stickleback Rise. Henry's aim, on the other hand, was to make love in animal fashion, with vigorous movements and heavy grunting and moaning. And although they were able to laugh at themselves and their excessive self-consciousness, a degree of tension and artificiality had entered into what had previously been delightfully natural between them.

Indeed, they felt a degree of tension and artificiality in the whole of their life in Perkin Warbeck Drive. The house, lacking a woman's touch due to Nadežda being chair-bound, seemed lifeless. The lounge, as Howard Lewthwaite felt that it was politically correct to call it, was heavily floral, almost luxurious, but lacking the sparkle that would have been given by real care on Nadežda's part. The dining room, too, with its dark mahogany table, brown Windsor chairs and brown Windsor soup, was an excessively careful room. Howard Lewthwaite did the cooking. Even under the circumstances of his wife's illness, he could not have equated his political conscience with having domestic servants, and if this seems hypocritical coming from one who hadn't been above a bit of town planning corruption on quite a major scale, well yes, Howard Lewthwaite was a hypocrite. Nice men often are.

And Howard Lewthwaite was a nice man whose natural good humour had been eroded by exhaustion, ill-luck, guilt and worry. His acts of corruption had been caused by his need for money to take Nadežda to live in a better climate. Because she was unable to stand up, she was developing a chest condition which was far more likely to kill her than her polio. It was impossible to emigrate while Sam was still at school. Howard Lewthwaite was worried that his drapery business in Market Street wouldn't last that long.

Sam, naturally, spent most of his time in his room, rocking round the clock with Bill Haley. His family, equally naturally, were happy for him to stay there.

So, the house that had seemed so full of life and love when Henry had first visited it last New Year's Eve – was it really less than a year ago? – seemed full of worry now. The rustic summer-house, where Henry and Hilary had discovered their love for each other, had yielded up all its mystery and romance in one go.

On the early evening of Tuesday, December 10th, shortly before their dinner that was called tea, Henry looked at his watch and said, 'Spotted dick just being served,' and, to his astonishment, Hilary said, 'I'm missing all that, you know,' and, to his even greater astonishment, he heard himself say, 'So am I.'

Every day Hilary wrote her novel and Henry pretended to write his, and every Wednesday afternoon Hilary said, 'Hush. Don't grunt so loudly,' and Henry grimaced. And British Home Stores, the British Council of Churches, and the Yorkshire Branch of the Institute of Quarrymen failed to recognise the latent genius of Henry Ezra Pratt.

Then it was almost Christmas, there were drinks in the heaving, dark, masculine back bar of the Lord Nelson with Henry's former colleagues on the *Thurmarsh Evening Argus*, all writing novels and dreaming of Fleet Street and/or literary fame. Ted Plunkett's seductive wife Helen said, 'Not pregnant yet, Hilary?' and raised an eyebrow, 'Didn't I miss much with Henry, then?' and Hilary said fiercely, 'You missed a lovely, lovely man,' and Ted sighed because he should have married Ginny Fenwick, and Ginny Fenwick blushed because she knew why Ted had sighed, and Henry felt a deep nostalgia for those busy, boozy days, and for the camaraderie of the workplace, and this disturbed him; and it worried him that so many things disturbed him, when he loved Hilary and was so happy with her.

On Christmas Day there were ingenious presents, there was turkey and Christmas pudding with threepenny bits in it, there were mince pies, there was plenty to drink, and although the obligatory nature of the enjoyment prevented true spontaneity, neither Henry nor Hilary felt any nostalgia for Cousin Hilda's that day.

Denzil Ackerman and Lampo Davey invited them to London for New Year's Eve, and they accepted, since they both knew that no New Year's Eve in Perkin Warbeck Drive could ever equal last year's in romantic intensity.

In Denzil and Lampo's *bijou* mews town house in Chelsea, tasteful decorations covered every available space, although there weren't many available spaces, since the house was bursting at the seams with pretty little *objets d'art*, notable among them being Denzil's unrivalled collection of vintage biscuit tins.

Denzil greeted them in a natty blue apron. Denzil and Lampo kissed both Hilary and Henry, and Henry was very pleasantly embarrassed.

'I'm doing the cooking. He's doing the worrying. We take it in turns,' said Denzil.

'I never worry,' said Lampo. 'He just likes to think I do, because he worries so much.'

Denzil gave an angry intake of breath, and wheeled from the room, narrowly avoiding knocking down two vases, a candlestick and a pomander. Henry flinched. He didn't like to see Lampo and Denzil arguing, since it was he who had brought them together, albeit inadvertently.

'We've a surprise for you,' said Lampo. 'Diana and Tosser are coming for drinks.'

Henry was horrified to feel the quickening of his heartbeat. At Dalton College he had fagged for Lampo and for Tosser Pilkington-Brick. Tosser had married Diana Hargreaves, sister of Henry's best friend, Paul. Henry had almost loved Diana once. Not now, though. No need for quickened heartbeats now.

Diana and Tosser were in evening dress. They would be. The last time Henry had seen Diana, at his wedding, she had been very pregnant. Now, although never slim, she looked quite shapely. The skin on her broad shoulders, though not as fine as Hilary's, was attractively brown and smooth. Henry didn't feel any desire for her, of course, but he felt a worryingly sharp hostility towards Tosser. He found himself hoping that they weren't happy, and this too disturbed him.

'We've left Benedict with Mummy,' said Diana. 'She sends her love, Henry. They both do. They miss you dreadfully.'

They drank champagne, and Tosser said, 'When you get a job, Henry, do come and see me for insurance and pensions advice.'

'Tosser!' said Diana.

'Diana, please, the name is Nigel,' said Tosser stuffily.

'The name is Tosser when you behave like a toss-pot,' said Diana.

Oh good, they were arguing. No, Henry, don't feel like that.

But it was difficult not to feel like that. Everyone seemed so fulfilled, Tosser doling out financial advice, Diana producing Benedicts, Lampo working for Sotheby's – or was it Christie's? –

Denzil still churning out his arty-farty cobblers for the *Thurmarsh Evening Argus*, Hilary starting work shortly *and* getting on so well with her bloody novel. Out, green-eyed monster.

'I've got a very promising interview next week,' said Henry.

He groaned inwardly. Why had he been so weak as to feel the need to compete? He didn't want to talk about his interview.

'Gorgeous. What's it for?' said Lampo, as he opened a second bottle of champagne, which fizzed out all over the inlaid marble top of a Georgian game table and sent Denzil white with anger.

Henry thought he had got away with it, but after ten minutes of frenzied cleaning, when Lampo turned to Denzil and said, 'Sorry. No harm done, I think,' Denzil, in order to ignore Lampo effectively, turned to Henry and said, 'Come on. You never told us what that interview was for.'

'It's with the Cucumber Marketing Board,' said Henry. 'They've relocated to Leeds. There's a vacancy for an Assistant Regional Co-ordinator, Northern Counties (Excluding Berwick-on-Tweed).'

There was a stunned silence in the little mews house in Chelsea.

Henry 'We admire your personality but are not convinced that you have the moral commitment that we as a religious body are seeking' Pratt sat in the foyer of the Cucumber Marketing Board, which was brilliantly user-unfriendly many years before the concept was put into words.

The Cucumber Marketing Board was housed in a four-storey Edwardian building in the business district of Leeds, among banks and solicitors' offices. The steel-armed chairs and the glass-topped table were far too small for the high-ceilinged room with its dusty chandelier and impressive ceiling rose. The table was strategically placed too far in front of his chair and too near the floor, so that he risked severe backache every time he bent down to pick up the out-of-date copies of *The Lady* and *The Vegetable Growers' Gazette*, which were the only reading matter provided.

'Mr Tubman-Edwards will see you now,' said the receptionist. 'Second floor. He'll meet you at the lift.'

Henry couldn't believe it. Could this possibly be the same Tubman-Edwards, the bully of Brasenose and Dalton, whom Tosser Pilkington-Brick, when he was a hero and not a financial consultant, had forced to smile on the other side of his face? If so, it was goodbye, cucumbers.

He wished he looked taller and more athletic. He wished that his dark grey suit didn't look crumpled.

He walked along a dark, uncarpeted corridor to the lift, which clanked precariously to the second floor, where he was met by a rather anxious man in his fifties, wearing a pin-striped suit and an MCC tie with a blob of egg yolk on it. A tiny piece of cotton wool had stuck to a cut on his neck.

'Dennis Tubman-Edwards,' he announced. 'It's Henry, isn't it? We're friendly people here.'

He smiled, seeming unaware that his smile gave a twisted, slightly sinister look to his face. Henry saw the resemblance to J. C. R. Tubman-Edwards (Plantaganet House) for the first time.

Mr Tubman-Edwards led him along a carpeted corridor, past the offices of the Director (Operations) and the Director (Admin.) and opened the door of Room 208, which carried the legend 'Head of Establishments'.

Mr Tubman-Edwards seated himself behind his very bare desk, and gestured to Henry to sit in the hard chair provided for interviewees. The office was not large and was almost entirely taken up with filing cabinets. There were just two pictures on the walls – a lurid portrait of the Queen and a school photograph of the Dalton College boys from Mr Tubman-Edwards's final year. His desk was bare except for a pen, a pad of lined paper, and two photograph holders.

'You were at school with my son, I believe,' said Mr Tubman-Edwards, turning one of the photographs round so that Henry could see the unprepossessing face of the ghastly boy.

'Yes, that's right,' said Henry, wondering desperately whether this was good news or bad.

Mr Tubman-Edwards winced and gasped. 'Sorry,' he said. 'Touch of shrapnel still lodged in the skull. Gives me gyp intermittently. Not to worry. Chums, were you?'

It might be a trap. Better be honest. Not too honest, though. Pity he needed the job. He would have loved to have said, 'Couldn't stand the great sack of blackmailing yak turd.'

'Er . . . not particularly,' he said.

'What's your ambition in life?' asked the father of the great sack of blackmailing yak turd in the same casual, conversational tone.

Henry realised that he had been thrown a conversational hand-grenade. To pitch his ambition too high – 'I'd like to feel that I'd helped to save Western civilisation' – would be to risk ridicule and, more seriously, rejection. To pitch it too low – 'I'd like to feel that I could support my family and give them double glazing for life' – might be even more disastrous.

'Er. . . ,' he began, more to show that he was still alive than anything, and as soon as he had stopped, he realised that to be indecisive would be the most fatal fault of all.

Too late. Oh well. Mr Tubman-Edwards smiled his slightly crooked smile and tapped his HB pencil on the desk. Must say something.

'I *suppose*,' he said, investing a deeply thoughtful inflection into his voice, to suggest that his long hesitation had been caused by deep thought, 'I *suppose* my ambition is to find an ambition that satisfies me.'

'I see,' said Mr Tubman-Edwards neutrally. 'I see. And what is your attitude to cucumbers?'

If this next abrupt change of subject was intended to jolt Henry, it failed. He felt on safer ground with cucumbers than with ambition.

'I like them,' he said, and then, to his horror, he heard himself add, 'I think they're the Cinderellas of the salad bowl.'

Fortunately, Mr Tubman-Edwards took him seriously.

'In what way?' he asked.

'Well what is a salad built around for most people?' said Henry. 'Lettuce and more lettuce. Tomatoes. Hard-boiled eggs. I think because it's the same colour as lettuce – green,' he wished he hadn't added the explanation, '. . . the cucumber is often added as an afterthought. I'd like to raise the profile of the cucumber, give it in post-war cuisine a prominence akin to its dominance of the teatime sandwich in the pre-war world.'

J. C. R. Tubman-Edwards's father seemed impressed, if also slightly stunned.

'Excellent,' he said. 'Excellent. Splendid.'

A wave of self-disgust swept over Henry. How could he sit there and pretend, for the sake of a measly job, that cucumbers were so important? Where was the fighting spirit on which he prided himself?

'Of course they aren't the be-all and end-all,' he said.

'I'm sorry, I'm not quite with you,' said Mr Tubman-Edwards. 'They aren't the be-all and end-all of what?'

'Of life,' said Henry.

He feared that, in that brave, reckless moment, he had lost all chance of working for the Cucumber Marketing Board. But he was wrong.

He would often wonder, in the years to come, if things would have been better if he'd been right.

2 The First, Faint Shadows

On Friday, January 10th, 1958, there was a second successful launch of the Air Force's Atlas Inter-Continental Ballistic Missile at Cape Canaveral, a burglar found so much wine and spirits in a director's room at an Edinburgh shop-fitting firm that he was found drunk at the director's desk when the work-force arrived, and Hilary left for the doctor's before the post came.

The moment Henry had read the letter, he wanted to stand in the middle of Perkin Warbeck Drive and announce the good tidings with such a yell of triumph that it would be heard in Lambert Simnel Avenue and Wat Tyler Crescent. But there was only Nadežda to tell, and he didn't want to tell her before he told Hilary.

He wheeled Nadežda to the French windows, from which she liked to watch the birds. A pair of chaffinches were foraging under the bird table, the male strikingly colourful, the female gently subtle. A jaundiced sun was filtering through high clouds. There was still a little frost under the conifers and in front of the summer-house, but in Henry's heart there was a warm glow. No matter that the call of the cucumber gave him no great sense of vocation. No matter that he would never know whether he had got the job on merit or because he'd been at school with Mr Tubman-Edwards's son. No matter that an unworthy little voice had already whispered to him that there was no need to tell anybody, not even Hilary, about the Tubman-Edwards connection. Pratt of the Argus was employable again. The world was a beautiful place.

He rehearsed the scene in which he would tell Hilary and she would admire him. He heard footsteps on the gravel path, but it was the heavy crunching feet of the nurse who would wash and dress Nadežda and give her the massage that did so little good.

He stood at the French windows, looking out at the summer-house, where they had discovered the depth of their love. Four starlings descended on the bird table, and the chaffinches flew away. How could a sore foot take a doctor so long?

At last he heard her light, quick steps. He opened the front door, and there she stood, his pale ethereal love, and her eyes sparkled, as if she already knew. He ushered her in with mock courtliness, closed the door, and said, 'I've got some news.'

'So have I,' said Hilary. 'I'm pregnant.'

He gawped. He couldn't grasp it. She couldn't be, his slender love.

'Good Lord,' he said, with more amazement than delight. And then the amazing fact of it filtered through, and he said 'Good Lord' again, with more delight than amazement, and he rushed to her and she to him and they hugged in the sadly impersonal hall, and he said, 'When?' and she said, 'Beginning of August,' and they laughed a bit and cried a bit and she said, 'I must tell Mummy.'

The nurse had finished washing and dressing Nadežda and had wheeled her back to her favourite position by the French windows.

'I'm going to have a baby, Mummy,' said Hilary, bending to kiss her mother's lifeless hair, while the nurse gently kneaded those deceptively perfect shoulders.

'Oh my darlings, I'm so happy for you,' said Nadežda with a gasp, and they both heard, in the silence that followed, her unspoken thought, 'I hope there's nothing wrong with it.'

Suddenly sobered, Hilary turned to Henry and said, 'Didn't you say you had some news?'

'Oh yes,' said Henry, as three magpies attacked the bird table, and the starlings flew off. 'I'd almost forgotten.' That'll teach me to rehearse scenes, he thought. 'Our baby will have no cause to be ashamed of its Daddy. Our son or daughter, when he or she goes to school, will be able to boast that their father is the Assistant Regional Co-ordinator, Northern Counties (Excluding Berwick-on-Tweed) of the Cucumber Marketing Board.'

Cousin Hilda sniffed.

'Cucumbers!' she said. 'I don't use them.'

'Is that all you can say?' said Hilary.

28

Henry and Cousin Hilda looked at Hilary in astonishment. Two milky cups of Camp coffee stood on the otherwise bare dining table in the basement room of number 66, Park View Road. Cousin Hilda had not indulged.

'Mrs Wedderburn'll be right glad you're fixed up,' she said.

'Never mind Mrs Wedderburn,' said Hilary. 'What about you? Aren't you pleased Henry's got a job?'

'Hilary!' said Henry.

'Leave this to me, darling,' said Hilary.

'I wouldn't say I'm pleased, no,' said Cousin Hilda carefully. 'It's nowt to get excited about. It's natural. I'd say I were displeased when he hadn't got one, and now I'm not displeased any more.'

'It's not the greatest job in the world,' said Henry. 'But I won't be in cucumbers for ever. It's just a launching pad. It does . . . er . . . it does mean we won't be coming back here to live.'

'I see,' said Cousin Hilda.

'We enjoyed being here. We missed it when we were with Hilary's family, even the spotted dick. Didn't we, darling?'

'Yes, we really did,' agreed Hilary.

'What do you mean – "Even the spotted dick"?' said Cousin Hilda. 'Is there summat wrong with me spotted dick?'

'Oh no,' said Henry. 'Not at all. It's the best spotted dick I've ever eaten.' He didn't tell her that the only other spotted dick he'd ever eaten had been at Brasenese College, where all the food had been inedible. 'We'll move into rented accommodation and start looking for a house.'

'I see,' said Cousin Hilda.

'Cousin Hilda? Do you love Henry?' asked Hilary.

Henry's astonishment was total now, but he knew better than to say, 'Hilary!' again. His heart was beating fast and he felt rivulets of embarrassment running down his back.

Cousin Hilda turned away abruptly and shovelled more coke into the roaring fire, although it was already stifling in the little room. The smell of hot glass from the panes in the front of the blue-tiled stove mingled with the remnants of battered cod, jam

29

roly-poly, and Mr O'Reilly's end-of-the-week feet.

As Cousin Hilda bent to her task, Henry saw the white dead skin of her thigh through a hole in her pale pink bloomers.

When she had finished her displacement activity, Cousin Hilda suddenly looked Hilary full in the face. Hilary didn't flinch. Henry held his breath.

'Of course I do,' she said. 'I've looked after him like a son, haven't I? He knows I do.'

'He doesn't actually,' said Hilary. 'He can never quite believe that anybody loves him. I'm not sure that he even realises how much I love him.'

'Hilary has a reason for feeling particularly emotional tonight, Cousin Hilda,' said Henry.

'Don't make excuses for me,' said Hilary.

'Well tell her.'

'All in good time. I thought there were things that should be said. Families ought to be able to say things.'

'We were brought up not to say things,' said Cousin Hilda. 'The longer it goes on, the harder it becomes to say things.'

'That's why I thought tonight might be a good time to start,' said Hilary.

It was extraordinary, but Henry had the impression that Cousin Hilda was actually quite pleased.

But she couldn't resist having one more parting shot. 'Some folk say too much. I could never be like the Dorises of this world. Her mother used to say, "I'm saying nowt." Doris should have taken heed.' Then she turned to Hilary and her face softened into something almost resembling a smile. 'It's time now, isn't it, Hilary?' she said. 'Time to find out why you have reasons for feeling emotional tonight.'

And Henry realised, to his amazement, that Cousin Hilda knew.

'I'm pregnant,' said Hilary.

Cousin Hilda's face didn't move, but a single tear ran down her cheek, and Henry recognised it for what it was. It was a tear for the life she might have led.

And maybe Hilary recognised it too, because she went over to Cousin Hilda and hugged her and held her close and planted a gentle kiss on her forehead, and Cousin Hilda's lips worked anxiously and at last she spoke.

'Give over,' she said. 'Don't be so daft.'

And then she sniffed.

Henry recognised it as a truly historic sniff.

It was the first time that Cousin Hilda had sniffed not out of disapproval, but because her nose was running.

During January, 1958, the National Union of Mineworkers claimed an extra ten shillings a week for its 382,000 day wage men, Dr Vivian Fuchs reached the South Pole and Sir Edmund Hillary flew in to greet him with the immortal words, 'Hello, Bunny,' scientists at Harwell, revealing secrets of their work on producing electricity through hydrogen power, predicted that the sea would provide a fuel supply sufficient to last mankind for a thousand million years at nominal cost, and Henry and Hilary Pratt both started new jobs.

On Hilary's first day at Thurmarsh Grammar School for Girls, Henry traipsed the cold pavements of Thurmarsh, looking at a succession of dismal flats. Her absence pierced him like a cruel frost. At lunchtime, on an impulse, he went to the Lord Nelson, in Leatherbottlers' Row, in the hope that he would run into some of his old colleagues from the *Evening Argus*. Nobody he knew came in. Even the bar staff were unfamiliar to him. He sat at their usual corner table in the brown, clubby back bar, and had a Scotch egg, a ham sandwich, two pints of bitter and a bout of melancholia. He wished that he could put up a notice explaining that 'Mr Henry Pratt isn't really lonely and pathetic. He is revisiting old haunts while waiting to take up one of the most prestigious appointments in the cucumber world.'

Just as he was about to leave, Peter Matheson, leader of the Conservative minority on Thurmarsh Borough Council, and father of Anna, Hilary's schoolfriend who lived with the bigamous Uncle Teddy in Cap Ferrat, entered the bar. He had been a prime mover in the saga of corruption which had seemed likely to make, but had ultimately been allowed to break, Henry's brief journalistic career. Henry disliked him intensely, yet felt so lonely without Hilary that he accepted a drink with eagerness.

'I don't usually drink at lunchtime,' said Peter Matheson, when they were settled at the corner table, 'but I've had some grave news about Anna. I haven't even told Olivia yet.'

Henry's blood ran cold. Had Peter Matheson discovered that she was married to Uncle Teddy? Or had she died?

'You remember that girlfriend of hers who was becoming a nun?'

'Yes,' said Henry cautiously, remembering the tale that Anna had told her parents to explain her presence in France.

'Well Anna's joined her. She's become a nun.'

Henry felt a surge of relief. Anna wasn't dead. And of course he knew that she hadn't become a nun.

'Oh I am sorry,' he said, hoping that he looked sufficiently grave.

'It's an extremely strict order. She isn't even allowed to see her parents. We've lost our only child.'

Henry was appalled, but also reluctantly impressed, by Anna's ruthlessness. He bought another round, didn't mention his own good news, and talked to Peter Matheson in a suitably muted manner.

For the remainder of the afternoon, back in Perkin Warbeck Drive, Henry counted the minutes till Hilary's return. He planned to kiss her, tell her how much he'd missed her, ask her about her day, take her to bed and lay his head against her still smooth stomach, trying to sense the developing foetus within.

In fact, perhaps because he had drunk two more pints than he had intended, he gave her only a perfunctory kiss and found it impossible to tell her how much he had missed her. He felt jealous of all the experiences from which he had been excluded, and managed to invest his, 'How did you get on?' with only a grudging expression of interest.

'It was a bit odd really,' said Hilary. 'The headmistress said, "Welcome to Thurmarsh Grammar. I hope you'll be very happy here," and I said, "Thank you very much. I'm sure I will. I'd like to give in my notice. I'll be leaving in July. I'm pregnant."'

'You didn't!'

'I did. I thought it only fair to make my position clear from the start.'

Henry shivered. He couldn't always cope with Hilary's directness.

On Henry's first day at work, Hilary found it difficult to concentrate on the subjunctive tense, and Act One of *Macbeth*, and Lily Rosewood being sick all over Jeannie Cosgrove's satchel. All day she was wondering how he was getting on. Her love had robbed her of her sense of proportion, and she felt sick with anxiety lest his new career be an instant fiasco. 'It can't be. They're bound to recognise his lovely talents. They're bound to take my lovely man to their hearts,' she told herself. But the tension persisted. She hung around the school as long as she could, and walked home slowly, to their charming, but tiny, one-bedroom flat in Copley Road. Her route took her down Market Street, past the beginnings of the new Fish Hill Shopping Complex, along the Doncaster Road, down Blonk Lane, past the football ground, up Ainsley Crescent, left into Bellamy Lane and right into Copley Road. A fine, penetrating drizzle was falling, and her unreasonable and absurd tension rose throughout the journey.

She set to, in the characterful but primitive little whitewashed kitchen, making fish pie and feeling that she never wanted to eat again.

At last he came in, her lovely man.

'Well?' she said.

'Well what?' he said.

'How did it go?'

'It was all right.'

She shivered. Sometimes, nowadays, it was as if a curtain had come down between them.

Every morning the Assistant Regional Co-ordinator, Northern Counties (Excluding Berwick-on-Tweed) caught the 7.48 from Thurmarsh (Midland Road) to Leeds City Station, crossed City

Square, with its sculpture of the Black Prince, walked up Park Row, turned left into South Parade, and entered the sombre brick building that housed the Cucumber Marketing Board.

Every morning, he walked along the uncarpeted corridor of the ground floor, past the offices of the Head of Services (Secretarial) and the Assistant Heads of Services (Secretarial), took the shuddering lift to the first floor, where the gloomy corridor was carpeted, but not as expensively as was the second floor, walked past the offices of the Head of Gherkins and the Deputy Head of Gherkins, and entered Room 106.

If an estate agent had been selling Room 106, he would have said that it was compact, enjoyed central heating and afforded substantial opportunities for improvement. He would not have pointed out that it had a splendid view over a courtyard on which the sun never set because it never rose on it either, and offered an unrivalled opportunity for the study of the changing styles of drainpipes over the last sixty years.

Henry was the proud possessor of a heavily scratched desk with three drawers, a telephone, adequate supplies of basic stationery, an in-tray, an out-tray, a pending-tray, and precious little else.

On that first morning, about which he had told Hilary so little, Henry had been in the process of discovering that all the filing cabinets were empty, when his telephone had rung with shocking shrillness.

'Assistant Regional Co-ordinator, Northern Counties (Excluding Berwick-on-Tweed),' he had said. 'How can I help you?'

'Henry Pratt?' a pleasant female voice had asked.

'Yes,' he had admitted cautiously.

'I'm Roland's wife.'

'Roland?'

'Roland Stagg. Regional Co-ordinator, Northern Counties.'

'Ah!'

'Roland has flu.'

'Oh dear.'

'He asked me to welcome you, and to ask you to take his messages and generally hold the fort.'

'Right. Right, I'll . . . I'll hold the fort.'

'Splendid.'

And so, for a week, little Henry sat in his little office, growing even paler than usual, and held the fort in almost complete isolation. He had no idea what he was supposed to do. Approximately five times a day the phone rang, and it was almost always a re-routed call for Roland Stagg. Of the twenty-five messages which Henry took down, eleven related to meeting people for drinks and only seven contained any reference to cucumbers. But he looked forward to taking these messages. They gave him something to do.

He went to the library, got out books on vegetables, and wrote down all the information he could find about cucumbers. He brought in five postcards from various friends, and pinned them to the wall beside his window. He bought photo frames and put two photographs of Hilary on the desk.

The rest of the time he sat at his desk, with pen, paper and reading glasses at the ready, so that he could pretend to be busy if anyone came in.

Only two people came in all week, but the first, the whistling post-boy, did come in four times a day, bringing no mail, peering at the empty out-tray, nodding pleasantly, and leaving the door annoyingly ajar. In the end Henry grew so ashamed of his empty out-tray that he sent letters to Cousin Hilda, Auntie Doris, Uncle Teddy, Lampo and Denzil, Howard and Nadežda, Ted and Helen, and Ginny Fenwick. The post-boy looked at him in surprise and almost said something.

The other visitor was a pleasant, matronly lady, who introduced herself as 'Janet McTavish, Head of Services (Secretarial). I should have called on you on Monday. I didn't realise you'd started.'

'Well there's not been much sign of it,' said Henry. 'Do sit down.'

'Oh no thank you!' said Janet McTavish fervently, as if horrified at the thought of such intimacy. 'I just wanted to welcome you.'

'Thank you.'

'And to tell you that you'll be sharing Andrea, and when Andrea isn't available you'll have second use of Jane.'

35

'Sorry?' said Henry. 'What for?'

'Well typing, of course,' said Janet McTavish.

'Ah yes. Of course. Right. Right. Well, thank you,' said Henry. 'No typing yet?'

'Not yet.'

Apart from the two visitors to his office, Henry only met three other people all week – the Director (Operations), the Director General, and the lady with the tea trolley.

The phone call from the Director (Operations) came on the Wednesday.

'Timothy Whitehouse, Director (Operations). Can you spare me a mo'?'

'Yes, I . . . er . . . I can spare you a mo'.'

He took the lift to the second floor, with its superior carpet.

Mr Whitehouse's office was considerably larger than Henry's, and decorated with reproductions of all the paintings by old masters that had ever included a cucumber.

The Director (Operations) was in his mid-forties, a lean, sharp man with a predatory nose, but tired eyes. He invited Henry to sit down and said, 'How are you settling in?'

'Very well,' said Henry, 'if a bit slowly.'

'A bit slowly?'

'Well, with Mr Stagg being ill this week. Obviously I'm holding the fort . . .'

'Good man.'

'But I'm not able to do a great deal till he returns.'

'No, of course. Now, Henry . . . you don't mind if I call you Henry, do you?'

'No, no. Not at all.'

'Good. We're friendly people here. A word about our structure, Henry. You are answerable to Roland Stagg departmentally, to Dennis Tubman-Edwards staff-wise, and to me operationally, and vice-versa. Is that clear?'

As mud. 'Oh yes. Very clear.'

'Good. May I offer you some advice, Henry?'

'Certainly, Timothy.'

'Ah!' Mr Whitehouse swivelled round to gaze out of the window. 'I may have given you a false impression when I said that we are friendly. *Mea culpa!*' He repeated the Latin tag, as if it was the apogee of learning. '*Mea culpa!* I address you as "Henry", you address me as "Mr Whitehouse". I might want you to call me Timothy, but we exist in a rather difficult limbo between the civil service and the free market economy, and in this quasi-governmental limbo it has been found that a degree of formality is, regrettably perhaps, appropriate. You understand, I hope?'

Like I understand Swahili. 'Oh yes!'

'Good.' The Director (Operations) swung back with disconcerting abruptness, and looked Henry straight in the eye. 'A word of advice, Henry. Be your own man, stick to your guns, be fearless, always speak the truth, and you won't go far wrong.' He lowered his voice. 'Roland Stagg's a good man, but between you, me and the mythical G.P., you should take everything he says with a pinch of salt.'

'Sorry? The mythical G.P.?'

'They told me you were bright.' Mr Whitehouse shook his head sadly. 'The gatepost.' He stood up. 'Good.' He limped round the desk, and shook Henry's hand. 'Sorry about the limp. A present from Jerry at Alamein. Come and see me if you need me. Never worry about wasting my time. Goodbye, Henry.'

The summons from the Director General, Vincent Ambrose, came on the Friday.

The lift clattered up to the third floor, where the carpet had a thick pile.

Mr Ambrose's office was much larger than Mr Whitehouse's, with a vast antique desk and leather armchairs. It had a standard lamp with a shade of a particularly succulent red, several pictures, none of which contained cucumbers, and an antique sideboard laden with bottles of drink, none of which Henry was offered.

Mr Ambrose – large, genial, vague – was very welcoming, however, sat him down, offered a cigar, and said, 'I make a point of seeing all new staff. We aren't an aloof bunch in cucumber marketing, Mr Bratt.'

'Pratt.'

'I'm *so* sorry. So sorry. Learning the ropes, are you?'

'Yes, I'm learning the ropes.'

'Finding your way around?'

'Yes.' Boldly, Henry ventured a little jest. 'Well, I've found out the route the tea trolley takes anyway.'

The Director General looked shocked.

'You don't use the trolley, do you?' he said. 'Don't you make your own?'

'Are we allowed to?'

'My dear chap! What do you think you have a kettle for?'

'I don't think I do have a kettle.'

Vincent Ambrose looked horrified.

'No kettle?' he said. 'No kettle? Take it up with Maurice Jesmond.'

'Maurice Jesmond?'

'Head of Facilities. Must have a kettle. Can't do decent work on trolley tea. Where do you live?'

'Thurmarsh.'

'Really? Really??'

Mr Ambrose seemed astounded that anybody would actually live in Thurmarsh.

There was a loud explosion from a car back-firing in the street.

'Duck!' shouted Vincent Ambrose, flinging himself onto the carpet.

Henry looked down at him in astonishment. The Director General picked himself up, dusted himself down, and grinned.

'So sorry,' he said. 'Last lingering effects of shell-shock. Please don't feel embarrassed. I'm not. Totally involuntary. So, you're learning the ropes?'

'Very much so.'

'Good man.'

Vincent Ambrose smiled benevolently, shook hands with Henry, and wished him luck. Henry returned to his office, phoned Maurice Jesmond, discovered that he was on leave, and spent the afternoon studying the changing styles of drainpipes over the last sixty years.

The prospect of two whole days together dispelled the slight shadows that had begun to hang over Henry and Hilary's relationship. They almost recaptured the rapture of their first moments of love. The thought of the developing baby excited Henry enormously. He woke in the middle of the Saturday night and put his ear to his wife's stomach while she slept, hoping to hear some noise from the foetus, maybe a gurgle or a rumble from its incipient stomach. He knew in his head that it was far too early for such a thing to be a possibility, but his heart was full of joy at the great miracle of life, and awe at the thought that he, podgy Henry Ezra Pratt, could father a child. It dawned on him that he was now completely content to accept the miracle as a miracle and seek no explanation of it.

He went to work on the Monday morning with dread. To his great relief, the Regional Co-ordinator, Northern Counties (Excluding Berwick-on-Tweed) had recovered from his flu, and sent for him almost immediately.

Roland Stagg was a large man of about fifty, with a double chin and a huge paunch over which his trousers drooped inelegantly. He smoked incessantly and always had ash on his clothes. His breathing was laboured, and he was in the middle of a coughing fit.

'Sorry,' he said. 'Burma.'

'Burma?'

'I was in Burma during the war. It didn't do much good for my lungs. Don't worry, no problem, only really affects me now when I've been ill. I shouldn't smoke. I *am* sorry about last week. Did you find your feet all right?'

'Well I didn't really know what to do,' admitted Henry.

His departmental boss looked irritated. 'Well, didn't you think?' he said. 'Aren't you capable of thought?'

'Yes, but I had nothing to go on, and I didn't want to queer your pitch.'

'Quite right. I don't like my pitch queered. But couldn't you have at least explored your predecessor's files?'

'There aren't any files. The filing cabinets are empty.'

'Oh my God,' said the Regional Co-ordinator. 'The bastard. He's destroyed your records *in toto*. Vindictive little beast.'

'I think he's taken my kettle as well.'

'Your kettle as well! And he was at Charterhouse. What's happening to the public school system?'

Henry judged that the question was rhetorical.

'You'll have to take my files, copy them, trace every grower in the North who isn't on my files and contact them all to get the history of the relationship,' said Mr Stagg. 'You can't operate without a history of the relationship. You'll find I'm a hands-off employer. I'll leave it to you. Chase Maurice Jesmond for a kettle. Come to me if you have problems. Right?'

'Right.'

Henry stood up. Suddenly, Mr Stagg smiled.

'You took my messages very diligently,' he said. 'You'll have gathered I'm a drinking man. Are you a drinking man?'

'Sometimes,' said Henry cautiously.

'Be here at twelve thirty. We'll have a noggin.'

Over their noggin in the large, lively Victoria, with its huge Victorian windows, Roland Stagg gave Henry the benefit of his advice. 'Be cautious, keep a low profile, and never commit yourself unless it's absolutely unavoidable.' He lowered his voice against the possibility of being overheard in the next booth. 'Old Shitehouse is a decent sort and a loyal boss, but take everything he says with a pinch of salt.' He raised his voice again. 'Keep your eyes skinned, your nose clean, your ear close to the ground and your mouth shut, and you won't go far wrong.'

Henry 'Deeply conscious of not having been in the war and distinctly guilty about being so healthy' Pratt threw himself into his work with enthusiasm. He was determined to make his mark in the cucumber world, so that his reputation would go before him and find him other work. 'I heard about this chap doing stirring things with cucumbers. Thought I ought to take a peep at him.' He also felt, as a self-confessed underdog, a degree of natural sympathy for the cucumber, seeing it as the Henry Pratt of the vegetable world.

In the early weeks he was kept busy compiling his missing records, contacting growers and retail outlets (shops to thee and me) and asking questions about the history of their relationship. He looked forward to travelling around his region, meeting cucumber folk.

He realised that, if he followed Mr Whitehouse's advice, he would be out on his ear within a month, whereas, if he listened to Mr Stagg, he would survive for a lifetime and get absolutely nowhere. He would need to steer a very careful course between the Scylla of Mr Whitehouse's boldness, and the Charybdis of Mr Stagg's caution. He felt confident that he could.

Even in his social life, Henry didn't neglect his new enthusiasm.

One Friday evening, in mid-March, he went with Hilary to the Lord Nelson to meet his old colleagues. Henry, who was having no great social life at work, felt a frisson of excitement and delicious regret as they walked into the back bar and saw the journalists gathered round their corner table.

Henry's journalistic disasters had slipped irrevocably into legend in the months since his departure. He greeted the humorous recollection of them now with a mixture of shame and pride, and was moved by the extent to which his former colleagues appeared to miss him.

'I had to stay over. Couldn't miss my dear Henry,' said Denzil.

'It's extraordinarily kind of you,' said Henry.

'Not at all. I'm glad to get a night away from Lampo. He finds my snoring revolting.' Denzil sighed. 'Lampo says snoring is tasteless. The truth is I'm getting old and he finds it disgusting. He's dreadfully selfish.'

Henry felt sad at the thought that one day, inevitably, Lampo and Denzil would part.

Helen Plunkett, née Cornish, pressed her thigh against him, and smiled her pert, seductive smile. Ted Plunkett, her brooding husband with the great bushy eyebrows, gave a theatrical scowl of mock jealousy. Henry recognised this now as double bluff. If Ted pretended to be jealous, people wouldn't realise how deeply hurt he was. Ginny Fenwick, bulky but sensual, and still hankering after becoming a war correspondent, did recognise it and was hurt, because she still loved Ted. Henry felt embarrassed by Helen's rampant thigh and by his excessive consciousness of it. Hilary gave him a wry smile, to assure him of her understanding of the situation. Helen, seeing the smile, scowled. Colin Edgeley hugged Henry hugely and said, 'We miss you, kid. What are you having?' Ben Watkinson asked him to name all the goalkeepers in the third division north. Even Terry Skipton, the slightly deformed news editor and Jehovah's Witness, had two glasses of orange squash before saying, 'It's been lovely to see you, Henry. I'll leave now. It pains me to see my children getting drunk.'

They went on, down memory lane, up Commercial Street, to the Devonshire, where Henry disgusted Hilary by suggesting that the dark patches under the arms of Sid Hallett and the Rundlemen might be the same ones that he had seen on the shirts of the resident jazz band when he'd last visited the pub almost a year ago.

'So Hilary's pregnant,' yelled Helen over 'Basin Street Blues'. 'I always knew you had it in you.'

Her hand stroked his private parts gently. He turned hurriedly to Ben, and reeled off all the goalkeepers except Halifax Town's.

Colin Edgeley hugged him again and said, 'Can I borrow a quid till next Thursday?' as if forgetting that Henry wasn't a colleague any more.

But Henry had a new life, and the evening cured him of nostalgia for the old one. Suddenly, during Sid Hallett's spirited if inaccurate rendition of 'South Rampart Street Parade', he longed to be in bed with Hilary. A wave of love swept through him, and his feet tingled.

But they were all incredibly hungry, and after closing time an irresistible force led him not to bed, but to that very inadequate substitute, the Shanghai Chinese Restaurant and Coffee Bar.

Over his glutinous beef curry, Henry gazed earnestly at his old friends and said, 'Who should I contact about cucumbers?'

There was a stunned silence.

'I want to give the cucumber a higher profile,' he said. 'I

thought somebody could do a feature about it. The forgotten vegetable kind of thing. Bring back the cucumber sandwich type of touch.'

'Well I should think Ted could fit it into his kiddies' column,' said Helen. 'He might even make a competition out of it. "Knit your own phallic symbol." '

'It was just an idea,' said Henry.

The following Friday, Henry met Martin Hammond in the Pigeon and Two Cushions. Martin, his friend ever since the days of the Paradise Lane Gang, had become the youngest ever Union Convener at the Splutt Vale Iron and Steel Company. He was tired. 'I'm knackered. It's a non-stop job, raising the level of political consciousness,' he explained, yawning and apologising owlishly.

'Have you heard anything about Tommy?' Henry asked. 'It's a bit strange. He wasn't even on the plane.'

Tommy Marsden, fellow member of the Paradise Lane Gang, ex-star of Thurmarsh United, had been transferred to Manchester United in December of 1956. Yet when the plane carrying Manchester United home from a European Cup match in Belgrade on February 6th, 1958 had crashed at Munich Airport, killing twenty-three people, including eight members of the first team, Tommy's name had not been mentioned.

'They say he doesn't hit it off with Matt Busby,' said Martin, 'but I don't really find time for chat about football.'

To Henry's joy, Oscar, the hypochrondriac waiter, came on duty at 7.30. He bore down on them in his white umpire's coat, beaming from mastoid to mastoid.

'It's good to see you again, gentlemen,' he said. 'I get this sore throat on and off, but it never seems to develop into anything. The doctor says I'm living with it symbiotically. Sounds disgusting. Where have you been? I wondered if you'd emigrated.'

'Hilary's pregnant,' said Henry.

'Oh, congratulations, sir,' said Oscar. 'Such a lovely young lady. Such a nice wedding. I almost forgot me sinuses. What's it to be, gentlemen?'

'A pint and a half of bitter,' said Martin stuffily.

'Do you like people?' asked Henry, when Oscar had gone.

'Of course I do,' said Martin Hammond.

'Oh,' said Henry. 'Only I thought you might be too busy improving their lot to have much time for them.'

Martin Hammond coloured, and Henry felt sorry.

'Only a half?' he said, when the drinks arrived.

'I don't drink much any more,' said Martin.

'Have you got a girlfriend?' asked Henry.

'I've no time,' said Martin Hammond.

'What's your attitude to cucumbers?' asked Henry.

'They give me indigestion,' said Martin Hammond.

'You know what you are?' said Henry. 'Old before your time.'

During the Easter holidays, Hilary resumed work on her novel. One evening, when Henry returned home tired after visiting the Selby and Osgodby areas to meet cucumber growers and 'show my face', Hilary told him that she had made good progress, and he said, 'Oh good. Thank goodness one of us is talented,' and she stared at him in dismay, and he stared at her in dismay, and said, 'No, I'm really pleased. Tell me about it.' But she couldn't. A curtain was drawn across a whole room in their lives.

They had been having driving lessons, and it didn't help Henry's mood when Hilary passed her test first time, even though it meant that they bought a very old Standard Eight, which Henry was able to drive at weekends, to improve his technique.

An enormous improvement in his driving did result. In fact, his examiner on his second test told him that he might have passed him if he hadn't hit the car while parking at the very end. 'What do you do now?' the examiner asked him. 'Try to find the owner and report the accident,' said Henry. 'Right,' said the examiner drily. 'Well, that bit's easy. I'm the owner.'

Hilary was becoming aware of a strong element of perversity in Henry's make-up. When he passed his test at the fourth attempt – we'll draw a veil over the third, since the greengrocer's has long been rebuilt – there was only one possible target for his first trip behind the wheel. Berwick-on-Tweed, the only town in the North of England for whose cucumbers he was not responsible.

It was an unseasonably warm Saturday in early July. On parts of the north-east coast the temperature was nudging 65. As the car nosed rustily up the A1, past Newcastle, with the sheep-rich Cheviots to their left and the great castles of Northumberland to their right, Henry's blood fizzed to the romance of the open road.

They reached Berwick in time for a sandwich lunch. As they wandered the sober Georgian streets of that estuarine gem, Henry was disturbed to see how full of cucumbers the greengrocers' were.

They drifted, hand in hand, along the Quay Walls, at the wide Tweed's edge. Under the great road and rail bridges, swans paddled gently against the current, so as to remain still for their lunch.

As they sauntered happily along the ramparts, they saw a tall, craggy, handsome young man and a bronzed young woman walking towards them, hand in hand. For an absurd moment Henry wished that it was a mirror image, and that *he* was tall, craggy and handsome. He almost wished that Hilary was sun-drenched and sensuous and sultry and fleshy like . . . 'Anna!' they both exclaimed.

Anna Matheson, best friend of Hilary at Thurmarsh Grammar, and unlawful wife of Uncle Teddy in Cap Ferrat, who had once bared her all for Henry in her little flat in Cardington Road, went the colour of milky coffee beneath her suntan.

'Oh hell,' she said. 'Oh Christ. Oh well. This is Jed.'

'Hi,' said Jed.

Jed! What sort of a name is that? thought Henry, and he found that he didn't want to be tall, craggy and handsome any more.

'These people are all right, Jed,' said Anna. 'Hillers was my best friend at school and Henry is Teddy's kind of adopted son.'

'Oh. Right,' said Jed.

'We can tell them, Jed. I have to.'

Jed thought for a moment. 'OK,' he said.

Anna led them along the dignified ramparts towards the sea, past the Customs House and the Guard House.

'You look wonderful, Hillers,' she said. 'Pregnancy really suits you. I can't believe it. You look lovely.'

'Thank you,' said Hilary drily. 'You do too.'

'Well I always did,' said Anna, 'but you were a mess.'

'Thank you very much.'

'No, not being rude, because now you aren't, not remotely, so that's great,' said Anna.

'Oh, I see,' said Hilary. 'Good.'

They had reached a grassy open space, sheltered from the on-shore breeze by the town walls. Anna plonked herself on the grass and brought her knees up almost to her chin, as if to flaunt the glory of her sun-kissed thighs. Jed, in his old oil-stained cords, lolled darkly, suspiciously.

Behind them, gentle rollers expired on the Northumberland coast, and an oyster-catcher's shrill alarm cry rang out. In front of them, gulls wheeled bad-temperedly over the slate- and red-tiled roofs. The sun shone on the sandstone and whitewash of the trim Georgian houses. Henry and Hilary waited patiently for an explanation.

'Jed has a boat,' said Anna.

Jed frowned.

'I have to tell them, Jed. They know about Teddy. It's nothing sinister, anyway. It isn't drugs or dead bodies or the white slave trade. Just Teddy's old business. Import–export. We import wine and brandy and export whisky. All right, it's illegal, but there's no harm done.'

Henry was amazed at the extent of the relief with which he greeted this story. Why should he still care so much about Uncle Teddy? Why should he care so little about Uncle Teddy's breaking of the law?

'I love Teddy,' said Anna. 'I'd never want to hurt him. Jed knows that.'

'Oh aye. Right. Oh, she loves Teddy,' said Jed.

'I'm no angel, but I do have feelings, and I'd never want to hurt Teddy,' said Anna.

'Never want to hurt him. I can vouch for that,' said Jed.

46

'Obviously it has to be me who comes to England,' said Anna. 'Teddy can't. He's supposed to be dead. Teddy knows I'm seeing Jed.'

'It'd be a trifle awkward if your parents happened to see you now, not wearing your nun's habit.' It was Henry's turn to be dry.

This time Anna gave a tanned blush.

'It is all a bit awful, isn't it?' she said. 'But what can I do? They'd be even more hurt by the truth.'

A huge gull, sitting on the middle of nine chimney-pots, disturbed that rare summer afternoon with a stream of raucous indignation.

'There's just . . . there's just one thing,' said Anna. 'It'd be nice if you could bear it in mind. Teddy thinks Jed's seventy.'

3 The Miracle of Life

As he walked along the corridor to the maternity ward, Henry again made the mistake of rehearsing the scene that was about to take place. Hilary would be sitting up in bed, beautiful and serene and sparkling, and little Kate would be gurgling happily in her arms, or perhaps sleeping peacefully after the ordeal of birth.

In fact Hilary was lying with her head resting against three pillows. Her face was strained and even paler than usual. There were dark patches under her deep-set eyes. Her hair, wet from her exertions, clung lankly and dankly to her scalp. She was holding their baby very gingerly. Kate's disproportionately large face was red, and a few strands of wispy blonde hair were almost invisible on her scalp. Her eyes were shut, her nose was wrinkled and she was yelling furiously at the ignominy of moving from her mother's womb to twentieth-century Thurmarsh.

Henry had imagined that he would bend down to kiss Hilary and say, 'Darling, I'm so proud of you. I love you so much. I'm the luckiest man in the world.' But his throat was tight with emotion and no words would come, and he felt himself dissolving into ten thousand receding pin-pricks. The floor of the ward came up to meet him. As his forehead crashed into the foot of Hilary's bed, he felt the pain as if it were outside himself, at the end of a long, dark tunnel.

The nurse looked at Hilary in alarm, and Hilary looked at the nurse in alarm.

'I think he's pleased,' said Hilary weakly.

Then she burst into tears, and the baby bawled and yelled and Henry stirred and moaned, and the nurse said, 'I've heard of post-natal depression, but this is ridiculous.'

Two burly men wheeled Henry to the Casualty Department, where the blood was washed off his face and the wound dressed. Then they wheeled him to the X-Ray Department, where his forehead was x-rayed. Then he tried to walk, but his legs were wobbly. They gave him a mug of sweet tea, and he tried again, and this time he was strong enough to walk carefully down the serpentine corridors, past wards and operating theatres and the Oncology and Pathology Departments, so that by the time he reached Hilary's bedside he felt a complete sham.

'How are you?' asked Hilary anxiously.

Henry groaned.

'That's what I should be asking you,' he said. 'This is your ordeal, not mine.'

Hilary clasped his hand.

'No, no,' he said. '*I* should be clasping *your* hand. It's you who were brave and suffered. It's you who has to bear the burden of being a woman. You were in labour six hours. I just . . . oh, I feel so guilty.' And then, at last, late but no less sincere, 'Darling, I'm so proud of you. I love you so much. I'm the luckiest man in the world.'

He squeezed Hilary's hand and she squeezed his back, and he said, 'You look lovely.'

'You don't.'

'Oh, thank you very much.'

'Well, you don't. You've got a huge swelling on your forehead and two black eyes.'

'Oh no,' he groaned. 'Oh, I haven't, have I? Oh God. I didn't want to steal your thunder.'

'How's your head?'

'Never mind my head. How are your . . . well, actually, I've got a splitting headache, but never mind that, how are your . . . well, your everything? Oh darling, you must be so sore.'

'I don't even want to think about it,' said Hilary weakly.

He gazed down at their sleeping daughter, and thought he could see echoes of Hilary in her nose and eyes and mouth.

'She's so beautiful,' he said.

'What happened?' asked Hilary, squeezing his hand again. 'Why did you faint?'

'I don't remember,' he said. 'I don't even remember coming in the ward.'

49

'Are you concussed?'

'Darling! Never mind about me. How . . . er . . . was it awfully . . . they say I am a bit concussed, actually, but never mind that, it'll pass, how about you, that's the point . . . I mean, don't talk about it if you don't want to.'

They sat in silence for a moment, holding hands. Their three-hour-old daughter stirred in her sleep and made a tiny noise.

'She's dreaming,' said Hilary. 'What can she have to dream about? What does she know?'

'Her lovely mummy's lovely insides,' said Henry. 'It's coming back. I remember, I came in, and I saw you lying there, looking so exhausted.' He saw Hilary's disappointment and added hurriedly, 'and so incredibly lovely and beautiful. And I saw . . . it . . . her . . . and she . . . I mean, people say babies are small, but she's huge, I mean all that, her head alone looks enormous, and I mean there's hardly room for my prick sometimes, and all that had to come out through that, and I was just overwhelmed with love and empathy with your suffering and I thought, "I'll never complain about anything again." '

'How's your head?'

'Awful.'

Hilary laughed.

'Oh God,' he said. 'That was wicked. Oh, darling, I . . . Oh God, I feel so ashamed. No!! Who cares what I think? How *do* you feel, really?'

'Tired,' said Hilary. 'So terribly tired. You'll just have to go on feeling ashamed. I don't have the energy to steal my thunder back.'

He kissed her very gently, and the doctor came in with the nurse.

'Aching,' said the nurse. 'Lost quite a lot of blood. Shocked.'

'Well, I'm not surprised,' said the doctor. 'What you poor women have to go through!'

'Oh I was speaking about the husband,' said the nurse.

Henry groaned.

When Cousin Hilda saw little Kate she said, 'She's got big ears, hasn't she?' and Henry and Hilary, translating this into praise for eyes, nose and mouth, smiled proudly. When Auntie Doris came, she said, 'Oh, look at her, bless her. Isn't she lovely, bless her?' It was difficult to think that Auntie Doris had once been Kate's size, and horrendous to think that one day Kate might be Auntie Doris's size.

The dreadful summer of 1958 drew blessedly to a close. The cod war raged between Britain and Iceland, the Russians fired two dogs into space and brought them back safely, the number of unemployed reached a ten-year high of 476,000, and Thurmarsh throbbed to the songs of Elvis Presley and Pat Boone.

They took Kate to London to spend a weekend with Mr and Mrs Hargreaves in their tall, narrow Georgian town house in Hampstead, where Elvis Presley was seldom heard, and Pat Boone never. Henry and Hilary were put in Diana's old room, with Kate next to them, in the room where Henry had made love with Diana, for the first and last time, less than three years ago.

'Diana and Nigel are coming to dinner,' Mrs Hargreaves announced. She was still amazingly graceful and attractive, and Henry almost blushed at the memory of the erections he'd been forced to hide on the beaches of Brittany when he was seventeen and hungry. 'They're bringing Benedict. And Paul's popping over.' Her voice dropped. 'Judy's left him.'

Thank God! Paul had been his best friend at Dalton College, but Henry had never liked Judy Miller. She had behaved like a barrister when she was still a student. When she actually became a barrister, goodness knew to what heights of arrogance she would aspire.

'Oh dear, I am sorry,' he said.

'It's kind of you to say so, but you aren't really,' said Mrs Hargreaves. 'She wasn't right for him. I just wish he'd had the sense to leave her before she left him. Oh, and we've invited Nigel's and your old sparring partner, Lampo Davey, and his . . . er . . . friend, whom you also know, I believe.'

It might have been Hampstead, but Mrs Hargreaves wasn't Bohemian enough to say 'lover'.

'Incidentally, you don't praise the food here,' said Henry to Hilary as they unpacked. 'You don't praise it at Cousin Hilda's because food isn't meant to be enjoyed, and you don't praise it here because it's assumed to be delicious and to praise it is to admit the possibility that it might not have been.'

Henry felt nervous as they got ready for dinner, and this surprised him. True, it was fourteen months since he'd last seen Mr and Mrs Hargreaves, at his wedding, but he hadn't expected, now that he was a husband and a father, that he would still feel an uncouth northern hick in these sophisticated surroundings. Now he wondered if those feelings would ever change. Would he always seek the approval of Mrs Hargreaves, because he found her elegance and unattainability so sexually attractive? Would he always feel inferior to Mr Hargreaves, because Mr Hargreaves was a brain surgeon and he was with the Cucumber Marketing Board?

Kate fell asleep on cue after being fed and changed. Hilary looked beautiful in a simple, beige, straight sheath dress, which reflected, subtly, the sack dresses that had come back into fashion. Henry realised that he was so very nervous tonight because he was so anxious for her to shine.

As they walked down the narrow stairs to the drawing room on the first floor, Henry resolved to be charming, to sparkle wittily, but to give Hilary the space to be even more charming and sparkle even more wittily. He wouldn't call Nigel 'Tosser' once.

The drawing room had a faintly Chinese air, and Mr and Mrs Hargreaves had the confidence to have allowed it to become just slightly shabby.

Even before the arrivals had been concluded, Henry was aware that his irritation level was high. He would have to be careful.

He was irritated that Lampo Davey and Denzil Ackerman were *both* wearing bow-ties. It seemed too showy a touch for this gentle, elegant house.

He was irritated that Lampo and Denzil were putting on such a show of courtly charm and togetherness, when he knew that they'd have spent most of the day arguing.

Lampo and Denzil always kissed women with exaggerated enthusiasm, and little murmurs of delight, as if they seriously thought that they could hide their homosexuality, but they seemed to kiss Hilary with special enthusiasm, and this also irritated Henry.

He was irritated at the realisation that Paul was deeply upset at the loss of the dreaded Judy.

He was irritated that Benedict Pilkington-Brick (what a mouthful!) had already inherited Tosser's complacent nose and self-satisfied mouth, and that Diana was pregnant again.

He was irritated by the understated beauty of Mrs Hargreaves's black dress and by Diana's baby-doll outfit.

He was irritated by Hilary's self-confidence. She rose to the civilised atmosphere, accepting a glass of white port as if she knew what it was. He realised, with a sickening thud, that the depressed, repressed girl had grown into a confident woman who could succeed in places where he was unable to follow.

'How's the novel coming on?' asked Denzil.

And Hilary, who hadn't mentioned the book to Henry for weeks, told him.

'Slowly,' she said. 'I have to break off to feed Kate and Henry at regular intervals. But I think it's developing its inner core, and whatever other merits it may lack, at least it's not autobiographical.' Did she know that Henry's novel would have been the story of his life? 'Upstairs, in the tiny back bedroom, Annie's pains began. Amos heard her first sharp cry at twenty-five to seven in the evening.' He shuddered at the thinness of the disguise.

Everybody was thrilled that she was writing a novel. When she left the room to check on the sleeping Kate and Benedict, Mrs Hargreaves said, 'I wondered if you'd ever find anybody good enough for you, Henry. Now I wonder if you're good enough for her.'

'So do I,' said Henry, with such feeling that there was an uneasy pause.

Enjoying the 1948 Pomerol, in the olive-green dining room, Henry remembered the first time he had eaten there, and had hated claret, and had called the *boeuf bourguignon* 'stew'. For a moment he felt warm and sophisticated, and then Hilary irritated him by saying, 'This soup's lovely.' He glared at her. She smiled with infuriating assumed innocence.

53

Mr Hargreaves asked Hilary about her novel again as he dissected his grouse with a disturbing lack of delicacy for a brain surgeon. They discussed Lampo's work at Christie's – or was it Sotheby's? – Denzil's recent interview with Frank Sinatra for the *Argus* – 'Have you ever been to Thurmarsh, Frank?' – the absence of Judy, which Paul, fooling nobody, described as a great release, and Paul's career. He announced that he was abandoning the law and taking up medicine. 'The law is so cynical,' he said. 'I could never defend a man I knew to be guilty. I want to feel I'm at least trying to do good in the world,' and Henry said, 'How can you say that, Paul? You're more motivated by money than anyone I know, except Tosser.'

With one fell swoop, Henry had offended Paul and Tosser, incurred the disapproval of Mr and Mrs Hargreaves, and caused Hilary to look at him in surprise, as if realising that there was a side of him that she hardly knew. Only Diana seemed pleased by his remark, giving Henry a quick grin and then wiping it off and looking exaggeratedly pompous for Tosser's benefit.

'Henry,' said Mrs Hargreaves with chilling politeness, 'we're *longing* to hear about these cucumbers.'

Henry decided that he had no option but to take her remark at face value, but that he mustn't be so naïve as to launch into a description of his work.

He decided to strike a more oblique and urbane note.

'Tiberius adored cucumbers,' he said.

There was silence.

'The king of the conversation-stoppers strikes again,' said Diana, looking like a sixteen-year-old schoolgirl once more.

Mrs Hargreaves gave Diana a look which said, 'Careful. Don't be rude to our guests, however rude they are.'

'Talking of Tiberius,' said Mr Hargreaves, as if to prove that it hadn't been a conversation-stopper, 'when you think of what went on in Ancient Rome, it's remarkable that two thousand years later what you two do in the privacy of your own home is still illegal.'

Lampo and Denzil smiled a little uneasily.

'What Lampo does is break my *objets d'art*,' said Denzil. 'I didn't know there was a law against that.'

'I've always maintained that you should be able to do what you like, as long as you don't frighten the horses,' said Tosser Pilkington-Brick.

'Good old Tosser,' said Henry. 'Everyone has one special talent. His is for coming out with clichés as if they're the product of deep and original thought.'

Hilary stood up abruptly.

'The food is delicious,' she said. 'The grouse is perfectly moist and gamey, the stuffing is extremely subtle, the celeriac purée is a revelation, but I must ask you to excuse me. I'm fed up with my husband being so graceless.'

Henry went red and mumbled, 'I'll go after her,' and there followed all the embarrassing business of his pleading with her, and their returning to the appalled dining room together, and everybody's finishing the meal with unbelievably careful conversation.

In bed that night, Hilary whispered, 'Are you in love with Diana?'

'Of course I'm not,' whispered Henry.

'Well you were very rude to Nigel.'

'One can hate Tosser without loving anybody. One needs no ulterior motive.'

'You were childish and stupid tonight. I was appalled.'

'Yes, well, you weren't, everybody adored you, so that's all right.'

'I thought you wanted me to shine. I tried to shine for my man.'

'Why did you keep praising the food, when I specifically asked you not to?'

'Because you specifically asked me not to. I don't like being given instructions, as if I'm a northern hick.'

They lay in silence for the rest of the night, side by side but not together. In the morning Henry apologised, and told Hilary how much he loved her, and everything was almost all right, and he apologised quite charmingly to Mr and Mrs Hargreaves, and everything was almost all right with them also.

Kate opened her eyes more frequently and gurgled more inventively and began to smile and went gently onto solids and cried when she had colic and when she burped they said, 'Clever little girl!' but when Henry burped Hilary said, 'Do you have to be so crude?' and Henry said, 'Don't forget I'm not a writer. I'm an inferior being,' but these little verbal spats were few and far between, and their love for each other was kept warm by their love of Kate.

They sent photographs of her to Uncle Teddy and Anna.

In his reply, Uncle Teddy said:

> Anna was so pleased to see you both in Berwick. I was glad to hear that Jed struck you as a reliable old boy. The first batch of you-know-what has arrived and is fetching high prices. I'm still an old rogue, Henry, and you're well shot of me, but if you ever feel like coming over, we'd love to see you all and I have two very good sauces of sea bass. Hilary looks far too lovely for you, what is it the girls see in you? Ouch, perhaps I shouldn't have said that! As for Kate, she looks just grand. What a belter! I never wanted kids, never could stand the little buggers, in one end and out the other and spend the rest of the time sleeping or crying. Minimal entertainment value. Age is a funny thing, though. When I see Kate I want to cry for the kids I never had. Too late now. I'd love kids by Anna but I'd be too old to play football with the little buggers and I'd drop dead or something equally silly and leave the poor girl stranded with them.

Hilary smiled after she'd read the letter and said, 'A bit sad, really.'
'Just a bit.'
'He spelt "sources" wrong.'
'A Freudian slip. In his mind he's cooking them already.'
'Let's go next summer.'
'Right.'

They moved into a two-up, two-down stone terrace house in an attractive but crumbling Victorian terrace in Newhaven Road, off the top end of York Road. The Rawlaston and Splutt Building

Society were worried by the condition of the house and thought the asking price of £3,250 excessive, but liked the security of Henry's position, and gave them their mortgage after careful consideration.

They invited Cousin Hilda for tea on their very first Saturday. That morning Henry banged a new name plate into position on the gate. Hilary bandaged his thumb, and they stood back and looked at the name with pride.

Cousin Hilda was less impressed.

'Paradise Villa!' she sniffed.

'What's wrong with it?' said Henry.

'Putting on airs,' said Cousin Hilda.

The living room had no carpets or curtains, and no furniture or decorations except for the art deco clock, a second-hand three-piece suite, a hard chair, and a very cheap nest of tables. A gas fire hissed gently.

Cousin Hilda gave the suite a dirty look, and plonked herself, legs akimbo and bloomers at half-mast, in the hard chair.

' "Paradise" is an echo of the back-to-back where I was born, of which I'm not ashamed,' explained Henry.

' "Villa" is meant to be humorous,' said Hilary. 'Anyone can see it isn't really a villa, but it also reflects the fact that Henry is thankful to have such an improvement on what his parents had.'

'Aye, well, I just hope Mrs Wedderburn'll be able to read all that into it,' said Cousin Hilda. 'I wouldn't want her to think you're putting on airs.'

Henry spread the nest of tables round the room, and Hilary brought in a tray of tea, crumpets and ginger cake.

'Oh no, nothing to eat, thank you. I must have an appetite for my gentlemen,' said Cousin Hilda.

'I beg your pardon?' said Henry.

'I owe it to my gentlemen to eat heartily,' said Cousin Hilda. 'If I just picked at my food, they'd think there was something wrong with it. I am, in my small way, a public figure. It carries responsibilities.'

'You must have something,' said Hilary. 'You're our very first guest.'

57

'We chose the house because it's nearer to you than the flat,' said Henry.

Cousin Hilda went pink, and Henry wondered how a lie could be bad, when it brought so much pleasure.

'Well all right,' said Cousin Hilda. 'Just one crumpet.'

She ate her crumpet with deliberation and concentration.

'Very palatable,' she said primly.

'Have you ever thought of using cucumbers?' asked Henry.

'I can't,' said Cousin Hilda. 'I share all my meals with my gentlemen. They know what to expect. They expect to know what to expect. I can't make changes. There'd be ructions.'

The art deco clock struck four. Kate stirred, opened her eyes, yawned, and gave Cousin Hilda a beautiful smile.

'She's smiling at you,' said Henry. 'She likes you.'

'Ee!' said Cousin Hilda. 'Mrs Wedderburn would love to see her. She'd be right thrilled to hold her.'

'Does that mean you'd like to hold her, Cousin Hilda?' asked Hilary, and Henry held his breath, and an amazing thing happened. Cousin Hilda smiled and said, 'Aye, well, I would.' So Kate was passed over to her very carefully, and Cousin Hilda held her with grim concentration, and tickled her chin self-consciously, and said to her, 'Who's a pretty baby, then?' Henry and Hilary looked at each other and smiled with their eyes, and there was a long silence, as nobody dared disturb the mood, and then Henry said, 'Do you think your gentlemen would like to see her?'

So Henry slipped home early on the following Thursday, and they took Kate to tea at Cousin Hilda's, and Kate slept as they ate their roast pork and tinned pears, and Mr O'Reilly said, 'There's a bit of you in her, Henry. And a bit of you, Miss Hilary, oh yes. She's a lovely little thing, that she is,' and Brian Ironside mumbled, 'She certainly is,' and Norman Pettifer said, 'Adrian had no Stilton at all today. Gorgonzola, Roquefort, Bleu de Bresse, Danish Blue, and no Stilton. There isn't an ounce of patriotism in that boy's body.'

That Saturday they took Kate to Troutwick to see Auntie Doris and Geoffrey Porringer. Auntie Doris said, 'Can I hold her, please?

Oh, isn't she gorgeous, love her?' And Geoffrey Porringer said, 'There's none of you in her at all, Henry,' and Auntie Doris said, 'Teddy!' and Geoffrey Porringer said, 'The name is Geoffrey, Doris. And why are you Geoffreying me anyway?' and Auntie Doris, who always made things worse by protesting about them, said, 'Because you're tactless, Geoffrey. I said she was gorgeous, and you said there's none of Henry in her at all, and you know how sensitive he is about not being good-looking.'

Auntie Doris seemed to Henry to be growing larger by the month and to be laughing almost too much now. He sensed that there was something rather desperate about her laughter and her drinking and about this deeply successful performance that she was giving as the landlady. He felt that if she didn't stop she would go on expanding until she exploded into little bits all over the antiques in the lounge bar one crowded Saturday night.

And, as Auntie Doris grew larger, it seemed that Geoffrey Porringer was growing smaller, hiding in her shadow. Henry could no longer dislike him enough to call him slimy.

He caught Auntie Doris pretending to pour herself a double gin. While she drank heavily, she didn't have quite the Rabelaisian capacity that she claimed. Geoffrey Porringer, on the other hand, pretended to be a moderate man, but slipped spirits into his beer at every opportunity, from whatever bottle happened to be most handy. Henry had the impression that, if something didn't change, the pub's popularity would kill them both.

They took Kate to Perkin Warbeck Drive. Nadežda said, 'I don't intend to do this business of saying whom she takes after. She's lovely, she's healthy, and she's herself.' Howard Lewthwaite said, 'We mustn't rest until we give this girl, and millions like her, true equality of opportunity.' Sam said, 'God, she's ugly!'

Donald Campbell achieved a world record 248.62 miles per hour on Coniston Water, the Preston by-pass became Britain's first stretch of motorway, and autumn slid irrevocably into winter.

Henry found himself increasingly desk-bound as the weather closed in. He sent letters to market gardeners who grew cucumbers, market gardeners who didn't grow cucumbers, farmers who might grow cucumbers, shops that sold cucumbers, shops that didn't sell cucumbers, restaurants that used cucumbers and restaurants that didn't use cucumbers. All these letters were typed by Andrea in the typing pool. When he discovered that Andrea was known as Deputy Head of Services (Secretarial), Henry realised that everybody in the Cucumber Marketing Board had a title, and there wasn't anything special in being the Assistant Regional Co-ordinator, Northern Counties (Excluding Berwick-on-Tweed).

One wild wet window-rattling, dustbin-lid-tormentor of a morning, Mr Whitehouse called Henry into his office, blew his predatory nose, and said, 'You're sending an awful lot of letters.'

'Well, yes,' said Henry. 'I'm aiming at blanket coverage.'

'M'm. There are two ways of looking at everything, Henry,' said the Director (Operations). 'On the one hand there is blanket coverage. On the other hand, there is saturation point. Point taken? Good. I'm delighted with your enthusiasm, Henry. Delighted. The fact is, though, because we all have to live in the real world, you've exceeded your budget.'

'I didn't even know I had a budget,' said Henry.

'Oh dear,' said the Director (Operations). 'Oh dear. I would never run a colleague down behind his back, not my style, not the Timothy Whitehouse way, but between you, me and the mythical G.P., Roland Stagg is getting a bit lax in his old age.'

Mr Whitehouse leant back in his chair, pulled his braces out, and let them fizz back into his chest. I wonder if he likes bondage, thought Henry.

'You did tell me to be my own man, stick to my guns and be fearless. I took that as an invitation to independence,' said Henry.

'I did indeed. A fair point. I sit rebuked. *Mea culpa. Mea culpa*! I should have told you to be your own man, stick to your guns and be fearless *within the budget*. Point taken, Henry?'

'Point taken, Mr Whitehouse.'

As Henry set off to return to Room 106, Roland Stagg shambled out of his office on the second floor, crumpled trousers hanging low over his obscene paunch, and said, 'I warned you, Henry. A low profile.'

'Yes,' said Henry, 'but he told me to be fearless and stick to my guns.'

'And I told you to take his advice with a pinch of salt.'

'Yes,' said Henry, 'but he told me to take your advice with a pinch of salt.'

'Yes, but I'm right and he's wrong. That's why he's the Director (Operations) and I'm only the Regional Co-ordinator, Northern Counties (Excluding Berwick-on-Tweed).'

Henry staggered, somewhat bemused, into his office, and sat behind his familiar desk, listening to the rain gushing from drainpipes of many styles. The telephone shrilled petulantly, and he jumped.

'Tubman-Edwards. I need to see you.'

Henry dragged himself to the office of the Head of Establishments.

Mr Tubman-Edwards looked at him sadly.

'Sit down,' he said.

So far so good! Henry had no problem in obeying the simple instruction.

'Oh dear,' said Mr Tubman-Edwards. 'Sid Pentelow is upset.'

'Sid Pentelow?'

'Director (Financial Services). He hates people exceeding their budget. As you're my appointee, it reflects badly on me. You've let me down, Henry.'

The rain was beating against Mr Tubman-Edwards's windows like furious bees.

'I'm very sorry,' said Henry, 'but I didn't even realise I had a budget.'

'There are budgets for everything. Postage, telephones, travel. My son's coming up next weekend. I know you weren't close chums, but I think you got on pretty well, didn't you?'

'Oh yes. Pretty well.'

'Tremendous. Well, we'd like it if you and your wife came to dinner next Saturday, if you aren't too busy getting ready for Christmas.'

'Well, thank you,' said Henry, appalled. 'We'd love to.'

61

'Excellent. These budgets are so generous that I simply never dreamt that anybody could exceed them. But you . . .' He looked at Henry sadly. 'You're a human dynamo.'

'Is that bad?'

'No, not within reason. But you must always remember that we are given finite tasks to perform. If we perform them too well, there's a danger that one day our work will be over. We'll have worked ourselves out of a job. None of us would want that, would we? Till next Saturday, then. Shall we say seven thirty for eight o'clock?'

The wind was playing badminton with fish-and-chip papers. A pigeon was tossed over the Queen's Hotel like a rag-doll. A taxi ploughed through a puddle and drenched Henry. His throat was sore and he thought he might be starting a cold. He only just caught the train and had to stand until Normanton. When he got home, Kate had colic and was screaming, and the stew had stuck and was slightly burnt. When the phone rang, he just knew it would be bad news.

'It's me,' said Helen Plunkett, née Cornish. 'Ted's away, and I've just had a bath, and I'm completely naked, and slightly pink all over from the heat, and I thought it was high time you came round and I did that interview about those cucumbers.'

Henry felt extremely nervous as his noisy wipers swished and screeched their way to Ted and Helen's flat in Coromandel Avenue.

He hadn't really wanted to go, but Hilary had insisted.

'She'll try to seduce me,' Henry had said. 'I know her.'

'Exactly. And you will not be tempted. I know you. We love each other utterly, don't we?'

'Of course we do.'

'Well, then. An ideal opportunity to re-dedicate our love.'

As he pulled up outside the unloved, leaf-sodden garden of number 12, Coromandel Avenue, and rushed up to the porch with its stained glass windows at either side of the door, Henry steeled himself to be strong against temptation.

It was a relief that Helen was no longer naked. Indeed, she was wearing a long, loose grey dress which did nothing for her body.

Large photographs of Helen and Ted at their wedding, of Ted's parents, of Helen's parents and of her sister Jill, yet another young woman after whom Henry had lusted, sat in silver frames on the heavy, ornate sideboard. The suite was brown leather. Helen made coffee, and plonked herself briskly and unsexily into a chair, leaving Henry alone on the settee.

'Right. To work,' she said, to Henry's relief. 'Why didn't you get on to me about the article? It's been months.'

'Because you didn't seem remotely keen.'

'I'm not. So, excite me. Persuade me. Where's my angle?'

'I just thought . . . a piece about how unjustly the cucumber is neglected,' said Henry as limply as an old salad.

'So why is it unjust?' She wrote busily in her elegant shorthand. Henry began to wish that she was looking a *bit* more seductive, so that he had something to fight against.

'Well . . . I mean . . . cucumbers are very nice. How's Jill?'

He hoped he wouldn't blush. He wondered if she had ever known just how much he had fancied her younger sister.

'Very well. Do they have any amazing nutritional value?'

'Still happy with Gordon?'

Jill had gone off with the enigmatic Gordon Carstairs, former lover of Ginny Fenwick and the only one out of all of Henry's ex-colleagues who had so far escaped to Fleet Street.

'Very happy. They come up occasionally. They're good sports. We have fun.'

Helen's pearly grey eyes met Henry's, and he saw the spark of mischief in them. Then it was switched off abruptly.

'Well come on,' she said. 'Do they have any nutritional value? Are they good defences against disease, like garlic and ginger?'

'Er . . . as far as I know they aren't really any use against disease, no. I mean, they are actually ninety per cent water, so they hardly have any nutritional value whatsoever.'

'OK. So that's out, then. So is it their incredible taste? Has this not been fully appreciated?'

'Well, I mean. . .' Oh God, I'm floundering. 'I mean, they're nice, of course . . . *very* nice . . . but I wouldn't say they have a particularly strong taste. A nice taste. Subtle. Not strong.'

'Well I suppose they wouldn't be if they're ninety per cent water.'

'Perhaps taste isn't the area we should concentrate on.'

'Well, is it their phallic symbolism? Do they have ritual value? Is there a Splutt Cucumber Dance? Or a midnight procession in which all the adult men in Rawlaston wear funny hats and march to the Trustee Savings Bank with cucumbers in their trousers?'

'Of course not,' said Henry stuffily. 'This isn't France.'

'You look tired. Love life too much for you?'

'No. It's the rest of life that's too much for me.'

'Poor Henry. You're a fighter, though. You'll keep going. Now, what do you want me to say about these bloody cucumbers?'

Henry wanted to tell her to forget it, but no, he *was* a fighter, he *would* keep going. He took a sip of coffee. It was fearsomely strong, and it gave him at least the illusion of energy.

'Perhaps what I'm seeking is to make them fashionable again. I mean, cucumber sandwiches were once synonymous with afternoon tea.'

'I'm afraid Thurmarsh prefers toasted tea-cake.'

'Oh, I'm not talking about afternoon tea specifically. What I'm saying is, I'd like to make the cucumber a little bit chic.'

'Terrific,' said Helen. 'What a shame I work for the *Thurmarsh Evening Argus*, not *Vogue*.'

All good fighters know that there are moments when it's best to concede defeat.

'I think I'd better go,' he said. 'Goodnight, Helen. Thank you for the coffee. Give my love to Ted.'

When he got home, Kate was asleep in front of the fire. Hilary looked tired but lovely. She kissed him warmly.

'You weren't long,' she said. 'But then I knew you wouldn't be.'

'Of course I wasn't,' he said. 'I love you too much.'

'Was she desperately disappointed by your strength and resolve?'

'Well . . . perhaps not *desperately*.'

As they undressed, Henry felt sad as well as exhausted. It had

64

been a long, tiring, thoroughly bad day, but he should still have told Hilary that Helen hadn't attempted to tempt him. He felt that he was in danger of losing something extremely valuable. He was in danger of losing himself.

4 The Whelping Season

Henry felt increasingly intimidated on the drive to Leeds. The formal invitation had made him uneasy. The address sticker on the back of the envelope had made him nervous. The address – Mr and Mrs D. F. C. Tubman-Edwards, the Dower House, Balmoral Road, Alwoodley, Leeds – had overawed him.

The Dower House was set between a stockbroker mock-Tudor excrescence and a turreted extravaganza that looked as if it had been hewn off one end of a Château of the Loire, in one of the most prestigious streets in North Leeds. The huge houses were set in suitably large gardens.

How could he have continued to feel overawed after he'd discovered, at the top of a long, curving drive, that the Dower House was a boxy little brick villa, dwarfed by its setting?

How could he have felt so intolerably stiff in his best suit? How could he have allowed himself to feel that his old school blackmailer was his social superior?

Why had it mattered so much that his rusting Standard Eight looked so pathetic parked between a Riley and a Rolls?

Why hadn't it occurred to him that, instead of feeling humiliated because J. C. R. Tubman-Edwards was a merchant banker and he was Assistant Regional Co-ordinator, Northern Counties (Excluding Berwick-on-Tweed) of the Cucumber Marketing Board, he should have realised that Mr and Mrs Tubman-Edwards, with their social pretensions, must be even more humiliated that, in his fifties, the merchant banker's father was merely the Head of Establishments of the Cucumber Marketing Board?

Henry, in his suit, and Hilary, smart in her short black and gold dress, were astonished to find that Mr and Mrs Tubman-Edwards, and their son, and the two other guests, Dougie and Jean Osmotherly, were in evening dress.

'It's a family tradition on Saturday nights,' said Margaret Tubman-Edwards.

'Frightfully pretentious, my people,' said J. C. R. Tubman-Edwards proudly.

'We don't tell people, because we don't want to embarrass them in case they haven't got any. Not all young people do, do they?' said Margaret Tubman-Edwards, whose voice could have cut glass at twenty paces. She was small and neat and looked as cold as the dead, immaculate drawing room in which they were drinking cheap sherry poured out of a very expensive decanter.

'We know because we live next door,' said Dougie Osmotherly, who turned out to be big in ball-bearings and the owner of the Rolls.

Fancy taking the Rolls to go next door, thought Henry.

'Next door?' said Hilary. 'Really? Tudor or turrets?'

Henry flinched, but Dougie and Jean Osmotherly were unperturbed.

'Tudor,' said Jean, who was wearing a diamond ring, a diamond necklace, a diamond bracelet, a brilliant ruby ring, and four other rings.

'I love your jewellery, Jean,' said Margaret Tubman-Edwards.

'So embarrassing,' said Jean Osmotherly. 'One hates to look showy, but it's so much safer on the person with all these burglaries around.'

'Turrets is a problem,' said J. C. R. Tubman-Edwards. 'A scrap-metal dealer lives there. Moved in from your neck of the woods actually, Henry. My folks are furious. Well, I mean, it's a bit off, isn't it, choosing a posh area like All-Yidley and finding oneself next to a scrap merchant.'

Henry went cold at this gratuitous piece of anti-Semitism. He longed to object, but in his dark suit which had gone from being over-dressed to being under-dressed in one second, he hadn't the confidence. Knowing that he must say something, he said, 'Scrap merchant? Not Bill Holliday, by any chance?'

'You don't actually know him, do you?' said Margaret Tubman-Edwards, as if to know Bill Holliday would be the ultimate solecism.

67

'Well only slightly,' said Henry hurriedly.

The thought of Bill Holliday, whom he had once believed to be trying to kill him, didn't do wonders for Henry's confidence.

'Henry and Josceleyn were chums at Brasenose and Dalton,' said Margaret Tubman-Edwards.

The mention of Brasenose and Dalton, and the memory of Josceleyn Tubman-Edwards blackmailing him and calling him Oiky, didn't do wonders for Henry's confidence.

'Well, not close chums,' he said.

'We ran into each other a few times, though, didn't we?' said Josceleyn Tubman-Edwards.

Later Henry would wonder why it was he and not Josceleyn Tubman-Edwards who'd been on the defensive in this conversation. It was Josceleyn who'd been the eventual loser in their battle, even if it had taken the looming presence of Tosser Pilkington-Brick to seal the victory.

What a shoot-out, Henry thought now, Tosser and Josceleyn staring at each other down the double barrels of their names.

But all he said was, 'Yes. A few times.'

A gong resounded through the boxy Dower House, with its frosted glass doors. Henry looked for self-mockery and found none.

The dining room was as cold as Josceleyn Tubman-Edwards's eyes. The stuffed fox over the brick fireplace struck an inappropriately rural note.

'I'm rather piqued with Josceleyn,' said Margaret Tubman-Edwards. 'He was supposed to bring his girlfriend. He's untidied my table.'

'I've given her the old heave-ho,' said Tubman-Edwards. 'Kept dragging me to the ballet. Trying to improve my mind.'

Not much use unless you have a mind to improve, thought Henry. Oh why oh why didn't he have the courage to say it?

'Not much use unless you have a mind to improve,' said Mr D. F. C. Tubman-Edwards.

Everybody laughed, but neither Josceleyn Tubman-Edwards nor his mother laughed with their eyes.

They ate insipid leek and potato soup out of Spode soup bowls, and tiny fillets of lukewarm shoe-leather *meunière* off Spode fish plates, washed down with cheap white wine poured from a very expensive decanter. They talked about Josceleyn's meteoric rise through the ranks of Pellet and Runciman. 'Wasn't there a Pellet and a Runciman at Dalton?' said Henry, and there was momentary family unease at the hint that Josceleyn had got his job through the old boy network rather than talent. Hilary suggested, politely, that merchant bankers were parasites. Josceleyn Tubman-Edwards flushed and Henry flinched and Dougie Osmotherly said, 'Well, I think you're all parasites except those of us at the sharp end, who make things,' and roared with laughter, as if someone else had said something very witty, and Josceleyn Tubman-Edwards said arrogantly, 'You're an anachronism, Dougie. In fifty years nobody'll make anything except money in this country.'

Over a pallid steak and kidney pudding, eaten off Spode meat plates, washed down with Bulgarian red wine poured out of a very expensive decanter, there was talk of Conservative fund-raising functions, and Jean Osmotherly invited Henry and Hilary to one and Hilary said, politely, that she was afraid that on principle she wasn't prepared to support the Conservatives, and Josceleyn Tubman-Edwards said, 'Well, they're all Conservatives in Allyidley,' and Hilary said, 'I'm sorry, Josceleyn, but I can't let that go. I just loathe anti-Semitism,' and Henry felt proud and horrified at the same time, and Josceleyn looked genuinely contrite and said, 'Oh Christ. You're not Jewish, are you?' and Hilary said, 'No,' and Josceleyn looked puzzled and said, 'Well, what are you complaining about, then?' and Hilary said, 'I hate racialism,' and Josceleyn said, 'Well, I was only bloody joking, for Christ's sake,' and Margaret Tubman-Edwards said, 'Josceleyn! That's enough,' and the stuffed fox stared, and Josceleyn Tubman-Edwards said, 'I see. Everybody's rude to me and when I defend myself it's all my bloody fault as usual. I'm going to the fucking pub. Coming, Henry, old mate?' and Henry said, 'Of course not, old mate. I'm invited to dinner,' and Josceleyn Tubman-Edwards stormed out, and Dennis Tubman-Edwards said, 'Well at least your table's tidy now, Margaret,' and Margaret Tubman-Edwards said, 'Shut up and pour some more wine, Dennis,' and Dennis Tubman-Edwards grumbled, 'Seems it's illegal to joke these days,' and Henry and Hilary exchanged glances which said, 'We seem to be becoming connoisseurs of dinner parties at which people walk out.'

For the rest of the evening they talked with careful banality about the rival charms of the Yorkshire Dales and the Peak District, the French way of life, the quality of the Thurmarsh shops, the best ways of hiding the hi-fi, and other safe subjects. Nobody dared leave early because that would have been to admit that the evening had not been an unqualified social success.

Shortly before midnight, Dougie Osmotherly stood up and said, 'Well, Jean needs her beauty sleep even if I don't, and we've a long way to go.'

'Yes, we must go too,' said Henry.

'Oh don't let us break the party up,' said Jean Osmotherly.

'Have one more port, Henry,' said his Head of Establishments, and it sounded suspiciously like a command.

Dougie Osmotherly pointed his Rolls towards next door, with many jokes about driving carefully and not falling asleep on the way home.

When Dougie and Jean had gone, Dennis and Margaret Tubman-Edwards sighed in unison and Margaret said, 'Sorry about them, but we owed them a meal desperately and what can one do when one lives in the land of the *nouveaux riches?*'

'We are of course the *anciens pauvres*,' said Dennis Tubman-Edwards.

His wife didn't laugh.

Henry drove off full of drink as many people did in those days. By the time they reached Thurmarsh he was fighting against sleep.

Paradise Villa seemed very lifeless without Kate, who was spending the night with Hilary's family.

'You were very quiet tonight,' said Hilary, as they sat at opposite sides of the bed and undressed like weary zombies.

'You weren't,' said Henry pointedly.

'Don't you want me to be what I am and say what I think?' said

Hilary. 'Do you want me to have no beliefs and no feelings and no social courage whatsoever?'

Henry wanted to say, 'God, your body's beautiful. Your skin is *so* lovely.' So why did he say, 'What do you mean by that? Is that what you're saying *I'm* like?'

'I think you're lovely and worth all those people put together and it makes me bloody livid that you can't see it,' said Hilary, and she slammed the bedroom door and locked herself in the bathroom and burst into tears.

Henry was very drunk, Hilary fairly drunk, Hilary crying in the bathroom, Henry pleading outside the bathroom door. Both utterly exhausted. Unpromising beginnings for a night of love.

Yet afterwards, when they counted, they were very nearly certain that it was on that night that Jack was conceived.

If Henry had written down his ideal list of guests for their first Christmas at home, it would not have consisted of Howard Lewthwaite, Nadežda Lewthwaite, Sam Lewthwaite, Cousin Hilda, Mrs Wedderburn, Liam O'Reilly and Norman Pettifer. After that dinner party at the Dower House, however, all social difficulties paled into insignificance.

They had roast turkey and all the trimmings, and everyone drank wine except for Cousin Hilda and Mrs Wedderburn. Cousin Hilda looked shocked when Norman Pettifer and especially Mr O'Reilly accepted, and Mr O'Reilly went puce with courage. Cousin Hilda even looked slightly shocked when Mrs Wedderburn said, in answer to Henry's attempts at persuasion, 'It's not that I disapprove. I just hate the taste.'

Kate slept and fed and watched and smiled and just might have been dimly aware that it was a special day. Sam described everything as 'grisly', it was his word of the month, but everyone else enjoyed themselves and Henry and Hilary worked as a splendid team, having been too busy to be unhappy. Their happiness, and Kate's, was toasted, and even Cousin Hilda raised her glass of water and almost smiled. Howard Lewthwaite occasionally looked sad and Nadežda occasionally looked distant and when the splendid cheese board was served Norman Pettifer made his only bitter remark of the day. 'Not bought from Adrian, clearly,' he said.

Everyone took turns at holding Kate, but Nadežda felt that she would be too heavy, and in the kitchen, as they made coffee, Hilary said, 'Perhaps we shouldn't have let them all hold Kate. It's brought her disability home to Mummy,' and Henry said, 'I think she must know it already, since she's in a wheelchair,' and then he apologised and kissed her and said, 'We had to do it. It's made Mrs Wedderburn's day and Mr O'Reilly's year,' and the brief shadow passed.

As the light faded, Henry and Nadežda and Howard and Sam played a long game of Monopoly, and Hilary, Cousin Hilda, Mrs Wedderburn, Mr O'Reilly and Norman Pettifer contested many a hard-fought bout of Snap.

In the evening, they had cold ham and salad, while they watched *Christmas Night with the Stars*, introduced by David Nixon. Then they watched Harry Belafonte with the George Mitchell Singers, and *Top Hat* with Fred Astaire and Ginger Rogers.

As the *News* began, Cousin Hilda said, 'Well, that were a right good night if you like singing and dancing.'

After the *News* there was a five-minute mental health appeal by Christopher Mayhew MP.

'Where's the sense of depressing us on Christmas Day?' said Cousin Hilda.

'Surely we can spare five minutes to think of those less fortunate than ourselves?' said Hilary, and Cousin Hilda blazed with Christian shame.

Norman Pettifer snored several times during *The Black Eye*, with David Kossoff, but afterwards he said he'd enjoyed it.

When *The Epilogue* began, Henry moved to switch the set off.

'You're never switching *The Epilogue* off on Christmas Day!' said Cousin Hilda.

'No,' lied Henry cravenly. 'There was a fly on the screen. I was going to brush it off.'

After *The Epilogue*, Henry and Hilary saw their guests to the door. It was past midnight.

'It's been the best day of my life,' said Liam O'Reilly. 'Definitely.'

Hilary turned away, to hide the tears in her eyes.

The fierce winter of 1959 held the British Isles in its grip. In London there was a return of the killer smog, in which 3,000 people had died in four days in 1952, and all eight and a half miles of Britain's first motorway were closed after just forty-eight days, due to rainwater and melted snow seeping under the surface.

In the Midlands, 10,000 girls who made nylon stockings took a twelve per cent wage cut to save jobs.

Tosser Pilkington-Brick phoned Henry and Hilary and said, 'We've got a little girl.'

'Terrific,' said Henry. 'What are you calling her?'

'Camilla,' said Tosser.

'Well never mind,' said Henry. 'I do hope all goes well for you, anyway.'

'Thanks,' said Tosser. 'Had any thoughts about pensions and insurance yet?'

Henry 'Incapable of thinking about pensions and insurance' Pratt caught the train from Thurmarsh to Leeds every morning, sent out more letters, collated more replies, produced a draft of a leaflet giving advice on the planting and care of indoor and outdoor cucumbers, accepted with simulated humility and gratitude Roland Stagg's suggestion that it become two booklets, one for indoors and one for outdoors, negotiated a leaflet budget with Sid Pentelow, made a little work go a long way, kept a low profile, produced a set of encouraging statistics, accepted Roland Stagg's suggestion that he make the statistics less encouraging, so that there would be more room for improvement and credit for the department later, felt that he was getting nowhere and that nothing whatsoever in the world of cucumbers had been changed one iota by his appointment to the Cucumber Marketing Board, and was warmly congratulated on his progress by the Director

(Operations), the Head of Establishments and the Regional Co-ordinator, Northern Counties (Excluding Berwick-on-Tweed).

Neither Mr Tubman-Edwards nor Henry ever mentioned the dinner party at the Dower House.

Hilary discovered that she was pregnant, and Kate began to crawl, backwards at first, then forwards.

Russ Conway became a star, Cliff Richard's career began, and Henry had three pieces of news, and all three depressed him, and it depressed him that they depressed him, and this disturbed him, and it disturbed him that so many things disturbed him.

The first piece of news was told him by Hilary, one late spring morning, while she was changing Kate's nappy in front of the gas fire, in the still uncarpeted living room.

'Darling?' she said, with ominous seriousness.

'Yes?' Henry's heart raced psychically.

'I've finished my novel.'

'What?'

'I've sent it to an agent somebody recommended.'

'Oh.'

'Is that all you can say – "oh"?'

'Of course not. Great. I'm thrilled.'

'No, you aren't. You're jealous.'

'Of course I'm not. I'm absolutely thrilled. I'm . . . I'm just surprised. I mean, you haven't said a word about it for months.'

'Because you get so jealous.'

'I don't. I'm just a bit annoyed because I would like not to have been so insulted by being kept in the dark.'

'I couldn't tell you. You make it impossible for me to tell you.'

'I see. I'm impossible.'

'I didn't say that. You see, you're angry.'

'How can you say that? What sort of a person do you think I am?'

'I don't know any more.'

'Oh. Great.'

They hardly spoke for the rest of the weekend. On Monday, in his office, looking out onto a courtyard full of offices full of people looking out at him, Henry felt deeply depressed and fought hard to find in himself the generosity to tell Hilary how much he hoped her book would be a success.

That evening, he did find the generosity.

'I hope it's a huge success,' he said. 'I hope it's a best-seller.'

They kissed, and later they made love, and Kate was fun, and they were happy, except . . . Henry knew that he hadn't found the generosity to mean what he said, and he suspected that Hilary knew this.

The second and third pieces of news that depressed him were both imparted in the heaving lounge bar of the White Hart, in which Kate was a sensation. Even hard-bitten seed merchants agreed that she was one of the most beautiful babies in the history of the human race.

As Henry struggled to the bar, he found his way blocked by the broad backs of a row of regulars, all taller than him. One of the backs, a member of the county set, turned to his neighbour and said, 'I hear Belinda's whelped,' and as he pushed through to get served, Henry said, 'Excuse me, are you referring to Belinda Boyce-Uppingham, by any chance?'

'What's it to you?' said County Set unpleasantly.

'I knew her well as a child.'

County Set looked as if he thought it unlikely.

'Well, she's had a little girl called Tessa,' he said, and turned his back on Henry.

Why should it depress me, pondered Henry, that Belinda Boyce-Uppingham, that frontispiece for *Country Life*, whom I foolishly adored when I knew no better, has whelped?

The third piece of news was that the baby of Lorna Lugg, his childhood sweetheart, was called Marlene.

Two monkeys, fired into space by the Americans, returned to earth safely. Four mice were less lucky, and circuited the earth until they died.

Golden summer covered Britain in a gentle haze. Henry chugged around his Northern Counties under skies of an unbroken pale blue. He spent little time in the more spectacular regions. Few cucumbers were grown in the Lake District, on the Cumbrian fells, on the sheep-rich Cheviots, in the Trough of Bowland and the Yorkshire Dales. But in flatter lands, in the Vale of York, County Durham, West Lancashire, Western Westmorland beyond the lakes, and around the Solway Firth, Henry would grind to a squeaky halt and hear folk hiss, 'It's the man from the Marketing Board. I'm out.' With sinking heart he doled out advice that wasn't wanted to folk who knew better. With sinking heart he rattled home to a house that was filled with the loud silence of unasked questions. 'What did the agent think of your novel?' And even, 'Do you love me?'

Abandoned villages appeared in the middle of shrinking reservoirs. Moorland fires clothed the Western suburbs of Sheffield in acrid smoke which could be smelt even in Thurmarsh. The House of Fraser acquired Harrods. The *Manchester Guardian* became the *Guardian*. Kate took her first step, said her first word. It was 'Mama'. Innocent, tactless Kate.

Henry couldn't have his holidays until September, and they decided that France would have to wait another year. The sun still blazed, they took a cottage near Helmsley, Kate loved the countryside and saved their holiday.

On Sunday, September 27th, 1959, the Ministry of Labour announced that 4,747,000 working days had been lost to strikes in the first eight months of the year, singing star Shani Wallis dashed into the sea in Brighton in a fifty-guinea dress to save a man from drowning, and Jack Pratt was born. They had christened him (in case he turned out to be religious) before they realised that at school he would be known as Jack Sprat.

Jack was big. Quite big even when he was born. The sight of him, the thought of his passing through Hilary's womb and vagina, caused Henry pain, but not with the same intensity that had attended Kate's birth. Poor second child. Already the incredible, the absurdly brilliant miracle of conception, development and birth had become commonplace.

It was impossible for anyone to say that Jack was beautiful. He was fat, bald, red and greedy. Kate had hated soiling her nappies.

Jack adored soiling his. Kate had been difficult to feed. Jack proved impossible to stop feeding. Yet there was very soon about him, turning his ugliness into beauty, a natural good humour that warmed the embers of his parents' flickering fires. He cried, but he never whined. Kate, knowing that he was ugly, sensing that he was deeply loved, grew intermittently querulous, though her growing vocabulary and evident intelligence thrilled them.

Hilary and Henry hosted another massed Christmas at Paradise Villa, because to have gone to the Lewthwaites' would have been to have been obliged to go to Cousin Hilda's the following year.

In Capetown, Harold Macmillan spoke of the 'wind of change blowing through Africa'. Jack went onto solids, and in Paradise Villa the wind of change acquired a less inspiring meaning. Dr Barbara Moore walked from Land's End to John o' Groats in twenty-three days. Jack crawled from the nest of tables, across the new green carpet, almost to the door, in one minute eleven seconds. Togo became independent. Kate yearned for independence and learned to use colouring books quite accurately.

On Saturday, June 28th, 1960, Henry and Hilary set off for France.

Slowly, the faithful Standard Eight slipped south. The Great North Road. The Dartford Tunnel. The Dover Road. The night ferry. Romantic words, monotonous reality. They chugged through ascetic old towns full of cafés and restaurants that they couldn't afford to enter, past vibrant games of *boules* under peaceful avenues of plane trees. As the road curved endlessly among the sunburnt hills of Provence, Kate grew restless. They'd promised her the sea, and although she wasn't quite sure what the sea was, she became deeply impatient to see it. Late on the second afternoon she *did* see it, but it was too big and too empty for her, and she felt betrayed, and cried bitterly.

But she liked Cap Ferrat, the glimpses of sea and mountain, the stunning villas, the huge, immaculate gardens.

Uncle Teddy's villa was set behind a row of colour-washed fishermen's cottages. It was just over three years since Henry had been there, on that momentous journey of discovery, when his whole world had seemed to turn upside-down. Now he could approach it calmly, happily, in holiday mood.

He pulled up neatly on the gravel outside the gate, got out of the car and gave himself a luxurious stretch.

Enjoy that stretch, Henry. Make it last. Your mood is about to change.

Uncle Teddy was at the door already, and Henry and Hilary both knew, before he opened his mouth, that something was very wrong.

'Anna left me yesterday,' he said.

5 A Difficult Holiday

It was cool and dark in the shuttered villa. Uncle Teddy opened the shutters and let in the smell of the South, the salty lethargy of the sea, the stale breath of the afternoon sun, and the herb-scented freshness of the evening breeze.

He flinched from the cruel light, which was merciless towards his greying hair, his ashen face, his hollow sleepless eyes, his thin ageing legs and his unlovely paunch. He smiled and said that he was fine. He showed them their room, large and cool, with shutters on to a balcony, and two hired cots. He tickled Jack's chin and made awkward remarks to Kate, who stared at him solemnly as if he frightened her. He made tea in the marble kitchen, and said, 'I thought we'd eat out tonight. I haven't been able to get myself organised to shop.'

'Of course not,' said Hilary. 'We'll shop and cook.'

Uncle Teddy handed them an envelope.

'She left a letter for you,' he said.

They read it in turn:

> Dear Henry and Hilary,
>
> I know this will come as a great shock to you, and I feel really bad about spoiling your holiday, but my first thought must be for Teddy. Don't give that hollow laugh. I mean it. I've known for some time that I've got to go. I just haven't got it in me to stay with an old man and I owe it to Teddy to get out before he becomes old. He still has a chance of somebody much more suitable than me, some rich widow or something, he's a sexy man and fun quite a lot of the time, but he's never really tried to understand me and how I tick. I really think the only woman he's ever really been interested in is Doris. He wanted a fling and an adventure. He wanted to seem to be a bit of an old rogue. He's done it and that's it.

Anyway, I can't feel too guilty because it was great fun while it lasted and we both have some fantastic memories. Well, all right, I shouldn't have gone with him, but I did and that's all there is to it. There isn't anybody else, no Jed or anybody, so I'm looking for Mr Right! Anyway, the point is, if I'd left him at any other time he'd have had nothing to occupy his days and I know you and the kids'll cheer him up for a couple of weeks and by then the worst'll be over. So I've done it at the best time, even though I feel rotten about it.

Washing stuff et cetera under the sink, foodstuffs fairly self-explanatory, brushes and mops in an *outside* cupboard at the back next to the third shower and loo.

I'll miss seeing you all very much. This isn't easy for me either.

With love,

Anna

PS Not a word to Daddy. I'll just tell them I couldn't cope with life as a nun. Anyway, they'll be so relieved that they won't ask too many questions.

Hilary said that the children were too tired to eat out that night, so they bought food in, and Hilary made chicken *provençale*, because if the food wasn't Mediterranean, they might as well have been in Thurmarsh.

When he came in for pre-dinner drinks, Henry caught Uncle Teddy holding a photograph of himself and Anna, and there were tears in his eyes. He put it down hurriedly as soon as he heard Henry, and gave a watery smile.

'We were happy that day,' he said.

'Would it be better to put the photos away?' suggested Henry.

There were photos of a scantily clad Anna all over the villa.

Uncle Teddy shook his head. 'I've only just lost her,' he said. 'I couldn't cope with losing the memory of her as well.'

Over their dinner, which he hardly tasted, Uncle Teddy said, 'Never should have done it, I suppose. Should have known better.'

'There's no point in thinking that,' said Hilary.

'I don't regret it, though. Not a moment of it.'

'Well, then.'

After the meal, as they sipped wine on the terrace, with the incessant clattering of ten thousand crickets challenging the velvet stillness of the southern night, Uncle Teddy said, 'How *is* Doris?'

'She's very well,' said Henry. 'She's put on quite a lot of weight.'

'She's never had a lot of self-discipline, hasn't Doris,' said Uncle Teddy. 'Not easy to, running a pub, mind.' He sighed. 'I can't believe she's ended up running a pub.' He sighed again. 'What a mess. Pub still doing all right, is it?'

'They get by,' said Henry.

They didn't tell Uncle Teddy that it was so popular that it was known throughout the Dales as 'Doris's'. They didn't think it would be what he wanted to hear.

'I don't blame her for not waiting,' said Uncle Teddy. 'My fault for getting sent to prison. Doris couldn't live without a man. No idea how to start.' He sighed. 'You'd think she'd have been able to get somebody better than Geoffrey Porringer, though.'

'I thought he was your friend,' said Henry.

'As a chap to do business with, fine,' said Uncle Teddy. 'Chap to eat with, grand. Chap to drink with, no problem. Chap to wake up to, all those blackheads on the pillow beside you, horrendous I'd have thought.'

'Well you couldn't be expected to fancy him,' said Henry. 'I mean, I can't believe that I would if I was a woman, but you never know. Women have strange tastes in men.'

'I know,' said Hilary. 'I married you.'

Henry assumed that it was a joke, and laughed not because it amused him, but in order to make it clear that it was a joke. But Uncle Teddy took it seriously.

'That's very true,' he said. 'I can't believe some of the fellers women take up with. Sidney Watson over at Mexborough. Hollow chest, halitosis, and an undertaker. They were queueing up. Tommy Simonsgate, the plumber. Wallet full of moths, and always had bits of cabbage sticking between his teeth. Married a model. I gave it two years. Ten years later, they'd three kids, she looks like a brick shithouse, and he's just the same, except a bit more sophisticated. It's broccoli instead of cabbage.' He fell silent for a reflective moment. 'I don't blame Anna for going. I'm getting an old man's legs. I'll end up looking like a punchball on matchsticks. I'm not bitter. She gave me some wonderful times. Always knew it had to end. I just wish we could have had one more year. Just one more year. I'd have settled for that.' His voice was choking. He blew his nose. 'May as well kill the bottle.'

He filled their glasses almost to the brim. A plane winked across their natural planetarium, and there was a soft whisper of wind.

'Grand kids,' he said. 'Grand. I'm going to love having them around. I'm so glad you came, son. And you, Hilary. You're a belter. I'm proud of him, winning you. Always knew he had it in him, mind.'

He paused. Neither Henry nor Hilary spoke. They didn't know what to say. They decided to let Uncle Teddy get it off his chest.

'I'm frightened of growing old. I had looks, you see. It's sad losing them. You're all right, Henry, because you've never had looks.'

Henry had to bite his tongue to stop himself saying, drily, 'Thank you very much.'

'So you've nothing to lose. Women find you irresistible because of your . . .'

Uncle Teddy paused for so long that Henry felt compelled to speak.

'Charisma?' he said hopefully.

'Vulnerability. They want to mother you and then when they realise you're a proper sexy man they're hooked.' He sighed again. 'I should have gone back to Doris when you gave me the chance. Tell me, would you say . . . would you say Doris and Geoffrey are . . . happy?'

Henry's head was swimming with wine and exhaustion. He longed for sleep. He couldn't think. He knew that it was important to answer carefully, but he simply hadn't the energy.

Luckily, Hilary had.

'No,' she said. 'They aren't happy, but they aren't unhappy either. They've formed a *modus vivendi*. A way of living.'

'Thank you for translating,' said Uncle Teddy, 'but I'm not completely ignorant.'

'Sorry.'

'Anna and I used to read Shakespeare's plays out loud.'

Henry and Hilary tried hard to hide their astonishment. Without success.

'You're stunned. We decided to expand our horizons. Couldn't get to grips at first. Then, suddenly, open sesame, we got it. Loved it. *Romeo and Juliet*, know it?'

'I know it,' said Hilary.

' "Romeo, Romeo, wherefore art thou, Romeo? We must defy our families, because . . . we've formed a *modus vivendi*." Not good enough, is it? Doris deserves better. Doris deserves love.' Uncle Teddy took a gulp of wine, not tasting it. 'I should have gone back to her when you gave me the chance.' He held his glass up against the night sky, as if surprised to have found that it was empty. 'I don't regret it, though. None of it.' He stood up. 'Starting to repeat myself. Time for bed. You've got a holiday to have.' He shook Henry's hand with strange formality. 'Good to see you, son.' He kissed Hilary. 'You're lovely.' He weaved his way back to the house, turned, said, 'I'm going to give you a wonderful holiday,' and disappeared into the house.

Kate and Jack slept through till seven. Uncle Teddy was already up, natty in white shorts and a blue shirt. Breakfast was laid on the terrace. The morning was as fresh as a washed dairy.

'Morning,' said Uncle Teddy heartily. 'Did you sleep well?'

'Very well. How about you?'

'Like a top,' lied Uncle Teddy. 'Right. Coffee?'

They nodded.

'Right. Coffee coming up.'

Uncle Teddy tried to make a great fuss of the children without quite knowing how to, and said, 'Oh well.'

They had no difficulty in supplying the missing sub-text: 'I wish I'd had children. Too late now.'

'We thought we'd go on the beach today,' said Henry, as he spread honey on a crisp, fresh roll. 'Jack isn't really ready, but Kate'll love it.'

'You will come, won't you?' said Hilary. They had decided that it would be better if *she* asked.

'Oh no,' said Uncle Teddy. 'I hate the sea.'

They looked at him in surprise. Uncle Teddy had no difficulty in supplying the missing sub-text: 'Then what on earth are you doing living by the bloody thing?'

'Oh, I love living by it,' he said. 'I love sea fronts, hotels, promenades, palms, seaside cafés, fish markets, children's happy faces, everything about it except the bloody thing itself. Well, I don't hate all seas. I love the Atlantic. That's my sea. Breakers rolling in. Sand-castles eaten up by the onrushing tide. Sand left glistening by the receding tide. Limpets drying out on the rocks. Streams to dam. Tongues of sea flecking their way in, sliding into rock-pools. Rock-pools coming to life again. Tides, change, drama, that's my sea. The Med just sits there, like a lukewarm soup. Disgusting.'

Henry looked at him in amazement, and Hilary looked at Henry in silent rebuke for not having told her that Uncle Teddy had a lyrical side.

'You're astounded. You think nothing excites me except sex and import–export,' said Uncle Teddy. 'I told you. We've expanded our horizons. Oh God, how could she go?' His face crumpled and then the mask returned. 'Out, damned self-pity. I'll leave you now. Enjoy your day.'

And Uncle Teddy got into his Rolls Royce and drove off.

Jack crawled over the sand, Kate loved being buried in the sand, light aeroplanes passed overhead trailing advertising banners, Jack and Kate loved the water, and the day passed pleasantly; and they shopped, and Hilary cooked, and the children were utterly exhausted and fell asleep, and Uncle Teddy returned home and said, 'Sun's over the yard-arm. Time for the first Pernod,' and they drank their *apéritifs* and ate *salade niçoise* and sea bass with fennel that Hilary had made very creditably, although the sea bass was slightly over-cooked.

Over dinner Uncle Teddy asked what they'd done that day and pretended to be interested in their replies. Then they asked him what he'd done and he said, 'Oh, you know, drove around the hills, put the roof down, felt the wind in my face, smelt the wild thyme, blew the cobwebs away.'

'Don't you have friends here?' asked Hilary with that social directness that Henry admired and feared.

'Oh yes. But you've heard of flags of convenience. These are friends of convenience. Friends of geography. I like the French, can't think why so many British can't stand them, but they're foreigners to us, we're foreigners to them, I don't think we ever quite make real friends. The British are all exiles, like me, so there's something wrong with them all, except the *bona fide* businessmen and diplomats, and the *bona fide* don't like me because I'm not *bona fide*. Nice sea bass this, Hilary.'

'It's over-cooked.'

'Barely. Damned good first effort. Anna took ages to get the hang of cooking.' He paused, thinking affectionately of past culinary disasters, and their hearts bled for him. 'No, the fact is, they aren't real friends, and I don't think I could face them now. All the explanations. All the sympathy.' He smiled wryly, and with more self-knowledge than they would have believed possible. 'Besides, I've always put myself across as a bit of a *roué*, young lady at my side, saucy remarks, suggestive inferences, all the gubbins. Bit of a gay dog, old Teddy Braithwaite. Seen it all, knows how to live. Be a shame to let them see me with the stuffing knocked out of me, the gay dog become a hang-dog. No, I have to reconstruct myself and move on. Never see any of them again. Chapter closed. More wine?'

So every day Uncle Teddy took to the hills. Some days Henry and Hilary went sightseeing. They went to Cannes and Nice and Menton and Monaco and Vence. But some days it was too hot for sightseeing, and some days it was even too hot for the beach. Henry and Hilary grew rather bored with the beach, and Jack and Kate grew sleepy with the sun, and, after lunch, when time stood still, they all went to bed. Occasionally, in those shuttered, insect-buzzing afternoons, Henry and Hilary made love, sleepily. More often they just slept, lovingly. Then there was shopping, and feeding of children, and cooking, because it turned out that they ate in almost every night. Uncle Teddy would return, the sun would go down over the yard-arm, there'd be Pernod and Kir and food and wine and Uncle Teddy repeating himself and apologising for ruining their holiday, and bursting the balloon of self-deception with the sharp pinprick of self-knowledge.

Yet over it all there hung a growing shadow, a shadow that had nothing to do with Uncle Teddy, but everything to do with Henry and Hilary. Henry didn't even know it existed, but Hilary did.

On the beach on their last morning, the hottest, the haziest, the stickiest, the soupiest, Hilary was almost shivering as she screwed herself up to speak.

'My book's been accepted by Wagstaff and Wagstaff,' she said.

Henry felt the great cancer of jealousy, the great lump. He also felt a surge of righteous indignation.

'And you never told me,' he said.

'I didn't dare.'

'Bollocks!'

Kate began to cry. Jack smiled. They had to take Kate to the water. The water was warm. Henry was very conscious of the slim, bronzed bodies all round. His podgy body had gone a blotchy red.

'Don't shout and upset them,' said Hilary.

'I won't. But I really do think it's awful that you waited until the last day of our holiday, and then you tell me as if it's bad news.'

'It is bad news to you.'

They all splashed each other and laughed.

'When did you find out?' said Henry.

'Three days before we left home. And then we were so busy and I thought you'd be upset and I thought I'd tell you on the first day here and then of course all this business blew up and somehow I couldn't do it. I'm sorry.'

Henry longed to be able to say, 'I understand completely, my darling. It's my fault, for giving you the wrong impression, but it is

86

a wrong impression. I'm absolutely thrilled. I hope the book's an enormous success, and my God your legs look good today,' but he couldn't. He said, 'So you should be. If you don't trust me I don't see what hope there is for us,' and he set off and swam almost a mile out to sea, and his chest ached with the anger and the exertion, and he thought he was starting a heart attack, and he was far out beyond everybody. He fought his panic and controlled it, and swam very slowly back, with his inimitably ungainly breast-stroke, towards the splashing, laughing, smoothly athletic swimmers and the great range of the Alpes Maritimes, barely scarred by all the corniche roads. Above the mountains clouds were gathering, clouds with dark angry centres, clouds like boils full of pus.

Hilary didn't speak. Henry found it impossible to apologise. He said, 'I suppose we'd better get ready for lunch,' in a low, lifeless voice. 'Yes,' said Hilary, in a similar voice.

All afternoon they communicated like that. That evening, Uncle Teddy suggested a posh restaurant for their last night. They ate outside, overlooking the sea, with Jack in his carry-cot. The staff were kind and warm to Kate and Jack. Henry and Hilary, used to being treated like germs when they took the children out in England, couldn't believe it.

They pretended that nothing was wrong, for Uncle Teddy's sake. And Uncle Teddy pretended that he was as happy as a sandboy, for their sake. They ate *bourride* and *langoustine mayonnaise* and lamb crusted with herbs, and because of the ghastly charade that they were playing out it might have been cotton wool.

'It's been a lovely fortnight, despite everything.'

'I hope everything works out.'

'It mustn't be so long next time.'

'I think you've taken it terribly well.'

'Thank you for everything.'

'I'll write very soon.'

'What a lot of flies there are tonight!'

'I hope none of them are mosquitoes.'

87

'It'll be a long journey tomorrow.'

'There are some nice places to stay just south of Paris.'

'The air's incredibly heavy tonight.'

'This raspberry mousse looks wonderful.'

'The wine is lovely.'

'Thank you. I will have another glass.'

'We sound like the conversations in those "Teach Yourself French" booklets.'

Which of them said what? It doesn't matter. They barely knew themselves.

One of the waiters held Kate's hand and took her to the water's edge. Another carried a delighted Jack on a tour of the kitchens.

In the sky, the boils grew, the pus throbbed. The first great fork of lightning broke the world in two. There was a huge rumble of thunder. Jack grinned. Kate cried.

The storm reached them at two o'clock. The thunder and lightning were almost continuous. It rained ferociously for forty minutes.

Then the rain stopped and the thunder and lightning moved away, although it would be more than two hours before they were free from distant rumbling.

Neither Henry nor Hilary had slept a wink. Jack slept throughout it all. Kate woke and cried but was brave when she was cuddled and soon went back to sleep again.

Henry and Hilary lay as stiff as boards, not touching.

'What you said was absolutely true,' he whispered, because he was very conscious of Uncle Teddy, also presumably unable to sleep. 'I *was* jealous.'

She didn't reply.

'Are you asleep?' he whispered.

'No.'

'Why not?'

'Because it's so awful. I'm so disappointed in you.'

'That sounds very priggish.'

'I *am* priggish. My dad's priggish.'

'I love you.'

'But not my book.'

'Oh fuck your book.'

'Exactly.'

Silence then.

A last faint rumble of thunder.

The first pale streak of dawn.

The first exclamation of delight at the glory of the privilege of existence from a passing thrush.

More silence then.

'I need your help,' whispered Henry.

'I don't believe it,' whispered Hilary. 'I create something, with great difficulty. I have no confidence in it. It's accepted. I'm overjoyed. I can't tell you. I tell you. I think, "Maybe I'm wrong. Maybe he isn't jealous." I'm not wrong. You hate my creativity. You hate the existence of my book that is a painful thing wrenched out of myself. My second greatest pride, my second greatest joy, for my first greatest pride and joy was you. I'm thrilled. I'm excited. I find I'm not useless after all. And you are angry. I'm so hurt. So hurt. And *you* ask *me* for help.'

'Don't you love me any more?' whispered Henry.

'Oh yes, I still love you,' whispered Hilary. 'But I don't *want* to love you any more.'

Two hands meet in a French bed. They clasp each other. They squeeze each other, once. They drop apart.

Silence then.

6 Count Your Blessings

One of the many benefits of having children is that one is too busy to have other crises. Henry and Hilary were very loving parents. Henry would hurry to catch the train from Leeds City Station of an evening, in order to be home for bath-time. Big, ugly yet appealing Jack, with his constant good nature, was almost always a delight. Pale, sensitive, excitable Kate, with her changes of mood and her sharp emotional needs, was altogether more difficult, but often deeply loving and affectionate. She listened to bedtime stories with a solemnity that no heart could have resisted. She laughed at Henry's funny voices with an abandon that touched them deeply.

Henry and Hilary were invited to dinner at the Lewthwaites' one Wednesday. They took Kate and Jack, and put them to bed upstairs. While Henry was reading Kate a story about a magical wellington boot, he was disappointed to hear other guests arriving with cheery 'hello's' and, 'Oh you shouldn't have. They're lovely. Find a vase, Howard.' They felt disappointed. They hadn't come prepared for other guests. They strained to catch the identity of the unwelcome strangers, but Sam began to play an Adam Faith record, and the chance was gone.

The other guests turned out to be unwelcome, but not strangers. They were Peter and Olivia Matheson, and their daughter Anna.

Peter Matheson turned upon them the massed floodlights of his social smile. Olivia's face was becoming deeply lined. Anna was wearing no make-up and an unsuccessful grey version of the sack dress. It simply looked as though she was wearing a grey sack. She went pale when she saw them, but soon recovered her colour.

'Hello, Hillers,' she said hurriedly. 'Hello, Henry. Oh it is good to see you. One of the worst things about being a novice nun was not seeing my friends.'

Henry's heart sank. They were in for an evening of play-acting.

'And your parents, surely?' said Olivia.

'Oh yes, of course,' said Anna. She flashed a defiant look at Henry and Hilary.

'I could never understand that,' said Peter Matheson. 'I should have thought you could have seen your parents.'

'You had to renounce the familiar,' said Anna. 'It was a test of strength. Unfortunately, I failed.'

'Well we're pleased you did,' said her father.

Henry accepted one of Howard Lewthwaite's splendidly strong gin and tonics. Hilary chose white wine, Peter Matheson whisky, Olivia sherry, Anna tonic water.

'I've got used to not having artificial stimulants,' she said. 'I'm not sure if I could cope with them now.'

'Well of course I think religion can be an artificial stimulant,' said Peter Matheson. He laughed at his own remark, which was just as well, if it was intended to be funny, because nobody else did.

Howard Lewthwaite departed to the kitchen.

Olivia Matheson approached Henry, and led him over to the window of the heavily floral lounge. There was still a gleam of light in the western sky.

'You're a man of the world,' she said. 'And Hilary's Anna's best friend. Will you help Anna come to terms with real life?'

Henry had a vision of Anna, on the one and only night when he had taken her out, sitting stark naked in a cheap brown armchair in her flat in Cardington Road, beneath a reproduction of 'Greylag Geese Rising', by Peter Scott. Nothing had risen that night, except the greylag geese.

'Yes,' he said. 'Yes, yes. We'll . . . er . . . try and help her come to terms with real life.'

'Thank you.' She patted his arm. 'My husband really likes you.'

The conversation became general again, and Henry didn't feel like letting Anna off the hook too easily.

'I'm shamefully ignorant about nuns,' he said. 'Tell us what you had to study, what devotions you had to perform, what disciplines were required of you, how you spent a typical day.'

Anna smiled. 'I'd like to,' she said, 'but we were sworn to secrecy, and although I've left, I'd like to respect that.'

Henry had to admire her, albeit reluctantly.

'I hate that kind of secrecy,' said Hilary. 'It sounds like a religious version of the Masons.'

'Yes, that's one of the things that disillusioned me,' said Anna.

Hilary had to admire her, albeit reluctantly.

Sam, in jeans and tee-shirt, put his head round the door and said, 'Hi. I'm out with some mates tonight. Have a great meal. Bye.'

Howard Lewthwaite, in a 'Ban the Bomb' apron, put his head round the door and said, 'Come and get it.'

Hilary wheeled her mother into the lifeless dining room. Howard Lewthwaite asked Henry to deal with the wine. Everybody had some, even Anna. 'I suppose I ought to try to get to like the stuff,' she said.

'You've been to France too, haven't you?' said Olivia Matheson to Henry and Hilary, over the beef casserole.

'Yes, but not near Anna,' said Henry. 'We stayed with my Uncle Teddy. It was rather sad. He'd been married to a woman thirty years younger than him, and she'd left the day before we got there.'

'Please, Henry,' said Peter Matheson. 'Anna's looking embarrassed. She's rather unworldly about these things.'

'It's all right, Daddy,' said Anna. 'I'm interested. I need to learn. How did the old man take it?'

'He's not exactly an old man,' said Hilary. 'He was devastated, of course, but . . . not bitter. Amazingly enough, he wasn't bitter.'

'Good,' said Anna. 'I'm glad of that. Bitterness is self-destructive. The nuns were very much against bitterness.'

'Careful,' said Henry. 'You're giving away secrets.'

'Oh Lord, yes,' said Anna. 'It's the wine, I expect.'

'Another glass?' said Henry.

'Well perhaps a little one,' said Anna. 'It's not quite as awful as I'd thought.'

Nadežda had a coughing fit over the trifle. Hilary wheeled her out. When she came back, Nadežda said, 'A bit of almond went down the wrong way', but her chest had sounded ominously wheezy to Henry.

After the cheese, Howard Lewthwaite stood and said, 'This meal is a kind of celebration, also a sort of postscript. As you know, we've sold Lewthwaite's to the developers of the Fish Hill Complex. A sad day, but none of us can stand in the way of progress, can we?' He looked at the ceiling, not wishing to meet Henry's eye or indeed Peter Matheson's. Peter Matheson looked at the floor, not wishing to meet Henry's eye or indeed Howard Lewthwaite's. Henry closed his eyes, not wishing to look at the ceiling or the floor or to meet Peter Matheson's eye or Howard Lewthwaite's eye or Hilary's eye or Anna's eye. 'We've bought a house in Spain, near Alicante. Naddy needs a drier climate and nothing else matters.' Howard Lewthwaite smiled at Nadežda, whose eyes were moist. 'Sam's at college, so it's the right time. We're going to sell the house, so it'll be the end of our life in Thurmarsh. I know Henry and Hilary will miss us, as baby-sitters if not as people.' Henry and Hilary dredged a laugh from the depths of their shock that this moment had suddenly come. 'You will of course be welcome to visit us, we'll be very upset if you don't. So, my family . . . my friends . . . cheers.'

The meal ended with forced jokes and slightly hysterical laughter, because otherwise everyone might have felt rather sad.

As they re-entered the floral lounge, Peter Matheson put an arm round Henry's shoulder. Henry could feel his power. He had to fight to remind himself that the deep affection the man was showing was totally simulated. Peter Matheson knew that Henry had wanted to expose his corruption, and he almost certainly hated Henry as much as Henry hated him.

He led Henry to the curtained window.

'You're a man of the world,' he said. 'Will you help Anna come to terms with her fear of sex? Because that's what's behind all this nun business. Scared stiff of it, poor girl. They're all the same, nuns. You only have to look at their faces. Pasty. Frightened of sex.'

Henry had to fight the temptation to say, 'Pull the other one, you corrupt, deluded twit. When I took her out she'd whipped her clothes off before I could say "Mother Superior". She's been having it off with my Uncle Teddy in Cap Ferrat, with tall, craggy Jed in Berwick, and probably with every able-bodied man from Berwick to Cap Ferrat between the ages of sixteen and eighty-two.'

He didn't, of course, but he did feel obliged to make a brief defence of the contemplative life against Peter Matheson's absurdly simplistic theories. 'Well I do think there are other, more positive reasons for joining a religious order than fear of sex,' he said.

'Not in Anna's case,' said Peter Matheson. 'So will you and Hilary befriend her, introduce her to people, give her a chance to . . . I don't know . . . blossom as a woman?'

'All right,' said Henry. 'We'll try to help her to blossom as a woman.'

'Good man!' He gave Henry a thump of gratitude which almost dislocated his collar bone. 'My wife's got a soft spot for you.'

'Did you or did you not give a market garden outside Cockermouth advice about gherkins?'

The expression on the face of the Director (Operations) was of disappointed regret rather than of anger.

'Well, yes, I did,' said Henry. 'It was a sloppy job. Some young lad was dealing with them. Hopeless. He hadn't been thinning out the seeds properly, he'd barely been training the laterals along the support canes, they were hanging down all over the place like willies in a snowstorm.'

Timothy Whitehouse raised his eyes to the ceiling, then swivelled round to take refuge in contemplating his reproduction of Constable's little-known 'Bringing Home the Cucumbers to Dedham'.

What on earth possessed me to say that, thought Henry, and to his fury he felt himself blushing.

'Yes, well, no doubt you gave good advice,' said the Director (Operations), 'but gherkins aren't your responsibility, are they?'

'Well not officially, no.'

'You've trodden on John Barrington's toes.'

'I'm sorry.'

'So you should be. John's a good man, but a touch temperamental and *very* territorial.'

'So what should I have done? Gone home and got him to go all the way to Cockermouth to deal with it?'

'You could have tried phoning to clear it with him. He *might* have agreed. Have you sent him a minute, explaining what happened?'

'No. I'm sorry. I've been very busy.'

'Well when you have a minute, will you send him a minute? He heard direct from Cockermouth. Naturally he was upset. Don't be so impulsive, Henry. Don't let your enthusiasms run away with you.'

'Right,' said Henry. 'Right. But you did tell me to be my own man, stick to my guns, be fearless and always speak the truth. I interpreted that as a recipe for action.'

'Quite right,' said the Director (Operations). 'Quite right. I should have qualified it. *Mea culpa.* I should have told you to be your own man, stick to your guns, be fearless and always speak the truth, *within the confines of your statutory responsibilities.* Point taken? Good. No reason any of this need set your career back for any *great* length of time.'

On November 2nd, 1960, Penguin Books were found not guilty of obscenity in publishing the unexpurgated version of *Lady Chatterley's Lover*, after a trial in which the prosecuting barrister asked the jury, 'Would you allow your wives and servants to read this book?'

Hilary spent the following weekend with her editor from Wagstaff and Wagstaff, discussing the revised but unexpurgated version of her first novel.

Her editor sounded very literary and bookish. Henry had visions of a stooping man in his fifties, with receding hair and thick glasses. It was kind of him to give up his weekend, and to invite Hilary to stay in his flat in Highgate, but there would have been no peace for them in Paradise Villa, and who would have looked after the children if she'd gone while Henry was working?

Henry enjoyed his weekend with the children, but it was tiring, and he was a little upset, on Hilary's return, when she refused to play with Kate because, 'I really am very tired. I've got no energy,' although he had to smile when Kate said, 'Well, I'm tired too. I've only got one energy.'

1961 saw Major Yuri Gagarin orbit the earth in a spaceship. For Britain, it was a less spectacular year, unless you were an aspiring taxi-driver given to gambling. Licensed betting shops and mini-cabs were legalised. For Henry, who wasn't an aspiring taxi-driver given to gambling, it was an even less spectacular year. He forced himself to work hard, to identify with the cucumber, to fight for the cucumber, and in so doing he rekindled his enthusiasm for the cucumber. The results of all this would not be apparent until 1962.

Hilary took so long to finalise the changes to her book that it proved impossible to publish it that year. It was scheduled for the spring of 1962.

It was not the love of their children alone that kept the marriage of Henry and Hilary on the rails in the months after their crisis in Cap Ferrat. Henry deserves some credit too. He fought valiantly against the jealousy that had sprung unbidden into his heart.

On the afternoon of Sunday, June 18th, 1961, Kate and Jack were, most unusually, both asleep at the same time. A stranger looking in at the living room of Paradise Villa, carpeted and curtained now but still sparsely furnished, would have witnessed a scene of apparent male dominance. Husband curled up on the settee, reading. Wife ironing. In fact, however, the husband was reading the finished version of the wife's novel, and the wife was ironing to ease the almost intolerable tension that she was feeling. She hadn't let him see the manuscript until it was finally polished, and hadn't been sure that she wanted him to read it even then, but he had insisted. 'I must. It's part of you. I can't shy away from it,' he had said.

He put the typescript down, and took off his glasses. He looked at Hilary gravely. Her heart was thumping.

'I think the character of Hubert is rather shadowy,' he said. 'I didn't quite understand him. I didn't feel you'd quite understood him.'

'Oh.'

'Cousin Hilda.'

'What?'

'I'm using Cousin Hilda's technique.'

'You don't mean . . . you can't mean. . . ?'

'I do mean. Everything else is absolutely magnificent. I think it's as near a masterpiece as dammit.'

'Oh darling.'

They kissed and hugged and wept. A smell of burning filled the room. Henry would never wear his mauve shirt again and, since she'd never liked it, Hilary's happiness was complete.

They had Anna to supper occasionally, to keep up for her parents' benefit the fiction that they were helping her to blossom as a woman. Twice she called their suppers off at the last moment, because she was blossoming as a woman elsewhere, but on one of the occasions when she did come, she said, 'I hear you've got a novel coming out, Hillers. Jolly good.'

'Yes, it is jolly good,' said Henry. 'It's a real work of the imagination. It's about a group of men in an old people's home. It's spare and elegant and truthful, with an icy wit but also with deep compassion.'

Henry had never seen Hilary blush before. They exchanged loving smiles, and Anna looked very wistful, as if she suddenly realised that Hilary *could* teach her something about blossoming as a woman.

1962 saw twenty-five people die of smallpox in Britain, the Liberals win a sensational victory in the Orpington by-election, and the arrest of 1,100 people in Parliament Square during a sit-down demonstration against nuclear weapons.

Henry received a long letter from Uncle Teddy:

Dear Henry,

I'm writing this to you alone and not to you both as it's family business and I want advice on something Hilary can't really help me about. Do show it to her if you want. She's a splendid girl, how you've captured anybody as good as that I just don't know. I hope her novel's a huge success, I'm sure it will be, she's so sensible.

Henry, things haven't worked out well for Doris and me, but I think about the old girl a great deal. When I was in clink, slopping out and resisting the amorous advances of burglars, wife-beaters and child-molesters, I'd never have thought that the Côte d'Azur would be like a prison, but I'm in another kind of prison here and because I'm free to leave and because there's no time limit to my sentence, and not even any point in behaving well because you don't get remission, it is in a funny sort of way more mentally disturbing than the other sort of prison.

I'm drinking Pernod as I sit here, trying to pretend I like it, why can't I drink G and T like all the other Brits? Anyway, what I'm delaying saying because it seems really silly is that I love Doris very much and realise that I always have. I don't regret Anna, she was great, best sex the old rascal ever had, but she was actually too good for me to want any other Doris substitute. I'm tired, Henry. Too tired to be an old rascal any more.

What I'm getting round to is asking if you think Doris is any happier with Geoffrey now than she was when you did all that go-between business. If she is happy, that's it, end of story. But if she isn't . . . well, could you bear to start all that up again?

Last time she wanted to get together and I didn't. Now I do and it'd be typical of life if she didn't.

I once thought Doris was an old bitch and life was lovely. Now I realise it's the other way round.

Love to Hilary and to you,
Teddy

PS I mean that. I realise now that I do love you. Probably I'd
never have been able to be emotional enough to tell you if I'd
not left England. So why do I want to come back so much?
PPS All the best to the Sniffer. I realise now that she can't
help being like she is.
PPPS If you do run into Anna, tell her I'm all right.

Henry did show Hilary the letter, and they decided that the
obvious thing to do was to go to Troutwick and try to find out just
how happy Auntie Doris really was.

It was Hilary's turn to drive, on a glorious spring morning. The
branches of the trees in the sodden gardens were furry with bud.
The sun shone on the windscreens of ice-cream vans making their
first trip of the year, and on the bald heads of old men as they
sauntered along to check if the bowling greens had dried out. In
the back of the car, Kate kept saying, 'Are we nearly there?' and
Jack echoed her, 'We near there?'

At last the long haul through the mill towns was over and they
were in the open country. There were still a few patches of snow
to the north of the dry-stone walls. A hundred thousand sheep
proclaimed the joy of spring. They were nearly there, and Kate
and Jack fell fast asleep.

Henry was aware, throughout the journey, of a great clash
between his head and his heart.

Please find that Doris and Geoffrey have discovered true peace
at last, said his head, because then there will be nothing more that
you need to do.

Oh I hope they aren't happy, said his heart. I'd love to see Doris
and Teddy together again, whatever the difficulties.

Henry gave the casting vote to his heart.

'Doris's' was dancing to the tune of spring. The bar windows
were open for the first time that year. Balmy zephyrs stirred the
pot plants on the piano top and the loins of young farmers at the
bar. Shoppers dumped their carrier bags under the antique tables.
Auntie Doris beamed.

99

They took their drinks into the garden, where Jack and Kate ran around and got very excited. It wasn't quite warm enough for sitting, but they didn't mind. Summer was coming to the high country. There was hope in their goose-pimples.

Auntie Doris sat with them for five minutes, but spent the whole time saying, 'Ah, bless them, aren't they lovely? Aren't you lovely children? Oh, Kate is pretty, love her. Oh and Jack's smile. That smile will turn women's knees to jelly. Oh, bless him.'

When Henry went to get more drinks, he managed to get served by Auntie Doris and said, 'On a lovely day like this, Auntie Doris, do you get the feeling, "My life is as wonderful as can be"?' but all Auntie Doris said was, 'No. I get the feeling, "Oh hell, I'm going to be rushed off my feet." '

It was half past three before the last customers had left. They went into Doris and Geoffrey's private quarters. Kate and Jack had eaten, but the adults were awash with drink and empty with hunger. Auntie Doris began to cook steak, fried onions and chips in her tiny kitchen. In their private living room, shabbier even than the pub and unadorned by antiques, Geoffrey Porringer snored obligingly, Hilary occupied the children with plasticine, and Henry went into the kitchen for a hurried chat with Auntie Doris.

'So, how are you really?' he enquired.

Auntie Doris looked at him in surprise.

'What's up with you today?' she asked. 'You're very interested in whether I'm happy all of a sudden.'

Henry cursed himself for his mistake even as he was making it. 'Well, Cousin Hilda asked me the other day if I thought you were happy. And this set me thinking about it.'

'What's it to do with her? I don't want my mental state discussed by the Sniffer. It's none of her business. Put some plates in the oven, there's a good lad.'

'Oh, I wasn't going to tell her.'

But voluble, indiscreet Auntie Doris was doing an impression of a clam.

They stayed till half past seven. Henry disliked driving home in the dark, but the children would sleep and with luck they wouldn't wake as they were carried to their beds back home.

Shortly before they left, in the quiet early evening bar, Henry said to Auntie Doris, in a low voice, 'That trouble you had with Geoffrey and the waitresses. Does he still . . . you know . . . touch them up?'

'I'm not telling you anything,' said Auntie Doris. 'You're too friendly with the Sniffer. You may not mean to tell her, but I know you, things'll slip out. Dried-up old cow.'

Henry felt that this was an implicit admission that things weren't all right, but it wasn't the definite answer that he needed. He realised, however, that he'd failed dismally in his secret investigations and he made a mental note not to set up a detective agency when at last he broke free from cucumbers.

He also felt that he couldn't let Auntie Doris's description of Cousin Hilda go unchallenged.

'You're unfair to Cousin Hilda,' he said. 'She's kind and loving, in her way.'

'I don't deny it,' said Auntie Doris. 'She's a kind, loving, dried-up old cow. Collect the empties for me, will you, there's a good lad?'

Henry hadn't thought of the possibility of seeking the truth from Geoffrey Porringer, but it was from Geoffrey that he learnt it.

Hilary was loading up the car with the children and all their paraphernalia, Henry was handing her things, including Jack, who was asleep, while also holding Kate's hand so that she didn't run into the road, and Geoffrey Porringer was watching them, with a soft smile on his face.

Auntie Doris leant out of the window and hissed, 'Help them, Teddy. Don't just stand there like a spare prick.'

'The name is Geoffrey, Doris, not Teddy,' hissed Geoffrey Porringer. He turned to Henry and said, 'Shall I take her hand?'

'No, no. It's quite all right. We've nearly finished,' said Henry.

'I get it all the time,' said Geoffrey Porringer. 'Do this, Teddy. Do that, Teddy. On her mind, you see. Dead for six years, and she still loves him. If I say, "I don't like kidneys, Doris," it's,

"Teddy liked kidneys." If I say, "I've got catarrh," it's, "Teddy never had catarrh," so I say nothing and it's, "Teddy never sulked, I'll say that for him." The man was my friend, Henry, so I know what he was like. A self-centred, inconsiderate rogue. Now he's a bloody saint. Death's immortalised the bastard.'

An American space-craft hit the moon, the last trolley bus ran in London and Coventry Cathedral was consecrated.

One Saturday morning towards the end of May, a couple of weeks before the publication of Hilary's novel, they left the children with Cousin Hilda, who was always secretly thrilled to have them, and went shopping for clothes, followed by a drink in the Pigeon and Two Cushions, and a meal at Thurmarsh's first Indian restaurant.

In the Pigeon and Two Cushions, Oscar welcomed Hilary ecstatically.

'Oh, madam!' he said. 'Madam! I've missed you. I thought you were dead. I nearly died the other day. Chest pains. I thought, "Hey up, Oscar Wintergreen, this is it, owd lad, your number's up, your time has come, the old ticker's finally had its chips." '

'I presume it hadn't,' said Hilary, 'since you're still here.'

'You deduce correctly,' said Oscar. 'Indigestion. Salami. Should have known better. Salami and me, we've never seen eye to eye. Anyroad, I were very sick. Oh sorry, madam. I shouldn't have brought that up. Oops! No joke intended. Anyroad, within two hours, right as rain, I were here as per usual that selfsame evening. So, where have you been?'

'Nowhere,' said Hilary. 'I've been having, and looking after, two children.'

Oscar's mouth opened, but no sound emerged, as he realised that he had never endured any health problems in that area. All he could do, therefore, was to fall back upon the question which, for all the pleasure of their reunion, they were longing to hear.

'What can I get you?' he said.

Henry had two pints of bitter, and Hilary had a gin and tonic, and they laughed at the suitability of Oscar having a surname that was also an ointment.

In the Taj Mahal, which was dark and empty as always on a Saturday morning, they sat in front of an enormous photograph of the eponymous edifice, and ate onion bhajis, lamb dhansak and chicken dopiaza, and Henry suddenly realised that Hilary was about to broach a difficult subject.

'Er. . . ,' she said.

'Er?' he said. 'What "er"?'

'The publishers want me to do a kind of promotional tour.'

'I see.'

'Just the major cities. London. Birmingham. Glasgow. Manchester.'

'How long would you be away?'

'A week.'

'What about the children?'

'Well that's obviously a problem. I suppose you'd have to take a week off and look after them.'

'But that'd mean using up my holiday.'

'I know. Obviously if you don't feel you can, there's no more to be said.'

The waiter saw the look on Henry's face, and approached hurriedly. He had a generous nature, a distinct talent on the sitar, a philosophical bent, a worrying pain in the left testicle, a desperate desire to be a doctor, fantasies about Petula Clark and a disturbing letter about the health of his mother in Hyderabad, but since all he said was, 'Is everything all right?' it is impossible, with the best will in the world, to reflect all these factors in dialogue.

'Yes, yes, everything's lovely,' said Henry. 'If I had a long face it's just . . . a personal problem.'

'Thank you, sir,' said the waiter inappropriately.

When the waiter had gone, Hilary said, 'I mean, I'd like to go, simply because they've put all their effort into my book and how can I expect them to do it if I'm not prepared to?'

'Not because you'd enjoy it?' said Henry as drily as a bhuna curry.

'Of course I'd enjoy it,' said Hilary. 'I love you very much, but it's only one week and it'd be interesting and, yes, I'd love to go.'

Henry grinned. 'Then you must go,' he said. 'It's a wonderful book and you deserve it.'

Hilary leant across and kissed him. The waiter beamed.

So Hilary went to London and Birmingham and Glasgow and Manchester and Henry got the children up and praised Jack for his success on the potty and dressed them and played with them and read them stories and Kate drew and painted and acted out little scenes she'd made up, and Jack put increasingly elaborate things together and pulled them to pieces again and laughed, and Henry cooked fish fingers and beans and dreamt of Hilary in French restaurants, and he said to himself, 'I am not jealous. I am not jealous. I am not jealous,' and sometimes it worked.

In the mornings he took the children to the Alderman Chandler Memorial Park, and it was there, sitting on a bench, watching them playing happily on the swings and roundabouts, that he fell into conversation with the Indian waiter.

'Have a sweet,' said the waiter. 'Indian sweet. Very sweet.'

'Thank you,' said Henry, taking the proffered delicacy. 'Oh yes. Very sweet.'

'Very sweet sweet.'

'Yes.'

They laughed.

'Life is an odd one, yes?' said the waiter.

'Well, yes. Very. Actually a very odd one.'

'Quite so. This morning, for instance. I have breakfast. I practise on the sitar.'

'Oh. You play the sitar?'

'Not very well.'

'I bet you do.'

'Well I suppose I have a talent. I play. I am happy. Then "ouch".'

'Ouch?'

'Back comes the worrying pain in my left testicle. I play a happy tune and I think, "Oh, if only I didn't have this pain," and I am happy and sad at the same time.'

They watched the children in silence for a few moments.

'Do you like being a waiter?' asked Henry.

'Not much. It is dreary work and many people are not like you. Many people are pigs,' said the waiter. 'I would much like to be a doctor.'

'One day, perhaps,' said Henry.

'Maybe, if I work hard. Your children?'

'Yes.'

'Very fine children.'

'Thank you.'

'I would love to have children by Petula Clark.'

'Good Lord.'

'I know, but she is a fine woman. I like Western women. Eastern women too. All women.'

'Sexy beast.'

'Alas, yes. But I ought not to wish for children by Petula Clark. It is impossible.'

'Unlikely, certainly.'

'One should never seek to attain the unattainable.'

'You have a philosophical bent.'

'Thank you.'

Kate fell and almost cried, but didn't, so Henry didn't interfere.

'Did you see me fall, Daddy?' she shouted.

'Yes.'

'Did you see me not cry?'

'Yes. Brave girl.'

'I inherited it from my mother in Hyderabad,' said the waiter.

'Sorry. What?' said Henry.

'My philosophical bent. She has eight children. Brings them up well. Her life is work. Work work work. In old age she gets her reward. Arthritis.' He stood up and shook Henry's hand. 'Count your blessings, my friend.'

7 The Contrasting Fortunes of Four Lovers

It was natural that on Hilary's return, the children should run to her with squeals of uninhibited delight, ignoring totally the person who'd looked after their every need for six long days. How wonderful, thought Henry, to be so oblivious of one's effect on other people.

'Tell me how helpful you've been to your wonderful daddy,' said Hilary.

Henry felt humiliated by her need to include him with such blatant tact. She was nervous, and this made him feel grumpy. The words that he'd planned – 'Oh, darling, I've missed you so much' – stuck in his craw. How often this seemed to happen to him.

'You're nervous,' he said. 'Why?'

'I was frightened you might be grumpy. And I was right to be frightened. You are grumpy.'

'I'm only grumpy because you didn't trust me not to be grumpy,' growled Henry.

Hilary made the mistake of laughing.

'It isn't funny,' said Henry. 'I see nothing funny in the break-up of a marriage.'

Hilary went even whiter than usual, and began to cry. Henry heard the voice of the Indian waiter, 'Count your blessings.'

He rushed over to her and said, 'Oh, I'm so sorry. I didn't mean it,' but she refused to let him kiss her properly.

He'd laid the table in the small, cosy kitchen, which at Hilary's suggestion he'd painted a cheery yellow. He'd even lit a candle. He'd made watercress soup and moussaka. Hilary said it was nice, and even the children ate a little, but it wasn't what he'd hoped for, and the fact that it was entirely his fault only made it worse.

At the end of the meal, Hilary said how lovely it had been.

'What, even after all the sophisticated food you've been having?'

'Best meal I've had all week.'

He didn't believe her, but he was pleased none the less.

'I'm sorry about earlier,' he said, as they washed up. 'I love you so much and I miss you so much that I can't cope sometimes.'

Hilary put her arms round him, lifted his 'Oxfam' apron, and touched his thigh gently.

He told her about the Indian waiter, and she laughed, and once again things were almost as they had once been.

During the summer of 1962, Hilary had a minor disappointment, and Henry had a minor success.

The minor disappointment was that Hilary's book, despite good reviews, was selling only modestly.

The minor success was that figures issued by Eddie Hapwood, Head of Research (Statistical), showed that in 1961, throughout the Northern Counties (Excluding Berwick-on-Tweed) production of cucumbers had risen by 1.932 per cent.

Hilary and the children came with Henry on one of his trips round the North Country, but the children grew bored in the car, and even the knowledge that they were passing through areas where people were growing 1.932 per cent more cucumbers failed to excite them for very long.

They flew to Spain for their holiday. Kate and Jack were incoherent with excitement. They ate paella and Spanish omelette and swam and grew brown and both Howard and Nadežda told Henry how much they loved him for making Hilary so happy, and Henry thought of the times when he'd made her miserable, and felt sick with guilt. He resolved, secretly, to be much better towards her when they returned home.

But all the time, whether lolling on the beach or being driven up into the dry hills, or catching the little train that wound painfully slowly through the orange groves near the coast, Henry was aware of the two important decisions that he must make – when to move out of cucumbers, and what to do about Uncle Teddy and Auntie Doris.

Shortly after their return, the Cuban Missile Crisis pushed the world to the brink of war. President Kennedy revealed that the United States had evidence of Russian missile bases in Cuba. He began a partial blockade of Cuba. Russian warships steamed towards Cuba. President Kennedy did not waver. The Russian warships turned back, the Russians agreed to remove the missile bases, America agreed to lift the blockade, and Henry decided, in this uncertain climate, not to move out of cucumbers until 1963.

He also decided that he *must* tell Auntie Doris about Uncle Teddy.

'I've no choice,' he told Hilary. 'He's unhappy, she's unhappy, even Geoffrey Porringer's unhappy.'

'I agree,' said Hilary. 'I'm surprised you've delayed so long.'

'It's a big responsibility, interfering in people's lives,' said Henry. 'It's a terrible responsibility. I think, before I actually do it, I'd better write to Uncle Teddy to check if it's still what he really wants.'

> Dear Uncle Teddy [he wrote],
>
> I'm sorry not to have been in touch before, but I just haven't known what to do. I've decided now that I will act as a go-between for you, if you solemnly swear that you really do love Auntie Doris and will commit yourself to her till death do you part.
>
> Kate is at school full time now and loving it, she's very bright. Jack is more the practical type. He's into everything, naughty but lovely. Hilary's getting on well with her second novel, set in a glue factory! She doesn't want me to read it before it's finished.
>
> Work is going pretty well for me too. Would you ever have guessed, when you took me into your home that snowy day in that awful winter of 1947, that fifteen years later I'd be responsible, virtually single-handed, for an increase of 1.932 per cent in cucumber yields in Northern England (Excluding Berwick-on-Tweed)?
>
> I look forward to your reply and hopefully setting the whole thing in motion very soon.

We hope you'll have a happy Christmas and that 1963 will see the beginning of a great new life for you.

Lots of love,

Henry and Hilary (not forgetting Kate and Jack)

They had a Christmas card from Uncle Teddy, but it had crossed Henry's letter. His message read:

> I hope you all have a lovely Christmas. Very disappointed not to have had any news re what we discussed. No news or bad news or you forgot or just got too busy? Sorry there's no lolly enclosed. Fings ain't wot they used t'be in import–export.

And then there was nothing. A year that was to leave the world a very changed place began with a giant freeze, with heavy snowfalls and frost night and day for several weeks. Henry rushed to the post each morning. Bills, giant carpet sales, one fan letter for Hilary – I wonder if you are a relation of Gloria Lewthwaite, who did water-colours, mainly of lighthouses, before the First World War – but nothing from Uncle Teddy.

And then at last, towards the end of February, there was a letter from France:

> Dear Henry,
>
> I'm sorry not to have replied to your letter. I went skiing at Megeve over Christmas [So much for fings not being wot they used to be import–export, thought Henry wryly] and had a most unfortunate accident and broke two legs, one of which was mine. I had to hang around in hospital for quite a while, also I had to make sure the other man, a postman from Rouen, was all right before I left. Luckily, both our legs are mending well, though I don't know how long it'll be before he's doing his rounds again.
>
> Anyway, to business. I simply can't give the promise you seek. I've had enough of broken promises. I've discovered that life is a miserable sod which can't be trusted for a

109

second. Rather like Geoffrey Porringer, really. What I do swear, on a bottle of the twenty-five-year-old Macallan, is that I love Doris very much, and I *intend* and *want* to commit myself to her till the old bastard of a reaper carries us to our respective destinations – her up, me down! If that's good enough for you, we're on with the great adventure. If not, well, common sense will have prevailed.

I'd like to return to England to live, with a new identity. I can get a false passport, no problem, in exchange for certain services.

Love to you all,
Uncle Teddy

Henry's reply, written on Cucumber Marketing Board paper, when he should have been writing a report on 'Late Cropping Ridge Cucumbers of the Solway Firth' for the *Vegetable Growers' Gazette*, was quite brief:

Dear Uncle Teddy,
Thank you very much for your letter. Sorry about the broken leg. Also about the postman's broken leg, although, since I don't know him and therefore can't love him except theoretically, I'm not as concerned about his leg as about yours.

I'm thrilled you want to go ahead, and am happy with your assurances. They're very honest and I respect that more than empty promises.

I have certain principles, boring though you may find them, and I have to ask you, before I go ahead, to promise that the 'certain services' that you can get a passport in exchange for are not addictive drugs, anything to do with armaments of any kind, or an introduction to the Masons.

With lots of love from us all as ever,
Henry.

John Profumo, Secretary of State for War, told the House of

Commons that he'd committed no impropriety with a girl called Christine Keeler. Dr Beeching announced his solution to Britain's traffic problem. He would close large numbers of railways. In April, Henry received his long-awaited reply from Uncle Teddy:

> Dear Henry,
> Again, sorry for the delay, but an opportunity came to mix business with pleasure in Barcelona, and I never look a gift horse in the mouth, in case all the others fall and it wins.
> I wouldn't touch drugs, I don't have the contacts for armaments, and I never liked the Masons. All that rolling-up of trouser legs plays havoc with your creases. I'll tell you what my little adventure consists of when we meet.
> I can't wait to see Doris again. Awaiting your reply eagerly, as ever.
> Lots of love,
> Uncle Teddy
> PS Better meet in 'the smoke'. Too many people know me in Yorkshire.

So there was no more reason to delay telling Auntie Doris. Waves of excitement and dread swept over Henry.

They met at the Fig Leaf, an expensive and enormously fashionable restaurant near Keighley, run by two retired furniture restorers, Daniel Westerbrook and Quentin Cloves, whose behaviour made Denzil and Lampo seem like heterosexual quantity surveyors. Only the fact that the wives of three senior police officers thought it the best food for fifty miles had saved them from investigation.

The place tinkled with prettiness. Cupids and cherubs abounded, private parts hidden by the eponymous leaves.

'Doris!' exclaimed Quentin Cloves, kissing her on both cheeks and some of her chins. 'Darling! Wonderful to see a human face!' He lowered his voice. 'The briefcase brigade everywhere today. So boring. The soup of the day is chervil, the fish of the day is red mullet baked with rosemary, and the lamb with mustard and honey crust is, like Dante's comedy, divine. And aren't you going to introduce me to your friend?'

'My nephew, Henry Pratt,' said Auntie Doris.

'Welcome to the Fig Leaf, Henry Pratt. You have a wonderful aunt,' said Quentin Cloves.

All this didn't make things any easier. Auntie Doris would have to give up all this celebrity if she went back to Uncle Teddy.

'I'd never have thought you'd find a place like this in Yorkshire,' said Henry.

'It's just the beginning,' said Auntie Doris. 'In the years to come, the broad acres will be awash with fashionable food.'

In the chummy bar, which was like an antique shop with drinks, Henry found it impossible to give his staggering news without being overheard, but as soon as they were at their table, he began.

'Auntie Doris?' he said. 'I asked you out to tell you something.'

'O'oh! I'm intrigued.'

'We must keep our voices down. Nobody must hear.'

'I'm *very* intrigued.'

'What I'm going to say may shock you.'

'You're not leaving Hilary for Quentin Cloves!'

'It's . . . it's about you, and it's . . . something very difficult to say.'

'I'm nervous, Henry. That's why I'm trying to joke.'

'There's no need to be nervous. It's not bad news.'

'Well thank God for that.'

'It's about Uncle Teddy.'

'Uncle Teddy? What news can there be about him? He's been dead seven years.'

'Yes, well . . . that's the point, you see. He . . . er . . . what? Oh the terrine . . . Thank you.'

Auntie Doris was giving him a strange, intense look. Had she guessed? He realised that, nervous though he was, he was enjoying being in possession of a sensational secret. He hadn't wanted her to guess. Damn the waitress.

As soon as the waitress had gone, he told her.

'He didn't die in that fire. He's still alive.'

'What? But they found the body.'

'That was . . . somebody else. Nobody you know.'

'Well where is he?'

'Cap Ferrat.'

'Cap Ferrat? That was our place.'

'Exactly. I think he's loved you all along.'

'Why are you telling me this now?'

'He wants you back, Auntie Doris. And so do I.'

'Good Lord! Well, I . . . Good Lord!' Auntie Doris took a mouthful of her *ballottine* of lobster, and chewed like an automaton. 'I feel dizzy,' she said. 'I feel faint.'

'I'm sure you do,' said Henry. 'Drink some wine.'

Auntie Doris took a gulp of Pouilly-Fuissé.

'That's better,' she said. 'I thought I was going to pass out. I thought, "I wish Henry was telling me this outside, on the moors, in the wind." I felt . . .'

'Claustrophobic.'

'Yes. You are serious, aren't you?'

'Would I joke about something so important?'

'So . . . why did he do all this?'

'It was all. . . ,' Henry lowered his voice still further, 'financial shenanigans. Property.'

'I told him he should get into property.'

'Well he did.'

'So whose was the body in the Cap Ferrat?'

'I can't tell you. People still living might get hurt. Nobody you know.'

Auntie Doris raised another piece of the *ballottine* to her mouth. Suddenly her fork stopped, and she asked the question Henry had dreaded. 'Why didn't he tell me?'

'He . . . er . . . I think I'd better tell you the whole truth.'

'People usually say that when they're about to tell you half the truth.'

'Well I'll tell the whole truth. There was a woman.'

'A younger woman?'

'Er . . . slightly.'

'Who was this slightly younger woman?'

'Oh Lord. I can't tell you that either.'

'People still living might get hurt?'

'Yes.'

'Is she dead too?'

'Oh no. She left him . . . with her tail between her legs after he'd thrown her out.'

'I see.'

'You're the only person he's ever loved, Auntie Doris.'

'Well, he's the only person I've ever loved, Henry. Have you seen him?'

'Yes, we stayed with him in Cap Ferrat just after this slightly younger woman had . . . been thrown out.'

'So! He took her to Cap Ferrat! That was our place. He shouldn't have taken her to Cap Ferrat.'

'A psychiatrist would say he took her there because subconsciously he wished she was you.'

'I'm sure he would if you paid him enough.'

'He has a nice villa, a good life, many friends, a thriving . . . import–export business. He wants to give all that up, and come back to England . . . and you.'

'Well!'

'I wish he could. I love you both, you see.'

'I still can't think why.'

'Neither can I, but we won't go into that.'

'What do you think I should do?'

'Meet him in London. See how it develops. Find out what you feel about him.'

'What'll I tell Geoffrey?'

'Shopping trip with Hilary.'

'You're a very resourceful liar.'

'Must have been my upbringing.'

'Oh God. Were we totally awful? Henry, I heard your friend Tommy Marsden on the telly, saying, "It hasn't really sunk in yet." I thought, "God, you must be thick, if you don't realise

114

you've scored the winning goal in the Cup Final." I see what he meant now. This hasn't sunk in. So many questions. What about Geoffrey? Where would we live?'

'Would you feel bad about giving up the White Hart?'

'Bad? I'd be thrilled. Don't get me wrong, I've loved it. It's done wonders for my self-confidence. But you've heard the phrase, "A legend in his own lunchtime." Well I have to drink the lunchtimes of my legend, and it'll kill me. Oh my God!'

'What?'

'Teddy can't see me like this, with all these chins. Oh my God.'

'He won't mind. He's got a paunch and his legs are going thin.'

'No, but . . . has he? Oh, poor Teddy. No, but I'm huge. It's served its purpose. I have to lose weight. Teddy will mind.'

'What do you mean, "It's served its purpose"?'

'Kept the customers happy – they think I've a huge personality because I'm huge – and put Geoffrey off sex. I don't like sex with Geoffrey any more. I keep thinking of those waitresses. And the blackheads are getting worse.'

'Well there you are, then.'

'Yes.'

Quentin Cloves had a curious ability to walk across a room without seeming to move his legs. He floated towards them now.

'And how was the famous Fig Leaf *ballottine d'homard*?' he asked.

'Wonderful,' said Auntie Doris. 'Magnificent. Supreme.'

Quentin Cloves looked gratified. But when he'd gone, Auntie Doris said, 'The sad thing is, what with all this, I just didn't taste it at all.'

Henry waited three weeks before replying to Uncle Teddy, to give Auntie Doris time to go to a health farm.

Her visit was an enormous success, or rather a ceasing to be enormous success, and she followed her strict regime impeccably even after her release, a day early, for good behaviour. But, as her weight dropped off, her face became gaunt. She aged, through dieting too quickly, and she lost energy. Geoffrey Porringer, at first enthusiastic over the venture, didn't enjoy its fruits, and the more fickle among the customers felt the place wasn't what it was, the beer wasn't kept as well, it wasn't as clean, service was more surly, it was resting on its laurels, when in fact nothing had changed except Auntie Doris's weight.

Auntie Doris was pleased, if also slightly offended, that Geoffrey Porringer's sexual appetite didn't increase as expected.

Then there was a delay before Uncle Teddy's reply – 'Sorry I didn't write sooner but an opportunity to visit Italy came up.'

In the meantime, Hilary was getting on well with her second novel. Although sales of *In the Dog House* had been modest, and the advance on *All Stick Together* hadn't been sensational, these sums, added to Henry's utterly secure if not startlingly large salary, had given them the confidence to make an offer for a larger house, with three bedrooms.

Dumbarton House was a 1930s property, more modern Georgian than mock-Georgian, in Waterloo Crescent, off Winstanley Road, slightly too near to the town centre to be truly part of the posh suburb of Winstanley, where they brought their fish and chips home in briefcases. Neither of them liked it as much as Paradise Villa, but it had the extra bedroom they needed, and a secure garden, and Cousin Hilda said, 'Mrs Wedderburn said, "It'll be further away for them." I said, "Yes, Mrs Wedderburn, but old houses just aren't synonymous with small children." "They'll still visit you regularly, though," she said. "Oh yes," I said, "though Henry has his cucumbers, which keep him right busy, and bringing up children is a full-time job even if you aren't writing a novel as well." She said, "I can't understand why she writes novels, a nice girl like her. I prefer biographies, me. At least you know they're true." She's very direct, is Mrs Wedderburn, but she has a heart of gold. Where I'd ever have found another friend like her I do not know.'

In the summer of 1963 the Profumo affair swept away old certainties about the probity of British public life. By the end of the summer, a society osteopath called Stephen Ward had revealed the truth about John Profumo's relationship with Christine Keeler. By the end of the year, Profumo would have resigned, Ward would have been found guilty of living on immoral earnings and died of a drugs overdose, the Prime Minister Harold Macmillan would have been succeeded by Sir Alex Douglas-Home, and Christine Keeler would be in prison for perjury over the trial of her West Indian associate, Aloysius 'Lucky' Gordon.

In the midst of all this, Henry 'not so lucky' Pratt sat at his desk on a sultry August day, and found no enthusiasm for his task – the preparation of the first draft of a consultative document to be presented to Roland Stagg (to be rejected by him if bad, and claimed as his own if good) under the snappy title 'The Way Forward – Cucumber Distribution in the Seventies. A centralised chilled store for the Northern Counties – a Study of Feasibility and Location.' On this summer dog day this podgy and exhausted young dog couldn't even summon up enthusiasm for his other great task – the scouring of the Situations Vacant columns for alternative employment.

This was because, in his mind, he was elsewhere.

Where was he, in his mind?

He was in the restaurant of the Hotel Magnifique, in London, with Uncle Teddy and Auntie Doris.

The Hotel Magnifique no longer exists, mercifully, but in 1963 it was the ideal venue for a romantic encounter. The restaurant was so large, and the customers were so few, and the service was so slow, that one achieved almost total privacy. The lights were so dim that the lines on ageing faces were invisible. The food was so bland that it couldn't possibly interrupt any train of thought or emotion. The bill was so enormous that the lady could never accuse the gentleman of meanness again.

Uncle Teddy gave a nervous, stiff smile, as if for a photograph he didn't want taken, and said, 'You look wonderful, Doris.'

'I don't,' said Auntie Doris, 'but thank you. But you *do* look wonderful.'

'I don't either, but thank *you*,' said Uncle Teddy.

'So, I'm a bigamist, like you, to add to my other crimes.'

'My God, I suppose you are. What other crimes?'

'Receiving stolen goods. Smuggling. Tax evasion. Fraud. All the things that came with living with you.'

'Doris!'

'Anyway, I've got a good defence if I'm ever arrested for bigamy. The fact that you were certified dead by a Coroner's Court should get me off.'

An elderly waiter limped towards them across the cavernous restaurant, which had the look of a ballroom on a liner. He carried menus which had the wingspans of giant condors.

'At last!' said Uncle Teddy.

'I beg your pardon, sir?' said the waiter.

'You aren't exactly Speedy Gonzales, are you?'

'Geoffrey!' hissed Auntie Doris. 'Tact.'

'The name is Teddy, Doris. And why are we Teddying, anyway?' said Uncle Teddy. 'Two minutes together and already I'm being Teddyed.'

'Well, honestly,' said Auntie Doris, who always made things worse by protesting about them. 'Fancy complaining about the speed of service to a man with a deformed foot.'

'Doris!'

It was as if Uncle Teddy had never gone to prison and come out to find Auntie Doris living with his best friend and pretended to be killed in a fire and gone to live in France with a slightly younger woman, aged nineteen, while Auntie Doris married his best friend. There were no great statements of love and regret, of guilt and shame. They just slipped back into the old ways, they Dorised and Teddyed together through a long, bad meal, and knew that they wanted to spend the rest of their lives together.

As the summer died, so did Henry's enthusiasm for finding another job. He was simply too busy. In the evenings and at weekends, he kept the children amused while Hilary finished her novel. Jack was almost four now, and soon he'd be as good at football as Henry. Kate rode her bicycle round the Alderman

Chandler Memorial Park at a pace which terrified him. Jack climbed with ease trees that other children and cats and firemen found difficult. Both children courted serious accidents and defied warnings. Neither ever suffered anything worse than grazed knees and elbows, but Henry's nerves were shattered. And when the children fell exhausted into bed, he fell exhausted into redecorating Dumbarton House. Small wonder that he was having difficulty concentrating on the second draft of 'The Way Forward – Cucumber Distribution in the Seventies. A centralised chilled store for the Northern Counties – a Study of Feasibility and Location.' They had a new car now, well a new used car, a Mini. It nosed its way to York and Tyneside and Wearside, to Lancaster and the Solway Firth, so that its proud owner could examine the nine possible sites that had been short-listed for the projected chilled store.

When Hilary's editor said that the ending of *All Stick Together* was slightly too farcical, he suggested that it was his turn to come to her. She, having no idea that Henry thought of her editor as a middle-aged, bespectacled, stooping, bookish wreck, suggested a Saturday, when she wouldn't have to fetch the children from school, and Henry could take them out for the day.

Henry took the children to York, leaving before the arrival of the editor. They had a good day, particularly enjoying the Railway Museum and the Castle Museum, which had a complete Victorian street. But the children grew tired, and they arrived home before the editor had left.

Henry's first sight of Nigel Clinton sent his whole world spinning. He had a strong sensation of falling and was astounded to find that he was actually standing absolutely normally on the stridently orange and purple carpet that they hated and couldn't yet afford to replace. Nigel Clinton was twenty-five, Oxford educated, tall and dark. It was only in Henry's mind that he was the most good-looking man who ever walked this earth, but he was undeniably handsome and, being determined to be a successful man of letters, he was seriously embarrassed by his looks, so that he smiled at new arrivals with a self-conscious shyness that merely increased his sex appeal.

'Are you all right, darling?' Hilary asked Henry anxiously.

'Fine. Just tired.'

She kissed him warmly – perhaps, he thought, a little too warmly. Had she something to hide?

Henry found himself absurdly anxious to impress this young man, and on the whole he was sorry that his next remark, 'Still at it, then?' was such a banal statement of the obvious, and when Nigel said, 'This is a nice house, Henry, and a lovely street,' with an air of surprise, Henry regretted responding with, 'Oh yes, Nigel. We have all sorts of things in the North – shops that sell books, theatres that put on plays. I could even show you an off-licence that stocks green chartreuse.'

He took the children into the formica-infested kitchen, and started to make their tea, regretting that it was something as unsophisticated as egg, sausage and baked beans.

Jack soon grew bored and said, 'I'm going to see Mummy.'

'Don't. She's working,' said Henry.

'I need to see her,' said Jack, who often said 'need' when he meant 'want'.

Henry, tired from the excursion and flustered by Nigel Clinton, broke his first rule of good parenthood. He made a threat that he couldn't sustain. 'If you do,' he said, 'you'll go straight to bed without your tea.'

Jack went to the living room.

Kate sighed.

'My brother can be a real pain sometimes,' she said.

Henry turned the gas off, went into the living room, and apologised to Hilary and Nigel for the interruption.

'It's all right,' said Hilary. 'He just wanted to say "hello". He loves his mummy.'

'Everybody loves his mummy,' growled Henry. 'Now come on, Jack. Please.'

'Will I get my tea?'

'Yes!!'

The little perisher gave Henry a triumphant look and said, 'Bye bye, Mummy. Have a good work. It's nice to meet you, Nigel.'

As he shut the door, Henry heard Nigel say, 'What a charming, well-mannered boy.'

Henry put the gas on again.

'Nigel's taller than you, isn't he, Daddy?' said Jack.

'Much taller,' agreed Henry grimly.

'Why is he taller than you, Daddy?' asked Kate.

'I expect he always ate his tea,' said Henry.

This glib piece of parental opportunism was greeted with the disgust it merited, and the doorbell rang.

It was Auntie Doris, with three large suitcases and no money for the taxi.

'I've done it,' she announced as she swept past Henry. 'I've told him. I've left him. Oh!'

She looked surprised and put out by the presence of Nigel. This was her big scene and there shouldn't be an unknown supporting player there.

'Tea's burning, Daddy,' called Kate.

'Oh shit,' quipped Henry stylishly, and he hurried to the kitchen.

'Auntie Doris, this is my editor, Nigel Clinton,' said Hilary. 'Nigel, Doris Porringer.'

Auntie Doris flinched. She hated being called Doris Porringer. She shook hands with Nigel, and wished that she'd done her make-up properly before leaving.

'I've just left my . . . nice to meet you, Nigel . . . my husband,' she said. 'Teddy's coming over on Monday and I've . . . oh, sorry, are you working? Am I interrupting? I should have rung, but I thought on a Saturday . . . and I'm all of a dither with everything.'

'Of course you are,' said Hilary. 'Are you in a desperate rush, Nigel?'

'No, no,' said Nigel, the almost impossibly obliging. 'We're almost through, and it'll do us good to take a break. Final little fine adjustments,' he explained to Auntie Doris.

'Ah!' said Auntie Doris blankly. 'Yes, I've told him, and I wondered if I could stay till Monday when I meet Teddy.'

Henry, having provided the children's tea at last, joined them.

'Well . . . er . . . well, yes, of course,' he said. 'We'll move Jack in with Kate.'

'Oh Lord. Is it a nuisance? I should have rung,' said Auntie Doris.

'It's no problem,' said Hilary.

'No problem at all,' said Henry.

'The kids'll love it,' said Hilary.

'They'll love it,' said Henry.

Oh my God. Bloody Nigel will think I have all the conversational sparkle of a rather dim parrot.

'Can I get you a drink, Auntie Doris?' said Henry. 'Do you mind if we have a drink, Nigel? It is a bit of a crisis.'

'No, no. I have all the time in the world. Honestly,' smiled Mr Too-Good-to-be-True.

'Let's all have a drink,' said Hilary. 'What have we got, Henry?'

'Gin but no tonic and whisky but no soda, and some unchilled white wine,' growled Henry 'Never Got Further than Thurmarsh Grammar, the Short-Arse of the Cucumber Cock-up Corporation' Pratt.

'Whisky and tap water sounds good to me,' said Nigel 'Oxford Graduate Bet He Got a Bloody Double First, Mr Smarm-Bomb' Clinton.

'Suits me too,' said Hilary.

'I could manage a bit of gin with . . . more gin,' said Auntie Doris.

Henry went to mix . . . to *get* the drinks, mix would be an exaggeration . . . but he could still hear every word.

'I've left my husband, Nigel,' explained Auntie Doris. 'We run the White Hart at Troutwick. You may know it.'

'No, but it sounds delightful.'

'I'm madly in love with a man called Miles Cricklewood.'

'Ah.'

'He's a retired vet.'

'Gosh. Sorry to sound a bit dense, but . . . er . . . if you're in love with this Miles Cricklewood, who's Teddy?'

'That's what I call Miles,' said Auntie Doris. 'I don't like his real name.'

'Your taste does you credit,' said Nigel Clinton. 'If Hilary called a character Miles Cricklewood, unless it was a false name adopted by some rather dodgy type, I'd throw it out.'

Hooray hooray hooray maybe there is a God after all Mr Perfecto has put his foot in it and called Uncle Teddy a dodgy type by implication! Henry almost danced in with the drinks and then he realised that it wasn't as much fun as all that because Nigel would never know that he'd put his foot in it.

'But real life fact is very different from fictional fact,' Hilary was saying. 'If I put an editor like you in one of my books he'd seem impossibly tactful and intelligent.'

'And handsome,' said Auntie Doris.

'And tall,' said Jack, entering with a half-eaten orange. 'Don't forget tall.'

'Thank you. Thank you, all of you,' said Nigel. 'If you put me in your book, I'd have to say, "This is all right if you're creating a character who's learning the ropes in order to become *extremely* successful later on." '

'If I gave him dialogue as conceited as that, I'd have to think he was *very* over-ambitious,' said Hilary.

'Touché,' said Nigel Clinton.

'Don't drop your orange on the carpet, Jack,' was Henry's sparkling contribution to the fanciful cut and thrust.

Auntie Doris, who looked completely bewildered, returned to her dramatic situation.

'Teddy and I are going to live in Suffolk, where he won't be recognised,' she said.

'Excuse me,' said Nigel Clinton, 'but why doesn't he want to be recognised?'

There was a pause.

Kate entered, also with a half-eaten orange.

'Get a plate, Kate,' said Henry.

'You're a poet and you know it,' said Kate.

Henry blushed for fear Nigel thought his childish rhyming had been deliberate.

'Sorry,' persisted Nigel, 'but why doesn't he want to be recognised?'

'He's very famous and very shy,' said Hilary.

'I've never heard of him,' said Nigel.

'You were amazingly right about the name not being real,' said Henry. 'Who's a clever editor? Except, of course, that he isn't a dodgy type.'

Whoopee!! Bull's eye. OXFORD GRADUATE LOSES COMPOSURE IN POST-DODGY TYPE-SMEAR BLUSHING CATASTROPHE.

'If we told you his real name, you'd know him,' said Hilary.

'Well, it wouldn't go any further,' said Nigel.

'Sorry,' said Henry. 'We can't make exceptions.'

'How did Geoffrey take it?' asked Hilary.

'With milk and sugar,' said Kate.

'Very good, very funny, but Auntie Doris is a bit upset, so hush, dear,' said Henry.

'Badly. I left him sitting there, just staring into space,' said Auntie Doris.

'Well, he isn't staring into space now,' said Henry. 'He's walking up the garden path.'

They hurried Auntie Doris upstairs. Nigel swept the children out into the garden for a game, and Henry let Geoffrey Porringer in. He almost stumbled into the living room, and sat down heavily.

'Doris has left me,' he mumbled.

'What??' exclaimed Henry.

'No!!' cried Hilary.

Henry and Hilary exchanged shamed looks at all this pretence which was sullying the genuine grief of Geoffrey Porringer.

'You didn't know?' said Geoffrey Porringer.

'Not an inkling,' lied Henry. 'When did this happen?'

'This afternoon.'

'Where's she gone?'

'To live with some bloody vet.'

'I don't believe it.'

They all became aware of the suitcases at the same time.

'Those are her suitcases!! Is she here?' said Geoffrey Porringer.

'What? No, of course not.'

'We have the same suitcases as hers,' said Hilary.

'We admired her suitcases,' said Henry, 'and she told us where she got them, and we got the same set.'

'Why are your suitcases in the middle of the floor?'

'We're going on holiday. We're catching the night ferry,' said Henry. 'We must be off soon, in fact.'

'Very soon,' said Hilary. 'I'm awfully sorry, but there it is.'

'But what'll I do?' said Geoffrey Porringer.

'I honestly don't see what you can do,' said Henry. 'Look, I feel really embarrassed about having to hurry you out, Uncle Geoffrey, but I'll come and see you when we get back.'

They couldn't bring themselves to say that they were sorry about the break-up, having engineered it. Nor could they bring themselves to point out that he'd brought it all on himself by his touching up of waitresses.

They led him gently to his car, and watched him drive off, jerkily, with much crashing of gears.

Auntie Doris came downstairs, and Nigel came in from the garden with Kate and Jack.

'Nigel's even more fun than he's tall, Daddy,' said Kate.

'No, he's taller than he's fun, but he *is* fun,' said Jack.

'I'm not sure that your book is too farcical after all,' said Nigel Clinton.

Auntie Doris and Uncle Teddy took a rented flat in Ipswich, and scoured Suffolk for their dream home, and Cousin Hilda greeted the news of Auntie Doris's running off from Geoffrey Porringer to Miles Cricklewood with a sniff and a 'Leopards never change their spots.' Henry wished he could have told her that Auntie Doris wasn't as loose as she imagined, but Cousin Hilda would tell Mrs Wedderburn, and if Mrs Wedderburn knew they might as well put an advertisement in the *Argus*. Cousin Hilda had told them only recently, 'Gossip is that woman's Achilles' heel.'

On the day after his imaginary holiday, Henry drove to Troutwick, rehearsing every detail of the holiday he hadn't had. He needn't have bothered, because Geoffrey Porringer was too wrapped up in his own affairs to ask anything.

As he entered the pub, Henry met a pregnant Lorna Lugg coming down the main stairs after taking a tray of drinks to the Residents' Lounge.

'You're still here!' he exclaimed.

'Only Sundays,' said Lorna Lugg, née Arrow. 'Eric cooks dinner Sundays.'

'Eric cooks!'

'Well he *was* in the Catering Corps.'

'Of course. What does he do now?'

'He's a quarryman. He sets off explosions.'

'Good Lord! I see you're expecting your second.'

'My fourth.'

'Your fourth! What have you got?'

'Two girls. Marlene and Doreen. One boy. Kevin.'

'Lorna!' called Geoffrey Porringer.

'I must go,' said Lorna Lugg. She smiled. 'He doesn't touch me up any more.'

I'm not surprised, thought Henry. You aren't a pretty girl any more. Oh, Eric, you've turned my pretty Lorna into a baby factory.

Henry ordered a pint, to make his visit look less like a mission of mercy, and also because he was thirsty.

'Quiet today,' he commented.

'Doris was the one with the personality,' said Geoffrey Porringer. 'But we'll get by.'

'How are you really?' asked Henry.

'The staff are being very supportive.' Geoffrey Porringer pulled Henry's pint. 'Ollie's been a tower of strength. My regulars have stood by me. We'll survive.'

'Well I wish you the very best of luck, Uncle Geoffrey.' Henry raised his glass.

'Thank you.' Geoffrey Porringer clinked glasses dully. 'I'd hate to offend you, young sir. I've always had a lot of time for you. But, you see, I have to look forward. So I'd rather you didn't call me Uncle Geoffrey any more.'

Henry did feel a little offended, especially as he'd only called him Uncle Geoffrey to please him.

'Not offended, I hope?'

'No, no. No, no.'

'Good. Wouldn't want to offend you. You've been a good friend, but, you see . . . your aunt was a wonderful woman, but . . . larger than life. I was in her shadow. I'm on my own now, like it or not, and I'm going to give it my best shot, so there's no family now and I'm not an uncle.'

'I understand.'

'I hope so. Would you understand, Henry, if I . . . if I said, "End of chapter. That particular album closed." If I said, and I mean it, I really do, thank you for coming, but I'd be happier, this sounds awful, I know, but there it is, happier if . . . well I suppose if I didn't see any of Doris's family any more. Give me more of a chance.'

'Well, if you're sure.'

'Oh yes. I'll tell you one thing, Henry. I don't like the smell of this Cricklewood fellow. Retired vet. Fishy. Wouldn't surprise me if the chap turned out to be a rotter. Wouldn't, Henry, not one bit. Well if Doris thinks she could ever come back to me she's got another think coming. Serve that gentleman, would you, Ollie? Thanks. Another think coming, Henry. Honestly.'

'Well, fair enough,' said Henry. 'Well, I'll be off, then. Good luck, Unc . . . Geoffrey. And, if you ever do change your mind, feel you do need me, get in touch, won't you?'

'Will do, young sir. Will do.'

President Kennedy was assassinated in Dallas on November 22nd, and Henry was the only person in Britain who couldn't remember where he was at the time. He did remember that it seemed like the end of innocence and hope, though that would change with time.

In time, President Kennedy's death would begin the modern world's loss of naïvety about its leaders, and that, at least, was a blessing.

The world lost Pope John XXIII, Hugh Gaitskell in his prime, and Edith Piaf, who could still have been in her prime. Frank Sinatra Junior and the Spanish footballer Alfredo Di Stefano were kidnapped. It needed federal troops to enforce the de-segregation of the University of Alabama, but at least it was done. Perhaps it was suitably bizarre that the year which witnessed the sensational rise of the Beatles should end with the American hit parade topped for the whole of December with a song called 'Dominique', sung by a Belgian nun.

By then, Hilary had finished her rewrites, and Henry was fighting hard against his jealousy of Nigel Clinton.

In the spring of 1964, Uncle Teddy and Auntie Doris found their dream cottage in a pretty village called Monks Eleigh. It was called 'Honeysuckle Cottage'. Uncle Teddy was all for renaming it 'Cap Ferrat'. 'Over my dead body,' said Auntie Doris. 'You took her there.' 'What do you want to call it, then, Doris? "Dunsmugglin"?' said Uncle Teddy. 'What's wrong with "Honeysuckle Cottage"?' said Auntie Doris. 'It's so unoriginal,' said Uncle Teddy. 'That's what I like about it,' said Auntie Doris. 'Our adventure is over. We're now going to enjoy the evening of our lives, in "Honeysuckle Cottage".'

All Stick Together was published in October. Advance sales were good, and the publishers wanted Hilary to embark on another tour, so Henry again took a week of his holidays to look after the children.

On his last day before his week's holiday, he felt quite important. His recommendation of two smaller chilled stores, in Darlington and Preston, had found favour and was to be implemented. He didn't feel bitter that it was being passed off as Roland Stagg's idea. He knew the kind of world he lived in. He too had lost some of his naïvety.

'Have a nice holiday,' said Roland Stagg, leaving half an hour early to miss the traffic.

'Thank you. I won't,' said Henry.

He didn't. As day succeeded day, as Hilary toured bookshops and radio stations, the figure of Nigel Clinton was everywhere. It waited for the children outside their schools, it played with them in the Alderman Chandler Memorial Park, it stirred the stew-pot and cooked fish fingers with them. Henry grew more and more certain that his jealousy was not irrational. At night, especially, he knew that Nigel Montgomery Clinton was kissing and touching where he had kissed and touched. It was instinct that made him get up at three thirty-five on the Thursday morning, and go to Hilary's second-best jeans, her writing jeans, and there in the back pocket he found the letter, as afterwards he believed that he had known he would:

> Dearest Hilary,
> I love you so much, darling. . . .

He asked Alastair and Fiona Blair, who had children at the same school, if they would fetch the children that day, and drove madly, wildly, tearfully, angrily, crazily, past Retford and Newark and Love You and Grantham and So Much and Stamford and Peterborough and Darling and Huntingdon and Cambridge and Love You So Much, my Newmarket and Lavenham, towards the nearest to parents that he knew, the nearest to a family that he had ever known.

Uncle Teddy and Auntie Doris were weeding the pretty garden of their sugar-loaf cottage as if the words 'import' and 'export' had never existed.

They greeted him ecstatically.

'Welcome to our domestic bliss,' said Uncle Teddy.

'We owe so much to you,' said Auntie Doris.

'Hilary has a lover,' said Henry.

8 The Swinging Sixties

'Don't forget how incredibly lucky you've been in landing a woman like Hilary,' said Uncle Teddy, over pâté and toast in the Aga-cosy kitchen.

'Teddy!' said Auntie Doris, who always made things worse by protesting about them. 'He'll think you're meaning he's not good-looking.'

'Doris!' said Uncle Teddy, who sometimes made things worse still by protesting about them as well. 'That won't upset him. He knows he isn't good-looking.'

'Teddy!' said Auntie Doris.

'What I'm meaning is,' said Uncle Teddy, 'that you confront her very calmly. Don't raise your voice, and risk letting the thing escalate into a shouting match.'

'Show her the letter,' said Auntie Doris. 'Confront her with it, but not in an angry way.'

'That's right,' said Uncle Teddy. 'Sorrow and regret at an isolated lapse. That's the style.'

Henry would often ask himself why he had believed that advice given by two people who had led such tortuous love lives could possibly be sound.

At last the children were asleep. The long charade of Hilary's home-coming was over.

'Now perhaps you'll tell me what's wrong,' she said.

' "Wrong"?' said Henry. 'What do you mean?'

'You've been polite but dead all evening.'

'It's been a nice evening.'

'It's been unbearably nice. Something's very wrong, and I want to know what it is.'

'Don't you know what it is?' said Henry quietly.

'Well, yes, I think I do. I think you're deeply jealous of my books and my success, such as it is, and I find that deeply ungenerous and very disappointing.'

'Books my arse.' No! Calm. Don't raise your voice. Confront her with the letter, but not in an angry way. 'I think you ought to know that I've found this,' he said in a calm, but wavering voice.

Hilary took the letter and stared at it wildly. He wouldn't have believed that she was capable of going as much paler as she did. So she was guilty. Her face extinguished his last desperate hope that it was all a dreadful misunderstanding.

'Where did you find this?' she said, in a strange, low, icy voice.

'In your pocket. Careless to leave it.' No. No gibes.

'Careless? Careless? I didn't think my husband would go through my pockets.'

'Obviously, or you wouldn't have left it. It's lucky I did, isn't it?' No! Sorrow and regret. 'Look, darling, I . . . things happen, and I can forgive if . . . er . . . give him up and we'll work harder together and . . . work something out. I'm prepared to try.'

'*You* are prepared to try? My God! Big of you.' Her words stung him. He flinched. If he hadn't known that she was hitting out in self-defence, he'd have believed that she really hated him.

She gave him a look that was dredged from the depths of her bruised eyes. He recognised the dry swirling of panic. A horribly dry look. A strangely sad look. He'd have preferred tears.

And then she swung round and simply walked out of the house. She didn't even shut the door.

He just stared, bemused, at the space where she had been. Nothing in the advice of Uncle Teddy and Auntie Doris had prepared him for this.

He hurried upstairs. The children were fast asleep, little chests rising and falling peacefully.

He had to go after her. He'd have to risk it.

He couldn't risk it. Kate and Jack were his absolute responsibility, and he loved them without reserve.

He phoned his neighbours, the Wiltons. They were in. They promised to come round immediately, without hesitation. He hadn't expected that, because he hardly knew them. He thanked them warmly, told them under which stone he'd leave the key, pulled on his tatty old duffel coat, slammed the door, left the key under the agreed stone, and rushed off down Waterloo Crescent.

He turned left into Winstanley Road, towards the town centre, because surely Hilary wouldn't have set off towards the countryside on such a dingy October night? He hurried, half-running, then walking till he got his breath back, he was so unfit.

Winstanley Road dipped towards the town centre, and became less prosperous with every frantic, gasping step. At the point where it became York Road it began to smell of decay, of rising damp and falling incomes, of struggle and strife.

At last he saw her, marching resolutely through the ill-lit town, marching wildly in the drizzle with no coat.

Past the grandiose brick shell of the shabby Midland Road Station he chased her, past the lavatorial marble of the Chronicle and Argus building, no time for memories now. Up Brunswick Road, past unloved, unlovely terraces, past the gabled fortress that had once been Brunswick Road Elementary School, in which, on a morning almost as awful as this night, Henry had won false fame with a fart. Now he merely wheezed. Wildly Hilary walked, and her wildness gave her strength. Although breaking into asthmastic trots at regular intervals, Henry was catching her up only slowly.

Down the other side of the hill she strode, as the road dipped into the Rundle Valley. On the right were the great steelworks of Crapp, Hawser and Kettlewell. Once, the nights had rung with their virility and glowed like the gates of Hell. Now they played a sadder, gentler tune.

Drizzle turned to rain and, as if to wound Henry with thoughts of the child he'd been and the man he had become, Hilary turned down Paradise Lane, past the little terraced house where he was born.

Through the gate onto the tow-path she strode, across the Rundle and Gadd Navigation, over the waste ground, onto the wide footbridge over the faintly phosphorescent Rundle. There, under a night sky turned orange by the massed street lights, Henry caught her.

'Hilary,' he implored. 'My darling! I'm sorry!'

Why am I saying I'm sorry, he wondered, when it's she who's been unfaithful to me? Because I love her and don't want to lose her.

She didn't even look at him, but turned away, along the river. The rain fell harder. Orange clouds scudded dimly across the sky.

'Hilary!' he repeated.

She turned and came towards him. Her face was deathly white. He thought she was going to hit him. She pushed him. He fell backwards, flailing wildly. The acid waters of the Rundle met over his head, as they had done when he was four years old. He was drowning, burning, dying. He forced himself upwards, desperately, his head broke the surface, he gulped air frantically, excruciatingly. Hilary had gone. He went under again. He surfaced again. He tried to touch the bottom, but couldn't. He told himself to keep calm. He began to swim. The river, swollen by the recent rains, swept him downstream towards the weir. He struck out for the bank, handicapped by bursting lungs, aching chest and sodden clothes. He heard the curiously comforting rattle of a long goods train, and the very uncomforting roar of the weir. He flung himself towards the bank as the weir approached. He dragged himself up over trapped driftwood and broken bottles, slipped in the mud, hauled himself slowly back up with rubbery arms, just managed to pull himself over the lip of the sodden bank, and lay there, gasping, spluttering, the least impressive beached whale in history.

Later, when he was standing for Parliament and all this could be looked back on in tranquillity, Henry would say, 'I was pushed into the Rundle in 1939. It was an open sewer. I was pushed into it in 1964. I realised instantly that pollution had increased over those twenty-five years. Elect me, and I will make it my life's work to rid our town of this pollution. Elect me, and I will give you a river into which it will be a positive pleasure to be pushed.'

But on this October night his mouth tasted foul, he felt sick and poisoned, his breath returned to normality only slowly, and Hilary had disappeared completely.

He stood up. Water dripped off him. He'd lost his left shoe and a used condom was hanging from his right shoe. He flung shoe and condom into the river.

He trudged back, in his soaking socks, over the river, over the waste ground, across the steep hump-backed bridge over the Rundle and Gadd Navigation, along the tow-path, through the gate into Paradise Lane, and past the house where he was born. He picked his way carefully, watching out for broken glass and dog turds.

There were no trams any more, and there were all sorts of rumours about how Bill Holliday had won the scrap contract. He didn't attempt to wait for a bus, stinking as he did of sewage and dead fish.

He wheezed on sore feet and jellied legs, up Brunswick Road, down the hill to the town centre, past the lit windows of Premier House, where production of the morning's *Chronicle* was in full swing, and along York Road, parts of which were as smelly as his clothes. Stragglers of the night gave him looks as dirty as his trousers. A drunk, urinating in the gutter, stared at him as at an inferior being.

As he limped up the garden path, he had a wild hope that Hilary would be there, remorseful. But she wasn't. The Wiltons greeted him as if his was the only way to dress, and left only reluctantly and after assurances that he would phone them if necessary.

He phoned the police, had a whisky, and a bath, and went to bed to toss through a long, lonely night.

In the morning, he told the children that Hilary had gone to see a friend, but they sensed that something was wrong, and were fractious.

The police phoned at nine forty-five. She'd been found wandering near Hoyland Common. She'd been taken to the General Hospital. She was suffering from exhaustion and hypothermia. She didn't know who she was.

She looked at Henry and showed no sign of recognition. She looked feverish. Her eyes were hot but blank. He tried to hold her hand, but she wouldn't let him. He phoned Howard Lewthwaite in Spain, and within half an hour he had booked himself on a plane to London that evening.

Even facing Howard Lewthwaite was better than inactivity. Henry told the children that Mummy had been taken ill, but would be all right. He arranged for them to spend the night with Alastair and Fiona Blair, who had become good friends, and he drove to London to meet Howard Lewthwaite off the plane.

Hilary's father looked old and ravaged beneath his suntan. Henry told him what had happened. It seemed the only course.

'I simply can't believe it,' said Howard Lewthwaite. 'She wouldn't.'

'I thought that,' said Henry. 'But she did.'

'Have you any proof?' asked Howard Lewthwaite.

'There was the letter,' said Henry, flicking the wipers on.

'That was him telling her that he loved her. You haven't seen a letter from her telling him that she loved him.'

This simple truth was a revelation to Henry. He realised that what he'd taken as proof was no kind of proof at all. But he couldn't yet face the implications of even the possibility that he'd been wrong.

'Then why did she keep the letter?' he said.

Howard Lewthwaite didn't reply.

Henry didn't tell him that before he'd seen the letter he'd been certain that she and Nigel were having an affair. The intensity of his jealousy was a very personal shame.

'When I showed her the letter she went absolutely white,' he said. 'I didn't need to ask her anything more.'

It was four in the morning when they reached the hospital. Henry realised that Howard Lewthwaite didn't want him to stay. So he went home and tried to sleep. He was utterly exhausted, but couldn't sleep. It was true, he hadn't got proof. For Hilary to be unfaithful was deeply painful, but if he'd got it wrong his guilt would be even more painful. He needed proof.

At half past six, unshaven and hollow-eyed, having had barely a wink of sleep for forty-seven hours, he set off for London again. There wasn't much on the roads that Sunday morning. He drove fast, barely conscious of the mechanics of driving, going through the events of the last two days again and again.

He found Nigel Clinton's flat in Highgate without difficulty. Hilary's editor was very surprised to see him, and shocked at his appearance.

'What on earth's up?' he said. 'You look awful. Has something happened to Hilary?'

Henry sank into an armchair and an enormous feeling of exhaustion swept over him. He'd intended to have an eyeball-to-eyeball confrontation, but since he was several inches shorter than Nigel it was perhaps just as well that he was seated, with Nigel towering over him, as he said, 'Have you been having an affair with my wife?'

'Of course I haven't,' said Nigel. 'Chance would be a fine thing.'

'Did you write to her, saying, "Dearest Hilary, I love you so much, darling"?'

'Oh yes.'

'Why?'

'Because I loved her. Sorry. I know I shouldn't have. I loved her from the first moment I met her, but I never stood a chance.'

'What?'

'She loves you. She's utterly faithful and always will be. I was so jealous that Saturday when I saw you all together. I've taught myself, with great difficulty, not to love her. I'm free again now.'

All his life Henry had experienced conflicting emotions, but in that flat, of which he would take away not the slightest visual memory, he was almost torn apart by them. Joy, relief, pain, shame, despair.

'I'm sorry,' he said. He stood up. He went dizzy, and felt that he was going to faint.

'Are you all right?' asked Nigel.

'Yes. Just very tired and very hungry.'

'You aren't going to hit me, then?'

'Why should I? You've done nothing wrong.'

'I tried, though. I tried hard to do something wrong. You look very pale.'

'I'm going to have to sit down again.'

'I only cook spaghetti bolognese. But I cook a very good spaghetti bolognese.'

136

Henry's return journey was horrific. It was the fourth time he had driven between London and Thurmarsh in two days, and he'd had no sleep at all during that time. He had cramp, back-ache, arm-ache, a headache, and a sense that his brain was too small to fit his head. He'd gone to London to make Nigel Clinton eat humble pie, and instead he'd eaten Nigel Clinton's spaghetti bolognese. And he'd made the worst mistake that he'd ever made in his life.

He recognised now that Hilary was innocent and his jealousy had been the mental illness of a possessed man. He realised now that when she'd gone white it was with anger at his hunting through her pockets and reading her mail and with disgust at his lack of trust.

The nights were drawing in, and the light faded early on that suitably sombre October evening. The clouds were heavy, but there was no rain. Smoke from wood fires rose straight into the still sky, and curls of mist licked the hedgerows. Half the time Henry was unaware that there was a road and that he was in his Mini. He was in the summer house in Perkin Warbeck Drive, with Hilary telling him of the boy who had left her and the man who had raped her. She'd told him what it was like to wake up in a hospital ward, among strangers, not knowing who you were, and to realise gradually that this was the same old you, the same old earth, the fight had to go on, you hadn't taken a large enough dose. Anna had told him that Hilary was mentally ill. 'I've had a lot of depression,' she'd said that night. 'And I tried to kill myself. And I went very inward. If that's mental illness, I'm mentally ill.'

He had sobbed, 'What a responsibility.' He had said, 'You're a complete fool, you know. I'm clumsy, insensitive, thoughtless, hopeless. I'm a case.' He was, and he'd failed utterly in his responsibility. The tears streamed, the mist turned to fog, the journey became a nightmare.

He reached the General Hospital at ten fifteen that night. He was told that Hilary was under sedation. Such was his physical state that a suspicious and brave nurse accompanied him to the car park and watched until she was certain that he had really left the area.

Henry slept for thirteen hours, had horrendous nightmares, and woke to realise that he had completely forgotten about his own children and was already three and a half hours late for work.

The Blairs had got the children to school without any problems. Timothy Whitehouse sympathised over what Henry called 'a little domestic upheaval', and accepted his absence with equanimity. 'The Cucumber Marketing Board will survive till you get things sorted out,' he said. And a visit to the hospital soon established that there was nothing Henry could do there.

Henry and Howard sat in the draughty Main Reception.

'She has pneumonia,' Howard told him. 'And a full-scale nervous breakdown.'

'Oh my God.'

'She's in no physical danger. She recognises me, but doesn't remember anything about that fateful night. The doctor thinks she *will* recover her memory when the shock wears off. To see you just yet would be far too dangerous.'

A man with his leg in plaster was wheeled through, and a woman with her arm in plaster said, 'Hello, gorgeous, shall we go out and get plastered together?'

The receptionist coughed without putting her hand in front of her mouth.

'Howard?' said Henry.

'Yes?'

Howard Lewthwaite's tired face was cautious. He'd been alerted by Henry's tone of impending confession.

'Hilary didn't sleep with Nigel Clinton.'

'Well I told you she didn't.'

'I know.'

A yellow van pulled up with a screech, and a man in blue overalls hurried in through the swing doors with a red fire extinguisher.

'All sorted,' he told the receptionist, who smiled and sneezed without getting a handkerchief out.

'Howard?' said Henry.

'Yes?'

'All this is my fault.'

'Henry! These things happen.' Hilary's father smiled wearily. There was no hostility in his smile, but no friendship either.

Henry collected the children from school. When they got home, he told them that their mummy was ill in hospital, and they would be able to see her when she was better. They looked very solemn, but didn't cry.

Next morning, he took the children to school, and Fiona Blair, dark, tall, handsome and very Scottish, offered to take them home from school each evening and give them their tea, so that Henry could return to work.

'That's incredibly kind of you,' said Henry.

'What are friends for?' said Fiona Blair. She touched his arm gently. 'We're so sorry. We love you both.'

Henry flinched from their love. He had caused so much pain. He needed self-abasement.

Nevertheless, he hoped he wouldn't need too much self-abasement at Cousin Hilda's.

He hurried round, to catch her before she went shopping.

As he walked up the gravel drive of number 66, Park View Road, he became a child again. His stomach sank with dread.

Cousin Hilda was very surprised to see him at five past nine in the morning.

'What's wrong?' she said.

If only nothing had been wrong, and he could have said, 'Why do you assume something must be wrong, just because I call at five past nine?'

The smell of Tuesday morning's sausage and tomato filled the little basement room. The stove was dying now that breakfast was over.

'We've had a bit of a tragedy,' he said, sitting at the table, in his old place.

Cousin Hilda gave an anticipatory sniff, and Henry launched into his tale of woe.

When he'd finished, Cousin Hilda looked at him sadly and said, 'How could you think owt like that of Hilary? She's a grand lass, is Hilary.'

Henry wanted to say, 'Why couldn't you ever have said that to her face? It's too late now,' but all he said was, 'I know.'

'Mrs Wedderburn were saying to me the other day, "That

woman is a saint. Henry has married a saint." She's never wrong about folk, isn't Mrs Wedderburn, even if her tongue does sometimes run away with her.'

'Anyway, I thought I'd come and let you know straight away,' said Henry.

'Thank you for that.'

Cousin Hilda made them a cup of Camp coffee, and they sat gloomily in the cooling room, no longer cheered by the warmth and glow of the stove.

She sniffed violently.

'Satire,' she said.

'I beg your pardon?' said Henry.

'That's what's behind it all. All this satire. There's no trust any more. That David Frost. Who does he think he is?'

'Well I do think people don't trust each other as much, and sometimes they're right not to, because they don't deserve trust, but I don't think satire can be held to blame. My problems with Hilary aren't caused by David Frost.'

'Well when I were a girl we didn't have satire, and we did perfectly well wi'out it.'

'You didn't have motor cars either.' Henry was briefly triumphant, believing that he'd scored a debating point.

'Exactly!' said Cousin Hilda. 'It's bound to affect the brain, is carbon monoxide poisoning. It's forced to.'

Henry remembered that, despite his troubles, he ought to continue to take an interest in Cousin Hilda's life.

'How are your gentlemen?' he asked.

'I've lost Mr Ironside. Well, it were only to be expected. His family have joined him up here. But I've lost Mr Pettifer and all.'

'Good Lord.'

'Aye, but it were only a stop-gap while he found a house, and he stayed eight years. The funny thing is, I were glad he was going, to say I'd had eight years of his bitterness. But now he's gone I miss him. I'd give owt now to hear him running down young Adrian's cheese counter and looking down on me because I never met Laurence Gielgud. I must be getting old. There's too much change in this business.'

'Who've you got now, then?'

'Well Mr O'Reilly, of course. And a Mr Travis. He's a widower and a liquidator.'

'A liquidator?'

'Bankruptcies and I don't know what. Says he may be here a while if things go well, by which he means if things go badly.' She sniffed. 'My other two rooms are empty. Folk are renting flats and buying ready-made packet meals these days.' She sniffed again. 'They don't want "digs" as such any more. An era is drawing to a close. Still, you have worse troubles.'

'Well . . . we'll get over them.'

'Well I won't rub it in. I know I can be a bit stern sometimes, but when folk are in trouble there's no point in rubbing it in,' said Cousin Hilda. 'You know you've been a complete and utter fool. There's no need for me to tell you.'

Dr Martin Luther King received the Nobel Peace Prize, Harold Wilson's new Labour government announced that prescriptions would be free of charge from February, the House of Commons voted to abolish the death penalty, and Hilary recovered slowly from her pneumonia and even more slowly from her nervous breakdown.

Shortly before Christmas, Howard Lewthwaite told Henry that the time was ripe for her to see the children.

'But not me?'

'Not you.'

The children were very subdued on their return from seeing their mother.

'She's very ill,' said Kate, 'but she's getting better, isn't she?'

'Oh yes.'

'Why didn't you come in too?' asked Jack.

'So that you could see her on your own,' said Henry.

Jack considered this, and nodded.

'We're going again on Christmas Day, aren't we?' said Kate.

They spent Christmas with the Blairs. In the afternoon, they took the children to see Hilary. Henry waited outside.

On their return, the children were a little less subdued.

'She's getting better,' said Kate.

'You let us see her on our own again,' said Jack.

'She'll be home soon,' said Kate.

Henry often asked Howard Lewthwaite if he would take Hilary a letter, but he said it was too soon.

Towards the middle of January, he said that he thought the time was ripe.

'Be tactful, won't you?' he said.

'What do you think I am?' said Henry.

Howard Lewthwaite didn't reply. Henry felt that any reply would have been preferable to that telling silence.

His letter told Hilary that he realised that she had been completely innocent and he was deeply sorry and he loved her very much and the children were looking forward to her coming home.

Howard Lewthwaite called round at Dumbarton House a few days later, and handed Henry Hilary's reply.

'Not good news, I'm afraid,' he said. 'Read it when the children aren't around.'

Henry put the children to bed, poured himself a large whisky, and settled down with Hilary's letter. It was written in a shaky hand.

> Dear Henry,
>
> I'm sorry about my writing. I'm not very strong yet. I was grateful for your letter, and I'm glad you now know that I was completely innocent. I wish you'd come to that conclusion from your knowledge of me, rather than finding out from Nigel. I suppose that, if you had, we might have found some trust together again.
>
> I've been very ill with pneumonia. Apparently I walked all night and was delirious. I remember nothing after walking out of our house. I've also had . . . they call it a nervous breakdown . . . just a total collapse of will and energy and hope. A blankness. I feel that there's nobody inside me, yet my hand moves and the pen writes, so there must be. I told you what it was like before and this is as bad, but I won't try to kill

myself this time, because I'll think of Mummy and Daddy and Sam and the children. Yes, and you, because I know you'd rather I was still alive. I'll go and live in Spain and I hope the children will come and visit me in the holidays.

I forgive you for your lack of trust. I can't pretend it didn't cause me deep pain and agony. I don't think I can ever forgive you for reading my private mail. I expect you wonder why I kept that letter. Because I'm vain. I accepted your love as natural because I thought we were made for each other and that's how the miracle of love works. But if another man also loves me, I must be attractive. I'd never thought so, so it pleased me, so I kept it, so I deserve what I got.

I am feeble, Henry. I am sick. I have a fragile grasp of mental stability. Not so fragile that I can't write about it, I was a novelist after all, but fragile nevertheless. Sometimes I've seemed to people to be strong, but that's the way I've had to be to cover my weakness. But I've always known that I wasn't good enough for you.

Imagine the shock, therefore, when I discover that you aren't good enough for me! Your sexual suspicion and jealousy, though horrible, are perhaps forgivable as a temporary madness. Your jealousy of my books was the real problem and although I won't write any more I could never cope with all that.

How can we live happily together if we're both not good enough for each other? I don't want you to feel that I hate you, but I know that I couldn't bear you to touch me and how could we live like that?

What it is really, darling – I hope you don't mind me still calling you darling – is that we had wonderful times and because of how it was and because it couldn't be like that again I think it's best if it isn't at all.

I've thought about trying for the children's sake and you must understand that I can't. It's a fact rather than a decision. That they will be happier with one hopefully happy parent than with two unhappy parents is probable, but not certain.

What is certain is that I couldn't do it. Don't be fooled by this letter into thinking that I'm really all right. I can cope with letters. They don't speak back. I'm still very ill. I couldn't face going out of doors even yet. The doctors say I couldn't have the children, so you'll have to have them, and I'm sure that you want to and I know that you'll be a good father.

They say it'll be very slow but that I will make a full recovery. I don't actually want to. I don't want a man again and I don't want to write a novel ever again. I think I'll pretend to make a full recovery.

Please don't feel guilty. You gave me a better life than I ever dreamt of and made me strong enough to know that I won't kill myself this time and maybe will even be at least sort of happy eventually. My poor mother will be sad for my sadness but, more so, happy to have my company. Ditto Dad.

I'll divorce you for mental cruelty, but that's really just legal, I don't mean it.

I hope you'll find somebody else and find something more worthy of your life than cucumbers. You're still very special, despite everything.

With love,
Hilary.

He found that he hadn't touched his whisky.

Henry wrote two more letters, but Hilary refused to accept them. Sir Winston Churchill died at the age of ninety. Hilary wasn't allowed newspapers. She couldn't read about the long, inexorable deepening of the conflict in Vietnam. America seemed determined to wipe communism off the face of the earth even if the face of the earth had to go with it. She couldn't read how in Alabama State troopers used tear-gas, night sticks and whips to break up an attempted Negro march from Selma to Montgomery or how President Johnson asked Congress for support for a new civil rights bill that would guarantee every Negro citizen the right to vote in all elections. She was still too frail to be fed the slow drip of history.

Winter gave way to spring with bad grace.

Henry's thirtieth birthday passed without celebration.

Six days after Henry's thirtieth birthday, Howard Lewthwaite took Hilary back to Spain with him.

Henry had to tell the children that their mummy wouldn't be coming home again.

He sat them at the kitchen table, and he sat down with them. He needed courage to launch himself into it. It was harder than doing a comedy act in front of all the boys in Dalton College.

'Mummy isn't going to come home,' he said. 'She's going to live in Spain with Granny and Grandpa Lewthwaite, because she's been ill. You'll be able to go to Spain to spend your holidays with her and you'll be by the sea and it's much warmer than Filey so it'll be very nice. And the rest of the time you'll be here with me and we'll do all sorts of nice things at weekends. I love you very much and Mummy loves you very much and you'll go on aeroplanes and it'll all be very nice.'

Excitable, highly strung six-year-old Kate remained passive and pale-faced and stared at him solemnly out of her deep dark eyes that reminded him so much of Hilary. It was burly, phlegmatic, ruddy-faced five-year-old Jack whose lower lip began to quiver. Oh please don't cry, thought Henry.

'Will Mummy come home when she's really better?' asked Kate.

Oh Lord.

'No,' he said quietly. 'I'm afraid she won't.'

Jack's lip quivered again.

'Mummy and Daddy want to do different things now. Mummy wants to live in Spain and Daddy has his work with the cucumbers. People sometimes do still like each other very much but don't want to be together all the time.'

'But you don't want to be together *any* of the time,' said Kate.

'Well . . . look . . . sometimes people, even grown-ups, especially grown-ups, do very silly things. Your daddy did a very silly thing and your mummy got cross. Mummy isn't cross any more but . . . she's decided she doesn't want to live with me any more.'

Jack's lip quivered again, but he still didn't quite cry.

'Did you throw a kipper at her?' asked Kate.

'Good heavens, no,' said Henry. 'Why do you say that?'

'Sally Cranston's daddy threw a kipper at Sally Cranston's mummy.'

'Oh dear. No, I didn't throw a kipper.'

'Was what you did as silly as throwing a kipper?'

Sometimes he cursed Kate's powers of persistence.

'It was much sillier.'

Jack's eyes widened in astonishment, and he forgot completely about his quivering lip.

'Much sillier than throwing a kipper!' he said, with deep awe. 'I can't imagine anything that's much sillier than throwing a kipper.'

Lucky you, thought Henry. I can, and I'm going to have to live with it for a very long time.

In May, Mr Tubman-Edwards reached retirement age. His retirement party was held in the Board Room on the third floor. One of the periodical economy drives was in full swing. The food was provided by the wives of staff members and brought in by car.

'Be very careful tonight,' Roland Stagg warned Henry. 'Many a promising career's been nipped in the bud because a copy-book was blotted at a retirement party.'

'Do I have a promising career?'

'Oh yes. You just have to be patient. Your hour of glory is at hand.'

Balloons in the shape of cucumbers, custom-made by Brighouse Balloons Limited, adorned the otherwise austere Board Room, whose walls were bare save for framed certificates of trophies won at international fairs by British cucumbers.

Three of the wives had made chicken and mushroom vol-au-vents.

'Typical of this lot. No consultation,' grumbled Maurice Jesmond, Head of Facilities.

The room soon filled up with cucumber folk and their better halves, but during the early stages of the party the atmosphere was rather stiff and formal. This was because of the presence of several members of the Board of Directors: mysterious men whom one met occasionally in the lift, farmers, growers, wholesalers and retailers of cucumbers.

The guests began to attack the food with gusto. Two trays of chicken and mushroom vol-au-vents went rapidly. The other hung fire.

Henry, aware of his depressed state of mind, drank sparingly even after the Directors had all made an early departure. He was determined not to blot his copy-book.

He attempted to be extremely charming to Mrs Tubman-Edwards.

A wasted effort!

His opening remark of, 'I should have written to thank you for a delightful dinner party,' was flung back at him with, 'I should have *known* you were stupid if you had. It was a nightmare. I have endured fifteen years in this city, because of cucumbers.' His, 'I believe you brought some vol-au-vents. They're lovely,' elicited the response of, 'Mine are the ones that aren't lovely. Mine are the ones that are being left.' But his *pièce de résistance* was undoubtedly, 'I expect you'll be glad to have Mr Tubman-Edwards at home more.' This was greeted by a snort of derision that resembled a rhinoceros attempting to clear a particularly nasty dose of catarrh.

He found himself, midway through the evening, trapped in a corner, beneath a framed certificate commemorating the winning of the third prize at the Foire Internationale de Légumes in Nantes, listening to the retiring Head of Establishments' woes.

'What am I going to do, Henry?' he said. 'All day, every day, at home with Margaret.'

'Polar exploration?'

'Possibly. I've tried golf. I just can't hit the damned thing and I lose my temper. Never marry a snob, Henry. You didn't marry a snob, did you?'

'No. I married a much too wonderful woman.'

'Well I married a snob. Margaret is a snob. She thought I'd have a glittering career. A mandarin of the civil service. What did I become?'

'A satsuma of the not-so-civil service?'

'Exactly. You need a sense of humour here. My son bullied you, didn't he? Josceleyn.'

'Well . . . yes . . . he blackmailed me.'

'No moral fibre. A sticky end predicted. I have an only son who was unlikeable even in the pram, a grotty little house full of all the Spode my wife inherited from her family and keeps on using to remind me that she's known better days, and there I sit between a scrap-metal dealer and a ball-bearings mogul, with a snobbish wife who's as sexy as a camshaft and can't even cook anything edible to put on her bloody Spode plates. I also have a deep sense of failure and futility. I've struggled through, keeping my nose clean, and now they say, "Thank you very much, here are some inedible vol-au-vents cooked by your wife, piss off." '

'I'm very sorry,' said Henry.

'Not your fault,' said Dennis Tubman-Edwards. 'My fault for marrying a snob.' He winced. 'The shrapnel. Always plays me up when I get angry. Did you read *Biggles*?'

'Yes. I loved *Biggles*.'

'Knew you would. I always wanted to be Biggles. Air Force turned me down. Bad eyesight. I hate my initials. D. F. C. Tubman-Edwards BA. I always wanted to be B. A. Tubman-Edwards DFC. A few gongs might have improved my sex life. My wife's a snob, you see. Did I tell you that?'

'Yes. Yes, you did.'

'You look depressed, Henry. Are you depressed?'

'Well I have to say I haven't found you a riot of laughs.'

'I suppose not.'

'I don't feel I'm getting anywhere.'

'Nonsense. You're serving your apprenticeship and managing not to blot your copy-book. People will begin to notice you.'

'Nobody's noticing me.'

'People will begin to notice that nobody is noticing you. People will begin to realise that you're a sound man. Be patient. Your hour of glory is at hand.'

Some of the staff became the worse for drink. The Deputy Head of Liaison (otherwise known as the post-boy) was sick.

At eleven o'clock all the balloons descended. Henry had managed not to blot his copy-book, but he still felt depressed.

So Henry got up, gave the children breakfast, took them to the Blairs, travelled to Leeds, sat in his dark little office waiting for his hour of glory, read the Situations Vacant column, travelled back to Thurmarsh, picked up the children from the Blairs, listened to them chattering about how much they were looking forward to seeing Mummy, put them to bed, read them a story about a bow-tie that didn't like the posh man who was wearing it and wanted to be worn by a farm labourer, drank a large, slow whisky, tossed and turned in his lonely bed, got up, gave the children breakfast, took them to the Blairs, travelled to Leeds, sent off applications for jobs, travelled back to Thurmarsh, picked up the children from the Blairs, listened to them chattering about how warm the sea would be in Spain, put them to bed, read them a story about a grandfather clock that laughed at a cuckoo clock because it was Swiss and got punished for its racialism and arrogance, had a large, slow brandy, recalled sadly in his lonely bed those fiercer days of masturbation at Dalton College, got up, gave the children breakfast, picked up his mail and discovered that he hadn't even been granted an interview by the people to whom he had applied for jobs.

Three months of the swinging sixties passed unswingingly in this way. The Commons voted for the renationalisation of steel, Ian Smith's Rhodesia Front Party was elected with an increased minority, Cassius Clay knocked out Sonny Liston in the first round, the Beatles received OBEs and Edward Heath became leader of the Conservatives.

The children went to Spain, beside themselves with excitement, to spend a month with Hilary.

On his return from the airport, Henry heated up a Vesta prawn curry, and ate it while watching *Coronation Street*. Then he went to the Winstanley and sat there on his own, slowly drinking pint after pint. At twenty-five past ten Peter Matheson came in and Henry was thrilled to see him. This must be my lowest ebb, he thought.

'So it's out every night, the bachelor life again, is it?' said Peter Matheson.

'Yes,' said Henry, accepting another pint. 'Yes, it's terrible.'

Peter Matheson looked at him as if he was deranged or Italian or something equally odd, but Henry didn't care. Whenever the macho men said, 'Bet you're living it up now you've offloaded the little horrors,' he told the truth. 'The house is so silent. I miss them desperately.'

He missed Hilary dreadfully too, but he knew that there was no hope there, so he looked for pastures new.

His first Friday evening without the children saw him in the Lord Nelson, in Leatherbottlers' Row. Seated at their old table in the back bar, looking as if they'd been there ever since Henry'd left the paper eight years ago, were Helen Plunkett, Ginny Fenwick, Colin Edgeley and Ben Watkinson.

Ben was almost fifty now, and they all looked older. But then so did Henry. His hair was just beginning to thin.

Colin Edgeley leapt up, said, 'Hello, kid. Great. Have a drink, kid,' hugged Henry, and said, 'Oh shit. I haven't any money.' Ben Watkinson said he'd buy him a drink if he could name the county grounds of all seventeen first-class cricket counties. Ginny Fenwick blushed and bought him a drink. Henry named sixteen of the seventeen grounds, and Ben said that was good enough. Helen put her hand on his knee under the table and he developed an erection. She ran her hands across his crotch, felt the erection and raised her eyes.

'Where's Ted?' enquired Henry.

'Walking in the Lakes with mates,' said Helen. 'I hate the Lakes in August.'

Henry felt very excited indeed.

'So are you on the loose tonight or are you going on somewhere?' asked Ginny.

'No. No plans,' said Henry.

'No. Nor me,' said Ginny. 'I don't much like making plans. I like to see how the evening develops.'

Henry said, 'My round. Same again?'

'Not for me,' said Ben. 'Time I went home and gave the wife one. Oh, all right, as I haven't seen you for so long.'

'Yes, just the one, then I must get back to Glenda,' said Colin.

'Well just the one,' said Ginny. 'I don't want to hang around the pub all night.'

'Yes, please,' said Helen. 'I'm in no hurry.'

Ben went home to give the wife one. Ginny said, 'Well, I fancy something to eat. Are you coming, anybody?'

'No, got to get back to Glenda,' said Colin.

'I'm not hungry,' said Helen.

'No, thanks, Ginny. I've eaten,' lied Henry.

Ginny Fenwick blushed again and stumbled out of the pub.

'It must be awful not to be attractive,' said Helen.

'If you lend me a quid, I can buy a round,' said Colin.

'I thought you were going home,' said Henry.

'Glenda won't mind. You're my mate,' said Colin.

'How is Glenda?' asked Henry.

'Very well,' said Colin. 'We're getting on much better now I don't drink.'

They told Henry all the office gossip. Terry Skipton, news editor and Jehovah's Witness, had retired. Neil Mallet, who had once plagued Henry with deliberate misprints, had been seen in Buenos Aires, where he was apparently working on an English-language newspaper.

'I'm starving,' announced Helen. 'Have you tried our Indian restaurant, Henry? At last we're catching up.'

'Yes, I have. I like it,' said Henry.

'Great idea,' said Colin. 'I could murder a vindaloo.'

'And Glenda'll murder you,' said Helen. 'Go on home, Colin, there's a good boy.'

'Oh,' said Colin Edgeley. 'Oh!! Message received. Never let it be said that Colin Edgeley came between a mate and a leg-over.'

Henry and Helen held hands on that warm summer's evening.

'Shall we pop into the Devonshire first?' said Helen.

'No, let's not. I quite fancy an early night,' said Henry meaningfully.

'Me too,' said Helen meaningfully.

The Taj Mahal was half full. Later, after the pubs closed, it would be full.

Henry's nice waiter, whom he always thought of as Count Your Blessings, beamed up to them and said, 'Nice to see you again, sir. And your lovely wi . . .'

He stopped, confused.

'You're quite right,' said Henry. 'This is not my lovely wife. My lovely wife has left me. This is my lovely non-wife, Helen.'

It was impossible to see if Count Your Blessings blushed. He showed them to a corner table, handed them menus, and asked what they'd like to drink.

'A pint of lager, please,' said Henry.

'Do you make lassi? I don't feel that I need any artificial stimulation tonight,' said Helen meaningfully.

They had finished their meal by five to ten. A light soft rain was falling on the darkening summer streets of the unprepossessing town.

'Do you fancy coming home for a drink?' said Henry Ezra Pratt.

'You've rejected my advances once too often,' said Helen Marigold Plunkett, née Cornish. 'I'm not suddenly going to become available now that you're on your own. A girl has her pride.'

The following Friday, Ted was in the Lord Nelson, but not Helen. Also present were Ginny, Colin and Ben.

'Helen not here?' asked Henry.

Ted looked round the bar.

'No. Can't see her,' he said.

'All right, it was a silly question,' said Henry. 'Working, is she?'

'Gone to see her parents,' said Ted. 'I don't go. Mr and Mrs Basil Cornish don't see eye to eye with their son-in-law. You must be very disappointed. I gather you had a curry with her last week.'

Ginny blushed. She seemed to have developed a blushing problem.

'Yes, I did,' said Henry.

'Jolly good,' said Ted. 'Got on well, did you?'

'Yes,' said Henry, 'but nothing happened.'

Ted Plunkett raised his bushy eyebrows.

'What do you mean, "Nothing happened"?' he said. 'Why do you need to tell me that? I assumed nothing happened. Helen is a married lady.'

Ben went home to give the wife one. Colin announced that he'd better go as he'd been in the doghouse last weekend, and Ted said, 'Well, I'm off. Two's company. Three's a crowd.'

Henry and Ginny smiled at each other a trifle nervously, now that they were alone.

'Fancy a curry?' said Henry.

'Yes, please, even though I'm second choice,' said Ginny.

'Oh Ginny!' said Henry.

'Oh I'm not offended,' said Ginny. 'You're third choice.'

Count Your Blessings greeted them warmly and said, 'Good to see you again, sir. It's been quite a while.'

'There's no need to be tactful,' said Henry. 'Ginny knows I was here last Friday.'

Count Your Blessings showed them to a corner table, handed them menus, and asked what they'd like to drink.

'A pint of lager, please,' said Henry.

'Do you mind if I have wine?' said Ginny. 'I'm feeling rather nervous tonight.'

They talked about the old days, when Ginny'd had the flat above him, in Winstanley Road.

'A dental mechanic has your flat now,' she said.

'Lucky man,' said Henry.

'He is a lucky man. He has a nice wife, a lovely daughter, and nobody upstairs keeping them awake with twanging bed-springs.' Ginny sighed. 'I loved Gordon so much. I love him still.'

'Is there no one in your life now?'

'No one in that way. I had two great ambitions, to become a war correspondent and find myself a gorgeous man. I've managed neither.'

'There's still time.'

'Henry, I'm thirty-five.'

'Maybe not for the war correspondent, I don't know about these things, but certainly for a gorgeous man.'

They finished their meal by twenty to ten. The air in the grey, dusty town was warm and stale as the summer's day faded.

'Do you fancy coming home for a drink?' said Henry.

'What a splendid idea,' said Ginny.

They took a taxi. In the taxi, Henry put his hand on Ginny's thigh. She had big thighs.

They sat on the settee and drank almost neat whisky. Henry wished that Hilary's grave beauty wasn't watching them from the telephone table. He wished Kate and Jack weren't watching them, cautiously and seriously from the mantelpiece, laughing delightedly from on top of the television. He went upstairs to the lavatory, hurried into his bedroom, took the family photographs off the bedside table, where they fuelled his self-pity each night, and put them in a drawer.

He had a sudden fear that Ginny, like Anna Matheson on that never-to-be-forgotten night, would be lounging naked in an armchair.

But she was standing, with her coat on, reading an invitation on the mantelpiece.

'Time I was off,' she said.

This was worse than her having taken all her clothes off.

'Oh, Ginny,' he said. 'Aren't you going to stay and come to bed with me?'

She put her arms round him, and kissed him solemnly.

'No,' she said. 'You don't want me enough. I don't want you enough. It might work at the time. It wouldn't work afterwards. I'd want to go home as soon as it was over. Neither of us would want to wake up beside the other. Will you walk me to my door, like a gentleman? I'd like to feel I'd been out with a gentleman, just once in my life.'

The invitation which Ginny had been reading on Henry's mantelpiece was to the engagement party of Paul Hargreaves, Henry's best friend at Dalton College, to Dr Christobel Farquhar.

It took place in the elegant Hampstead home of Paul's parents. Henry told himself, with every mile of the long journey from Thurmarsh, that this was another social event at which it was important for him not to blot his copy-book. He would be witty, gracious, generous, sober – well, fairly sober. It was ridiculous to have a best friend whom you no longer liked very much. He would find in his heart the warmth to rekindle his affection for Paul.

Dr Christobel Farquhar was, as was to be expected, strikingly attractive. 'Paul's a lucky man,' Henry told her, and he told Paul, 'You're a lucky man.' Low marks for originality, but his reward was a warm smile from Paul which almost persuaded him that he really did like him.

There was champagne, but Henry drank carefully. There was a salmon buffet, and Henry ate carefully. With his suit unsullied by mayonnaise, and his senses barely affected by champagne, he sailed through the elegant rooms, crowded with surgeons and radiologists and neurologists and psychiatrists and a couple of Hampstead artists to give just a slight piquancy of bohemianism.

It was less than halfway through the party when he overheard the exchange. 'Who *is* that?' 'That's Paul's funny little friend. You know, the cucumber man.'

The cucumber man's heart raced, his pulse hammered, but he refused to feel humiliated. He was a fighter. He had always been a fighter. He would regain his fighting form.

So, when he had a minute or two with Paul and Christobel, he didn't say, 'Going to be a lawyer, get engaged to a lawyer. Going to be a doctor, get engaged to a doctor. Is your whole life programmed?' He said, 'I hope you'll be very happy and I hope you'll visit me in Thurmarsh. I haven't seen nearly enough of Paul over the years.'

When Mr Hargreaves, eminent brain surgeon, said, 'I'm retiring next year. Let some of the younger chaps in. No point in being greedy,' Henry didn't say, 'You don't need to be, you've got enough salted away to live in luxury for fifty years.' He said, 'An admirable sentiment. I wish you a long and happy retirement.' Mr Hargreaves thanked him warmly. It was nice to be thanked warmly.

When Mrs Hargreaves bore down on him, she imposed a critical test on his new-found social solidity. He felt an absurd temptation to say, 'I bet you look wonderful with nothing on.' He fought it off valiantly, and said, 'You look as young and elegant and beautiful as ever,' and was rewarded by a blush of pleasure and embarrassment that sent an exquisite shiver through his genitals.

Henry was surprised and delighted to see Denzil and Lampo. They weren't speaking to each other. 'A contretemps over a tantalus.' Lampo had put on weight. He looked solidly successful, as well he might, since he was regarded as a golden boy at Sotheby's – or was it Christie's? Denzil remained slender and trim, his limp had grown no worse over the years, and his parchment skin, stretched and flecked with age, had barely changed in the ten years that Henry had known him. He had aged young, and in his early sixties he was gently ripening into distinction.

'Still with cucumbers?' asked Lampo.

'Still with cucumbers.'

'Priceless. Oh my God. Tosser!'

Tosser Pilkington-Brick entered *en famille*. He too had put on weight, and lost the fitness of his rugger years. Diana looked pleasantly chunky, but tired. Benedict, who was almost eight, looked like Little Ford Fauntleroy. Camilla, who was six, looked like a very small horse.

Henry longed to talk to Diana. The intensity of his longing astounded him. He moved towards her, but got waylaid by Belinda Boyce-Uppingham.

'My God,' he said. 'This party's registering seven on the reunion scale . . .'

'Lovely to see you,' said Belinda. 'I heard something about you the other day. Now what was it? Oh yes. You've given up scribbling and are in radishes. That's right.'

'Well actually I gave up scribbling eight years ago, and it's cucumbers.'

'That's right.'

'And how about you?'

'I've got two,' said Belinda Boyce-Uppingham, as if there was no other subject but children. 'Tessa and Vanessa. Robin would love a son, but never mind, they're good girls. Ah, speak of the devil. Robin, you remember Henry Pratt.'

'Er . . . oh yes,' said Robin. 'The refugee chap who's in tomatoes.'

'Cucumbers, actually,' said Henry.

'I said "radishes",' said Belinda.

They all had a laugh over that.

'Oh, well, they're all veg, I suppose,' said Robin.

Henry was tempted to say, 'Shrewd of you to spot that. Who says you're as thick as two short planks?' but he fought it off, smiled a self-deprecatory smile, and said, 'Actually I sometimes forget what I'm in myself,' and they all laughed again, in the way people do, at parties, at things that aren't remotely amusing.

At last he was at Diana's side.

'It's so good to see you,' he said.

She flushed slightly.

'You know Benedict and Camilla, don't you?' she said.

'We have met but you were much younger then,' said Henry.

'So were you,' said Camilla.

'Camilla! Don't be rude,' said Diana.

'No, she's absolutely right. It was a silly remark,' said Henry.

He smiled at Camilla. If he'd hoped to win her over, it was a dismal failure.

'I remember you,' said Benedict. 'I'm nearly eight. Much older than Camilla. You were at Dalton College with Daddy, weren't you?'

'That's right.'

'I'm going to Dalton College after I've been to Brasenose College.'

'Really? I was at Brasenose too. You'll be following in my footsteps.'

'Will you excuse me?' said Benedict. 'I've spotted a friend. Nice to meet you.'

Benedict moved off.

'Bloody twit!' said Camilla.

'Please don't swear, Camilla,' said Diana.

'Gosh. Nosh,' said Camilla. 'That's good, isn't it? "Gosh. Nosh." '

'It's very good,' said Henry. 'Why don't you go and eat some?'

Camilla gave him a cool look, and stalked off.

'Where's Nigel?' said Henry, looking round, and remembering, on this his first day of total social smoothness, not to call him 'Tosser'.

'Tosser,' said Diana. 'Would you believe he's gone to phone a client?'

'Oh my God. He's monstrous. Sorry. I shouldn't have said that.'

'Yes, you should. He is.'

'But you're happy?'

'No.'

'Oh Diana, I wish you were happy.'

'That's nice.'

'Actually I wish everybody was happy tonight.'

'Oh.'

'But you particularly.'

'That's nice.'

It was so nice, Henry found, to smile at people and be smiled at by people. He wished the party would go on for ever and he would never have to go back to his lonely life.

The children returned, and Henry 'Can I have permission to get something out of the Permissive Society?' Pratt wasn't nearly as lonely when they were around. They said they'd had a wonderful time but didn't say much about Hilary, and he refused to stoop to using them in a search for information. They were very brown and looked extremely fit. To his enormous, his stupendous, his tear-wrenching, his heart-stopping relief, they seemed thrilled to see him and not unhappy to be home.

Folk music swept the land. Even in Thurmarsh there were hippies. Henry bought a Bob Dylan record, but he sensed that the whole movement was passing him by.

The Regional Co-ordinator, Northern Counties (Excluding

Berwick-on-Tweed) reached retirement age. His successor was named, and he was not the Assistant Regional Co-ordinator Northern Counties (Excluding Berwick-on-Tweed) but John Barrington, Head of Gherkins.

Once again, the party was held in the Board Room, but this time there were no balloons. 'A bad idea. *Mea culpa*,' had been Timothy Whitehouse's verdict on the balloons.

Maybe Henry 'Nonpareil at avoiding blotted copy-books' Pratt had become complacent. Maybe the pain of being passed over for his boss's job was greater than he could bear with equilibrium. Maybe the depression he had felt at Dennis Tubman-Edwards's retirement party had given him a morbid fear of retirement parties. Maybe he had a subconscious dread of finding that he had given his whole life to cucumbers and would end up at his own retirement party. Whatever it was, Henry couldn't face Roland Stagg's retirement party without having a couple of drinks first.

By the time he arrived, the party was already in full swing. He took a large glass of red wine and found his retiring boss bearing down on him, trousers at half-mast round his enormous paunch.

'I'd like a brief word, Henry,' he said. 'I've decided to come clean. I was asked if I thought you should succeed me. Now I'm very pleased with your progress. You've been keeping a really low profile.'

'So low that sometimes I wonder if I'm clinically dead,' said Henry.

'Excellent. Truly excellent.' He gave his painful, Burmese cough. 'Anyway, I said, "No. I don't think Henry should succeed me. He's ready for promotion, but he needs to move to a different department. He needs a challenge." Be patient, Henry. Hang on in there, avoid blotting your copy-book, and the world can be your oyster. Your hour of glory is at hand. Have you met my wife Laura?'

Laura Stagg was quite unreasonably pretty. Men with vast paunches shouldn't have such pretty wives. Where was the justice in the world? She was wearing a surprisingly low-cut dress and Henry was transfixed by her splendid cleavage. He felt an absurd temptation to say something outrageously sexy to her. Desperately, he said, 'How are you feeling about having Mr Stagg at home all day?'

'You're the one who was at school with Tommy Marsden, aren't you?' she said. 'When I heard him on the radio being asked what it was like to win the first division championship and he said, "It hasn't sunk in yet," I thought he must be some kind of prize idiot. But you know, I feel the same. It simply hasn't sunk in.'

She smiled and looked straight into Henry's eyes. He scuttled off in search of safer ground, and poured himself another large red wine.

He found himself face to face with Vincent Ambrose, the Director General. He hadn't spoken to Mr Ambrose since his first week, and doubted if the Director General would remember him, but there he did him an injustice.

'Get that kettle all right, did you?' said Vincent Ambrose genially.

'Absolutely.' Henry wished he hadn't said 'absolutely' so absolutely meaninglessly, when 'yes' would have sufficed.

'Jolly good.' The Director General paused, searching for something to say. 'Well, keep up the good work,' he said, and moved on.

When Henry spilt coronation chicken all down his suit front, he knew that he was sinking.

He took another large glass of red wine, to soothe his nerves.

He tried hard, that evening, to hang on in there, to keep a clear head, to avoid blotting his copy-book.

In vain!

He tried hard, that evening, having learnt for all time the dangers of jealousy, not to feel bitter about the promotion of John Barrington.

To no avail!

Somewhere, along the line, he had had one glass of red wine too many.

He awoke with a steam-hammer in his head and an unwashed wart-hog in his mouth. He could remember only three of the things that he had said during the rest of that awful evening.

He recalled countering John Barrington's, 'I hope we'll work well together. I certainly relish the prospect,' with, 'Well, I don't. You're a little prick, and you should have stayed with gherkins.'

He remembered saying, 'I bet you look gorgeous with no clothes on,' to the unexpectedly pretty wife of Roland Stagg.

He saw, vividly, horribly, the expression on the face of the Director (Operations), as he limped off after Henry had said, 'I know why you haven't promoted me. Because the face doesn't fit, does it, Mr Timothy Shitehouse?'

Slowly, Henry's physical state improved. By lunchtime, he only felt as if he had a face flannel stuck in his throat, and managed to phone his ex-boss to apologise.

'Oh dear oh dear oh dear,' said Roland Stagg. 'Who didn't keep a low profile, then? Who blotted his copy-book?'

'I know,' said Henry. 'I just wanted to say I'm sorry if I spoilt your party.'

'Not at all, except that I was sorry for you. It's never nice to see a good man disappearing up his own arse-hole.'

'I . . . er . . . I'm sorry if I said anything untoward to your wife.'

'I don't think you did.' Roland Stagg seemed puzzled. 'I said you'd disgraced yourself all round and she said, "Well, he said some very nice things to me." '

'Oh! Ah! Yes! Sorry! That's right.' Henry floundered wildly. 'Yes, I remember now. It was someone else's wife I said awful things to. That's right.'

At half past two, the Director (Operations) sent for him.

Timothy Whitehouse twitched his predatory nose, gave a half-smile and said, 'Don't look so miserable.'

'I am miserable,' said Henry. 'I said some awful things last night.'

The Director (Operations) swivelled in his chair and sought solace in his reproduction of Albrecht Dürer's little-known masterpiece, 'The Cucumber'.

'I'm not inhuman,' he said at last. 'I don't hold what people say at parties against them, otherwise nobody would come to our parties and I enjoy our parties. I note that you are upset at not being given Roland's job. I'm not so naïve as to believe that I'm never referred to as Shitehouse, but in your case I shall assume that it was a slip of the tongue caused by hearing lesser men use the expression about me. Is that correct?'

'Absolutely. Oh, absolutely.'

'I'm glad to hear it. I'll attempt to forget that you said it although, since no one has ever said it to my face before, that will be difficult.' The Director (Operations) swivelled round again, this time to look Henry straight in the eye. 'In ten years' time, when I hope you will still be with us, we'll look back on Roland's retirement party, and we'll split our collective sides. I hope that's a comfort.'

'Well it is, Mr Whitehouse, and I think you've been very generous, Mr Whitehouse, but . . . er . . . may I say something, Mr Whitehouse?'

'Of course. Didn't I advise you always to be your own man, stick to your guns and be fearless? Although I should have qualified that. I should have advised you to be your own man, stick to your guns and be fearless *when sober*. *Mea culpa*. So, what is it? Ask away.'

'I'm not sure that I want to be here in ten years' time.'

'I know. You've applied for other jobs. I've supplied references. You haven't got them. Bad luck.'

'I wouldn't want to stay unless . . . unless I felt it was worth my while.'

'Bravely spoken, for a man who said the things you said yesterday, which of course I'll try to forget. I understand. Point taken. Henry, my advice is this. Cease looking for other jobs, commit yourself fully to us, avoid saying the sort of things you said yesterday, which of course I'll try to forget, and be patient. Your hour of glory is at hand.'

'That's what Mr Tubman-Edwards and Mr Stagg said.'

'Well why don't you believe us?' said Timothy Whitehouse. 'We are Englishmen, after all.'

Henry found himself dismissed rather abruptly. He steeled himself to call on John Barrington.

John Barrington had only been in his office for six hours, but already he had plastered it with photographs of his family. Henry could see them canoeing, sailing, surfing, skiing. He felt even more unathletic than usual.

John Barrington ushered him into a chair rather offhandedly.

'I must apologise for what I said last night,' said Henry.

'Yes, I think you must,' said John Barrington.

'I hope we *can* work well together,' said Henry.

'Well so do, I, Henry. So do I.' John Barrington just happened, as if by chance, to pick up the bronze gherkin given him by the Gherkin Growers' Federation as Gherkin Man of the Year for 1962. He fingered it delicately. Henry wondered who on earth they had found to be Gherkin Man of the Year for 1963 and 1964. 'I'll lead by example, I'll ask for your help when required, and if you give it we'll have no problems. Now I am rather busy, if you don't mind. My first day. I'm sure you'll understand.'

1965 drew towards its close. The largest power failure in history blacked out New York City, parts of eight North Eastern states, and parts of Ontario and Quebec. Henry wondered if it had also disconnected his phone.

He sought an interview with John Barrington and was granted one.

'I feel I'm being under-used,' he said. 'I feel I'm being victimised for an unwise drunken remark at a party.'

John Barrington picked up his award. As a dummy is to a baby, so was his bronze gherkin to the new Regional Co-ordinator, Northern Counties (Excluding Berwick-on-Tweed). 'I'm not a petty man. The fact is, my predecessor ran a lazy ship. Too much devolved on you.'

'I didn't mind it devolving on me.'

'That does you credit, but it doesn't make it right. I run a tight ship. The responsibilities are mine.'

'I realise that, but I get nothing to do whatsoever. Sometimes I wonder why I've got this job at all.'

'I shouldn't speculate along those lines out loud, if I were you,' said John Barrington.

Henry intended to take the matter up with the Director (Operations), but then the children got flu, and then he got flu, and then the Director (Operations) got flu, and then it was too near Christmas.

The children went to Spain for Christmas, and Henry considered all the poverty in the world and thought, 'There are millions of people who'd be grateful for roast turkey and ginger cordial and three hours of Snap in a stifling basement room with Cousin Hilda and Mrs Wedderburn and Liam O'Reilly.'

That Christmas night Henry cried for Hilary as he had never cried before.

The children returned, life resumed its even keel, and Henry told the Director (Operations) of his displeasure at his inactivity.

'I'll have a word with John Barrington,' said Mr Whitehouse. 'Delegation is not weakness.'

Britain announced a complete trade ban against Rhodesia, the Soviet spacecraft Luna 9 made a soft landing on the moon, and the word that Timothy Whitehouse had with John Barrington produced only a marginal increase in Henry's workload.

My life is draining away, he thought. I'll be thirty-one soon.

Sales of the paperback of *All Stick Together* had suddenly accelerated over the Christmas period. The publishers told Henry that Hilary's book was a big success, but they were getting no reply to their letters. He wrote and begged her to write to them. They told him that she had written to say that she was very pleased on the author's behalf but that she no longer considered herself the author.

She didn't write to Henry.

In the early hours of Sunday, March 13th, 1966, Henry had a disturbing dream. He dreamt that he was in a glorious, baroque opera house, but all the seats were on the stage, and all the scenery was in the auditorium. And there was only one person in the twelve rows of seats on the stage. Henry, in immaculate evening dress, was sitting in the third seat from the left in the third row.

He looked down on magnificent painted sets which suggested that the performance was to consist of a cross between *Swan Lake* and *The Barber of Seville*.

Into the auditorium came Helen Plunkett, née Cornish. She was naked. She smiled at Henry and took up a stilted theatrical pose. Her legs were magnificent.

Next came Diana, also naked, chunkily sexy. She was accompanied by Benedict and Camilla, who were dressed as page boys. Diana waved at him cheerily, but the faces of Benedict and Camilla broke into derisive smiles.

Next came the eighteen-year-old Lorna Arrow, also stark naked. She smiled shyly at Henry. Her four children, Marlene, Doreen, Kevin and Sharon, ran on behind her, all dressed as Beefeaters, and she turned into the Lorna Lugg who had lost her looks, breasts sagging and stretch marks forming like cracks on a mirror.

Helen's naked sister Jill followed with her three boys, dressed as Chelsea pensioners. Then came Mrs Hargreaves, also naked and extraordinarily well-preserved, with a fifteen-year-old Paul and a fourteen-year-old Diana, both dressed as onion sellers. Young Diana blew a kiss to present-day Diana.

Next came Ginny Fenwick, stark naked, sturdy, running to fat, and carrying a Bren gun. She was followed by Anna Matheson, who slid on, seated naked on the very armchair on which she had been naked for Henry all those years ago.

Belinda Boyce-Uppingham was posing as a frontispiece for *Country Life*, except that frontispieces for *Country Life* wear clothes. Tessa and Vanessa wore jodhpurs and carried riding whips.

And out of the lake there arose Boadicea's chariot, and on it, naked and palely lovely, was Hilary, with Kate and Jack at her side, dressed as bullfighters.

All the women held out their arms towards Henry, and all the children smiled. The band struck up 'Happy Birthday to You' and they all sang, 'Happy birthday to you, Happy birthday to you, Happy birthday, dear Henry, Happy birthday to you.' Then all the women's breasts sagged and stretch marks formed on all their thighs and five hundred balloons shaped like cucumbers descended from the ornate ceiling, and the flesh fell off all the women to whom Henry had ever been deeply attracted, and the clothes and the flesh fell off all the children that they had borne, and they all became horrible smiling skeletons.

Henry awoke, drenched in sweat, to hear the telephone ringing with tinny insistence in the deep silence of the house. And he knew, with utter certainty, that it would be Hilary, disturbed by the aura given off by his dream, ringing to say that she still loved him. As he rushed to the phone, at ten past three on his thirty-first birthday on the 13th, having dreamt that he was the only one on the stage sitting in the third seat in the third row, the numbers three and one had sharp and lucky significance for him. He dived for the phone, terrified that she would ring off.

'Hello,' he said.

'Dyno-Rod?' said a deep male voice. 'Sorry to ring you at this unearthly hour, but I've got water pouring through my back passage.'

Two months later, Henry's phone rang again at ten past three in the morning. He felt certain, even though he no longer had any belief in his psychic powers, that it would be another crossed line for Dyno-Rod.

'Hello,' he said wearily.

'Henry?'

'Yes.'

'It's Diana. Are you alone?'

'Of course I'm alone.'

'I'm sorry to ring you at this unearthly hour. Tosser's left me and you're the only person I can talk to.'

9 For Better, For Worse

On Saturday, June 10th, 1967, the Middle East War ended after just six days with a cease-fire between Israel and Syria, Spencer Tracey died of a heart attack, and Dr Paul Hargreaves married Dr Christobel Farquhar.

The reception was held in a huge marquee in the vast garden of Brigadier and Mrs Roderick Farquhar, near Alresford in Hampshire.

The sun glinted in the grey streaks that were beginning to fleck Henry's slowly thinning hair. He was standing with Diana in a queue outside the marquee, waiting to tell the happy couple that they looked wonderful and it had been worth waiting almost two years to get Winchester Cathedral on a Saturday in June.

Behind them were a close friend of the bride, the lovely Annabel Porchester, and her fiancé, the unlovely Josceleyn Tubman-Edwards, of the merchant bankers, Pellet and Runciman.

'It's Henry!' said Josceleyn Tubman-Edwards. 'Good Lord! Darling, this is Henry Pratt, a chum of mine. We were at Dalton College together, and then Henry got a job with my father at the Cucumber Marketing Board. Henry, this is Annabel Porchester. She's one of the Suffolk Porchesters.'

'I always thought they were a breed of pig,' said Henry.

Diana giggled. It was one of her most endearing qualities that she had never quite grown up.

'I should have warned you that Henry is awful,' said Josceleyn Tubman-Edwards.

'Henry has a dreadful thing about posh social events,' said Diana. 'They make him panic and he fights back by being incredibly rude. He hasn't even introduced me.'

'Oh, sorry,' said Henry. 'Diana Pilkington-Brick. Paul's sister. She married Tosser Pilkington-Brick, who was also a "chum" at school. You remember Tosser, don't you, Josceleyn?'

Josceleyn Tubman-Edwards tried to smile. A piece of saliva remained attached to both his lips even as they parted, but they didn't part very far.

'Yes, I . . . er . . . I remember Pilkington-Brick,' said Josceleyn. 'Is . . . er . . . I mean . . . er . . . ?'

'We're separated,' said Diana. 'I'm divorcing him for adultery.'

'I'm sorry,' said Josceleyn.

'I'm not,' said Diana. 'I'm going to marry Henry.'

'Good Lord,' said Josceleyn. 'I mean, congratulations.'

'Yes, congratulations,' said Annabel.

'What do you do, Annabel?' asked Henry.

'Not a lot. I only came out last year,' said Annabel.

'Really! What were you in for?'

'Henry!' said Diana.

They edged slowly forward, a queue of hats wilting in the summer sun. It was so boring. They couldn't wait for the champagne and the food.

'So where will you get married?' asked Josceleyn.

'I've no idea,' said Diana. 'I was just thinking, "How do you follow this?" '

'Probably a church hall in Thurmarsh,' said Henry.

'Ugh!' said Josceleyn.

'Well don't worry,' said Henry. 'You won't be invited.'

'Henry! Why are you being so awful to the poor man?' said Diana.

Henry lowered his voice, to spare Annabel from his reply.

'He introduced me as his chum. The great bag of rancid lizard droppings blackmailed me over that business of pretending my father'd been a test pilot.'

'Oh! That was him!' said Diana. 'Oh well, that's all right, then. Poor girl. She must be after his money.'

'Well I'd hate to think she was after his sex appeal.'

At last it was their turn to greet the happy couple. Paul looked magnificent in morning dress, while Christobel looked the very essence of beauty, sophistication and, more surprisingly, virginity, in a high-necked, full-sleeved, full-length white silk dress with cape-effect back and matching pillbox hat. She carried a bouquet of white roses.

'You look stunningly wonderful. Any man could fancy you,' said Henry. 'And you don't look too bad either, Christobel.'

Paul and Christobel gave Henry cheerily disgusted looks.

'Seriously, you're a stunner, Christobel,' said Henry, kissing her gently on the cheek.

They moved on, took champagne, located their positions on the seating plan, and mingled. It really was a big wedding. There were more than three hundred guests. Henry wondered if they should run away to Gretna Green for theirs.

Mr Hargreaves, magnificent in morning dress, approached.

Henry felt that he alone did not look magnificent in morning dress. His hired suit was slightly too long and slightly too tight.

'Be nice to Daddy, won't you?' urged Diana.

'Of course.'

'He's still in shock.'

It had only been on the previous evening that Henry had told his future father-in-law. Well, he'd only proposed two days ago. His reunion with Diana had been a success from the start – comfortable, sexy and, above all, fun. But they had never thought of marriage. Henry couldn't imagine being father to Benedict and Camilla. And he didn't believe that the possibility had crossed Diana's mind. But he'd found it such a wrench to part from her, and so delightful to be with her, that he had suddenly decided, on the telephone, the day before coming down for the festivities, to propose. There had been a long, astonished silence, and then, to *his* astonishment, Diana had accepted him with the stunningly romantic words, 'I don't see why not. It could be rather fun.'

And now here was Mr Hargreaves, brain surgeon, bearing down on them and smiling warmly.

Henry smiled back, thinking wryly of the previous evening, when he'd said, 'Do you remember my asking to see you the day after Tosser lost England the Welsh match, in 1956? You thought I was going to ask for Diana's hand. And I was actually asking to

169

borrow fifty quid. You were so relieved that you'd have gladly given me a hundred quid.'

'Oh, Henry! I wasn't relieved,' Mr Hargreaves had said. 'Of course I wouldn't have minded if you were going to marry Diana.'

'Oh good,' Henry had said. 'Because I am going to marry her.'

'What??'

Mr Hargreaves had gone white. His mouth had opened and closed silently just once, like a disconcerted turbot. He'd regained his equilibrium rapidly, but not quite rapidly enough.

'Well, congratulations,' he'd said. 'When's the happy day?'

'Well she has to get divorced first.'

'Yes. Of course. Of course.'

Now, in the champagne buzz of the wedding marquee, Mr Hargreaves was also remembering last night's encounter.

'Hello!' he said warmly. 'You know, when I saw your friend Tommy Marsden on the idiot box the other day – I very rarely watch, but it happened to be on – and he was asked, "How does it feel to score the winning goal for England at Wembley?" and he said, "It hasn't really sunk in yet," I thought he must be really dense, but now I know what he meant. Last night it didn't sink in. Today it has. I hope you'll both be very happy.'

'Thank you, sir,' said Henry. He hadn't expected to say 'sir', he didn't think he was capable of it, unless it slipped out unintentionally, but, having said it, he was quite glad that it *had* slipped out unintentionally.

'Thank you, Daddy.'

Diana kissed her father.

'Any thoughts about the shindig?'

'Modest, we thought,' said Diana. 'No attempt to compete.'

'Good. Good. Any thoughts about where you'll live?'

'We thought London,' said Henry. 'I can't quite see Diana in the North. Too far from Harrods.'

'Well . . . good . . . yes, quite, huh! . . . good. You'll . . . er . . . you'll abandon the cucumbers, then?'

'Oh yes! They just aren't giving me a chance there.'

'Good. Good. Well that's splendid.'

'Henry'll get a job in London. There's bound to be something for a man of his talents.'

'Yes,' said Mr Hargreaves doubtfully. 'Yes,' he repeated more positively. 'Oh yes, yes, bound to be.'

'Henry has such a lot to offer the world, Daddy. He can't just throw himself away on cucumbers.'

Mr Hargreaves looked at his daughter in surprise at her fervour, then he looked at Henry as if reassessing him.

'Good,' he said. 'Good. Well, good.'

Mrs Hargreaves might have been designed for this day. She looked stunning in a green, pink, blue and orange-red double-breasted organza coat with roll collar and flap pockets, over a plain, vivid green sleeveless shift with matching green broad-rimmed straw hat from Christian Dior, gold earclips, and black patent pumps from Charles Jourdan at nine guineas. She approached them with two very excited pageboys and two even more excited bridesmaids.

'Shall we tell our children now?' said Diana.

'Why not?' said Henry. 'Darlings. Kate. Jack. Diana and I have something to tell you.'

'Benedict. Camilla. This is for you too,' said Diana.

'Diana and I are going to be married,' said Henry.

He clutched Diana's hand.

All around there was a roar of conversation, but in the middle of the marquee, in the eye of that champagne cyclone, there was silence.

Kate was the first to break it.

'You mean,' she said, her voice laden with gloom, 'Benedict and Camilla are going to be our brother and sister?'

'And Kate and Jack are going to be ours,' said Benedict. 'Bloody hell!'

Homosexuality between consenting adults in private was legalised. Henry couldn't help wondering what Lampo and Denzil would consent to do in private that night by way of celebration.

In San Francisco, during the long, hot 'summer of love',

peaceful hippies lit joss-sticks and placed flowers in the rifle barrels of bemused National Guardsmen. Elsewhere in America, in the long, hot summer of hate, the racial riots were terrifying, and other soldiers were still using flowerless guns all over Vietnam.

There was a military coup in Greece. The long night of the colonels had begun.

During the long, not-so-hot nights in Britain, motorists found themselves compulsorily breath-tested. Cousin Hilda wasn't affected, Uncle Teddy walked to the pub, and the journalists on the *Thurmarsh Evening Argus* took no notice.

The Director (Operations) of the Cucumber Marketing Board sent for Henry, swivelled happily in his chair and, looking him full in the face, gave him the good news.

'Your hour of glory has arrived,' he said.

On Saturday, July 13th, 1968, fierce fighting broke out between police and several thousand young people in Paris, teenage members of four Glasgow gangs surrendered meat cleavers, knives, a sword and an open razor during a one-hour amnesty arranged by Frankie Vaughan, the sea turned orange between Folkestone and Hythe as a result of dumped sheep dip, and Henry Ezra Pratt and Diana Jennifer Pilkington-Brick, née Hargreaves, held their wedding reception in the Hospitality Suite of the exclusive Regent Clinic, where Mr Hargreaves had saved the brains of the extremely rich for more than twenty years.

Before they all sat down, there was champagne in the slightly antiseptic ante-room, though not as much champagne, and not such good champagne, as there would have been if Diana had been marrying the tall, handsome son of one of the many medical luminaries who had graced the Hargreaves table over the years, rather than Paul's funny little friend, the cucumber man.

Nobody wore morning dress, but Henry looked almost smart in the best of his three dark cucumber suits, and Diana looked charming in a knee-length Pierre Balmain-style navy and white dress. The guests wore dresses of many different lengths, Mary

Quant having described the mini as boring, the maxi having failed to take off, and the midi being seen as a dull compromise.

The best man, Lampo Davey, wore a velvet suit with frilled burgundy shirt, while his legalised partner, Denzil Ackerman, plumped for a lime green shirt and a dazzling white suit. Anything went, as the sixties swung towards their close.

Nobody cut a more dashing figure than Auntie Doris, who wore a huge scarlet hat she had last put on in 1938. Cousin Hilda sniffed the moment she saw it, and Henry was on tenterhooks over how the conversation would go when she talked to Auntie Doris for the first time since his first marriage eleven years ago.

Unfortunately for Cousin Hilda, Lampo Davey buttonholed her before she'd spoken to Auntie Doris. 'I don't believe you've met my lover, Denzil, have you?' he said, and Cousin Hilda sniffed so violently that she developed a nose bleed. It soon subsided, but for some time she walked with her nose pointing towards the ceiling. She was therefore unable to sniff with any force when she came face to face with Auntie Doris's hat or when Auntie Doris said, 'Have you had a nose bleed, Hilda, or are you communing with your maker?'

'Is the vet not here?' countered Cousin Hilda icily.

'The vet??' said Auntie Doris. 'Why, has somebody brought a sick dog?'

'I were informed your latest amour was with a retired vet,' said Cousin Hilda. 'If I've got the wrong end of the stick, I'm sorry.'

'Oh, that vet! Yes, he is. Is a vet, I mean. No, he isn't. Isn't here, I mean. He's got this summer flu thing.' Auntie Doris was furious at having to tell everyone that he was ill. Ill as well as retired. They'd think she'd thrown herself away on some broken reed of an elderly vet. She longed to tell them that she was living with the man she'd always loved, her husband Teddy. 'I forget he was a vet sometimes. It was before I knew him. You needn't sniff, anyway. He's a fine man.'

'As fine as Geoffrey Porringer?' said Cousin Hilda grimly.

'Incomparably finer,' said Auntie Doris stoutly.

'As fine as Teddy Braithwaite?'

173

'No finer, but Teddy's equal in every respect.'

Cousin Hilda managed another cautious sniff.

'Can I lend you a handkerchief, Hilda?' offered Auntie Doris. 'I have a fine lace one from Harrods.'

'No doubt you do,' said Cousin Hilda. 'No doubt you do. I have one, thank you. A nice plain one from Woolworth's. There are folk starving in Pakistan. I don't think I should waste my money on tarts' hankies.'

'Hilda!' said Auntie Doris. 'It's Henry's wedding day.'

'Oh, dinna worrit thasen,' said Cousin Hilda, dusting down her dialect for Auntie Doris's benefit. 'I won't show Henry up.'

Henry approached and kissed them both, to Auntie Doris's delight and Cousin Hilda's embarrassment.

Auntie Doris came over all emotional suddenly.

'Auntie Doris! What's wrong?' said Henry.

She couldn't tell them that she was upset because she was living in sin with a man whom she couldn't marry because he was supposed to be dead and because she was already married to him, and she had a husband whom she couldn't divorce because she wasn't married to him. 'I'm in a cleft stick with no paddle,' she had told him once over a post-prandial game of Scrabble in Honeysuckle Cottage.

'It's just . . . Teddy would have loved to see this day,' she said, and she hurried off to the Ladies to repair her mascara.

'I think Doris is failing,' said Cousin Hilda. 'She'd forgotten her new man's a retired vet.'

'Oh well,' said Henry feebly. 'You remember Paul Hargreaves, Diana's brother, do you? And this is Christobel, his wife.'

As he left them to it, Henry heard Paul say, 'I've never forgotten your spotted dick,' and Cousin Hilda reply, 'Oh! That's very kind of you.'

He stopped to chat to Belinda Boyce-Uppingham.

'How's Robin?'

'Marvellous.'

'How are Tessa and Vanessa and Clarissa?'

'Blooming. Robin wants to go on till he has an heir. We'll

probably end up with a ladies' football team. So, you're bringing Diana up north? Good show.'

'Well, yes, I was coming south, but the Cucumber Marketing Board made me an offer I couldn't refuse.'

'Really? What of?'

'I'm their Chief Controlling Officer (Diseases and Pests).'

Belinda Boyce-Uppingham tried hard to look impressed.

'I am solely responsible for the nationwide fight against diseases of the cucumber. Did you know that there are more than forty major diseases of cucumbers?'

'Golly!'

' "Golly!" indeed!'

Henry was a bit worried about Tommy Marsden, who was knocking back the champagne. He hoped what they said in the papers wasn't true.

'Hello, Tommy,' he said. 'Far cry from the Paradise Lane Gang.'

'Too right,' said Tommy Marsden.

'Is everything all right with you still?' asked Henry.

'You mustn't believe what you read in the papers,' said Tommy Marsden. 'I got pissed and slept in once. If you believe the papers, I never train, I play when I'm drunk, and I've thrown a boot at the manager. I'd be out, wouldn't I, if I did? All that business with that tart in Bratislava was set up, too. They just wanted us out of the European Cup. Hey up, here's another member of the gang. Martin Fucking Hammond.'

'Please, Tommy, great to have you here, but can you avoid saying "fucking",' said Henry.

'Henry!' said Cousin Hilda, passing by in search of more pineapple juice.

'You two allus were stuck-up bastards,' said Tommy Marsden. 'I'm a footballer. They expect me to be uncouth. The chicks like me to be uncouth.'

Tommy Marsden moved on, and Henry knew that if he caused an embarrassing scene it was his fault for asking him; he'd asked him because he'd get some kudos from having such a famous friend.

'Hello, Martin. Hello, Mandy,' he said. 'How's married life?'

'Very life-enhancing,' said Mandy Hammond, née Haltwhistle.

'Good. I'm pleased to hear that.'

'This do could feed a whole province in Guatemala,' said Martin.

'Oh, Martin, I wouldn't have invited you if I'd known you were going to depress me,' said Henry.

'Just joking,' said Martin Hammond. 'I know you think I'm a bore. I thought I'd show you I can let my hair down when the occasion demands it.'

The gathering drifted *en masse* to the main room, which exactly suited the size of the guest list. The ceiling was high and had impressive mouldings, and there was a lovely chandelier which, if it fell, would crush Cousin Hilda, who was giving occasional uneasy looks towards it, not being used to sitting under chandeliers. The whole do was elegant enough to pass muster in a brain surgeon's world, but modest enough to suit what was a second marriage for both parties.

The top table, while following the rules of etiquette, had a somewhat eccentric look, since Henry's parents were represented by Cousin Hilda and Auntie Doris. Since there were two bridesmaids, Kate at one end and Camilla at the other, there were at the table six females, two of them children, and only three males, one of them homosexual.

The meal was cold, but delicious. Rough pâté, followed by Scotch salmon and tarragon chicken with new potatoes and various salads, and strawberries and cream. There was good flinty Mâcon Blanc, rather than the Chablis that a doctor's son would have merited.

Henry, seated between Diana and her mother, knew that he'd got the best of the table arrangement. Mrs Hargreaves told him how happy they were to welcome him as a son-in-law, although Mr Hargreaves flirted dangerously with tactlessness when he leant across and said, 'We were disappointed in Nigel. We had such high hopes. With you, I have a feeling it's going to be the other way about.'

176

The salmon was the proper stuff, not the farmed kind that poisons lochs and dulls taste buds. The chicken had enjoyed the open air and the fields of Sussex. The tarragon sauce was delicious. Henry wished that he could relax, wished that he didn't feel so anxious about his surrogate parents, about whether the Director (Operations) and the Regional Co-ordinator, Northern Counties (Excluding Berwick-on-Tweed) and their wives were enjoying themselves, about whether Tommy Marsden would disgrace himself, about whether Kate and Camilla would behave with dignity, and whether Benedict and Jack would come to blows at the children's table over at the far right.

He felt Diana's hand on his.

'Happy, darling?'

'Very happy.'

'Truly?'

'Truly.'

'*I* am.'

'What?'

'Happy.'

'Good. But why do you say, "*I* am," as if I'm not? I am.'

'You don't look happy.'

'I'm just anxious, that's all. I want everything to go well.'

'It will. And if it doesn't it's not your fault. You're too self-important.'

'Self-important? Me?'

'You take responsibility for the whole world.'

'Oh. Sorry.'

'Don't look so hurt. It's one of the reasons why I love you.'

'What are the others?'

'I can't tell you in public. Do you love me?'

'Of course I do.'

'Then tell me.'

'I love you.'

'No regrets?'

'No regrets.'

He did try not to worry. He could hear Mrs Hargreaves asking

Auntie Doris all about Miles Cricklewood, where he'd been a vet, what size of practice he'd had, about his parents and his family home. She was showing her broad-mindedness about what was still fairly unusual even in 1968, two mature adults living 'in sin'. Auntie Doris didn't have time to worry about the moral aspects. She was too anxious not to contradict herself with the mythical *curriculum vitae* she provided for her absent vet. She couldn't remember if she'd placed his practice in Surrey or Sussex. Her memory wasn't quite what it had been, and it was all too difficult.

Cousin Hilda, on Henry's other side, between Mr Hargreaves and Lampo, was putting up a surprisingly animated show. She was appalled that Henry was marrying for the second time – she had sniffed several times when he'd told her, and hadn't known how she would tell Mrs Wedderburn– but now that the event was upon them she would do her level best not to show him up, even if her motivation was largely not to show herself up, her limestone grit coming out in the face of all this soft southern soil. Unfortunately she had no idea what were considered interesting conversational topics in the big world. Every now and then Henry could hear Mr Hargreaves responding with excruciating politeness to her remarks. 'Moved from the cheese counter to tins! How distressing.' 'Well, if they don't like spotted dick they needn't be in for tea on a Tuesday, need they?' and he went hot under the collar at Mr Hargreaves's boredom, though knowing perfectly well that Mr Hargreaves could cope.

For a while, both Diana and Mrs Hargreaves were speaking to their neighbours and there was nobody for him to speak to. He looked down at the buzzing, cheery room. People were enjoying themselves at all the tables. Nobody was interested in him or in whether he had anybody to speak to.

Shortly before the end of the main course, Auntie Doris passed out and had to be brought round with a cold dishcloth. She couldn't tell Mrs Hargreaves that the strain of her questions about Miles Cricklewood had been the cause. She blamed the heat.

Nobody blamed the heat when Tommy Marsden passed out. Henry leapt to his feet, and hurried out into the heart of the reception, determined not to look embarrassed. He and Martin Hammond carried Tommy Marsden out, the two members of the Paradise Lane gang who had gone to the grammar school helping the one who didn't.

Henry returned to his seat and tried to look natural, as though his friends passed out around him every day.

'I hope nobody else passes out,' he said. 'Only they say things go in threes.'

Just after he'd sat down, he heard Cousin Hilda say to Mr Hargreaves, 'I know very little about brain surgery,' and throughout the strawberries and cream he could hear Mr Hargreaves talking about brain damage, and defunct areas of the brain, and he could see Cousin Hilda nodding sagely, as if she understood, and he had visions of horrible accidents, of Diana lying with her head smashed, of knives in brains, and he felt faint. The sweat was pouring down his back. Diana from a long way off asked him if he was all right, and he said, 'Kiss me. Please, kiss me,' so urgently that Diana gave him a passionate kiss, and he kissed her back. They kissed long and hard at the top table in front of all their guests, as though they were on their own, and people laughed and clapped and Lampo cried, 'Bravo!' and Paul shouted, 'Dirty beast!' and Cousin Hilda looked horrified, and Jack looked at Benedict and said, 'Yuk!' and Benedict said, 'Double yuk!' and Jack said, 'Twenty-seven thousand four hundred and ninety-third yuk!' and Benedict said, 'Thirteen trillion four billion seven million three hundred and ninety-fifth yuk!' and just for a moment it looked as if it might be possible for them to become friends.

Henry felt better. The glasses were charged for the toasts. Lampo stood up and began to read the telegrams.

' "My love, my blessing, and my hopes for your happiness – Hilary," ' read Lampo.

Henry passed out.

10 Kate and Jack and Benedict and Camilla

If you've never driven an elderly Mini from London to Thurmarsh with four children between the ages of eight and eleven crammed into the back, two of whom have the natural arrogance of southern prep-school children, and one of whom might eat the chip on her shoulder if she wasn't feeling car sick, you'll have to imagine the first day proper of Henry and Diana's marital idyll.

'Haven't seen anybody spitting on pavements yet,' said Benedict, just after they had passed through Newark.

'Just because it's all horrendously sordid doesn't mean we're in the proper North yet,' said Camilla.

Kate began to hit out at Camilla, losing control and yelling.

Jack put a calming hand on Kate, but she hurled his gesture back at him.

'Won't bloody try to help in future,' he grumbled.

Diana shouted, 'Shut up, the lot of you,' and Henry stopped the car with a jerk. Camilla was shoved forward, and banged her head, precocity dissolving into tears straight away, and Kate clambered miserably out of the car and was violently sick on the verge.

Diana wanted Kate to sit in the front after that, but she refused, knowing what hostility such a favour would arouse.

'Don't want her in the back,' said Benedict. 'She smells of sick.'

Diana leant across and hit Benedict, harder than she intended. Henry winced.

Benedict went very quiet, but Henry and Diana could sense his fury and himiliation.

Henry wished the sun was shining. The countryside looked grey and drab, the houses poor and dusty. He longed for his beloved North Country to shine, but it refused. They sidled in, between collieries and clapped-out steelworks, through a land in limbo between an ugly, virile past and a flat, uncertain future. How he wished that there were just himself and Diana and his beloved Kate and Jack in the car, and not these two southern children with their assumptions about lifestyles, their contempt for his old car, their scorn of the North. He wondered if Diana was wishing that there were just herself and Henry and her beloved children, and not highly strung, super-sensitive, carsick Kate and infuriatingly placid Jack. How well did they really know each other? Was this a dreadful mistake? Had they rushed in too quickly, on the rebound? He looked at Diana's strained face, and wondered if she was thinking the same thing, and panic gripped him.

The puncture was the final humiliation.

'How quaint,' said Benedict. 'I didn't realise people actually *had* punctures any more.'

How good it was, in that difficult time, to fight the diseases of the cucumber. Henry's new office was in the basement with no carpet and no windows, but there was no sense of demotion in his move underground. Here in this large, bunker-like room he was king. How exciting it was, in those first stressful weeks of his new marriage, to stick flags in a large relief map of the United Kingdom. Basal rot in Myton-on-Swale. Green mottle mosaic intermittent from Beverley to Market Weighton. Downy mildew prevalent around Kettering. Fusarium wilt particularly common from Wimborne to Dorchester.

Henry knew that his enthusiasm was at least faintly ridiculous. He wasn't at all surprised when John Barrington wandered into his long, low-ceilinged basement room, looked at all the flags with the diseases written on them, and said, 'How's the war going, Winston?'

'Pretty damn well, John,' he said. 'Pretty bad genetic yellowing in parts of Essex, casualties are inevitable, but some of the cucumbers'll get through.'

'Damn good show,' said John Barrington, and Henry smiled a slow, half-pleased smile.

Jack and Benedict shared one bedroom, Kate and Camilla another. The children were too old for mixed-sex sharing, and in any case they were anxious not to polarise the southern and the northern children.

Benedict had been imbued with the social assumptions of Tosser Pilkington-Brick. White upper-middle-class Conservative rugby-playing English males were superior to every other form of intelligent and unintelligent life. Whippet-fanciers, miners, socialists, Henry, immigrants and women were on a par with maggots. He felt hostile to Henry, but even more hostile to Diana, who had betrayed him and his beloved father.

Jack's deep good nature meant that he could endure an enormous amount of Benedict's sarcasm without rising to the bait. This infuriated Benedict, who became taut with rage, and this amused Jack. Because Jack was so very tolerant, the argument could be pushed to quite an extreme point before his slow, slow fuse began to burn. If it ever did come to a fight, it would be a serious one. Benedict would have to back off, because he could hardly win any glory from beating a boy two years younger than himself, and he could conceivably lose, since Jack was a big, strong lad. To an extent, therefore, Jack had the upper hand. This infuriated Benedict, but it did give him a degree of respect for Jack.

It wasn't clear what Jack thought about the relationship between Henry and Diana. He never spoke of it.

Henry and Diana felt that Camilla's social arrogance was not nearly as deep as Benedict's, and that she'd like to make friends with Kate if she could do so without incurring her brother's scorn. She wasn't at all hostile to Diana, blaming her father for the break-up to the point where if he hadn't had a Jaguar and a big house with a swimming pool she might not have even wanted to visit him.

Kate was deeply protective of, and loving towards, Henry. She was also more developed intellectually than Camilla, and never ceased to point this out. She wasn't doing this entirely for her own glory. She was doing it out of loyalty to Henry and Thurmarsh and the North of England and Winstanley Primary School and Mrs Williams, who was her best teacher ever. It was very upsetting, therefore, to be rebuked by Henry for saying, 'I'm not surprised you like horses, Camilla. You're pretty thick really,' and it made it impossible for Camilla to show any friendly overtures to Kate.

Henry and Diana hunted for a larger house, but couldn't afford one that cost a great deal more than Dumbarton House would fetch. This meant, inevitably, that, if it had five bedrooms, it would be in a worse area or fairly dilapidated. They put their names on the list of every estate agent in Thurmarsh.

HEALTH WARNING: THE NEXT PARAGRAPH COULD BE DISTRESSING TO ESTATE AGENTS OF A SENSITIVE DISPOSITION.

Three estate agents didn't send anything. One sent everything twice, which was a shame, as all their details were of half-built three-bedroom bungalows in cul-de-sacs, and went straight into the bin. Another sent details of country mansions costing £25,000. From another they did get details of the right kind of houses, but only in Hull and Goole. Only one offered them the right house in the right place at the right price, but the details were sent to the wrong address, and the house was sold by the time Henry and Diana read about it.

They considered moving nearer to Leeds, but decided against it, because Kate and Jack were settled in their schools.

It has to be admitted that, loving parents though they both were, it was a great relief to them when Kate and Jack set off for their annual summer holiday with Hilary in Spain, and, a week later, Benedict and Camilla were taken to Menton by Tosser.

Left on their own in Thurmarsh, Henry and Diana led as civilised a life as their shortage of money would allow. Henry was very conscious that Diana had never been short of money before, and more than once made her angry by harping on the subject. She was upset that he should think money mattered to her, and stated how unimportant she found it, sometimes in words that pleased him – 'I love you. I don't care about wealth. You are my wealth' – and sometimes in words that pleased him slightly less – 'I'm a grown-up. I knew what I was letting myself in for.'

They ate an occasional modest meal at Sandro and Mario's,

Thurmarsh's first Italian restaurant, and at the Taj Mahal – 'You had a lovely lady. Now you have another lovely lady. What is the secret, please?' Henry was always pleased to see Count Your Blessings.

They went to dinner with Alastair and Fiona Blair, with the Mathesons, though rarely now that Anna had emigrated to Canada, and with new friends from the Crescent, Joe and Molly Enwright. Joe was a teacher, Molly a painter.

Russian tanks rolled into Czechoslovakia. France exploded its first hydrogen bomb. Henry gave Diana her first full-scale Thurmarsh Friday night experience. First stop, the Lord Nelson. Helen sniffy, Ginny sad, Colin maudlin, Ted sarcastic and Ben astounded that Diana didn't know *any* of the grounds of *any* of the teams in the second division. Second stop, the Devonshire. Sid Hallett and the Rundlemen wearing flowery shirts in distant homage to flower power, and longer grey hair in an attempt to look vaguely hippy. But the music was the same, and so were the damp patches under their arms. Third stop, the Yang Sing, Thurmarsh's first proper Chinese restaurant, which had superseded the Shanghai Chinese Restaurant and Coffee Bar, now that the era of frothy coffee had ended.

'Well, what did you think?' asked Henry as they undressed in the silent house.

'It's a bit different from Hampstead,' was Diana's Delphic reply.

For three hectic days they had all the children with them, brown with memories, sullen in the Thurmarsh monsoon. Then Camilla was off to St Ethelred's in Devizes, and Benedict to Brasenose College in Surrey, both paid for by Tosser, who insisted on continuing their private education. Henry thought that at eleven and nine they were too young to go to boarding school, but he had to admit that he was glad they did and, to his slight shame, he didn't attempt to persuade Tosser to change his mind.

Benedict and Camilla were glad to leave the overcrowded house and meet their friends and be in their proper environment again, but they resented the fact that Kate and Jack would still be enjoying home comforts when they weren't, and in a house that was no longer overcrowded. Kate and Jack were happy to be staying at home, and fiercely loyal to the schools of Thurmarsh, but also resentful that so much money was being spent on Benedict's and Camilla's education, and feeling diminished by being excluded from their adventure in the great world outside.

In that great world outside, US officials in Saigon announced that defoliation in South Vietnam had produced no harmful results, and Mickey Mouse was forty. There was not necessarily any connection between the two events.

Henry and Diana's life settled into the next pattern, of Henry travelling to Leeds and of Diana taking Kate and Jack to school and fetching them home again. They gave occasional dinner parties. Diana was both a plainer and more confident cook than Hilary. Where Hilary would have produced delicious tandoori chicken with diffidence, Diana plonked down a decent but uninspired steak and kidney pudding as if it was ambrosia for the gods.

Henry forswore comparisons, and found himself making them all the time.

In his bunker in the basement of the Cucumber Marketing Board, Sir Winston Pratt prepared his strategy for 1969's attack on the diseases of the cucumber. Graphs were made, correlations were pursued, comparisons were studied. Did the level of acidity in the soil affect the incidence of angular leaf spot? Was there any discernible connection between altitude and grey mould? So many questions. So few answers. Such a challenge.

'Mrs Wedderburn's not been herself lately.'
   'Oh dear. What's wrong?'
   'It's nothing you can put your finger on.'
   Henry felt ashamed of thinking that there wasn't much of Mrs Wedderburn that he would want to put his finger on.
   'She's just a bit off colour, I suppose.'
   'Oh dear.'
   This was just one of the many sparkling exchanges between Cousin Hilda, Henry and Diana, in the stifling little blue-stoved,

pink-bloomered basement of 66, Park View Road. Autumn had moved all too readily to accommodate winter.

Henry and Diana were engaged in a difficult task.

'Er . . . about Christmas,' said Henry.

Cousin Hilda sniffed psychically.

'Er . . . we . . . er . . . obviously this is our first Christmas, and . . . er . . . obviously things aren't entirely easy with the two different lots of children.'

Cousin Hilda sniffed again. 'If you can't stand the heat, don't move into the house,' her eloquent sniff announced.

'And . . . er . . . we . . . er . . . obviously we . . . er . . . want to give the children a very good Christmas. They are the top priority. And it isn't a large house. Not when you've four children in it.'

Cousin Hilda remained silent. 'Spare me the excuses,' her telling silence screeched.

'So, the thing is . . . er . . . we . . . much as we'd like to normally . . . and hopefully in other years . . . and if we get the house we're going for . . . we . . .'

Cousin Hilda sniffed yet again.

'What house?' she said. 'I don't know owt about a house.'

'Oh, didn't we tell you?' said Diana. 'We meant to. We've seen a house, in Lordship Road, a big Victorian house, and nearer here than we are now. We've made an offer.'

'Lordship Road!' Cousin Hilda sniffed. 'Which end of Lordship Road?'

'This end,' said Diana. 'It's between the Alma and the Gleneagles.'

Cousin Hilda sniffed twice, once for each private hotel.

'The Gleneagles used to be good,' she said, praising the Alma by omission.

Silence fell. The subject of Lordship Road had been exhausted. Henry would have to return to his main theme, and he received no help from Cousin Hilda or Diana.

'So . . . er . . . the thing is . . .' he said. 'I don't think we're going to be able to invite you this year.'

'There's no reason why you should,' said Cousin Hilda sharply.

'Diana's children are used to posh people. They wouldn't want to spend Christmas with me. Anyroad, I've got Mr O'Reilly to think of. He'd be a square peg out of water on Christmas day wi'out me. And I couldn't neglect Mrs Wedderburn. Not when she's off colour.'

They chatted briefly of other things after that, of the spiralling cost of crackers, the demise of the tram, and the golden age of corsets.

'Don't forget to send a card to Mrs Wedderburn,' said Cousin Hilda as they left. 'And if it isn't too much trouble, pop in a few words. She were right thoughtful that time lending you her camp-bed like that.'

Henry felt deeply ashamed of wishing that he could shove the camp-bed up Mrs Wedderburn's backside. What sort of person am I, he thought.

Henry helped Kate and Jack choose presents for Benedict and Camilla, and Diana helped Benedict and Camilla choose presents for Kate and Jack. All the children had stockings, filled with things of such careful originality that it didn't strike even Benedict how cheap they were. Christmas dinner was good, and the children played Monopoly, which goes on a long time, which was a good thing. Benedict won, which was fortunate, as he was the one to whom it was most important to win. Major incidents and tears were miraculously avoided, and in the evening they watched *Christmas Night With the Stars*, which went on a long time, which was a good thing, and included Petula Clark, which set Henry wondering what sort of Christmas Count Your Blessings was having. Then they had cold ham and turkey, and then they watched *Some Like It Hot*, which went on a long time, which was a good thing.

The newsroom of the *Thurmarsh Chronicle* and *Argus* throbbed with painful memories. The reporters attacking their typewriters with feverish urgency, the shirt-sleeved sub-editors searching for snappy headlines round the subs' table, the news editor isolated like the conductor of an orchestra at his paper-strewn desk between the reporters and the subs. The long rows of windows were as streaked with grime as ever, save for one. A window-cleaner on a cradle was just about to attack a second window. Henry couldn't imagine what the room would look like without its grimy windows.

An impossibly young reporter was seated at his old desk. It wasn't only policemen who were looking younger, now that Henry was thirty-three.

He made a drinking mime to Ted and Colin as he passed through, and they nodded enthusiastically.

He entered Interview Room B. Helen was wearing a short skirt and had her legs crossed. The blood had drained from her right knee.

'Sorry I'm a bit late,' he said. 'Anthracnose at Maltby.'

'What?'

'I have a new job. I thought it might interest you.'

'Aren't you going to kiss me?'

'Oh . . . er . . . here?'

'Nobody's watching except the pigeons.'

Henry tried to give Helen a polite kiss on the cheek. She reached for his mouth and plonked a great kiss on it, lips working hungrily. She'd been eating butterscotch.

A row of pigeons, puffed up against the approaching night, watched from a slate roof sprinkled with snow and showed no curiosity whatsoever.

'That's better,' said Helen. 'I wondered if you'd gone off me.'

'I'm a happily married man,' said Henry.

'I know. I've met your wife.'

'You were pretty sniffy that night.'

'Was I? Maybe I was disappointed that you hadn't turned to me after your marriage broke up. You know I'm not happy with Ted.'

'What? I did turn to you, and you said you weren't suddenly going to be available when I was on my own. "A girl has her pride," you said.'

'Well, exactly. I wanted to be wooed, and chased. You could have pursued me.'

'I like Ted.'

188

'Ted would have been thrilled if I'd gone off with you. He'd have married Ginny, which he should have done all along, and everyone would have lived happily ever after. Too late now.'

'Yes.' There wasn't any point in saying that he wouldn't marry Helen if she was the last woman left on the planet.

'Do I gather from your attitude that you don't approve of Diana?'

'On the contrary. I think she's a great improvement.'

'What?'

'Let's face it, Henry, Hilary could be heavy going. Diana's fun. She might have possibilities.'

'What do you mean, "possibilities"?'

'Come off it. You know. Adult dinners. Nice company. Nice food. Good wine. A bit of swapping. Everyone enjoying themselves and no harm done. How about it, Henry? Then you'd see my legs at last.'

'I'm not into that sort of thing, Helen.'

'Oh, don't be so priggish and superior.'

The light was fading fast. Henry wondered if the pigeons would stay there all night. Where do birds sleep? It was one of life's many mysteries. He realised that he didn't want to continue the conversation, he wanted to be at home with Diana, or anywhere rather than the bleak cell that masqueraded as Interview Room B.

'I don't feel in any way superior,' he said. 'I've made quite a mess of my emotional life, but I do still try to lead a good life. If that's priggish, I'm priggish. Now, shall we do the interview?'

Helen opened her notebook and waited.

Is Your Cucumber Wilting? Henry's your man!
by Helen Cornish

Do you have trouble keeping your cucumbers straight and firm?

Are you having problems with Damping-off, False Damping-off, Gummosis, Scab or Topple?

If you are, Thurmarsh-born Henry Pratt (33) is the man to help you.

For Henry, a one-time reporter on the *Argus*, is now Chief Controlling Officer (Diseases and Pests) for the Cucumber Marketing Board, the Leeds-based organisation which aims to give the humble British cucumber a high profile.

Henry, who recently moved into a big Victorian house in Lordship Road, Thurmarsh with his second wife, Diana, his two children, Kate and Jack, and his step-children, Benedict and Camilla, is passionate about cucumbers and their diseases.

Bent

'I seem to have given my life to cucumbers. Perhaps it's my natural bent. Not that I've any time for bent cucumbers,' he joked to me yesterday.

'I suppose I am a bit of a fanatic,' he enthused. 'But then my job is probably one that needs a fanatic.'

Henry, who is not tall and lean like a good cucumber, but short and podgy and a self-confessed unathletic slob, believes that the British public are shamefully ignorant about cucumbers, that they take them for granted and even regard them as objects of slight derision.

'I think the cucumber's a bit of an underdog in the salad world,' he reflects. 'I'm a bit of an underdog myself, so maybe I have a natural affinity for it.'

Fairy Butter

In his fight to bring healthy cucumbers to our tables, Henry has to battle against no less than 42 different diseases of cucumbers, ranging from three different kinds of wilt and four different kinds of mildew to such romantically named complaints as Angular Leaf Spot, Fairy Butter and Root Mat.

'If you think it's all a load of rot, it certainly is,' he quips. 'There are at least six different forms of cucumber rot.'

Henry is spending the winter preparing booklets, pamphlets and leaflets for growers and gardeners, giving advice on how to recognise and deal with all their diseases.

'It's like a military operation,' he explains. 'I have all sorts of little flags dotted all over a map of Britain. The chaps josh me a bit about it, but all in good humour. They're a terrific bunch.'

If you think the cucumbers in your local shop are a terrific bunch this summer, and you can't see any Leaf Spot, Mildew or Rot, you'll know who to thank. That unsung hero, Paradise Lane-born Henry Pratt, the man who stops the cucumbers wilting.

'It's made us a laughing stock.'

'It's made *me* a laughing stock. I can't go in a pub in Thurmarsh without people asking me if my cucumber's wilting.'

'It's set our image back ten years.'

'I'm very sorry, sir.' Henry felt that the 'sir' was justified on this occasion. 'I never dreamt she'd make fun of us. I didn't realise how far the press has sunk since I left.'

Timothy Whitehouse swivelled round to gaze at his reproduction of Van Gogh's little-known 'Sunflower with Cucumbers', as if anything was preferable to looking at Henry.

'Did you clear it with Angela?' he asked.

'No. Sorry.'

'What's the point of having a press officer if you don't consult her?'

'I'm afraid I tend to get excited and forget I'm an organisation man.'

The Director (Operations) wheeled round and looked at Henry sadly.

'There's no room for mavericks or lone wolves in an organisation like ours,' he said. 'You've blotted your copy-book again.'

'I realise that,' said Henry.

'Blot after blot, Henry. What am I going to do with you?'

'May I just say in my defence that when I joined you did tell me to be my own man, be fearless and always speak the truth?'

'I did. I did. Point taken. *Mea culpa*! I should have said, "Be your own man, be fearless and always speak the truth *except to the press*." Let me spell it out once and for all, Henry.' He pulled his braces forward, let them go thwack against his chest, leant forward, predatory nose pointing straight at Henry, and smiled with his teeth but not his eyes. 'We're a team here. We expect our staff to show discipline and team spirit. In working for us you have to accept authority as a force beyond individuality.'

'That's just what my headmaster at my prep school said.'

'And you thought, "Silly old buffer. What does he know?" But he was right. What school was this? I must recommend it.'

'Brasenose College in Surrey. The headmaster was Mr A. B. Noon BA.'

'Aha!'

'That's funny, because his name is palindromic, the same backwards as forwards, and so was your "aha!"!'

'I do know what palindromic means, I did recognise A. B. Noon BA as palindromic, and I said "Aha!" deliberately with what I hoped was a flash of rather neat wit,' said the Director (Operations). 'I'm not stupid, but I'm beginning to think you are, so maybe I won't recommend Brasenose College after all.'

As Henry drove up the drive towards the creepered fortress that held Brasenose College in its grim grip, he saw the palindromic headmaster, Mr A. B. Noon BA, balding and stooping now, striding towards the playing fields with his two palindromic daughters, Hannah and Eve, steaming pallidly in his wake, both stooping prematurely. Had they been walking like that, staring at the ground, for twenty-one years?

Benedict's face turned white when he saw the rusting Mini parked alongside the Daimlers and Bentleys of the other parents. He stood in the pillared portico of the main entrance and came no further.

'Well come on,' called Henry.

Benedict shook his head.

Henry approached the school building with dread, lest he catch something of its old smell of rissoles and fear. Swifts were screeching joyously round the roof.

'I asked you not to bring that thing here,' hissed Benedict.

'I have no other means of transport,' said Henry. 'I'm not rich and you'll have to accept that.'

Benedict stared into the distance, loftily. His eleven-year-old face was stony.

'Material possessions aren't what matter, Benedict. It's moral values that count. And love and affection and fun. We can have all these if we try.'

'Try telling that to the chaps in the dorm.'

'I did, once. It wasn't much use, I admit.'

'I'm not getting in that thing.'

'Oh, come on. Be strong. Be your own man.'

'I am my own man, and I'm not coming. I've better things to do.'

'We've come a long way to see you.'

'Miracle you got here.'

'Well we did, and your mother wants to see you.'

'She should have thought of that before she married you.'

Henry looked into Benedict's hot, blazing eyes, and thought he could see the potential for madness there.

He almost felt the potential for madness in himself. His heart was pounding with barely controllable fury.

Benedict's face turned from deathly white to bright red.

'I don't want you sticking your cucumber into my mother,' he said. 'I bet it's got downy mildew.'

He turned abruptly and disappeared into the darkness of the school. Henry walked slowly back in the sunshine, feet crunching wearily.

Diana gave him an anxious smile. He shrugged his shoulders.

'Won't come,' he said.

He got back into the car, started the engine, and turned to smile at Camilla.

'Come on, Camilla,' he said. 'Let's go and look at some horses.'

11 A Surfeit of Cucumbers

Poverty is a tragedy. Wealth is a problem. Being able to earn just enough money to make ends meet concentrates the mind wonderfully.

Apollo II landed on the moon, Neil Armstrong and Edward Aldrin Junior walked on the moon's surface for two and three quarter hours; the Isle of Wight music festival attracted 250,000 spectators and left the surface of the island looking like the moon; Spiro Agnew, who could well have been educated on the moon, launched a rich tradition of idiotic statements by US Vice-Presidents, when he told an audience at a New Orleans dinner that those who supported a moratorium on the Vietnam War were 'encouraged by an effete corps of impudent snobs who characterize themselves as intellectuals'; and Henry concentrated wonderfully on the diseases of the cucumber.

Not to the neglect of its pests, I hope, the anxious reader cries.

Alas, anxious reader, I have to dash your hopes. In January, 1970, Henry realised that he had neglected the pests shamefully.

Never mind, he told himself, that's all water under the bridge now, and it gives me a target for the summer.

His target would be no less than the elimination of the glasshouse red spider mite and the glasshouse whitefly. From Land's End to John o' Groats there would be no resting place for the little bastards.

In number 83, Lordship Road, life was a constant struggle against cold and damp. The solid Victorian house was on the verge of crumbling. It was extremely difficult to keep warm, and had sinister damp patches on the walls. In this unpromising setting, between the Alma and the Gleneagles private hotels, the Pratt family life proceeded by fits and starts.

For thirty-four weeks, Benedict and Camilla were away at school, and Henry had to admit that it was an enormous relief.

For much of the summer holidays, and for the Christmas and New Year period, Kate and Jack were in Spain, Benedict and Camilla in France or Austria, skiing. Diana didn't want to hear about Tosser and was told his every banal thought, his every greedy mouthful, his every rich client. Henry wanted to know everything about Hilary and received only the sketchiest information that she was 'all right'.

Henry calculated that it was only for twenty-five days in the year that all four of the children's bedrooms were occupied at once. For these twenty-five days he felt that he was carrying the North/South divide around with him, in an atmosphere that was never less than tense, although there were no major eruptions. Benedict seemed almost unnaturally calm, and even allowed himself to be driven round Thurmarsh in Henry's Mini.

The children covered the damp patches on the walls of their bedrooms with posters and blown-up photographs. They chose contrasting subjects, and Henry was amazed and delighted that none of them concentrated on pop stars, although Benedict's choice did make him feel rather uneasy.

Kate chose great ballet dancers, romantic men with white faces and hollow cheeks, who looked as if they were dying of consumption.

In Jack's room the posters were of footballers – Bobby Charlton, Bobby Moore, Jimmy Greaves, Denis Law. Not Tommy Marsden. Tommy Marsden wasn't a hero any more.

Camilla's pictures were of horses.

Benedict plumped for Mussolini, Rasputin, John Lennon, Nietzsche and Dr Crippen.

Uncle Teddy rushed to the garden gate.

'You'll find her a bit changed,' he said.

'Changed?' said Henry.

'Her memory's a bit patchy sometimes. She's a bit obsessive.'

'Obsessive?'

'You'll see.'

The garden of Honeysuckle Cottage was rich with sweet william and wallflowers and lupins and marigolds and the eponymous honeysuckle. The tilting, peach-washed thatched cottage was an impossible dream.

Auntie Doris came out to meet them, smiling broadly. Henry could see nothing wrong, except perhaps that her eyes had become slightly deep-set.

'Hello, darling,' she said, hugging Henry. 'Hello, Hilary.'

'It's Diana, actually,' said Henry.

'Of course it is. Silly me. Would you like a cup of tea?'

They had tea in the garden. Blackbirds pinked, insects buzzed, fighter planes screamed, lawnmowers droned. Everything was as it should be, in the early days of summer.

'It was just a slip of the tongue when I said Hilary,' said Auntie Doris. 'I knew who you were.'

'Of course you did,' said Diana.

'I was at your wedding,' said Auntie Doris. 'I fainted, Henry fainted, that footballer passed out.'

'Your memory's very sharp,' said Henry.

'What do you mean?' said Auntie Doris. 'Why do you say that? You think it isn't, don't you?'

'Of course not.'

'I'd hardly be likely to forget three people passing out at a wedding, including the groom. That's hardly evidence of a sharp memory. You're humouring me.'

'Not at all,' said Diana. 'Henry doesn't humour people.'

'Would you like a cup of tea?' asked Auntie Doris.

'They've just had a cup of tea,' said Uncle Teddy.

'I know that,' said Auntie Doris. 'I'm not stupid. I made it for them. I thought they might want another one. It's a warm afternoon.'

After their second pot of tea, Uncle Teddy mooted a walk with Henry, and Henry realised that there was an ulterior motive for the suggestion.

Flower baskets hung from the thatched eaves of pink-washed and white-washed cottages. The larger houses had magnificent brick chimney-stacks.

On the green that led up to the church, Henry stopped to read the notice on an old Victorian pump: 'TAKE NOTE THAT BOYS OR OTHER PERSONS DAMAGING THIS PUMP WILL BE PROSECUTED AS THE LAW DIRECTS.'

Uncle Teddy waited impatiently, and as soon as they moved on, he said, 'Will you do me a small favour, Henry? Will you take some packages to Derek Parsonage for me?'

Henry's heart sank.

'What sort of packages?'

'Oh, just odds and ends. Safer for you not to know what's in them. Nothing illegal.'

'What do you mean, "Nothing illegal"?'

'Nothing stolen. Nothing harmful. Just things that, in this drearily bureaucratic world, should go through the customs, that's all. Security for our old age. Security for Doris's old age. Bit in it for you.'

'Oh, I wouldn't want any money from it,' said Henry, as they sauntered up the lane towards the open country.

'You mean you'd do it, but only for nothing?' said Uncle Teddy.

They stopped to look over a five-barred gate at a pleasant view over gently undulating farmland. A lone skylark was singing. Henry tried hard to refuse.

'Yes,' he found himself saying.

'Good man,' said Uncle Teddy. 'Good man. Sorry it has to be so cloak-and-dagger, but Doris has an unfortunate habit of remembering things she's not supposed to remember.'

'I thought her memory was bad.'

'Exactly. She forgets what it is she's not supposed to remember. Calls me Teddy sometimes in front of other people. I just tell people that was her husband. Died in a fire. Won't marry me because she's still carrying a torch for him. Touching story. Gets people in tears down the pub.'

They set off, more briskly, for home. Uncle Teddy wasn't interested in views and cottages now that he'd achieved his purpose.

As they approached Honeysuckle Cottage, Uncle Teddy slowed down and said, 'Er . . . just one thing. We'll probably play

Scrabble this evening. Usually do. The old girl's spelling's not always too hot these days. Best not to point her mistakes out, I find.'

Auntie Doris offered to make a pot of tea. Uncle Teddy said the sun was almost over the yard-arm, so they had gin and tonic instead. Auntie Doris had cooked chicken-and-ham pie but had forgotten the ham, and she'd made rhubarb crumble with salt instead of sugar. 'Bloody repulsive, but there's no point in upsetting the old girl,' said Uncle Teddy. They drank malt whisky and played Scrabble. Auntie Doris only made two spelling mistakes – Doezn for Dozen and Seequin instead of Sequin. She won, largely because, due to her mistakes, her Z and her Q both fell on triple letter squares. 'Bit of luck for the old girl there,' said Uncle Teddy. 'Nice to see it. Deserves it after living with that arse Porringer. Wish I could run into the bastard again. I'd give him two black eyes to match his blackheads.'

At first, Henry believed that the weather had played the major role in the creation of the cucumber mountain. His natural modesty and lack of self-confidence led him to underestimate his part. But as the summer of 1970 drifted on, evidence began to pile up which suggested that the major responsibility belonged to him. Rot was rare, wilt was minimal, mildew was almost entirely confined to the Celtic fringes. As for the glasshouse red spider mite and the glasshouse whitefly, the little bastards didn't know what had hit them.

The dual northern chilled stores at Preston and Darlington were overflowing.

When Henry was summoned before the Director (Operations), he expected praise for his achievements.

'You look strangely contented,' said Timothy Whitehouse.

'Well, I . . . er . . . yes.' The Chief Controlling Officer (Diseases and Pests) was puzzled. 'Yes, I . . . er . . . yes.'

'I see,' said Mr Whitehouse, somewhat surprisingly. 'Henry, we have a glut of cucumbers. A cucumber mountain.'

'Or, since they're ninety per cent water, a cucumber lake.'

'This is no time for levity.' Timothy Whitehouse looked at Henry sadly. 'We have a disaster on our hands.'

'How can that be? There are millions of cheap cucumbers around.'

The Director (Operations) gave Henry another sad look and, as if he couldn't bear to look at him any more, swung round and gazed at Rembrandt's little-known and deeply compassionate 'Old woman with cucumber'.

'How can you be so naïve?' he said. 'Who are we responsible to?'

'The public?'

'No!!! They have no voice. They're amorphous. They don't, in the final analysis, exist.'

'The growers?'

'Better. They have a voice. We have to make sure they're reasonably contented and don't go dumping cucumber mountains outside Number Ten. Not that it's likely. They aren't French. But no, we as employees are ultimately responsible to our Board of Directors. And who are they responsible to? The government. They are our pay-masters. Have you heard of support buying?'

'Well, yes, of course. Can you remind me how it works?'

'Can I remind you? How long have you been with us?'

'Er . . .'

'Never mind. I haven't time to wait for your brain.' The Director (Operations) pulled his braces to their full extent and let them thud back into his chest. 'We're desperately buying up cucumbers, using up our budget, and destroying them to keep up the price. They don't burn very well.'

'Can't we persuade people to buy more cucumbers?'

'Well there is a limit. It's their crisp freshness that appeals. They don't freeze well.'

'You can freeze cucumber soup.'

'Take a walk through Holbeck. Take a walk through Beeston. Take a walk through Seacroft. Look at the people. Are they going to freeze cucumber soup?'

'I think that's a rather degrading cultural assumption.'

'It's not necessarily criticism. Maybe they aren't poncey enough to freeze cucumber soup. We have a catastrophic glut, and I hold you responsible.'

'Doesn't the weather have something to do with it?'

'Very possibly, but God is not within my remit and you are.'

'I thought I was supposed to control diseases and pests.'

'You are. But not eliminate them overnight. What we seek to achieve, Henry, as I thought you understood, is equilibrium. Stability. Stable levels of production. Stable incomes. Stable prices.'

'So, I'm just to sit there and do nothing.'

Timothy Whitehouse leant forward, and Henry realised that he was about to receive one of those smiles that didn't reach the eyes. 'Who knows what the future holds in store? Some vast new cucumber plague, perhaps. Dutch cucumber disease. French rot. German measles. If that day comes, you will stand alone between us and annihilation.' He smiled again, persuasively, comfortingly, patronisingly.

'And if that day never comes?'

'They also serve who only stand and wait.'

'But you told me to be my own man, stick to my guns, and always speak the truth.'

'How old are you, Henry?' asked the Director (Operations).

'Thirty-five,' said the Chief Controlling Officer (Diseases and Pests).

'And you still believe what the authorities tell you.' Timothy Whitehouse shook his head sadly.

On Tuesday, September 1st, 1970, Concorde boomed over Britain for the first time. The damage was not as great as had been feared. A fluorescent lighting tube fell from the ceiling of a house in Wales, and two pencils, placed on a bridge by scientists in Oban, fell over. No other incidents were reported.

On the same day, King Hussein of Jordan escaped an assassination attempt, Benedict and Camilla returned home from Mykonos, US senators voted fifty-five to thirty-nine against ending the Vietnam War, Henry took two large parcels to Derek Parsonage's exotic brothel in Commercial Road, Britons were criticised for buying millions of useless vitamin pills, and Mrs Wedderburn died.

Derek Parsonage's brothel was situated in a Victorian town house that was marginally more decrepit even than 83, Lordship Road. A brass plate at the side of the door announced, 'World-Wide Religious Literature Inc.'

The entrance hall was piled with religious literature, and gave no hint of the female underclothes, chain-mail, black bags, whips, studded belts, schoolgirls' uniforms, harnesses, electric leads, dustbins, oranges, nooses, trapdoors, soft brooms, hard brooms and water hoses that lay in wait for the deviant men of Thurmarsh.

Derek Parsonage came out of his office and greeted Henry warmly, if sanctimoniously.

'So good to see you, Henry,' he said. 'Come into my office.'

When they were in the office, he said, very unsanctimoniously, 'I didn't realise you were into this kind of thing. What is your preference?'

'Oh no,' said Henry, feeling insulted yet also slightly flattered. 'I've seen Uncle Teddy and I've got a couple of parcels.'

'Say no more,' said Derek Parsonage, whose blackheads had got worse. 'Just drive them round the back. How is the old rogue?'

'Very well,' said Henry. 'Playing a lot of Scrabble.'

Uncle Teddy's old partner in crime, whose brothel had been involved in the deception over the burnt-down Cap Ferrat, gawped at this news.

As Henry drove his car round the back, he was horrified to see a police car lurking in the alley between the Pet Boutique and the Commercial Café.

As he opened the front door of number 83 after delivering his parcels, Henry could hear the phone ringing. 'I wonder if you'd come down the station of your own free will and save us all a lot of trouble, sir.' When he heard Diana say, 'Oh hello, Cousin Hilda,' Henry's relief was so great that he said, 'Hello, Cousin Hilda,' so heartily that her 'Hello, Henry. Bad news, I'm afraid. Brace yourself,' rocked him on his heels and he said, 'What is it?' in a croak, and when she said, 'Mrs Wedderburn's dead,' he felt such a wave of relief and such appalling guilt at feeling relief, that when she said, 'The cremation's on Wednesday. She were right thoughtful lending you that camp-bed. You will come, won't you?' he said, 'Of course we will,' without hesitation or annoyance.

Henry feared that he, Diana and Cousin Hilda would be the only mourners. He'd forgotten that Mrs Wedderburn had three sons. Judge then of his astonishment when there were in the gleaming, spotless clinical chapel of Thurmarsh Crematorium, off the Doncaster Road, not only the three sons and two of their wives, but also a sister, a sister's husband, two cousins, a nephew, nine people from her church, three from her sewing circle, two neighbours, her whist partner, her medium and her chiropodist.

'Quite a send-off,' said Cousin Hilda.

After the service, as they stood outside the chapel, not liking to rush away, but not wanting to talk to anybody, Henry found himself beside Mrs Wedderburn's sister, a small plump lady in black.

'A sad day,' said Mrs Wedderburn's sister.

'Very sad,' said Henry. 'A generous woman, who lends you her camp-bed with no strings attached, all her life to live for, gets crushed beneath a JCB. It makes you wonder what life is all about.'

'It's the driver I'm sorry for,' said Mrs Wedderburn's sister. 'He's going to have to live with that for the rest of his days.'

As they drove away from the crematorium, Cousin Hilda gave a deep sigh. It was the only emotion she allowed herself to show at the death of her one close friend.

'You made a hit with Mrs Wedderburn's sister,' she said. ' "What a nice young man," she said.'

It was her way of thanking them for coming.

There were several deaths in the second half of 1970, in addition to Mrs Wedderburn's. Antonio Salazar, Portuguese Chief of State for forty years, died in Lisbon. President Nasser died in Cairo. General de Gaulle died at Colombey-Les-Deux-Eglises. Henry felt as if something had died in him as well. There wasn't any point in sticking flags into maps any more. He began applying for jobs again, without success. He was in a Catch-22 situation. He'd been too long in cucumbers, so he needed a new job, but nobody would give him a new job, because he'd been too long in cucumbers.

Being a new boy at Dalton College did wonders for Benedict's confidence. In fact it removed it entirely for months. Kate's school reports remained good, and she took a keen interest in almost every subject. Jack plodded along, bulkily ugly, in the middle of the class if his teacher managed to stimulate him, towards the bottom if he didn't. But he was good at sport and immensely practical. Camilla lived, breathed and, sad to say, resembled horses.

1971 saw Britain's first national postal strike. It lasted almost two months, and helped Henry to slow down his fight against the diseases and pests of cucumbers while preventing him from applying for any more jobs. Decimal currency was introduced, and the price of everything, including cucumbers, went up. Unemployment in Britain reached 3.4 per cent, the highest figure since 1940. Sanity was restored to the production of cucumbers. Henry resumed his job hunting, to no avail.

On Saturday, October 23rd, 1971, Henry and Diana set off at 5.30 in the morning, in order to reach Dalton College in Somerset by twelve. Kate and Jack were staying with the Blairs, and Camilla was tucked up in a dormitory at St Ethelred's. They would take her out for Sunday lunch before returning exhausted to Yorkshire.

It promised to be quite a day. Lunch with Benedict at the Bald-Headed Angel, followed by the big rugby match against their arch rivals, Sherborne, and then a Grand Reunion Tea in School Hall for old boys who began their school career between 1945 and 1950.

Henry parked his new second-hand Ford Escort in the car park of the Bald-Headed Angel, for fear that if he drove it to the school gates Benedict would refuse to get in it. He and Diana walked to the school. The air was raw and damp.

Tosser Pilkington-Brick was standing beside his Jaguar in a very smart new overcoat. His second wife, Felicity, was sitting in the car, looking, as Henry and Diana decided later, pretty but vapid.

'Hello!' said Tosser, surprised. 'What are you doing here?'

'Taking Benedict out,' said Henry.

'There must be some mistake,' said Tosser. 'We're taking him out.'

Benedict sauntered jauntily towards them. His confidence, now that he was fourteen, and no longer in his first year, was coming back all too quickly. He looked from his father to his stepfather and said, casually, 'Oh lawks. Contretemps. Did I forget to tell you, Mummy, that I was going to lunch with Daddy? I only knew he was coming the other day. Frightfully sorry.' He kissed his mother casually. 'See you two at the match. Pity it's such a cold day for it. Right, Dad, let's get this Jag going.'

It had been on another cold late October day, twenty-three years ago, in the restaurant of the Bald-Headed Angel, that Diana, on the very first occasion that Henry had met her, had said, 'Isn't embarrassment embarrassing. This is the most embarrassing meal I've ever been to.' And now here she was, sitting with Henry at a table laid for three, next to the table where her son was sitting with her ex-husband and his second wife. The restaurant had recently been revamped, inexplicably, as a German *gaststaette*, which went with its character as an English coaching inn about as well as the cauliflower au gratin and carrots went with the badly trimmed, tough *wienerschnitzel*.

All around them, in the crowded restaurant, were parents and children. Henry and Diana alone had no pupil with them.

Henry reached across the table and clasped Diana's hand. She gave his hand an answering squeeze.

Benedict frowned on seeing this, and said, to his father, 'Any thoughts about this year's skiing?'

Tosser looked uneasily at Felicity, and it dawned on Henry that Benedict might be trying to embarrass Tosser and Felicity just as much as himself and Diana. This made him feel better.

Benedict leant across towards them. He had an unhealthy gleam in his eyes. 'Everything all right for you two?' he asked.

'Amazing,' said Henry cheerfully. 'The food here is incredible. One never believes it could get worse and it always does.'

'You fagged for my dad, didn't you?' said Benedict in an unnecessarily loud voice.

'Yes, I am younger than him, that is true,' said Henry. He raised his glass and clinked it with Diana's. The indifferent Piesporter swished gently. He turned to Tosser's table, raised his glass to the three of them, and said, 'Your good health, and your continued happiness and wealth.'

Neither Tosser nor Felicity seemed to know quite how to respond to this. They raised their glasses and smiled uneasily.

'You're happier this time round, I hope, Tosser,' said Diana.

Tosser tried to hide his fury at the use of his nickname.

'You didn't tell me you were called Tosser,' said Felicity. 'Why were you called Tosser?'

'No significant reason,' said Tosser pompously.

Henry saw Benedict give Tosser a malicious look. He felt an unworthy surge of pleasure.

Later, as he walked arm in arm with Diana towards the school, through the market-place whose charming jumble of old buildings was now dwarfed by a concrete and rust shopping centre, he realised that he'd been quite exhausted by the effort of not being embarrassed. A keen wind bore the faintest traces of rain. He shivered.

'Cold?' said Diana.

'No. Thinking about the look in Benedict's eye. There's so much anger in that boy.'

'And we're all angry with him, although it's mainly our fault,' said Diana.

'We're angry *because* it's our fault.'

'Come on. This afternoon's going to be hell if we don't throw ourselves into it. Let's cheer our heads off.'

The West Country is warm, wet and soft, with just three exceptions – Land's End, Lower Boggle and Middle Boggle. That afternoon, at Dalton College, Middle Boggle was at its most spiteful. The wind cut into eyes, painted noses red, and forced its way up trouser legs. Tosser went mad, reliving his glory days, shouting, 'Bolly bolly bolly, Dalton Dalton Dalton, play up shant, bolly bolly bolly,' in the time-honoured way. Diana shouted, 'Come on Dalton,' and waved her arms around. Felicity scowled and froze. Henry gradually got excited, but just couldn't bring himself to shout, 'Bolly bolly bolly, Dalton Dalton Dalton, play up shant, bolly bolly bolly.' Lampo and Denzil walked past them, hands touching. 'How the cretins roar,' said Lampo.

Dalton took a 13–8 lead early in the second half, and clung on for a victory that was unexpected and brave, albeit slightly fortunate. A great roar greeted the final whistle. Only cold Felicity and caustic Lampo remained aloof.

A great chatter of old boys wended its way down to School Hall, flushed with triumph: solicitors with hoarse voices, merchant bankers with chapped lips, and the cucumber man re-entering the scene of his past triumph.

The seats, which all those years ago had been packed with schoolboys laughing at Henry's comic act in the end-of-term concert, had been removed and stored under the stage. On the stage were trestle tables, laden with sandwiches and cakes. The old boys and their wives queued good-humouredly to be given name stickers. 'H. E. Pratt, Orange House 1948–50' and 'Mrs Pratt'. 'P. K. R. Davey, Orange House 1945–50' and 'Mrs Davey'. Denzil wore his 'Mrs Davey' sticker proudly. Doctors, bankers and accountants frowned at it and moved on. Vicars smiled, to show how broad-minded they were.

By the time he'd been forced to leave Dalton so abruptly, Henry had been on the point of feeling that he belonged there. Now, twenty-one years later, that confidence was hard to recreate. The words of his comic turn reverberated through his head – ''Ow do, I'm t'new headmaster, tha knows' – but they carried memories not only of his triumph but also of his shame at the betrayal of his father. In any case the ghostly words were soon drowned under the very real hum as hundreds of old boys greeted old friends. Most of them were taller than him and apart from the vicars they all looked more prosperous. He was Oiky Pratt masquerading in the over-careful tweed jacket and overweight creased body of a thirty-six-year-old man.

As he was walking away from the stage with a cup of tea and a slice of date-and-nut loaf, Henry was approached by a man whom he knew by his sticker to be F. L. Barnes, Plantagenet House 1946–51.

'H. E. Pratt,' announced F. L. Barnes, stooping to read Henry's sticker.

'That's me,' admitted Henry.

'I wondered if I'd see you,' said F. L. Barnes. 'You applied for a job with us not long ago. I'm in personnel at McVitie's.'

'Yes, I did. Didn't even get an interview. Frightened of employing another Daltonian, were you? Worried about charges of nepotism.'

'No, no,' said F. L. Barnes. 'Absolutely the reverse. Trouble was, you'd been given the most awful reference I've ever read.'

Henry felt as if he'd been punched in the stomach. He was still feeling shocked when N. T. A. Pilkington-Brick, Orange House 1945–50 arrived on the arm of Mrs Pilkington-Brick. Tosser looked so bulky, and Felicity so small and frail, that Henry flinched inwardly at the thought of them making love.

'I hope you didn't find the lunch *too* embarrassing,' said Tosser.

'I hope *you* didn't,' said Diana.

'Do you think we ought to talk about Benedict some time?' said Tosser. 'We think he's turning out a bit strange. Are you happy with the way you're managing him?'

'You sound as though he's a portfolio,' said Diana, 'and he is at school thirty-four weeks of the year and with you almost half of the rest.'

'Yes, but yours is his home. You are the prime influence upon him.'

'You could apply for custody if you want,' said Henry.

Tosser's fading Madagascan suntan faded still further. 'No, no. No, no. We're happy as we are. In fact . . . er . . . now that I'm married. . . ,' he gave Felicity a little smile and she simpered back, '. . . we . . . er . . . well, let's say, I *have* been having them *almost every* holiday, Camilla's fine, of course, but Benedict *is* a problem. This coming year too I have business commitments which . . . and I don't want to be greedy. He's your son as well, Diana.'

'Felicity isn't all that keen on him, is that it?' said Diana.

Felicity didn't move a muscle. They had no idea what she was thinking or indeed *if* she was thinking.

'No, no, you've got it all wrong, it isn't that at all,' said Tosser. 'I just think he doesn't know where his real home is and he ought to. That's all. I'm only thinking of him.'

'Of course,' said Henry.

Paul and Christobel joined the family circle. They were both practising gynaecologists now, and childless. Paul was putting on weight and developing gravitas. Christobel was still beautiful but Henry didn't feel that he knew her at all. Their voices always sounded as if they were comforting an elderly patient of limited intelligence. In his friskier moments Henry referred to their Georgian house outside Farnham as Bedsyde Manor. But this was not one of his friskier moments.

'No more problems with fainting, then?' asked Christobel. 'I know it's not our field, but it did concern us.'

'Fainting?' said Tosser.

'Henry fainted at his wedding,' said Paul. 'Went spark out during the telegrams, poor chap.'

'I was overcome with love for Diana,' said Henry uneasily.

J. C. R. Tubman-Edwards, Tudor House 1948–53, approached.

'Hello, mates,' he said. 'How are you, Tosser? Long time no see.'

'Thank God,' said Tosser, 'and the name's Nigel, and you never were my mate. You were rotten to Henry.'

'And I didn't like people being rotten to my little fatty faggy-chops,' said Lampo, joining the gathering along with Denzil.

Henry flinched. This wasn't what he wanted to remember.

' "Mrs Davey"!' said Josceleyn Tubman-Edwards. 'I think that's rather tasteless.'

'Yes, it's splendid, isn't it?' said Henry, revived by the prospect of teasing Josceleyn. 'How's your lovely debutante lady?'

'I've no idea,' said Josceleyn Tubman-Edwards. 'She jilted me two days before my wedding.'

Life can be a pig. A group of old boys are enjoying getting their own back on a bully, and suddenly they all have to feel sympathy for the poor bloke.

'Oh, I'm really sorry,' said Henry, and meant it.

Mr Lennox, Henry's old English master, a pedantic soul known to the boys as Droopy L., approached through a wall of conversation. His hair and skin were grey and he had frown lines the way other people have laugh lines.

'I'm afraid I'm going to have to ask you to remove your name badge,' he told Denzil.

'Oh come off it, Mr Lennox,' said Lampo. 'You always were a little Hitler.'

'There's no need to be rude,' said Droopy L.

'What's the use of reunions if we can't be nasty to masters we didn't like?' said Henry, with a boldness he didn't feel.

'Take it off, please. I really do insist,' said Droopy L.

'Please don't, Denzil,' said Lampo. 'I love Denzil, Mr Lennox. We argue like mad but live together more faithfully than most husbands and wives.'

'That's your problem,' said Droopy L.

'Oh no, it's your problem,' said Denzil. 'It's legal now and we're doing no harm.'

'I've had complaints,' said Mr Lennox, 'and I must ask you to remove it or leave. Where do you think this is – Marlborough?'

'Quite right,' said Tosser.

'Oh, come off it, Tosser, don't be such a pompous ass. You fancied Henry almost as much as I did,' said Lampo.

'Lampo!' hissed Tosser.

'Do we really need to go into all this?' said Henry.

'I'm very interested,' said Felicity.

'Come on, Denzil, my love,' said Lampo. 'We aren't welcome here.'

'We're coming too,' said Henry. 'It's outrageous.'

'Henry!' said Diana.'

'What?'

'You said we're going. You haven't consulted me.'

'Sorry, darling. You will come, won't you?'

'No. Not because I think it's disgusting, I think it's funny, but Denzil isn't actually Mrs Davey so he hasn't got a leg to stand on, and I'm not going to get steamed up about it.'

'I'm not steamed up. I care about my friends.'

'I care about my brother, and I haven't seen him for ages.'

'It's all right, Henry,' said Denzil. 'We'll see you later. Thank you for your support. I shall always wear it.'

'And with that hoary old joke, I leave with my hoary old lover,' said Lampo. 'Farewell, Droopy L. Farewell, Dalton.'

'Absolutely disgusting,' said Droopy L. 'I sometimes wonder why we bothered to educate you all.'

'It's true,' said the Director (Operations). 'Absolutely true.' He looked Henry straight in the eye at a moment when Henry would have expected him to gaze at one of his old masters for comfort. 'I didn't want to lose you.'

'I beg your pardon?'

'I give good references to people I want to get rid of and bad references for people I want to keep.'

'That's outrageous.'

'I have to protect my interests. And the interests of the organisation.'

'How can I ever trust you again?'

'I shouldn't, if I were you. Then we'll understand each other perfectly.'

'I'm very unhappy about it,' said Henry. 'I don't know if I can work with you any more.'

Now Mr Whitehouse did look away, gazing at Vermeer's exquisite but little-known 'Preparation of salad in a house in Delft'.

'I'll be sorry if you do resign,' he said. 'Though no doubt you'd find a good job eventually.'

'How could I, with your stinking references?'

'Oh, I'd give you good references once I'd lost you. I'm not a complete bastard. I'd tell the truth.'

'What is the truth?'

'That you're reliable, intelligent, enthusiastic and talented, with a deep sense of loyalty, who gets on well with other people, forms a useful member of the team and was being groomed for higher office at the time of your resignation.'

'Good Lord. Am I really being groomed for higher office?'

'Don't you believe me?'

'No. You told me not to.'

'As I say, you're intelligent.'

'I thought maybe I'd blotted my copy-book once too often.'

'Sometimes people who cause difficulties at lower levels are moved up, where they can do less damage. Sometimes rebels are embraced into the heart of the establishment, where they are rapidly persuaded that it isn't in their interests to be rebellious any more. Promotion is a minefield, and even you wouldn't be so naïve as to assume that it's usually given on merit.'

It was a deeply confused Henry Pratt who left the office of the Director (Operations). He couldn't face the lift, so he took the cold, bare, bleak steps down to the basement and his increasingly isolated bunker.

'To leave without having another job to go to is a terrible risk,' said Henry next Sunday afternoon, when they had the house to themselves and were lying in bed, cuddling sleepily, after making love. 'But if I stay and apply for other jobs, I won't get them because I'll get a stinking reference. I really am a square peg in a vicious circle.'

There was a burst of loud banging from the Gleneagles. They were refurbishing their bedrooms, not before time, and seemed to be doing the bulk of the work at weekends, presumably because they weren't using proper builders.

'I want to do something more with my life,' said Henry. 'I can't wait much longer.'

Somebody, somewhere, will recognise a good man when he sees one.

The banging stopped as suddenly as it had begun. Blissful peace returned. It was starting to get dark. The slightest flush of pink touched the mackerel sky.

Henry cuddled gently into the curve of his wife's body. Very slowly, he began to feel sexy. He ran his hands slowly up her wide, strong thighs. And then, sad to relate, he fell asleep.

Liam O'Reilly died on Christmas Day, after his Christmas dinner, suffering a massive heart attack during a game of Snap. There aren't many better ways to go. He was sixty-nine.

On an impulse, Cousin Hilda, who wasn't given to impulses, wrote to the latest addresses that she had for all her gentlemen, telling them of the funeral arrangements. 'Well,' she told Henry, 'I feel it's the end of an era.' She also wrote to an address in Ireland, which she found in Mr O'Reilly's wallet.

There was more of a turn-out at the funeral than might have been expected for such a reclusive man, but the mourners still felt dwarfed by the great, dark, incense-heavy vault of St Mary's Catholic Church.

Two obscure relatives from Ireland arrived, full of praise for Cousin Hilda's kindness, 'of which Liam was always most appreciative'. They each gave her a bottle of Jameson's whisky, and she was too moved by their kindness to refuse the gifts, which she passed on to Henry with a sniff.

Tony Preece also came, with his pale ash-blonde fiancée, Stella, whom he had still not married after an engagement lasting more than fourteen years. Tony had made quite a success of his act as Cavin O'Rourke, the Winsome Wit from Wicklow. He had the grace to feel embarrassed about his Irish jokes at Liam O'Reilly's funeral.

Another of the gentlemen to reappear was Neville Chamberlain, who had retired six weeks before after selling paint for forty-seven years, in England and Kenya.

Also present was Norman Pettifer. 'It's a sad day,' he said. 'A sad, sad day. And yet I can't feel sad, such is the selfishness of human nature. I heard this morning, this very morning, that young Adrian has been sacked.'

Also present, and increasingly prosperous, was Mr Travis, the liquidator.

Cousin Hilda invited all nine mourners back to her house 'for a little something'. The two Irishman, anticipating a wake, licked their lips.

There were ham sandwiches, cheese sandwiches, sausage rolls, and a choice of tea or Camp coffee.

When nobody could manage another bite, Cousin Hilda said, 'Now, I've summat special to see poor Mr O'Reilly off to a better world. I think he deserves to go out in style.'

Oh God, I hope it's something small, thought Henry. They were going out to supper at Joe and Molly Enwright's.

Cousin Hilda disappeared to her little kitchen.

'A funeral I'd like to have been present at was that of Dame Sybil Thorndike,' said Norman Pettifer. 'She was a trooper if ever there was one.'

'I expect there was drink at that funeral,' said one of the Irishman.

'Hush, Seamus,' said the other.

'I suppose selling paint has changed over the years,' said Henry.

'You can say that again,' said Neville Chamberlain.

But Henry didn't. He felt that it had been boring enough the first time.

Cousin Hilda entered with a tray on which there were five steaming bowls. Then she returned to the kitchen and brought another tray, on which there were also five steaming bowls.

Henry realised that he had been over-optimistic when he'd believed that he'd eaten his last spotted dick ever.

'Well, it is a Tuesday,' said Cousin Hilda.

12 Happy Families

Benedict, almost fifteen, started wanting to stay away with friends. Diana, Henry, Tosser and Felicity welcomed this. They were pleased that he was happy. They hoped that, if they took no action, the problems that they had seen deep in his eyes would go away.

Kate was beginning the long build-up towards her O levels. Great success was anticipated. She had matured into a lovely girl, if slightly moody.

Jack was becoming increasingly unacademic. He was good at football and cricket, but not at lessons. Henry told his teachers that he thought that academic education was failing those of a more practical nature. 'Tell the government,' was the response.

Camilla had her horses.

1972 moved inexorably into 1973. The Americans withdrew from Vietnam after the Paris peace talks reached agreement, but the violence continued.

Benedict got eight O levels. He announced that, if he got three A levels, his father would buy him a car.

Kate got nine mock O levels.

Jack played football for the under-fourteens and scored several goals.

Camilla had her horses.

One Sunday in late September, 1973, Cousin Hilda called round after church. Benedict was back at Dalton and Camilla had gone to Benningdean, a very posh school in Kent, but Kate and Jack were in. Kate was doing homework in her room, and Jack was building a bike in the garden out of old bits.

Cousin Hilda sniffed, because it was obvious to her that nobody at number 83 had gone to church.

They invited her to stay for lunch, and told her it would be early because Kate and Jack were going out. She sniffed again. 'In my day young people weren't allowed to have Sunday lunch early so they could go out,' her eloquent sniff attested.

To their astonishment, she accepted the invitation.

'You seem surprised,' she said.

'Well I am,' said Henry.

'You shouldn't issue invitations unless you mean them.'

'Oh, we meant it,' said Diana. 'And we're pleased. It's just that we thought you wouldn't be able to because of your gentlemen.'

'I have no gentlemen now,' said Cousin Hilda. 'I've hung up my boots.'

They stared at her in astonishment.

'I told Mr Travis, the liquidator, "I'm sixty-seven. I'm going into liquidation." He laughed.'

They realised that they should have laughed, and did so belatedly, then stared at each other in astonishment. Cousin Hilda had made a joke.

Cousin Hilda sniffed.

'There's no need to look surprised,' she said. 'I am human.'

'Oh, very much so,' said Henry hurriedly.

'I've realised for quite a while that I've been swimming against the tide. And I've a bit put by. I don't live particularly extravagantly.'

'Will you move?' asked Diana.

'No. It'll be nice to have the whole house to myself. I'll indulge myself.'

There was more laughter over lunch. Diana told Jack not to eat with his mouth full, when she meant not to talk with his mouth full.

'That was a good one,' said Cousin Hilda. 'That were a right comical slip, weren't it, Kate?'

'Very funny,' agreed Kate, who was always nice to Cousin Hilda.

'I must tell that to my . . . oh. . . I haven't got anyone to tell it to any more, have I?' said Cousin Hilda.

'You knew Tommy Marsden, didn't you, Dad?' said Jack.

'Yes. Why?'

'He's been sacked by Farsley Celtic.'

'Well, he's thirty-eight, like me.'

'He's sacked because he's a piss-artist.'

Henry held his breath. Cousin Hilda didn't appear to understand, but her lips tightened and he knew she was only pretending.

'You can chart his ups and downs by his clubs,' said Jack. 'Thurmarsh United, Manchester United, Leeds United, Luton Town, Stockport County, Halifax Town, Northwich Victoria, Farsley Celtic.'

'A sad story,' said Henry.

When the children had gone out, they sat by the fire and Cousin Hilda said, 'Do you know what decided me to retire?'

Henry and Diana, lolling full of beef, shook lazy heads.

'I'll tell you,' said Cousin Hilda. 'Mr O'Reilly. Liam.'

Astonishment roused them from their torpor.

'He never said much,' said Cousin Hilda. 'He had more sense. I see no need for all the conversation that goes on. Natter, natter, natter. What about? Nowt. You might have thought, he's not really made much mark on this globe, hasn't Liam O'Reilly. A "yes, please" and "thank you very much", and that was about all it amounted to. But I've been thinking, and I've been thinking about life, and it's a right funny thing, is life, when you think about it. You see, he never did much with his life, not to say *did*, but without him, well, it's just not the same. What it is is, he didn't have much of a presence, but he has a very powerful absence. It's funny, is that, isn't it? Odd, I mean. I reckon so, anyroad.'

A few weeks later, Henry and Diana chugged to Monks Eleigh through a golden autumn haze.

When they arrived, Henry saw that Auntie Doris couldn't remember who he was. 'Haven't you got a kiss for your little nephew Henry?' he prompted, and he saw the panic die from her eyes.

After a supper of tinned mulligatawny soup and Marks and Spencer's lasagne – neither Auntie Doris nor Uncle Teddy were up to proper cooking any more – they settled down to a good game of Scrabble. Henry found it both endearing and sad (mixed emotions number 84) to see this old rogue and this ultra-glamorous sexy painted lady getting so excited over a game of Scrabble.

During the game, Auntie Doris proudly produced the word Quonge. After a brief silence, Henry said, 'Sorry. What's Quonge?' 'A Mexican hat,' said Uncle Teddy. Diana pointed out that foreign words don't count. 'It's English for a Mexican hat,' said Uncle Teddy. 'The Mexican for a Mexican hat is *Quonja*.' With the Q happening to fall on a triple letter square, Auntie Doris established a lead which she maintained to the end. When she'd left the room, Uncle Teddy said, 'All guff about the hat, of course, but the old girl loves to win. Not a word, eh?' and Henry said, 'Oh no. We'll keep it under our *quonja*, don't you worry.' 'Very good,' said Uncle Teddy, as Auntie Doris returned. 'Humour always was your saving grace,' and Auntie Doris, who still made things worse by protesting about them, said, 'Teddy! Tact. Don't remind him that there's practically nothing else he's any good at.'

Towards the end of June, 1974, the wife of a market gardener in Country Durham informed Henry that her husband had been in hospital for several weeks, and their cucumbers had widespread rot, which she couldn't identify, and she didn't want to worry her husband over it, not with his kidneys.

Henry, who had been getting increasingly office-bound over the years, thought this the perfect excuse for an expedition, and pottered off up the A1.

The market garden was set just inland, north of Hartlepool, and not far from the looming, steaming, throbbing bulk of Blackhall Nuclear Power Station. It sat on heavy soil, in an almost flat, featureless landscape. Mr Wilberforce and his wife, Gertie, were clearly only just making a living in this unpromising spot. Some of their cucumbers were growing out of doors, others in primitive greenhouses. The greenhouses had their windows open on this sultry day.

Henry examined the diseased cucumbers, and to his relief the diagnosis was simple. A lesion had developed at the distal end, and the rot was becoming black as the pycnidia and perithecia of the pathogen were produced. Readers with more than a very limited knowledge of diseases of the cucumber will have deduced that this was black stem rot. Henry prescribed reduced humidity as the cure and, just to be on the safe side, took examples of the diseased cucumbers for analysis.

A mile or two down the road, he stopped for a pint of bitter and a sandwich in a pub, and overheard a remark about leukaemia. He began to wonder if there could be a link between the diseased cucumbers and the proximity of the nuclear power station. Excitement gripped him. Supposing he could prove a connection. BIOLOGISTS IN FERMENT OVER CUCUMBER MAN'S RADIATION AND LESION LINK.

The following morning, he took his cucumbers to Dave Wilkins in the Lab. The Head of Analysis (Practical) had long, unkempt greying hair and a beard that was almost white, even though he was only thirty-six. He had round shoulders and a paunch, and if he'd analysed his tee-shirt, he'd have found traces of fried egg, baked beans and Tetley's bitter on it. But he was extremely good at his job.

Henry asked Dave to look for evidence of radiation or any other abnormality which might be connected to the proximity of the power station, and which might have caused the black stem rot.

'Phew!' said Dave Wilkins. 'Radiation! We could burn our fingers with this one. I'm not sure it's within our remit, Henry.'

'Well whose remit is it within, then?' asked Henry. 'We don't have a Head of Analysis (Radiation).'

'I just don't want to tread on anyone's toes,' said the Head of Analysis (Practical).

'Oh God. Well, look, shall I clear it with the Director (Operations)?' suggested the Chief Controlling Officer (Diseases and Pests).

'Grateful if you would, Henry.'

Henry suddenly found that it was very difficult to ask to see Timothy Whitehouse to talk about radiation from a nuclear power station. He felt, as he walked down the corridor, that he was walking under the shadow of that vast industrial complex on the Durham coast.

He explained to the Director (Operations) how he'd heard a chance remark about leukaemia. He saw Mr Whitehouse's lips tighten and realised that he'd made a major error of judgement.

'I mean obviously I'm not suggesting that eating cucumbers could cause leukaemia,' he said.

'I should hope not.' The Director (Operations) thwacked his braces fiercely. 'That'd be great publicity. Just what we need. What are you suggesting?'

'That we check to make sure these cucumbers are absolutely safe to eat. That's our moral duty, wouldn't you say?'

'Right. Absolutely right.' Mr Whitehouse dialled an internal number. 'Dave? . . . I've got Henry here, Dave. Obviously it's vital to eliminate any possibility that licensed growers are selling radiated cucumbers. Check this one very thoroughly, will you? . . . Do you need written authority? . . . You'll have it. Thanks, Dave.' The Director smiled, and stroked his predatory nose thoughtfully. 'Your diligence is to be commended,' he said, but he said it through slightly clenched teeth.

That Saturday, Cousin Hilda arrived round about teatime, unexpectedly. A pile of old mattresses lay on the ground outside the Gleneagles. She gave a heartfelt sniff.

'What are those mattresses doing?' she asked.

'They're throwing them out,' said Diana.

'I should hope so. They look infested,' said Cousin Hilda.

They sat her down and offered her tea.

'Well, just one cup,' she said, 'and nowt to eat. I don't want to be a nuisance.'

'Of course you aren't a nuisance,' said Henry. 'It annoys me when you say that.'

'Well I were brought up to be polite,' said Cousin Hilda. 'It's a disgrace, those mattresses. I couldn't be doing with it, me. I'd have the council round. They're probably riddled with fleas. I don't know what this country's coming to sometimes. I get right choked up with it when I think on it. There are times when I'm glad Mrs Wedderburn isn't alive to see it.'

Diana poured tea. Only Cousin Hilda took sugar, and this discomfited her slightly.

'I've come wi' a request,' she said. 'I want to see our Doris.'

Henry and Diana were stunned.

'But you don't get on,' said Henry.

'Blood is thicker than water. I have more time to think now I've not got my gentlemen. I've never liked the sound of this Miles Cricklewood. I've always thought he sounds a bad lot. And then I thought, "Hilda, tha's a Christian. Tha shouldn't pre-judge." '

'Have some tea-cake,' said Henry, but Cousin Hilda shook her head. He took the piece instead, and savoured every mouthful, like a condemned man eating his last breakfast. How could he tell her about Uncle Teddy? Hilary would have helped him. Diana, splendid though she was, left such things to him. He decided to approach it gently, with subtlety and tact. As often happened, the words that came out weren't exactly what he planned. 'Miles Cricklewood isn't a bad lot,' he said. 'He isn't Miles Cricklewood either. He's Uncle Teddy.'

There was silence. Diana held a slice of lemon cake towards Cousin Hilda. She shook her head.

How would she react to such momentous news? Henry held his breath. When her reaction came, he was amazed that he hadn't realised what it would be.

She sniffed.

'Black stem rot,' said the Director (Operations), swivelling gently in his chair, and glancing at Dave Wilkins's report.

'And?'

'And nothing. Absolutely normal, thank goodness.'

Mixed emotions number 101 – H. Pratt feels enormous relief tempered with grave disappointment.

The tricks that the human mind plays never ceased to amaze Henry.

Well, the tricks that his mind played, anyway.

He was extremely nervous as the Ford Escort chugged its way

from Thurmarsh to Monks Eleigh. Several weeks had passed since Mr Whitehouse had told him that the cucumbers were normal apart from black stem rot.

Now, when Kate and Jack had gone to Spain, and Benedict and Camilla were with their father in Mauritius (their only visit to their father that year), it was at last possible to take Cousin Hilda to see Auntie Doris and Uncle Teddy.

Henry cared a great deal about Cousin Hilda. It was awful to think of her living alone, without a friend in the world. She hadn't moved into the rest of the house. The bed-sitting rooms where her gentlemen had lived and slept and, did she but know it, masturbated, were cold and dank. She inhabited only the basement – her little bedroom, her kitchen and scullery, her immaculate lavatory, and her cosy living room, where the smell of spotted dick no longer lingered but the absence of her gentlemen still seemed like a gaping hole. She went upstairs only twice a week, once to clean rooms that weren't dirty, and once for her bath. It was awful to think of her seven pairs of pink bloomers on the line every Monday morning, hanging limp in the rain, or fluttering bravely in the sunshine, or being hurled skywards by the gales. It was awful, and yet he loved her.

He cared a great deal about Auntie Doris and Uncle Teddy, alias Miles Cricklewood. It was awful taking packages from Uncle Teddy to Derek Parsonage, and from Derek Parsonage to Uncle Teddy, but he hadn't the heart to stop. It was awful to witness the slow but inexorable decline in Auntie Doris's mental powers. It was awful, because it was so touching that it took him to depths of emotion that he didn't always welcome, being an Englishman and a Yorkshireman, to witness Uncle Teddy's patience and kindness. It had been awful to be the regular unintended butt of Auntie Doris's tactlessness, and to be sent away to Brasenose and Dalton because Uncle Teddy and Auntie Doris were social climbers and didn't want to cramp their lifestyle. It was awful, and yet he loved them, especially now that they weren't bothering to be social climbers any more, and their lifestyle was gin and tonic, smuggled burgundy, wallflowers in a Suffolk garden, and Scrabble.

So Henry was deeply anxious about the coming meeting. Would a decent reconciliation be effected? And, in his search for something to take his mind off these worries, he faced up resolutely to a suspicion that he'd been resisting for two months.

The Director (Operations) and the Head of Analysis (Practical) were lying. The cucumbers had been affected by radiation. He didn't know quite how he knew. It was a matter of Dave Wilkins's uncharacteristic unease, and something about Timothy Whitehouse's smile, and he knew that the two men were in collusion.

Before he could work out the implications of this discovery, they were in Monks Eleigh, and pulling up outside the fairy-tale cottage, and Henry was saying to Cousin Hilda, 'You'll find Auntie Doris changed.'

'What's happened?' said Diana. 'There are no flowers.'

Uncle Teddy hurried down the drive to meet them, past wallflower plants, sunflower plants, sweet william plants, sweet pea plants, lupins and geraniums, and not one of them flowering in the whole garden.

'She's picked all the flowers to make the house look lovely for you,' he said. 'Not a word, eh? Business as usual. Savvy?'

He bent down to kiss Cousin Hilda, and to Henry's and Diana's astonishment, she accepted the kiss with good grace, albeit blushing slightly.

Auntie Doris came rushing out in a wave of scent.

'Hilda!' she said, and hugged her.

'Well I never,' said Cousin Hilda. 'Well I never.'

'Exactly,' said Uncle Teddy. 'Jolly good.'

'Terrific,' said Henry.

And so, on a tide of meaninglessness, they entered the cottage. There were flowers everywhere, in vases, jars, bowls, glasses, mugs, even eggcups. On window sills and occasional tables and bedside tables they stood in their profusion.

Henry and Diana stared at them in amazement, and Cousin Hilda sniffed.

Oh no, thought Henry.

Cousin Hilda sniffed again.

Don't be rude, please. She meant it for the best.

Cousin Hilda sniffed a third time.

'What a lovely scent,' she said.

Henry and Diana and Uncle Teddy tried to hide their astonishment, and Auntie Doris beamed.

'You've got the house really lovely for us, Auntie Doris,' said Diana.

'Thank you, Diana,' said Auntie Doris, and they were pleased that she hadn't said 'Hilary', but then she said, 'Don't just stand there, Geoffrey. Get them a drink.'

Cousin Hilda sniffed at the appearance of every gin and tonic and there was an awkward moment when Uncle Teddy said, 'What's all this sniffing, Hilda? Is it hay fever? Are the flowers upsetting you?'

'You know it isn't that, Teddy Braithwaite,' said Cousin Hilda. 'It's the drink. I can't change at my time of life.'

'Nor can we,' said Uncle Teddy.

'I don't think I expect you to any more,' said Cousin Hilda. 'But I can't pretend to like it. Shall we make a pact, Teddy? I don't comment on your drinking and you don't comment on my sniffing.'

'Fair enough, Hilda,' said Uncle Teddy. 'Spot on.'

They lunched on ham salads, which Auntie Doris carried in as if she'd prepared them, although they all knew that Uncle Teddy had.

As the afternoon rolled somnolently by, to the tune of bees and combine harvesters, they played Scrabble in the flowerless garden. Cousin Hilda had never played before, but Uncle Teddy insisted that she played instead of him.

'I'll umpire,' he said.

Cousin Hilda began, and after much delay she produced the word Tart.

Henry held his breath.

'What kind of tart?' said Auntie Doris.

'Tha what?' said Cousin Hilda.

'It's nice to know what you have in mind when you choose a word,' said Auntie Doris.

'A Bakewell tart,' said Cousin Hilda.

'Very good,' said Auntie Doris.

Henry produced Trained, Diana made Bottom, at which Cousin Hilda sniffed, and after much thought Auntie Doris plonked down Cow.

'What sort of cow?' said Cousin Hilda.

'Black and white Friesian,' said Auntie Doris.

Cousin Hilda's second word was Bed, and Auntie Doris said, 'Who's in the bed, Hilda?' and Henry held his breath, and Cousin Hilda said, 'I am. And I'm on my own, Doris,' and Auntie Doris said, 'Very wise.'

Henry made Grain, Diana Amber, and Auntie Doris, after much thought, Quurm.

'What's Quurm?' asked Cousin Hilda.

'A fruit,' said Uncle Teddy. 'It's a cross between a quince and a plum.'

'Perhaps my tart were a quurm tart,' said Cousin Hilda drily.

'Could have been, Hilda,' said Uncle Teddy uneasily. 'Could have been. Q on a triple-letter score. You've got thirty-six, Doris. Well done.'

Cousin Hilda struggled to make her third word, settling eventually on Rat.

'I'm sorry I'm so dull,' she said.

'Not at all,' said Uncle Teddy. 'A bit on the short side, but not half bad. Double word score too. You score six.'

Henry used the T of rat to produce Truffle. Diana used the L of truffle to make Lean and Auntie Doris used the N of Lean to form Zenoxiac.

'Very good,' said Uncle Teddy. 'That's *very* good. X on a double letter score is 16, so your word total is 34, Z on a treble word score, 34 times 3 is 102, C also on a treble word score, 102 times 3 is 306, 50 bonus for using all your letters, 356.'

'Oh my,' said Auntie Doris. 'What luck!'

'What's Zenoxiac mean?' asked Cousin Hilda.

'Containing foreign bodies,' said Uncle Teddy.

'How would you use it?' persisted Cousin Hilda.

'Well if a loaf of bread was found to contain a dead mouse, I'd say, "Goodness me. This loaf's very zenoxiac," ' said Uncle Teddy.

'How awful!' said Auntie Doris. 'Send it back.'

'No, no,' said Uncle Teddy. 'This is a hypothetical loaf and a hypothetical dead mouse.'

'Well mice frighten me,' said Auntie Doris. 'I wish you wouldn't invent hypothetical ones. Can't you invent something nice, like a hypothetical squirrel?'

'It wouldn't suit my example, dear,' said Uncle Teddy. 'You wouldn't find a dead squirrel in a loaf of bread.'

'Or a dead mouse,' said Auntie Doris, 'so stop being silly, Geoffrey.'

'Quite right,' said Uncle Teddy. 'Your go, Hilda.'

Cousin Hilda made the word Run.

'Well done, Hilda,' said Uncle Teddy. 'You score three.'

The game proceeded smoothly, if slowly, the afternoon drowsed, and Uncle Teddy announced the score. 'Well, Doris has won,' he said, 'with 677. Henry's a very good second, 166. Diana nudging him strongly, 161, and Hilda bringing up the rear, but not bad for a first time, 42.'

They had a pot of tea, and by the time they'd finished that, the sun had gone down over the yard-arm. They drank, and Cousin Hilda sniffed, and they didn't make any comment on her sniffing, and she didn't make any comment on their drinking, and they had chicken supreme, which Auntie Doris served but Uncle Teddy had bought and heated up, and at the end of the meal, when Auntie Doris went to put some more flowers in Cousin Hilda's bedroom, Uncle Teddy said, 'I don't want to pull the wool over your eyes, Hilda. You've been a sport today. There's no such word as Zenoxiac.'

'Well, Teddy,' said Cousin Hilda, 'tha's done a lot of things I can't forgive . . .'

'Admitted!' said Uncle Teddy.

'Tha's told disgraceful untruths and made dreadful deceptions.'

'No defence submitted!' said Uncle Teddy.

'So one little white lie isn't going to make much difference on the Day of Judgement,' said Cousin Hilda.

When Auntie Doris returned, Uncle Teddy said, 'Shall we have another game, seeing we're all one big happy family?'

'Now that's a right good game, that is,' said Cousin Hilda. 'Let's play Happy Families.

Henry and Diana's attempt to play Happy Families wasn't helped by the disappearance of Benedict. Camilla phoned from St Pancras in floods of tears.

'I went to buy a paper. When I came back he'd gone,' she said. 'That was an hour ago, and there's a suitcase missing. I just don't know what to do.'

'Have you rung your father?' asked Henry.

'Well, no. He's just said goodbye, and I think he's going out somewhere, and I knew you were expecting us, so I rang you, and my money's running out. Oh Henry, I'm so scared!'

'You just sit there, Camilla, with the luggage. I'll phone somebody to fetch you, and I'll drive down. Don't move till somebody comes that you know. OK?'

'Yes.'

'Good girl.'

'Sorry.'

'It's not your . . .'

But her money had run out.

Henry got no reply from Tosser's, but Mr Hargreaves was at home and said he'd cancel everything and go straight to St Pancras and rescue Camilla.

Henry phoned the police, gave a description of Benedict, left Diana at home in case he contacted her there, and set off on another nightmare drive. All the way down the M1 he rebuked himself. He'd done nothing. He'd hoped the Benedict problem would go away. Now it hadn't, but Benedict had. If only . . . if only . . . he arrived at Hampstead with an aching head full of 'if only's.

Camilla looked so much younger than her fifteen years, and so much less like a horse than she had ever looked, and to Henry's amazement she rushed up and dissolved into a flood of tears in his arms.

'We've tried Nigel, but no luck,' said Mrs Hargreaves, who looked worried but exquisite.

'It doesn't really matter now,' said Camilla. 'I'm with you. I want to go home, Henry.'

Henry found it disturbing that he could feel such gratification and joy in the midst of such worry. He phoned the police, who'd found nothing, and then, so keen was Camilla to get home, he set off after a quick bite of pâté and toast.

At half past eight on a tired late summer's evening Henry was on the M1 again. Camilla slept some of the way, and talked a bit about Mauritius, and said that looking back on it Benedict had been very quiet and serene but rather triumphant, as if he had something planned, so with that in mind and the suitcase gone she was sure that whatever had happened was of his own doing and that he'd be safe.

'Thank you,' said Henry. 'You're a wonderful girl.'

Camilla burst into tears, so he knew that she was pleased.

The following day, after a night of deeply disturbed sleep, Henry answered the telephone with no premonition.

It was Jack, ringing from Heathrow.

'Kate's disappeared, Dad,' he said, still almost phlegmatic. 'Vanished. Bit of a bugger, isn't it?'

The police issued photographs of both children, but they weren't given wide publicity, and nothing resulted.

Camilla and Jack, thrust into a situation not of their making, were amazingly good with Henry and Diana and with each other. Camilla didn't go riding, her heart just wasn't in it, and Jack abandoned, without any apparent regret, a trip to the Lakes with the Blairs. Between them, they even did the shopping and cooked simple meals, and they seemed to grow up almost by the hour. Cousin Hilda said, 'I'm just glad Mrs Wedderburn has been spared the worry,' and Henry and Diana lived through long nights where time made cruel sport with them. They told themselves that Benedict was seventeen and Kate sixteen. That was quite adult these days. But they knew in their hearts that on their own they were two children who knew nothing of the world and its many dangers.

On the fourth afternoon of their shared ordeal, Kate phoned.

'It's Kate, Henry,' screamed Diana.

'We're all right,' said Kate, and rang off.

They both went weak at the knees then, and began to cry with deep, deep relief, but it wasn't long before their relief became anxiety again. Where were they? What were they doing? Had Benedict known that Kate was phoning? How was Benedict behaving? What sort of boy was he, deep down behind the anger in his eyes? Would Kate get pregnant? And . . . oh, oh, oh but it was possible . . . would Benedict get violent? And . . . oh oh oh . . . oh oh oh oh oh . . . was it all their fault?

Kate phoned again on the eighth day and said, 'I'm coming home. I'm at Dartmouth police station.'

Longer and longer were Henry's rescue drives across England.

Kate looked at him, white-faced, and wild-eyed and shrivelled, like a cornered cat. He hugged her and said nothing, except, 'Where's Benedict?'

'I don't know,' she gasped between tears. 'I ran away.'

'They slept in an old hut up around the moor,' said the paternal, old-fashioned police officer. 'We've got search parties out. He'll be found.'

Sometimes Kate slept, and sometimes she cried, on the long, long journey home.

'Did he hurt you?' Henry asked very gently.

'No, no,' said Kate. 'He never hit me.' Then she burst into great sobs.

Henry pulled up at the roadside and held her tight and kissed the top of her head. Her hair smelt dirty.

'He told me he loved me,' she wailed. 'He didn't love me. He did it all to hurt you.'

Benedict didn't run away when the police found him. He turned and walked towards them, proudly. There were no charges. Kate had gone of her own free will, and he had used her, but not abused her, except that using is abusing.

He phoned Henry the next day, cool as a . . . as anything but a cucumber. Henry couldn't think of cucumbers as cool, now that there were suspicions about radiation lurking deep in the underground storage caverns of his mind.

'I'd like to come up tomorrow to collect my things,' said Benedict. 'I don't think I should stay in the same house as Kate any more. It'd be too awkward.'

So the next day Kate went to the Blairs. She was full of remorse and hurt and grief and anger, but the very enormity of Benedict's betrayal at such a tender age contained the seeds of her cure. It made home seem a very desirable place. It made simple childish pleasures like boiled eggs with toast soldiers very reassuring. It made her, briefly, into a girl again.

Jack also went out for the day. If he stayed he'd have been tempted to thump Benedict, and although he was two years younger he had such strength that he might have succeeded. It would be a disaster whether he won or not, so Henry gave him the money to go to the Scarborough Cricket Festival with his friend, Slim Micklewhite.

Benedict walked up the garden path, outwardly as cool as a lettuce.

Diana opened the door and faced her son. Henry stood just behind her, ready to give moral support if needed.

'Hi there,' said Benedict. 'I've come for my things. Those mattresses next door are *disgusting*.'

He refused their offers of tea, coffee and food, and he wouldn't meet their eyes.

'You should at least eat something,' said Henry.

'Not hungry.'

'What do you plan to do?'

'Go to Dad's. Frankly, I can't bear this grotty little town or your grotty little husband any more, Mum.'

Camilla stood in the kitchen doorway, a glass of milk in her hand, gawping in horror.

'That's an absolutely ridiculous thing to say, and you know it,' said Diana. 'Henry has done so much for you.'

'Has he fuck!' said Benedict.

229

'Ben!' implored Camilla.

'Stay out of this, Camilla. This is grown-up stuff,' said Ben.

Camilla went very red and tears welled into her eyes. She tossed her long hair angrily and stormed back into the kitchen.

Benedict moved towards the stairs. Henry was blocking his way.

'Are you going to hit me?' asked Benedict.

'I wouldn't hit a child,' said Henry.

'A child!' said Benedict. 'That's a good one.'

He pushed Henry out of the way and stalked up the stairs.

A moment or two later, Camilla followed him. She soon came downstairs in tears, and wailed, 'He told me to get out from under his feet. He said I'm a distinct pain. Brothers!'

She subsided into Diana's arms. Henry put his arm on hers. She kissed Diana and then Henry, and the three of them were still standing in the hall, arm in arm, when Benedict came downstairs with a suitcase and a hold-all.

'Oh my God!' he said. 'All happy together. A typical English family. Ugh!' His face twisted into fury. 'Don't you realise that he hates us, Camilla? Mum can't see it because she's so besotted. Surely you can?'

'I don't hate you,' said Henry in a voice which he hoped was cool, but which he knew had a crack in it, 'but I'll never forgive you for what you've done to Kate.'

Benedict put his cases down and moved towards Henry threateningly.

'Benedict!' cried Diana.

'That's right. Hit me. That'll solve everything,' said Henry.

Benedict stopped about three inches in front of Henry, and looked down at him. Henry had never wished for those few extra inches more.

'I'm not going to hit you,' said Benedict, suddenly loftily cool again. 'I don't hit wankers.'

'Oh good,' said Henry. 'At least we know you won't be punching yourself in the face, then.'

'Very witty,' said Benedict. 'Why don't you go and do another comic turn at Dalton? They're just about your level.'

He picked up his cases and moved towards the door.

'I'll be back for the rest of my stuff,' he said.

'Aren't you going to kiss me goodbye?' said Diana.

Benedict hesitated, looked as if he wanted to, then said, 'Not just now, Mummy. When you've left Henry, big kiss then.'

He opened the door with dignity, tried to walk through it with dignity, got his feet caught round his hold-all, stumbled out onto the path, and slammed the door furiously behind him. The china tinkled in the display cabinet in the hall, and then there was silence.

About twenty stunned unhappy minutes later Diana said, 'I hate to say this about my own son, but do you think we're wise to trust him? Should we check with Nigel that he really is going there?'

'Oh my God, of course we should,' said Henry. 'We're panicking. We're not thinking.'

Diana rang her ex-husband's number. Henry sat on the settee, holding her hand and listening. Camilla watched them earnestly from an armchair, and Henry noticed how her new maturity had changed her face. She was almost beautiful, and might become so.

'The Pilkington-Brick residence,' trilled Felicity, and Diana made a face.

'Hello, Felicity,' she said. 'Is Nigel by any chance in residence in his residence?'

'I'll fetch him,' said Felicity coldly.

Camilla gave her mother a brief, fond grin.

'Hello.'

'Nigel, it's Diana. Are you expecting Benedict?'

'No. Why?'

'Oh my God.'

'What's happened, Diana?'

'He's been here to collect his things. He says he's coming to live with you.'

'Oh. Well it's all very well for him to say that, but I'm not sure he can. He hasn't discussed it with us. I mean, truth to tell, he resents Felicity.'

'He resents everybody, including himself, but don't worry your tiny little mind about that, he isn't actually coming, your lifestyles are safe, if he was he'd have told you. He's lied to us and he's obviously going off somewhere.'

'Oh God. What's he up to now?'

'May I?' said Henry, pointing at the phone.

'Hang on, Nigel, Henry wants a word,' said Diana.

She handed the phone to Henry.

'Hello, Nigel,' said Henry. It was too serious a moment to call him Tosser.

'Hello, Henry. This is all a bloody bore, isn't it?'

'Listen, Nigel. Benedict left here about half an hour ago. Our only chance is to try the trains. I'm going to the station now. If I don't catch him and a train's gone that he might have caught, will you go to St Pancras and meet it?'

'St Pancras. That's miles away.'

'I know it's miles away but he's your son for God's sake.'

'Yours is his home and you've made a mess of dealing with him, that's the truth, isn't it?'

'There isn't time to argue, for God's sake. We must rush. Will you?'

'It's not as easy as that, Henry. I'm guest of honour at a dinner tonight. I'm Top Pensions Salesman of the Year.'

'I don't believe what I'm hearing. He's your son!'

'I'm not thinking of myself.'

'Huh!'

'Well, not only myself. There's Felicity. There's all the guests. The chap presenting the trophy's coming all the way from our Cardiff office.'

'You were my hero once. I'm off to the station. Here's Diana.'

Henry handed the phone to Diana and hurried out of the house.

He drove to Thurmarsh (Midland Road) Station like a maniac.

The London train had gone five minutes ago. He tried the bus station without luck, and then drove along Commercial Road towards Splutt, which was Benedict's most likely route if he was hitchhiking. There was no sign of him.

When he got home he phoned Tosser again.

'He might have got the 4.12,' he said. 'It gets to St Pancras at 7.57.'

'Look,' said Tosser. 'I see no reason why I should go, he's seventeen, he knows what he's doing, I'm not sure if it would do any good if I did go, though I hasten to add that I would go any other night despite that, but this whole event is about me and not to be there would be an enormous insult to a lot of good people, who've paid a lot of money.' He lowered his voice. 'Felicity is not a very strong or stable woman emotionally. Having Benedict here is not an option. I know it sounds brutal, but I have to think of Felicity's health. She's my ultimate responsibility.'

'Goodbye, Tosser,' said Henry.

'I want to change my name to Pratt,' said Camilla Pilkington-Brick.

There was still some hope for Henry and the world as 1974 drew towards its close. Life in 83, Lordship Road proceeded smoothly and the mattresses had finally been removed from the front of the Gleneagles. In Portugal, a bloodless military coup had overthrown President Tomas and Prime Minister Caetano, had seen the Socialist leader Mario Soares return from exile, and the end of censorship and the disbandment of the secret police. In Greece the long night of the colonels was over. Democracy returned joyously in a fizz of fireworks and a cacophony of car horns. 'What a fragile and precious gift democracy is, and how carelessly and apathetically we guard ours,' Henry told John Barrington in the pub one lunchtime, and John Barrington made his point perfectly without knowing it, saying, 'True. Better get those sandwiches ordered if we want a decent choice.'

There were clouds of course. The IRA bombed two pubs in Birmingham, killing nineteen people. And Benedict didn't return to collect the rest of his things. He didn't return to Dalton College either. The school heard nothing. Henry and Diana heard nothing. Tosser heard nothing. Camilla heard nothing and was very hurt. The police heard nothing and had more serious concerns on their hands.

233

Henry's contempt for Tosser was modified, during those winter months, by his knowledge of the way in which he himself salved his conscience with the thought that Benedict's absence was a good thing for every other member of the family.

Kate recovered from her experience slowly but steadily. The news that she had got nine O levels had boosted her ego at a vital time. She met a nice lad called Brian, who worshipped her, and she kept him at arm's length without being cruel. She would survive.

Jack was doing very well at football, was unlikely to do well in his exams, was known to frequent the Golden Ball in Gasworks Road, although he was more than two years under age, relished being the only boy in the house, and remained good-natured and cheery.

Camilla wanted to leave boarding school and join Kate at Thurmarsh Grammar School for Girls. Tosser resented this. 'I want her to have the best. I'm happy to pay. I did everything for Benedict.' In the end it was decided, democratically, in line with events in Western Europe, that she should stay at Benningdean until the end of the school year and then go to Thurmarsh Grammar if a) she was accepted and b) she still wanted to. She was becoming much more interested in boys and correspondingly less interested in horses.

Henry dreaded the end of winter. The conviction that he'd been lied to about his suspect cucumbers seeped out of the storage cavern of his subconscious. He knew that he'd find it difficult to live with himself if he ignored the issue, but he was nervous of the problems he might face if he didn't. Is this the fighter who learnt to laugh at himself and performed a comic act to the whole school at the age of fifteen? you ask most reasonably. Do not forget, gentle reader, that since that day Henry had experienced a failed career in newspapers, a rocky career in cucumbers, a failed marriage and a failed step-fatherhood. His confidence was low. Fighting wasn't so easy now.

On March 13th, 1975, actress Viviane Ventura won her court battle to prove that millionaire financier John Bentley was the father of her love child, Schehezerazade. Mr Bentley, seemingly ignorant of British politics, said, 'I was considering joining the Conservative party before this came up – now perhaps I ought to join the anarchists.' Seven-foot-tall US actor Rik Van Nutter opened a warehouse to sell off the spoils of his broken marriage with Anita Ekberg. Henry Ezra Pratt celebrated his fortieth birthday in modest fashion with a meal at the Taj Mahal restaurant with Diana, Kate, Jack and the Blair family.

Did life begin at forty for our hero? No. It merely continued.

Early in May he went up to County Durham again, and asked Mr Wilberforce, happily recovered from his kidney problems, if he could take a ridge cucumber and a hot house cucumber for analysis, 'Just to monitor the situation.' Mr Wilberforce, anxious to avoid further black stem rot, raised no objections.

That evening, Henry met Martin Hammond in the Pigeon and Two Cushions. There were still bells round the walls of the gleaming little black bar, but Oscar had long gone. During his forty years Henry had seen eras end as quickly as the promises of Prime Ministers. Golden ages had died like hares at harvest time. Halcyon days had disappeared like dissidents in Argentina. Now another golden age had gone. Another era had ended. The halcyon days of waiters in northern pubs had gone for ever. And, to add insult to injury, there was a fruit machine.

'Awful news about Tommy Marsden,' said Henry.

'Dreadful. If I'd said to you, twenty years ago, when he had the world at his feet, "I wouldn't be surprised if he ends up driving his car into a gravel pit outside Newark while blind drunk," you'd have thought I was mad.'

'I went to the funeral. It was a bleak little affair really.'

'I'd have liked to. It clashed with an absolutely vital Highways and By-ways Committee.'

'No idea what happened to Ian Lowson and Billy Erpingham, I suppose?'

'Ian Lowson emigrated to Australia. I've not heard a word about Billy Erpingham.'

'That's it then. The Paradise Lane Gang. It's just thee and me now.'

They recalled the good, bad, indifferent old days in silence for a few moments. Then Henry broached the matter in hand.

235

'Martin? Do you, with your industrial contacts and your political contacts, know of a laboratory where I could have something very important analysed in secret?'

'I might,' said Martin Hammond cautiously. 'What is it?'

'Two cucumbers.'

'What??'

They waited while a fruit machine repairer and his fiancée walked past to the far corner. The fruit machine repairer gave the fruit machine a nervous glance, as if fearing that it might go wrong and spoil his evening out.

Henry lowered his voice to a whisper.

'They were grown near a nuclear power station. I want them tested for radiation. You could be helping to uncover a web of corruption and deception in which the great British public are cast in the role of suckers yet again. You could help rock a major industry and embarrass its leaders.'

'You're speaking my language,' said Martin Hammond. 'Can it be that your political consciousness is waking up at last?'

Henry scoffed, but Martin was right.

On Monday, May 26th, 1975, head teachers demanded protection from angry parents, Evel Knievel retired after crashing while riding his motor bike over thirteen London buses, and Henry discovered that the cucumber grown outdoors in County Durham contained more than five times the amount of radiation permitted by Government regulations.

That night, after Kate and Jack had gone exhausted to bed, Henry and Diana talked long and hard in the old-fashioned kitchen of number 83, with its battered free-standing dresser picked up cheap at auction.

'I think I'll have to resign,' Henry said. 'I don't think I've any option.'

'Well, there's no more to be said then, is there?'

'You don't sound pleased.'

'I'm not, but does it matter? Your mind's made up.'

236

'Diana! I didn't say that. Obviously I want to talk it over with you, or we wouldn't be sitting here.'

The kettle was boiling. Henry expected that Diana would go to it, but she showed no sign.

'What do you think I should do?' he asked.

'I think you should make a real, hard, long, thorough effort to find another job, and then resign.'

The kitchen, damp enough at the best of times, was filling with steam. Henry hurried to the kettle.

'If I get another job first, I'll be leaving as a career move, not as a matter of principle,' he said. 'Doesn't principle matter to you?'

'Well I suppose all life's a compromise, Henry. I think it's all very well having principles, but one has to eat, and how could we survive if you lost your salary?'

'Oh, Diana!'

'Hilary had her novels. I don't have anything.'

'Because you never wanted to have anything, and please let's keep Hilary out of this.'

He plonked her coffee down on the plain, inelegantly knotted pine table, picked up cheap at auction.

'I didn't work because Nigel hated the idea of my working,' said Diana coolly.

'And what Nigel said went, because you don't have a mind of your own.'

They stared at each other in silence.

'I see,' said Diana. 'I thought I had an amazing marriage in which we never had rows. I thought we loved and respected each other. That's what made living in Thurmash and having draughty houses and clapped-out cars and odd battered furniture picked up at auctions and skimping and scraping and not being able to see my schoolfriends and having to shop at Binns of Thurmarsh instead of Harrods and Harvey Nichols worthwhile. That's why I never once complained. All for nothing. When the crunch comes, you're no better than Tosser.'

Henry looked at her in horror.

'I don't want to argue,' he said. 'The last thing I want to do is

237

argue. Oh my God, Diana darling, I didn't realise you'd felt like that all these years.'

'Because I didn't tell you, because I loved you, so it didn't matter. So I'm a not completely empty-headed person. I do have a mind of my own.'

'I'm sorry. Of course you do.'

'I care about people, Henry. You, the children, our friends, Auntie Doris, Uncle Teddy, Cousin Hilda. I care passionately about other people, and I don't think I'm selfish.'

'You're not! Oh, darling, you're not.'

He tried to kiss her. She wouldn't have it.

'No. Listen to me,' she said. 'Hear me out. I don't think I'm capable of being roused by abstract issues. It isn't in me. So I can't be excited by matters of principle as you can. I'm just not made that way. Of course people shouldn't be eating radiated cucumbers. You should try to do something about it. I agree. But not resign.'

'Well, I'll try, but I have to accuse the Director (Operations) of deceiving me, and that won't go down well. It might end up with my being sacked. I'd rather resign than that.'

'Well yes.'

'I mean, what is life all about? Just to eat, sleep, make love, bring up children so they can eat, sleep, make love and bring up children to eat, sleep and make love? I'm forty. Shouldn't I be ready to act like a man? Isn't it important for you to know that your husband is strong and resolute?'

'Not terribly, frankly. If it was I wouldn't have married you.'

'Diana!'

'I loved you for your warmth, humour, generosity and sexuality, not necessarily in that order.'

The clock on the living room mantelpiece, bought cheap at auction, struck thirteen. Midnight already!

'More coffee?'

'May as well. I won't sleep anyway.'

Over the next cup of coffee, Henry made the point that, if he did resign, he could tell the newspapers and become a bit of a celebrity. 'That'd help me get other jobs.'

'It might label you as a troublemaker.'

'I can't be as pessimistic and cowardly as that.'

'You want your moment of glory, don't you?'

'Well I must admit I'd quite enjoy it. Wouldn't you?'

'Oh dear,' said Diana. 'No, I really don't think I would. I think I believe that glory is an illusion.'

They finished their coffee in silence. There didn't seem to be any more to be said.

The Director (Operations) read the laboratory report on Henry's cucumber and then leant forward, his expression grim, his nose more predatory than ever.

'So you sent this to an outside lab,' he said, 'and not to us.'

'Yes.'

The sun came out from behind a puffy little cloud and set the dust dancing in Timothy Whitehouse's office. It was an inappropriately delightful early summer's day.

'Do you believe our labs to be inefficient, Henry?'

'No.'

'Do you believe our labs to be *dishonest*, Henry?'

Henry gulped. The moment he'd dreaded had arrived. Be brave, Henry.

'Yes.'

'I see. Oh dear,' said Mr Whitehouse gravely. 'Well now! In that case . . .'

'I resign.'

'What?'

'I resign.'

'That's a bit hasty, isn't it?'

'Well, I thought you were going to sack me, and I thought I'd better get my resignation in first.'

'Sack you?' The Director (Operations) smiled. 'No, no. I wasn't going to sack you.'

'You weren't?'

'No!' A laugh played briefly on the Director's thin lips, then disappeared. 'We hardly ever sack people, Henry. It can mean such trouble. Tribunals, lawsuits, strikes, compensation. Oh dear no. I suppose if I found that a member of my staff was systematically murdering his . . . or her, we mustn't be biased . . . colleagues, I might seriously consider dismissal. In your case, no!'

'Oh. Well . . . er . . . what . . . er . . . what *were* you going to say?'

'I was going to say, "Well, in that case I don't see how I can recommend you as my deputy." '

'What? I didn't think you had a deputy.'

'I don't. But our masters in Whitehall have calculated that since the Board was created the paperwork has increased by 142 per cent, and three new posts need to be created. One of them is my deputy. In seven years' time I will retire. You would have been the man *in situ*. I can't say you'd have succeeded to my post. I can only say it would have been likely.'

Henry swallowed. Be brave, Henry.

'Why should I believe you?' he asked.

'Don't you trust me?'

The sun went behind another inoffensive little cloud. The room became dark and grim.

'You told me not to trust you,' said Henry stoutly.

'So I did. So I did. *Mea culpa! Mea culpa!* I should have told you not to trust me *over small and personal matters*. Over the great issues of our business I am probity personified. Oh dear, Henry. This is all a storm in a tea-cup.'

The sun streamed into the office again. 'Henry!' Mr Whitehouse's tone became deeply persuasive. 'One cucumber has shown evidence of radiation. One grower has vegetables that are affected. Cucumbers are distributed centrally. If one person ate a hundred of these cucumbers, I agree, wooden box time. Nobody will! Nobody is in danger. So why alarm the inhabitants of a whole region, of the whole nation, threaten a whole industry, on which so many jobs depend, because of one cucumber?'

Mr Whitehouse paused, waiting for Henry to speak. Henry hesitated. Oh yes, he did hesitate. And, because he hesitated, Mr Whitehouse felt compelled to continue.

'Between you, me and the mythical G.P., Vincent Ambrose retires in six years. It's not in the realms of fantasy that you might end up as Chief Executive.'

'Me, Chief Executive!' scoffed Henry. 'I haven't even been to university.'

'The tides of egalitarianism are licking at the saltmarsh of privilege even here, Henry. How would you like to be Chief Executive?'

'It seems a complete sinecure. I've only met him twice and each time all he talked about was my kettle.'

'Exactly. An easy job. A nice salary. A guaranteed smooth passage through this rocky existence. How is your kettle, incidentally?'

'Fine. No problem.'

'Good. I should have asked before. *Mea culpa!*' Timothy Whitehouse leant forward across his desk, predatory nose pointing at Henry. He pulled his braces out as far as they would go, and smiled with all the magnetism that he could muster, and it still didn't reach his eyes. 'Withdraw your resignation, Henry. Please.'

This was it. The turning point of Henry's life. He thought about his easy existence in the protection of the Cucumber Marketing Board. He thought about Diana. About the children. About the long search for work that might ensue, in the increasingly cold world outside. He thought how easy it would be to devote the rest of his working life to cucumbers. He thought about the excitement of existence, the privilege of existence, the brevity of existence.

'I'm sorry,' he said. 'I can't.'

'Oh well,' said the Director (Operations), letting his braces thwack back viciously against his chest.

'I did it,' said Henry. 'I resigned.'

'I knew you would,' said Diana. 'I don't know why you bothered to consult me.'

'Would you have rathered I didn't consult you?'

'No.'

'Well then. Are you really very upset?'

'I still love you, but yes, I am. Very upset.'

'Oh, Diana. I . . . er . . . I rang Ginny. I'm going to have to see her later tonight.'

'Of course you are!'

'To give her my story!'

'Not to Helen this time?'

'Of course not. She made a fool of me.'

'Still a woman, though. Always a woman.'

'Diana! This isn't like you. You've never said things like that to me before.'

Diana turned wearily towards him. She was wearing a Fortnum and Masons apron given to her by her mother. She held a half-peeled potato in her left hand.

'I've never been deeply upset with you before,' she said.

'Oh God.'

Henry met Ginny Fenwick in the Winstanley, which was the nearest pub to her flat. She was forty-four now. She had never been beautiful, but there had been a sexuality in her appearance which had always attracted men. She was hiding her sexuality nowadays, dressing unattractively, not using make-up, so that men wouldn't find her attractive, so that they wouldn't, ultimately, reject her. What a delicate property is confidence.

Henry wished that he didn't have a story to tell, that they could just sit and reminisce.

He also wished that she was more impressed with his story.

'We've got a new editor,' she said. 'He's a real weed. I don't think he'd be impressed by your cucumber. As for your resignation, you aren't a well-known figure. It's a Leeds organisation, not Thurmarsh. It's not got a great deal going for it.'

'But they falsified results last year.'

'You've no proof of that. You don't have last year's cucumber.'

'Well of course not. It'd have rotted. People could be dying because they live near a nuclear power station.'

' "Could be." I need proof.'

'Well go and find it. Dig.'

242

'I'm on a local paper, Henry. This is a story for the nationals, or for the local papers in County Durham, not for us. Oh dear, you look so crestfallen.'

Henry was crestfallen. He accepted Ginny's offer of a drink, but really he felt like running away to sea and never seeing anybody he knew again.

'Won't you do the story?' he said.

'Oh yes, I'll do it. For you, Henry dear, I'll do it. I'm just warning you that it may not get much of a spread.'

'That's a bit defeatist, isn't it?'

'I never got that job as war correspondent, as you may have noticed. Next week I'll review my eleventh amateur operatic company production of *Oklahoma*. I feel a bit defeatist.'

'Oh, Ginny.'

Ginny's story didn't make the paper. The local papers in County Durham were interested, and said that they'd monitor the situation. The *Yorkshire Post* was polite and took all the details. Some of the nationals expressed keen interest, and the *Daily Express* said, 'We're very grateful. It'll help us build up our dossier.' Nothing was ever printed.

Nothing had changed, except that Henry no longer had a job, he no longer had any confidence that he would get a job, and he no longer had any real confidence in his relationship with Diana.

Had it all been a dreadful mistake?

'Of course not,' said Martin Hammond, pompous, self-righteous, somewhat tedious Martin Hammond, who was now his only contact with the Paradise Lane Gang. 'Of course not. Not if you feel better in yourself.'

'I do and I don't,' said Henry. 'I feel worried. I lack confidence. Yet I feel I have a new inner strength.'

'Well, that's marvellous,' said Martin Hammond, in the Oscar-less bar of the Pigeon and Two Cushions.

'It's not much use if I can't do anything with my new inner strength,' said Henry. 'What can I do with it?'

'Go into politics,' said Martin Hammond.

13 Wider Prospects

On New Year's Day, 1976, an unemployed, perhaps unemployable Socialist called Henry Ezra Pratt awoke with a severe hangover and wouldn't have believed anyone who'd told him that within three years he'd have been adopted as Liberal candidate for the Parlimentary Constituency of Thurmarsh.

Nor would he have believed, as he crawled out of the bed from which his wife had long departed, and staggered ashen and ashamed into the bathroom, where he took twice the recommended dose of paracetamol, turned on the stiff cold water tap with great difficulty, and drank seven toothbrush mugs of fluoride and chlorine into which a little water appeared to have filtered accidentally, that within a week he would have been offered a job for which he hadn't even applied.

And, as he attempted to find in his right wrist enough strength to turn *off* the stiff cold-water tap in the ugly cold bathroom of his new and unloved home, he certainly wouldn't have been able to guess what the job would entail, and, if he had guessed, he'd have been astounded if he could have foreseen that he'd accept it.

A new and unloved home? Financial circumstances had forced them to sell the large, crumbling house in Lordship Road and buy a much smaller characterless box in Splutt Prospect, high above Commercial Road. What town other than Thurmarsh could possibly boast a street that afforded a view of Splutt?

A bed from which his wife had long departed? Diana had gone to bed white with anger and had fizzed out of bed like a firework while he was still pretending to be asleep. She'd said nothing unpleasant to him throughout his long fruitless search for a decent job. She'd supported his rejection of the post of attendant at the magnificent new gents' toilet in the bus station. She'd accepted, with quiet misery, that a bedroom for Benedict was no longer a necessity and they must move to a smaller house. It might have been easier if she'd fulminated furiously against her humiliation. Henry knew that she'd never allow her parents, or Paul and Christobel, to see 22, Splutt Prospect. She was becoming even more of an exile from her family.

Ashen and ashamed? All the frustrations and agony of his disappointments had come to the surface last night. Henry had wept – oh God, it was all coming back. He'd told her he'd have more respect for her if she showed anger – oh God, it was all coming back, that had been so unfair. He'd eaten all the Brie and practically demolished the bottle of calvados that Paul and Christobel had brought them from France. Oh God, it was all coming back. He hurried to the ugly cold bathroom and got there just before it all came back.

A bedroom for Benedict was no longer a necessity? Nothing had been heard of him by anybody. His disappearance was with them every day.

Kate was sad but staunchly supportive. 'Cheer up, Dad,' she'd say. 'Surroundings don't matter. Being a happy family is what matters.'

Jack had left school at sixteen, was working for a builder, learning the trade, and Henry hadn't the heart to blame him if he spent more time in the Golden Ball than in Splutt Prospect.

Camilla hadn't left Benningdean or changed her name to Pratt. She loved her mother and Henry. She didn't love Splutt Prospect. She loved Tosser's splendid house in Virginia Water. She didn't love Tosser or Felicity. She had a boyfriend in Chichester. She loved Chichester. Tosser paid for her to travel to Thurmarsh and school and Virginia Water, but not to Chichester. Her boyfriend's father was a butcher.

Kate had gone to Brian's for New Year's Eve, and Camilla to Chichester. Jack had been at a party. Joe and Molly Enwright had invited Henry and Diana to a party, but they couldn't face social gatherings just then. The Blairs had cooled towards them since Henry's resignation. Every life crisis attracts its unexpected defections.

It was twelve o'clock before Henry felt well enough to stagger downstairs.

Diana looked at him sadly over her mug of coffee.

'I'm very, very sorry,' he said. 'A new year. Shall we make it a new start?'

'I think we'll have to,' said Diana.

It was Henry's habit, in those long days without work, to trudge the streets of Thurmarsh every afternoon. A few days into January, as he was struggling up Commercial Road with a cruel easterly blowing him homewards and lifting the flap of what Jack called his 'flasher's mac', Henry met Derek Parsonage struggling down the hill but into the wind.

'Henry Pratt!' said Derek Parsonage. 'Fancy a drink?'

'It's half past three. They're closed,' said Henry.

'I'm a member of a drinking club.'

'Well I really ought to be getting home,' gasped Henry, the wind plucking the words from his mouth.

'Not yet sunk to drinking with villains?' said Derek Parsonage.

Any suggestion of priggishness was anathema to Henry, and within minutes he was being signed in, in almost pitch darkness, to a basement den called the Kilroy Club, in Agincourt Lane.

The bar room of the Kilroy Club was only slightly lighter than the lobby. Thick, dark curtains covered the windows. The lights were dark red and feeble. This was a room for those who were allergic to daylight.

There were only three customers, a villainous-looking trio seated in a corner with pints of John Smiths.

Henry recognised the owner immediately. He was Cecil E. Jenkinson, formerly of the Navigation Inn. He was badly shaven, had bloodshot eyes, a thin strand of greasy grey hair on an otherwise bald pate, a gap in his teeth and a huge paunch. He'd gone to seed.

But his brain was still sharp. 'Henry Pratt, may the gods preserve us,' he said.

'Yes. Sorry,' said Henry.

Cecil E. Jenkinson had banned Henry's father because he upset the other customers by going on about the war. Later, Henry had shopped him for allowing under-age drinking, and he'd banned Henry as well.

'Oh, what the hell?' he said. 'That's water under the bridge. What's your pleasure, gentlemen?'

'Something you can't provide, but while we're dreaming about it we'll have two large whiskies,' said Derek Parsonage, whose blackheads were worse than ever.

Cecil E. Jenkinson handed them their whiskies with a smile, but his eyes told Henry that he would never be forgiven.

'I've seen one of those men in the corner before,' said Henry in a low voice.

'Police,' said Derek Parsonage. 'Watching.'

'Watching?' said Henry.

'Villains,' said Derek Parsonage. 'Most of the villains in Thurmarsh get in here.'

'They look like villains themselves,' said Henry.

'Camouflage,' said Derek Parsonage.

'Camouflage?' said Henry.

'So that they look like villains and blend into the background.'

'There aren't any villains.'

'If there were they'd look like them and blend into the background.'

'Henry Pratt,' said one of the policemen.

'I beg your pardon?' said Henry.

'Bloody hell, everybody knows him,' said Derek Parsonage, seeming put out by this phenomenon.

'I took you home when you'd immersed yourself in the Rundle,' said the policeman.

'Oh yes!'

'Barely out of short trousers, you were, and very religious. But the second time I took you home you were a piss-artist.'

'How are the mighty fallen!' said a second policeman.

The three policemen laughed.

A huge man with orange hair and a scar down his cheek entered.

'A villain,' mouthed Henry.

'Police,' whispered Derek Parsonage.

The huge man sat at the other side of the bar from the trio.

'Why aren't they talking to each other?' whispered Henry.

'They're at loggerheads,' whispered Derek Parsonage. 'He's Rotherham. They're Thurmarsh. There's bad blood. Will you take a very important package to Teddy on Saturday?'

'Derek! The place is crawling with police!'

'Don't worry. They wouldn't recognise a crime if it leapt up and bit them in the arse.'

'Oh all right. I suppose so.'

'Good man.'

Bill Holliday entered.

'Henry Pratt, or I'm a Dutchman,' said the scrap king.

'Bloody knows everybody,' grumbled Derek Parsonage.

'It's called personality,' said Henry.

'Well, well, well,' said Bill Holliday. He slapped Henry on the back, bought him a double whisky, and lit a big cigar.

'I thought you were trying to kill me once,' said Henry.

'So I was told,' said Bill Holliday. 'I laughed. Thought I'd die. I'm not one of the real villains, am I, Derek? We all know who they are.'

Derek Parsonage flushed.

'Please, Bill,' mumbled Derek Parsonage. 'This place is crawling with police.'

'Spice of life, a bit of danger,' said Bill Holliday.

A red-faced, rather bloated man entered. Henry knew that he knew him, but he didn't know how he knew him.

'It's Henry Pratt,' said the bloated man.

'Bloody hell, I don't believe it,' said Derek Parsonage.

'You don't remember me, do you?' said the bloated man.

'No. Sorry,' admitted Henry.

'Market Rasen Market Garden,' said the bloated man. 'Eric Mabberley. You're with the Cucumber Marketing Board.'

'Was,' said Henry. 'I resigned on a matter of principle.'

'Good for you,' said Eric Mabberley. 'What are you doing now?'

'Drinking,' said Henry.

'Nice one,' said Eric Mabberley. 'Have a whisky.'

'Well, thank you.'

'Large whisky for my friend Henry,' said Eric Mabberley.

'Quite a character, our Henry,' said Bill Holliday. 'Knows everybody who's anybody.'

Derek Parsonage sulked.

Henry's head began to swim, but it was nice to be a bit of a character. Life was strange. Sometimes you were a nobody, and knew nobody, and sometimes you turned out to be a bit of a character, who knew everybody who was anybody.

'Fancy a job with us?' said Eric Mabberley.

'Are you serious?' said Henry.

'Very much so. We've just bought Market Weighton Market Garden, we need new staff, and I like the cut of your jib.'

'Well, that's very nice of you.'

'Besides, you have the one thing we lack.'

'Oh,' said Henry, pleased. 'What's that?'

'Knowledge of cucumbers,' said Eric Mabberley. 'We need a cucumber man.'

So Henry was reunited with the only things that he knew about – cucumbers. But it was pleasant work, with plenty of fresh air, and there was the challenge of the opening of the Market Weighton Market Garden, and it was pleasant to be a member of a smaller and less bureaucratic organisation.

They moved from 22, Splutt Prospect after only a year, buying a pleasant if simple stone cottage on the outskirts of Nether Bibbington, a hamlet to the east of Thurmarsh. 'We'll be able to invite your parents here,' said Henry to Diana, and she smiled, grateful that this was the nearest he'd ever come to acknowledging that she'd been ashamed for them to see 22, Splutt Prospect. The cottage's setting scarcely justified its name of Waters Meet Cottage, the meeting waters being little more than wet ditches, but the prospect was infinitely more pleasant than that of Splutt.

Kate could still get to Thurmarsh quite easily, and Jack lodged with his boss during the week and came back for weekends. In the summer he played cricket for Upper Bibbington, and there were riding stables nearby, and Camilla took up riding again in the school holidays.

It was a wonderful summer. The temperature reached the nineties on more than one occasion, and they often ate outside. Kate took her A levels on magnificent summer days, the like of which Britain rarely sees. There was a water shortage, and it was a trying time for cucumber growers, but the Cucumber Marketing Board stepped in with subsidies to prevent the price becoming uneconomic. Henry's attitude to the Board was much more positive now that he was on the growing side of things. He realised at last how right the Board was to be more on the side of the growers than of the public.

There was still no news of Benedict, and when they visited Monks Eleigh they lost heavily at Scrabble, Auntie Doris being able to make several unusual words, including Crunk, Yaggle, Zomad and Anquest, but all in all it was a good summer for the Pratts. And yet . . .

And yet, things weren't quite the same between Henry and Diana. There were no more serious arguments, there were happy times, but the closeness never quite came back. Their relationship had become a framework within which their separate lives could flourish, rather than being the centre into which all their other activities flowed.

Kate got her three A levels and was accepted by Bristol University. Diana took bridge and needlework lessons. Henry, never before a pub husband, became part of the early evening crowd at the Lamb and Flag in Upper Bibbington. Often, he'd get home just as Diana was going out to her evening class. It wasn't a bone of contention, and yet . . .

And yet Henry knew that there was something missing from his life, and when Martin Hammond suggested that he put his name forward as a Labour candidate for the Rawlaston Ward of Thurmarsh Borough Council, he accepted without hesitation.

'It's just a formality, of course, but there'll be an interview.'

'Fair enough,' said Henry. 'I hope in the Labour party it's what you know and not who you know that counts.'

'You're speaking my language,' said Martin Hammond.

The interview took place in the committee room of the Labour Club. Henry found himself sitting at a long trestle table, facing two men and a woman. Behind them was a portrait of Harold Wilson. The painter wasn't awfully good at people, but did pipes wonderfully.

Henry hadn't done much preparation for the interview, partly because he knew that it was a formality, and partly because something which he didn't quite understand was preventing him from giving serious consideration to his political views. His answers, therefore, were as much of a surprise to him as to anybody.

'You knew my old deputy, Howard Lewthwaite, didn't you?' said the Leader of the Council, Walter Plumcroft.

'Yes. I was married to his daughter,' said Henry.

A grave wave of longing for Hilary swept over him. Oh God, how he missed her. And now he'd missed a question.

'Sorry,' he said, 'I missed that. I was thinking about her. How . . . er . . . have you any . . . er . . . perhaps afterwards, Mr Plumcroft, we could have a chat?'

'Certainly. No problem,' said Walter Plumcroft, who was a sewage works manager. 'A few questions. Just a formality. Are you sound on unilateral nuclear disarmament?'

'Well, no, I'm not sure that I am,' said Henry. 'I think it would be obscene ever to use nuclear weapons first, but no, I'm not sure if we should concede all our strength at the negotiating table.'

There was a stunned silence.

'Are you steadfast against being in Europe?' ventured Len Pickford, no relation of the removals people.

'Well, no, I'm not,' said Henry. 'I don't think you can ever defy geography successfully. We're part of Europe and we have to be in there, shaping it.'

The silence deepened. Janey Middleton, who was a school meals superintendent, was the first to rally.

'We aim to nationalise a third of British industry in the next Parliament. Don't tell us you aren't in favour of that,' she said.

'Well, no, I'm not,' said Henry. 'I believe all our services should be nationalised, but none of our production.'

A wren's alarm call shattered the deep silence that followed this reply.

'Are you in favour of replacing the traffic lights at the end of Market Street with a mini-roundabout?' asked Walter Plumcroft.

'I don't know enough about it to have an opinion,' said Henry.

'I think you'd better tell us what you do believe in,' said Len Pickford.

'I believe in moderation and compromise,' said Henry. 'I believe in a balance between unions and management, between planning controls and the free market, between men and women.'

A bicycle bell, rather fiercely rung out in the street, caused Walter Plumcroft to jump.

'You aren't a Socialist,' said Janey Middleton. 'You're a wishy-washy Liberal.'

'I know,' said Henry. 'I've only just realised it. I'm awfully sorry for wasting your time.'

After the interview, Henry went to the Globe and Artichoke with Walter Plumcroft. The pub was next door to the playhouse and on the faded red walls there were signed photographs of theatrical luminaries, notably Dickie Henderson, Francis Matthews and Marius Goring.

As he sat at a corner table with Walter Plumcroft, Henry could feel his heart going like a pump at Mr Plumcroft's sewage works.

'So . . . er . . . are you . . . er . . . are you in contact with the Lewthwaites?' he asked.

'Oh yes. Yes,' said Walter Plumcroft.

'How are they?'

'Naddy's pretty poorly, I think. Spain's given her a few extra years, but it can't be long now. It's very sad.'

'Very sad. And . . . er . . . how's Hilary?'

'Fine, as far as I know. I don't know if she does a lot, but, yes, fine.'

'Is there . . . er . . . would you happen to know if there's . . . er . . . anybody in her life at all?'

'I couldn't say. I could ask.'

'Well, if you are in touch, that would be very kind. Obviously I care a lot about her, and I hope there is.'

Well, if he was thinking of going into politics, he might as well get used to lying.

The more Henry thought about it, the more he liked the idea of being a Liberal. He liked underdogs. He'd always felt a rapport with cucumbers because he saw them as underdogs, the Henry Pratts of the salad. The Liberals seemed to him to be the cucumbers of British politics. They would form a useful underdog triumvirate – the Liberal Party, cucumbers, and Henry.

He telephoned the Liberal Club and told them he wanted to join. They took his name and suggested he call in for a drink.

At the Club he was introduced to a committee member, Ron Prendergast, of Prendergast and Dwomkin, funeral directors. They sat in the bar, in a quiet recess, below a portrait of Asquith. They could heard the clunk of snooker balls from the back room. Henry had once thought that the carpet couldn't decide whether to be orange or green. Now he liked it. How our perspectives change, he thought. How little absolute truth there is.

'I looked you up in our records,' said Ron Prendergast cheerfully. 'You gave us the privilege of burying your father. Everything satisfactory, was it?'

'Well it *was* over twenty years ago,' said Henry, 'and I was only eleven at the time.'

'So you want to join the club? Splendid. We have a nice snooker room. We're open seven days a . . .'

'No, no. Well I mean, yes, I will join, but no, what I meant I wanted was to be involved politically.'

'Ah!' said Ron Prendergast. 'Well, I'll give you a form and you can fill in what you're prepared to do – address envelopes, man polling stations, canvass . . .'

'No, no. I mean, yes, yes, I'm happy to do those things but I meant that I actually wanted to get involved. I'd like to become a councillor.'

'Oh! Well! That's tremendous! We only actually have one councillor at the moment. South Yorkshire's a bit of a Liberal black spot, truth to tell. I mean, we're always looking for candidates. Well, you know, grand.'

'I'm not . . . to tell you the truth this has all come as a bit of a spur-of-the-moment job . . . I'm not actually terribly *au fait* with our current policies.' He liked the use of 'our'. It made him feel a Liberal already. 'Could we discuss policies a bit?'

'Ah!' said Ron Prendergast. 'Policies aren't really my forte. I'm more on the snooker side of things. Archie Postlethwaite would be your man for policies. He's our councillor.'

Two days later Henry met Archie Postlethwaite, who worked for an insurance company. He was small and sallow and had a grey goatee beard faintly tinged with orange, as if it had dipped into tinned tomato soup. They sat under Joe Grimond, and Archie Postlethwaite seemed as bemused as Ron Prendergast by his question about policies.

'My policy is to give satisfaction on local issues. Find out what people want, and fight for it. Democracy in action.' He clearly liked that phrase, so he repeated it. 'Democracy in action. We build our power base from the local issues upwards. That's the secret of our success.'

'But we don't have much success.'

'Not in Thurmarsh. Thurmarsh is a black spot.'

A white-haired old man with a stick hobbled to the bar and ordered a pint of bitter and a whisky chaser.

'So what about our policies at national level?'

'I leave that to the boys in London. That's the beauty of the Liberal Party. You don't have all the political baggage to carry around with you. Look at the trouble the other two parties have got into by having policies.'

The white-haired old man hobbled over to them.

'It is!' he said. 'It's Henry Pratt!'

It was the blackheads that did it. Without them, Henry would never have recognised Geoffrey Porringer.

'Geoffrey!' he said. 'Well well well!'

The very fact that one hasn't seen somebody for a long time can lead to a reunion begun with unsustainable warmth and enthusiasm. Seeing Henry and Geoffrey Porringer greeting each other like long-lost brothers, Archie Postlethwaite hurriedly eased himself away from further awkward questions about policies.

'So how long is it?' said Geoffrey Porringer.

Henry worked out that it was more than thirteen years.

'Thirteen years! Is it really? And you haven't changed a bit, young sir.'

Henry couldn't bring himself to say that Geoffrey Porringer hadn't changed, so he said, 'Oh! I have.' He patted his stomach. 'A bit more there.'

'Well, maybe,' said Geoffrey Porringer. 'Oh, it is good to see you.'

Henry thought this a bit odd, since the last time they met, Geoffrey Porringer had said, 'End of chapter. That particular album closed. I'd be happier if I didn't see any of Doris's family any more.'

'It's amazing that we should run into each other here,' he said.

'Not really. I come every day. Very set in my ways now. I didn't realise you used it.'

'I don't. I want to become involved in Liberal politics.'

'Are you mad? Keep out of politics, young sir.'

'I never liked you calling me "young sir". Now that it's so obviously untrue I like it,' said Henry.

'You're young to me.' Geoffrey Porringer took a sip of his whisky and winced.

'Pain?' said Henry.

'It's nothing. How's Hilary?'

Henry winced.

'Pain?' said Geoffrey Porringer. 'Are none of us immune?'

'Mine's emotional.' He gave Geoffrey Porringer a brief résumé of his emotional life.

'Oh well, life goes on,' was Geoffrey Porringer's considered comment on all the anguish and joy through which Henry had lived.

255

'I deduce you're no longer at the White Hart.'

'Oh no. Sold that years ago. Well, it almost killed me. Made me an old man.' A bitter tone was creeping into Geoffrey Porringer's voice. 'Doris, you see. I couldn't fill her shoes. Nobody could. Everything was as good as ever. I promise you it was. But would those twat-arses acknowledge it? Never. "You should have seen it in Doris's day." If I had a fiver for every time I heard that I'd be a rich man. All said in front of me, as if because I'm on the other side of the bar I can't hear, or because it doesn't matter because I'm not a real person. Twat-arses, customers, apart from a few. Twat-arses.'

Henry bought a round. Silence fell between them. The false warmth of their reunion was evaporating, and there was still the subject of Miles Cricklewood to broach.

'Cheers,' said Geoffrey Porringer. 'Well . . . tell me, young sir . . . how is the old girl? Still with that bloody vet, or has she found greener pastures?'

'She isn't like that.' He longed to tell him that Miles Cricklewood was Uncle Teddy. 'She's . . . er . . . she's in a bad way.'

'Oh?'

'Her memory's going. She's going slowly senile.'

'Oh dear.'

'It's a very trying situation, but Miles is immensely patient.'

'Is he really? Good old Miles.' Geoffrey Porringer let out a long sigh that was almost a whisper. 'Well well well.'

'What?'

'I've grieved over Doris for years, and all the time I should have been counting my blessings. I've had a lucky escape.'

'Oh no,' said Henry. 'It's she that's had the lucky escape.'

Henry wrote to the Liberal Headquarters in London, announcing his desire to become actively involved in Liberal politics 'at grass-roots level', because he thought that phrase would go down well. He got a nice letter back, assuring him that he was on file. He knew that he ought to pop in for an occasional drink at the Liberal Club, but he couldn't face another meeting with Geoffrey Porringer. It would untidy his curtain line.

One evening, as he returned from the Lamb and Flag in Upper Bibbington and met Diana leaving the house for her bridge, he heard the telephone ringing and got there just in time.

'Walter Plumcroft here.'

'Oh yes?' Who the hell was Walter Plumcroft? Oh yes! Labour Leader of the Council.

'You asked me to ring you if I found out anything.'

What? What about? Oh!! Hilary!

'Yes. Yes, I did. About Hilary.'

'Yes. It's good news.'

'Oh good.' His heart was thumping. She was free. She loved him.

'I spoke to her myself. She's in a relationship and it's very very stable. All's well.'

Henry's heart sank.

'Are you still there?' asked Walter Plumcroft. 'Have we been cut off?'

'No, no. No, no. Oh, that's terrific. Oh, that's a great relief.'

'Thought it would be.'

So that was that.

Henry took a week's holiday at the end of October, and went down south with Diana. A whole week together. Maybe their sex life would resume its former glory. But their Ford Escort was ageing, travelling was tiring, and it never quite did.

They stayed with the Hargreaveses for a few days. Mr and Mrs Hargreaves were sailing elegantly into the sunset together in a glory that was fading only slowly. Mrs Hargreaves contrived to make the lines on her face enhance her beauty. Mr Hargreaves remained handsome and serene. At the end of a dinner of baked aubergine and roast turbot, as they left the olive-green dining room, Mr Hargreaves hung back, and Henry realised that he wanted a word with him. 'I just wanted to say,' he said, 'that when you told me you were going to marry Diana I had my reservations. When you took her up north I had my reservations. I have none now. My daughter has never been as happy as she is with you.' Henry felt as if he'd been sandbagged. Why couldn't Mr Hargreaves have said that in the years when Henry had made Diana truly happy, instead of now, when he knew that her happiness was just a pretence?

They drove down to Benningdean and took Camilla out with her friend Sally Harper. At the end of a splendid lunch in the Rose and Crown at Spewelthorpe, as they were getting their coats, Henry heard Sally whisper, 'I like him. He may be a funny little cucumber man, but he's very sweet.' They visited Penshurst Place, and as they walked back to the car through the golden russet of a Kentish autumn, Henry said to Camilla, 'I gather you told Sally I was a funny little cucumber man.' Camilla went red and said, 'Yes, but only because I didn't know if she'd be able to see what I can see in you. I'd only really seen her with people out of the top drawer before,' and she went even more red, and Henry said, 'It doesn't matter, darling. I love you,' and Camilla said, 'I love you too . . . Daddy,' and tears sprang into Henry's eyes and slid down his face and he brushed them away and said, 'Oh dear. Aren't people silly?'

Back in London, they went to dinner with Lampo and Denzil. It was Denzil's turn to cook. It had dawned on Henry only gradually that nowadays it was always Denzil's turn to cook. He pointed this out to Lampo, who said, 'He won't let me in the kitchen. He's a little Hitler.' Denzil and Lampo were barely speaking when they arrived. Lampo had broken a tea-cup. 'He's absolutely livid,' said Lampo, who was now very senior in Christie's – or was it Sotheby's? 'It's literally a storm in a tea-cup,' and Denzil hissed, 'It's ruined the set. It's a storm in twelve tea-cups.' During the meal, Denzil irritated Henry with his fussiness, always doing bits of washing up between courses and coming to the table late for the next course, but Lampo showed no sign of irritation whatsoever, and after all, Denzil was in his seventies. It had dawned on Henry only gradually over their long friendship that, beneath their almost constant arguments, Lampo and Denzil loved each other very much. So it was an enormous delight to enter their stuffed, impossible little house, although it was also an enormous relief to leave, knowing that one hadn't broken anything.

On their way to Bristol, they spent a night in Paul and

Christobel's exquisite Georgian house. Christobel's food was lovely, and there was beautiful claret and port. In his gentle cups, Paul said, 'I really moved into medicine because I noticed how many holidays my father had,' in that low, exquisitely modulated voice that he had developed over the years. Every time Paul spoke, he sounded as though he was saying, 'Don't worry, Mrs Welkin. It's only a harmless cyst and we'll have you up and about again in no time.' This bedside manner worked on Henry so effectively that he said, 'Well, you do work hard when you're not on holiday, don't you?' instead of, 'You spoilt bastard. You don't know what work is.' When Paul said, 'We made a conscious decision not to have children. They interfere with one's work, and we neither of us really like children,' Henry was tempted to say, 'A person who doesn't like children only likes people when they're convenient to them. It's a real give-away of selfishness,' but he didn't, he said, feebly, 'Well, that's your choice, fair enough.'

There was only one minor contretemps. Christobel said, 'I hear you're involving yourself with the Liberals,' and Henry said, 'Yes,' and Christobel said, 'Well at least it isn't the other lot,' and Henry said, 'Well, I wouldn't. I hate the Tories,' and Christobel said, 'Oh, I meant Labour,' and then realised that Henry had known that, and Henry said, 'What a delightful ceiling rose that is,' and the tactful gear-change was so blatant that everybody laughed, and the awkward moment passed. In their exquisitely elegant spare bedroom, Diana thanked Henry for being so nice to Paul. 'I knew what you wanted to say. I can read you like a book,' and they held each other very close, and almost made love.

In Bristol they met Kate's new boyfriend, who was called Edward. He was handsome and intelligent, but intended to be an actor. Already, he had involved Kate in stage management. She was blissfully happy and looked extremely pretty despite all the hard work she had put in to conceal the fact. It was becoming politically incorrect to be pretty. Henry felt that this was a shame and had no relevance to the injustices and abuses which plagued the world. He also felt a wave of sympathy for poor Brian in Thurmarsh and hoped that Kate had let him down lightly. Not that he had any doubts.

Kate was kind. He found it difficult, in a long evening of pub followed by moderate Anglo-French restaurant, not to feel a certain jealousy of Edward, who had taken so much of his daughter's affection, but he resisted it with all the force he could muster. Edward made it clear from his attitude to Henry how warmly Kate had spoken of her father, and although Edward had been to Winchester, he was deeply ashamed of the fact, of his height and looks and talent, and would much rather, or so he thought from his lofty, privileged position, be a funny little cucumber man from Thurmarsh.

They arrived back at Waters Meet Cottage exhausted, and resumed the even tenor of their lives. Henry worked at the market gardens and drank in the Lamb and Flag, Diana learnt bridge, played bridge and went to Highland Dancing classes, and every now and then they saw each other and were pleasant to each other, and in this way an English winter passed.

The summer of 1977 saw the British climate return to normal after the unseemly excesses of 1975 and 1976.

Spain held its first general election for more than forty years. General Franco's long dictatorship was over at last.

In the newly democratic Spain, Nadežda Lewthwaite died.

Lightning plunged New York into darkness for one long, terrible night. Fires were started, thousands of stores were looted of everything from food to new cars. 3,200 looters were arrested, but the authorities couldn't contain the rampaging mobs. How fragile is our civilisation! How miraculous it is that democracy should ever be introduced!

How disappointing it was that Henry heard nothing from the Liberal Party!

Elvis Presley died.

Henry and Diana discovered that Benedict was not dead.

One morning in September there was a letter from Tosser:

Dear Henry and Diana,
I've been endeavouring to make telephonic communi-

cation with you, but it seems that you're always out. What a social whirl it must be up there in Nether Bibbington. I'm quite envious.

The reason I'm contacting you is that I've had a letter from Benedict. He's working in a bar in Spain and is all right. His letter is very unsatisfactory, but I think you ought to hear it. I'm reluctant to send a copy as he might interpret this as a breach of confidence.

I hope you're both well.

With all best wishes,

Nigel.

Diana rang him immediately. Both their hearts were thumping. Henry sat on the settee beside her and was able to hear most of what Tosser said.

'The Pilkington-Brick residence.'

'Oh hello, Felicity, it's Diana.'

'I'll get him.'

'Thank you.'

'Hello, Diana.'

'Hello, Nigel.'

'This'll have to be brief. I'm due at a client's.'

'I'll be thrilled if it's brief, Nigel. Perhaps you'll read the letter.'

'Right.' They heard him call to Felicity. 'Darlesy-Warlesy, have you got the letter?'

Diana mimed being sick at 'Darlesy-Warlesy'.

Henry grinned.

'Thanks, Darlesy. Hello, Diana, are you still there?'

'Still here, Nigey-Wigey.'

'What? Oh! Diana! No, he says, and I must say it's all pretty unsatisfactory:

'Dear Dad,

'I thought it was about time I let you know that I'm all right. I hope you've been worried, but somehow I doubt it. I've been doing all sorts of things – helping in the wine harvest, et cetera

261

– and have finally settled running a bar with a friend near Malaga. That's all you need to know. I could do with a bit of dosh, and you were always decent in that department. I won't beg, but if you've got any spare from all your over-charging of your suckers, a cheque which I can cash here would be welcome. You can send it to Poste Restante, Malaga. I suppose I hope Felicity's well, she never did me any good, but she never did me harm either. I can hear you saying that I'm being pretty insulting if I want money. Well I hope you'd rather the truth than a lot of old poloney (is that the right word? The old vocab rusts a bit when you're abroad) about family and love just to get money from you.

'I hope that mother of mine is all right. I'll be happy to write to her when she's got tired of the cucumber man. Please give all my best to Camilla. I think that by the standards of this bastard world she's an OK person. Too OK for me to suggest she sees me here.

'I'll be grateful, in my way, for any dosh you can spare.

'Bye for now.

'Benedict.'

'Oh my God,' said Diana.

'Exactly. What do you think he means by "too OK for me to suggest she sees me here"?'

'I dread to think. You will tell Camilla what he says about her being OK, won't you?'

'Well I wasn't going to. It's hardly ringing praise, is it?'

'It is from him, you stupid oaf, and she'll be absolutely thrilled, she worships him still.'

'More fool her, and I did hope we might be able to discuss this in civilised language, Diana. I hope we're civilised people.'

Diana made a face at Henry. He grinned. Much more of this and they'd be in love again.

'Are you going to send any money, Nigel?' she asked.

'I don't know. I don't feel like it. It's a bloody arrogant letter.'

'You spend a fortune to get him taught to be arrogant, and then you complain. At least it's honest, though.'

'In its horrible way, I suppose. All that, "I hope you've been worried, but somehow I doubt it." That's an awful thing to say to a father.'

'It's an awful thing to have to say to a father.'

'Diana! Don't be so beastly.'

'I am beastly. You're so lucky to be with your magnificent Darlesy-Warlesy. Do you put a flag up when you're in residence? Or only when you're indulging in your brief, unsubtle love-making?' She slammed the phone down and burst into tears. 'Oh Benedict,' she wailed. 'Oh Ben!'

Henry hugged her, but couldn't comfort her. She needed other comfort now.

Henry had a week's holiday left. They flew to Malaga and toured every resort and every bar for fifty miles in each direction, showing a photograph of Benedict wherever they went. They found no trace of him, and arrived home exhausted, depressed and broke.

In October, Henry received a letter from a man called Magnus Willis.

> Dear Mr Pratt,
>
> I have read your letter about the Liberal Party and your desire to become involved. I've an idea of what form that involvement might take. I'll be in Yorkshire next week and wondered if you might be able to spare the time from your busy life to meet me for a drink at the Midland Hotel at 6.30 on Friday next, the 22nd.
>
> I must apologise for the short notice, but my travel plans have only recently been fixed.

So Henry found himself once more in that ungainly red-brick pile, the Midland Hotel, Thurmarsh. It was more than twenty-one years ago that he'd entered the hotel, twenty years old and aching with love, to spend a night with his childhood sweetheart, Lorna Arrow.

At the last count Lorna had had six children, and he was into his second marriage, but the Midland Hotel seemed to be in a time warp. The same vast armchairs, sagging terminally. The same huge, ugly chandeliers. The same photographs from the halcyon days of steam. Only the carpet, a light red, claret to the former's port, had changed.

Magnus Willis unfolded himself from an armchair, bounded across like a sex-starved wallaby, shook hands fiercely, said, 'Absolutely delighted to meet you,' took Henry into the bar, and said, 'What's your poison?'

'A pint of bitter, please.'

'Ah me!' sighed Magnus Willis. 'A bitter man. The common touch. I wish I was a bitter man.' He plumped for a glass of tonic water.

They installed themselves in an alcove.

'I thought this was better than the Liberal Club,' said Magnus Willis. 'Wagging tongues. Now, tell me your life story.'

Magnus Willis curled himself in his chair, legs tucked up in a pose that was at once strikingly foetal and so aggressively that of the fascinated listener that to his astonishment Henry found himself telling his life history.

'Absolutely excellent. First rate. Well done,' enthused Magnus Willis when he'd finished. 'Perfect. Needn't go into the first wife scenario too closely, but otherwise absolutely spot-on. Gloss over the newspaper connection, but otherwise tremendous. Needn't emphasise the cucumbers too much, but apart from that I don't think one could pick too many holes in it. And Thurmarsh through and through, that's what I like. Tell me why you're a Liberal.'

'Basically because I don't believe in dogma and I believe that interference by politicians in the running of the country should be kept to a minimum.'

'Go on.'

'I think we desperately need common sense and compromise in this country. I believe in moderation. There's nothing wishy-washy in being middle-of-the-road. It's a dangerous place to stand. I'm a passionate moderate.'

'You'll do,' said Magnus Willis.

'Sorry,' said Henry. 'What'll I do for?'

'Oh, didn't I tell you?' said Magnus Willis. 'Sorry. You'll do for our short-list of candidates for the Parliamentary Constituency of Thurmarsh.'

Henry gawped.

'It's nothing to write home about. We only have one councillor and he's useless. We've no local candidate who's remotely astute politically, and we must have one local candidate on the short-list. We've no chance of winning, but if you are chosen as candidate, if you put up a good show, a plum may follow. A nice by-election seat. Quite possibly a victory. We're rather good at by-elections.'

The 230,000 ton *Amoco Cadiz*, carrying oil from the Persian Gulf to England, broke in half in heavy seas off the coast of Brittany and caused the world's worst pollution disaster . . . so far. In Rome the body of Aldo Moro, the kidnapped and murdered ex-Prime Minister, was found in the boot of a car. The world's first 'test-tube' baby was born in Lancashire. Pope Paul VI died, his successor, Pope John Paul I, died after thirty-four days in office, and Karol Wojtyla, Archbishop of Krakow, became the first non-Italian pope for four centuries.

Henry had a quiet year. Kate was doing well at Bristol; Camilla surprised everybody by applying to go to art school and being accepted; Jack was building and drinking; Henry and Diana led not unpleasing but largely separate lives in Nether Bibbington, and the market garden company continued its expansion down eastern England, opening the Market Deeping Market Garden and the Downham Market Market Garden.

Just two things broke the even tenor of Henry's life.

The first occurred in May. He met Hilary in Fish Hill, right in the middle of the redevelopment that he'd fought to prevent. His heart stood still, and he fancied hers did too.

'What are you doing here?' he said.

'Looking for houses,' she said. 'We're hoping to come back. Dad hates Spain.'

'And you?'

'It doesn't really matter where I live.'

Her face was unlined. She hardly seemed to have aged. In fact she looked as if she had hardly lived.

'I often think of you,' he said.

'Do you?' she said. 'I often think of you.'

'Shall we have a coffee?' he said. 'Or a drink?'

'I don't think that's a very good idea,' she said.

'Are you . . . er . . . I heard there was a chap . . . are you still . . . er . . .?'

'Still happy? Yes. Yes, it's a very satisfactory relationship.' She held out her hand. 'Goodbye, Henry,' she said. 'I'm glad I've seen you. You look well.'

That was all. But his heart thumped and his stomach sank and his veins throbbed and he could hardly breathe and he felt that he was going to faint. He leant against the wall of Marks and Spencers and waited until it no longer felt as if his world was disintegrating into ten thousand pieces, and then he set off slowly and sadly on the long path back to real life.

The other thing that occurred was equally unexpected. After a gently polite but thorough grilling by the selection committee, he was elected as Liberal candidate for the Parliamentary Constituency of Thurmarsh.

Three days after he'd been elected, he opened the *Thurmarsh Morning Chronicle* and said, 'I don't believe it. I just don't believe it.'

'What?' said Diana.

'They've named the Labour candidate. It's Martin Hammond.'

'Oh dear.'

'Yes. A bit embarrassing.'

Five days after Henry had opened the *Morning Chronicle* and said, 'I don't believe it, I just don't believe it,' Diana opened the *Morning Chronicle* and said, 'I don't believe it, I just don't believe it.'

'What?' said Henry.

'They've named the Conservative candidate. It's Tosser.'
'Oh dear.'
'Yes. A bit embarrassing.'

14 A Dirty Campaign

On Tuesday, April 3rd, 1979, Mrs Thatcher opened the General Election campaign, promising tax cuts and warning the nation not to accept the attempt of James Callaghan, the Labour Prime Minister, to blame Britain's problems on the world recession.

On Wednesday, April 4th, the BBC admitted that their exclusive film of the Loch Ness Monster had in fact been film of a duck.

On Thursday, April 5th, Henry sat on a raised platform in the Committee Room above the Liberal Club, and listened to Mr Stanley Potts, Chairman of the Thurmarsh Liberals, introducing him to the small gathering of the faithful who had turned up for his adoption meeting.

Suddenly, all the nerves which had plagued him for the last weeks left him and he felt that he could even face the House of Commons without fear.

There were several familiar faces in the audience. Magnus Willis, who had turned out to be his agent. Archie Postlethwaite, the lone councillor. Diana, nervous and embarrassed. Jack, awkward but relaxed. Ron Prendergast, wishing he was downstairs playing snooker. Ginny Fenwick, hoping for fireworks. Eric Mabberley, a lifelong Liberal. Oscar, the redundant waiter from the Pigeon and Two Cushions. Mr Gibbins, six foot two, almost eighty, and as bald as a coot, in whose class, in the days when he'd been six foot four, Henry had emitted a legendary fart. And . . . it couldn't be. But it was . . . Cousin Hilda, who looked . . . yes . . . proud!

He stood up, to loud applause.

In a dark suit and orange shirt that matched his rosette, forty-four years old and becoming a bit of a roly-poly, with his hair streaked with grey and a bald patch on the top of his head, Henry was a comforting rather than an impressive figure. But he spoke well and with passion.

'Ladies and gentlemen,' he began. 'I'm grateful to you all for turning out tonight. I am Thurmarsh born and Thurmarsh bred.' There was applause. His old headmaster, Mr E. F. Crowther, from whom he'd stolen the phrase, had known a thing or two. 'I promise you that, if I am elected, I will serve the people of Thurmarsh with dedication, but I will not be a purely parochial politician. Better street lighting in the York Road area. . . , ' he paused, forcing them to applaud, '. . . will sit alongside the economy, the arts, the reform of our constitution and the conservation of our planet.'

He spoke briefly about the party's policies, about proportional representation, about a federal solution to Welsh and Scottish devolution, about democracy in industry, about replacing the House of Lords with an elected second chamber, about switching taxes from incomes to wealth and expenditure. There was laughter when he spoke of being thrown into the Rundle.

He concluded, 'I said at the beginning, "If I am elected." We start from a low base, but I don't believe that we have no chance. I wouldn't be standing if I did. I believe that the people of Britain are fed up with the counter-productive shuttle between Conservative and Labour dogmas. I believe that the people are hungry for change. I believe that, if we can make people believe that we believe, our hopes will not be make-believe. If we can inspire this town, we can win. I hate the complacent, easy patriotism of those who say that this is the best country in the world. If it is, with its incompetence and apathy, its prejudice and pettiness, its aggression and selfishness, God help the rest of the world. I suggest to you a greater, more honest, more difficult patriotism. Let's begin, here today, our battle to rid this country of its weaknesses. Let us say, "If we care enough, if we work together enough, this country *can become* the best country in the world." '

There was loud applause. Afterwards, people were warm with their congratulations.

'We've made the right choice,' said Magnus Willis.

'It's just dawned on me. You're the farter. Well, it's turned out not to be your only talent after all,' said Mr Gibbins.

'While you talked, I could almost believe I could be a political wife,' said Diana.

'I was proud of you. The whole market garden will be proud of you,' said Eric Mabberley.

'I shouldn't be out, not with my tubes. I've been bronchial since Christmas. But it were worth it,' said Oscar.

'It were very nice. I only wish Mrs Wedderburn had lived to see this day,' said Cousin Hilda.

On Monday, April 9th, Henry ran into Martin Hammond outside the Thurmarsh and Rawlaston Cooperative Society.

'Let's have a clean fight,' said Henry.

'I've nowt to say to thee,' said Martin Hammond, whose dialect was becoming more pronounced as polling day loomed.

Martin had telephoned Henry months ago, and said, 'I can't think how you can do this. You're a turncoat.'

'I've found that my true position is left of centre,' Henry'd said. 'I have to be true to myself, Martin. I believe Britain needs non-dogmatic, non-centralist government.'

'Cobblers.'

'Yes, I believe Britain needs cobblers too. We must support the dying crafts. Good point.'

Martin had rung off, leaving Henry to regret his cheap joke. He didn't want to argue with his old friend, and a couple of weeks later had written to Martin:

> Dear Martin,
> I'm sorry that at our last conversation I was so frivolous. It was to cover my embarrassment. I'd like to feel that during this campaign we can be gentlemen, and when it's over we can be friends. I respect your convictions, though I don't any longer believe they're the right way forward. I'm deeply opposed to the Tory Party, and will have no mercy for Tosser, but I'll oppose you honourably.
> With love and friendship,
> Your old mate from the Paradise Lane Gang,
> Henry

Martin hadn't replied.

On Wednesday, April 11th, Henry sat next to Tosser in the directors' box at Blonk Lane. All three major candidates declared their support for 'the Reds' though Martin hadn't been to a match for twenty-seven years, and Tosser had never been.

'Who'd have thought,' said Henry at half-time, 'all those years ago at Dalton, that you and I would share a wife and a constituency?'

'I asked you to keep Diana out of it,' said Tosser. 'But I suppose one can't expect honour from a grammar-school boy.'

Tosser was referring to a phone call he'd made to Henry several weeks before.

'Well, this is a funny situation, Henry,' he'd said.

'Yes.' Henry had been very dry. 'Did you ever get out to Malaga to try and find Benedict?'

'Well it's been difficult. I have sent money.'

'Money's easy for you. He might appreciate a bit of time spent on him.'

'He doesn't deserve it, Henry. Life's a two-way process. But this is what I wanted to talk to you about. Can we keep our families out of this?'

'If you wanted to keep your family out of it, it might have been better not to come to the constituency where your wife's second husband is standing.'

'I didn't know you were going to stand. And I hadn't told them Diana lived in Thurmarsh. Why should I? I never dreamt I'd be sent to your God-forsaken hole, and when I was, I thought it best to let sleeping dogs lie. I mean, I didn't have a choice of constituency, so what was the point of mentioning it? The aim of the exercise is to groom me, Henry. Lose with honour, get myself a nice seat somewhere in civilisation, with a nice fat majority.'

'Well I'll do all I can to make sure you lose without honour,' Henry'd said. 'I'll wipe you off the face of the map. I love my home town. I don't like to see it being used.'

Somehow, it didn't look as though it was going to be an overwhelmingly friendly campaign.

The opinion polls gave the Conservatives 49 per cent, Labour 38½ per cent, the Liberals 9 per cent!

All three candidates toured Thurmarsh in cars with loud-hailers. They toured the parts of the town where they might expect to win most votes. Canvassing wasn't about changing people's minds. It was about persuading your supporters to get up off their backsides and vote.

There were areas around Paradise and Splutt and York Road into which it was inadvisable for Tosser to venture, even though he'd been a rugby international.

There were areas like Winstanley and the streets around the Alderman Chandler Memorial Park where it would be a waste of time for Martin to canvass.

Henry's supporters were more difficult to locate. They could be anywhere. He had the hardest task, and he approached it with an energy and dedication which fired the enthusiasm of his helpers. He could charm people on the doorsteps. The canvassing returns were surprisingly good. He couldn't imagine that Tosser had a clue about talking to ordinary people, and Martin could hardly be described as inspiring. His confidence grew.

Every morning Henry held a press conference. He was never at a loss for a word. When his former colleague, Ted Plunkett, asked him where he stood on Europe, there was just a little smugness in his voice, as if he hoped to discomfit Henry.

'I believe in Europe,' said Henry. 'We must fight against its absurdities – uniform envelope sizes, Euro-sausages and standardised tomatoes – but we can never afford to be against its principles. I'll tell you why. Portugal has recently become a democracy after fifty years, Spain after forty years, Greece has emerged from the rule of the military junta, Germany and Austria were under the mad rule of Hitler not so long ago, while Italy had Mussolini. Six major Western European countries with dictatorships in my lifetime. If we're all together in Europe, that cannot happen again.'

Ted looked disappointed at that fluent answer from the man whom his wife had been known to fancy. Henry's confidence grew.

As polling day grew closer a report recommended a 100 per cent pay rise for MPs.

Mr Callaghan said that the defeat of inflation and unemployment took top priority.

Mrs Thatcher promised greater respect for law and order, improved education, a fair balance between rights and duties for trade unions, and the stopping of the stifling of individuality by the state.

Mr David Colclough, President of the National Hairdressers' Association, said in Bournemouth that windblown and unkempt hair could lose votes.

At the beginning of the evening of Friday, April 20th, Henry's hair was not windblown. Indeed, it was positively kempt.

By the end of the evening, Mr Callaghan, Mrs Thatcher and David Colclough would have been united in their disgust for him.

And the evening had started so well!

Henry was walking along Commercial Road, alone, after canvassing in Rawlaston. He'd told his team that he needed a few minutes on his own, to clear his head and marshal his thoughts.

To his amazement, to his disgust, to his utter and total joy, he saw Tosser Pilkington-Brick emerge furtively from the premises of 'World-Wide Religious Literature Inc.'

The Conservative candidate had been visiting a male brothel!

All sorts of lurid headlines passed through the mind of the former journalist. TORY CANDIDATE IN ARMOUR ORGASM SHOCK. PERVERT PILKINGTON DROPS A BRICK. BROTHEL BLOW GIVES BLUES THE BLUES. WHAT A GORY TORY STORY. No, he'd settle for something straightforward. CANDIDATE IN SEX SCANDAL SENSATION.

That evening, as chance would have it, Henry was embarking on a whistle-stop tour of the town's pubs. He was used to pubs. He was known in some of these pubs. He would do well.

Magnus Willis hated pubs and drank tonic water, a vote loser if ever Henry had seen one. So Henry's companion and minder was Ron Prendergast.

The pubs were quite busy almost from opening time. They

always were on a Friday night, which was why Friday had been chosen for this particular exercise.

They went to old haunts of Henry's – the Lord Nelson, the Pigeon and Two Cushions, the Devonshire, where the jazz had not yet started. They popped in at the Globe and Artichoke, the Artisan's Rest, the Coach and Horses, the Jubilee Tavern, the Nag's Head, the Tap and Spile, the Three Horseshoes, the Commercial, the Tipsy Gipsy and the Baker's Arms. In each pub, Henry had half a pint. He had to. It was part of his vote-catching exercise. It was his duty to his party.

He didn't discuss the issues, but chatted to people, told the landlords their beer was nicely kept, except in the Artisan's Rest, where nobody would have believed him. He called out, 'Good luck. Happy drinking. A vote for me is a vote for a good pub man,' and spoke of the old days when the pub had been one of his locals. All thirteen appeared to have been his locals, but he had been in eleven of them, and a bit of exaggeration is permissible during an election.

Ron Prendergast admitted defeat at the Baker's Arms, and Henry moved on alone to the Grenadier's Elbow, where he was to meet Magnus Willis.

Magnus, who'd been doing a major canvass in Splutt, entered the pub nervously but bouncily. There was a gleam in his eyes.

'Excellent returns in Splutt,' he said. 'People like you.' He sounded envious, about which Henry was sorry, and surprised, about which Henry was even more sorry. ' "He's like one of us," they say, and, "He's so ordinary," and, "I could imagine giving him his breakfast." You've got the common touch. We could be making history here.' He looked at Henry more closely. Some of the gleam disappeared. 'How many have you had?'

'Only thirteen.'

'Thirteen!!'

'Halves. Only halves. I'm as fit as a daisy. Magnus, I have great news.'

Magnus braced himself for the great news. All the gleam had gone.

He told Magnus about Tosser and the exotic brothel.

Magnus whistled.

'Are you absolutely certain?' he said.

'Absolutely certain.'

'We've got him! Not a word about this tonight, Henry. Leave it to me. I have to work out how to handle it. Oh, well done!'

The gleam had come back.

'Fancy a drink?' said Henry.

'No. No! Home now, there's a good chap.'

'Henry! My old mate!'

Colin Edgeley emerged from the roughish crowd at the bar, carrying a full pint with care.

'Have a drink, kid,' said Colin Edgeley.

'Just a half,' said Henry.

Magnus groaned.

'I'm not drunk, Magnus. One drink, then home like a good boy.'

'Right. I'm ordering you a taxi,' said Magnus.

Magnus went off to order a taxi, Colin returned, borrowed a pound from Henry, and bought him his half.

'A half used to be a "glass" of beer round here, and there were waiters,' said the Liberal candidate. 'What's happening to the world?'

'You ask them in Whitehall when you get there.'

'Too right. I will.'

'Are you coming up to the Devonshire for the jazz?'

'No. I'm going home.'

'It's not even ten yet.'

'I'm under orders.'

'Taxi ordered,' said Magnus, returning. 'Ten minutes.'

'Just time for the other half,' said Henry.

Magnus groaned.

When the taxi arrived, his agent took him firmly by the arm and frogmarched him to the door.

At the door, Henry wriggled free and turned round.

'I'm being sent home,' he shouted. 'I've been a naughty boy.

Would you vote for a naughty boy? 'Course you would. 'Cos you're all naughty boys too, aren't you?'

Magnus groaned.

'Waters Meet Cottage, Nether Bibbington,' Magnus told the taxi-driver.

He pushed Henry in and slammed the door gratefully. His job was done for the day.

As soon as they were out of sight of Magnus, Henry said, 'I don't want to go to Nether Bibbington or Upper Bibbington or any Bibbington. I don't want to go to Waters Meet. I don't like water. I want to go to Bitters Meet, otherwise known as the Commercial Arms in Devonshire Street.'

'Or even the Devonshire Arms in Commercial Street,' said the taxi-driver.

'That'll do.'

'I'm supposed to take you to Nether Bibbington. I've got a chitty.'

'Well I'll sign your chitty and give you a fiver.'

'Fair enough, Chief.'

So Henry found himself in the jazz club. It wasn't as crowded as in the old days. Sid Hallett and two of his Rundlemen were drawing the state pension now, and jazz wasn't hard enough for the new world that was coming.

He saw the journalists immediately. They were in a good strategic position, at a table close to the bar. Ginny Fenwick was there, and Helen Plunkett, née Cornish, and Ben Watkinson and his shy, no longer so petite wife Cynthia. Just the four of them. Not like the old days.

They greeted Henry warmly and with great surprise. A pint of bitter and a whisky chaser had been ordered before they realised how drunk he was. Colin arrived and said, 'How the hell did you get here?' and Henry said, 'Turned the taxi round,' and Colin said, 'You old rogue.' Henry couldn't finish his beer, but he accepted another whisky. It was extremely pleasant to sit with old colleagues in a bar and listen to ageing jazzmen greeting closing time with energy. Helen smiled at him and he smiled back and . . . and . . . ?

He was in bed. He was alive. His head hurt. The telephone was ringing. Where was he? The telephone had stopped ringing. He recognised that wardrobe. Where had he seen it before? At home! He was at home! How had he got home? He sat up and his head swam and he lay down again hurriedly. The telephone was ringing. What had happened? A blackbird was singing. It was morning! The telephone had stopped ringing. How had he got here? Where had he been last night? He remembered touring pubs and oh God yes turning the taxi round. The Devonshire. The blackbird had stopped singing. He remembered sitting in the Devonshire listening to Sid Hallett and the Rundlemen approaching what passed for a climax in their performance. He remembered Ginny leaving abruptly. Had he said something to upset her? He remembered Helen smiling. Had he upset Ginny by saying something to Helen?

The telephone was ringing. Why did the telephone keep ringing? It hurt his head.

It stopped.

He remembered a corridor. A dark corridor. A lawn. But indoors. Strange there should be a lawn indoors.

He remembered flashlights. Voices. Intruders. A lavatory. He hadn't felt well in the lavatory. He didn't feel well now.

The door opened.

Diana stood at the door.

She wasn't happy.

What had happened?

She gave him a look, half angry, half pitying. What did it mean?

'I'll stand by you until after the election or until you resign,' she said. Her voice was icy. Why was her voice icy? What did her words mean? The telephone was ringing.

'Why does the phone keep ringing?'

'Why do you think it keeps ringing?'

'What's happened? I must know what's happened.'

'Don't you know what's happened?'

'No!!'

She gave a hoarse, humourless laugh. He didn't like her laugh. He didn't like anything about this morning. He'd come out in a cold sweat.

'You'd better read the paper,' she said.

She handed him the *Thurmarsh Morning Chronicle*, which was to cease publication at the end of May.

He read the main headline. 'CANDIDATE IN SEX SCANDAL SENSATION.'

'Hurrah!' he cried. 'They got him.'

'What do you mean, "Hurrah!"?' said Diana.

He read on.

> The election campaign of Henry Pratt, the 44-year-old Liberal candidate for Thurmarsh, was in tatters last night after he was found in a naked love tryst on a pub's snooker table.

His blood ran cold. Icy sweat covered his body. He gawped at his icy wife. He remembered nothing. He read on.

> With him 'on the green baize' in the back room of the popular Devonshire Arms public house in Commercial Street was a well-known married Thurmarsh journalist, Mrs Helen Plunkett, who works for our sister paper, the *Evening Argus*.
>
> The couple, who have known each other for more than twenty years, were caught 'in the act' by Inspector William Bovis, after the police had responded to an anonymous tip-off.
>
> Another message, also anonymous, was received by this newspaper. There is as yet no indication of the identity of the caller, who was male and 'didn't have a strong accent'.
>
> Inspector Bovis said that the couple had both been naked, and charges might follow. 'I actually witnessed them engaged in an indoor sporting activity not normally associated with snooker tables,' Inspector Bovis told our reporter. 'There is no doubt in my mind that what I saw was sexual congress.'
>
> The landlord of the Devonshire Arms, Mr Wilf Cottenham (aged 52), said that the couple had been drinking in the bar

earlier in the evening. Mrs Plunkett had arrived with friends at about nine o'clock and Mr Pratt had arrived on his own more than an hour later.

'They'd both been drinking, but they weren't drunk or I wouldn't have served them,' he said. 'It's not that kind of pub.'

'I locked up at approximately eleven twenty-five, but didn't look in the Billiard Room,' he added. 'It's closed on jazz nights, so I had no reason to look.'

'I'm right choked about the table. It's torn in more than one place. They must have been at it hammer and tongs. It'll be a long time before anyone pockets any more balls on it.'

Mr Pratt appeared to our reporter to be very drunk indeed. 'Where's Chick Zamick?' he mumbled. 'In bed with Flory Van Donck, I'll be bound.' This was understood to be a reference to an ice hockey star and a Belgian golfer.

Mrs Plunkett said after the incident, 'Henry had been canvassing in pubs and was very definitely inebriated. He made certain suggestions and was very insistent. I'd been drinking and I yielded. I'm deeply ashamed of myself and just hope that I'll be able to patch things up with my husband.'

Rumours that Mr Pratt might resign were described as premature by Mr Pratt's agent, Magnus Willis. He said, 'It's a disaster. No question of it. But we'll assess the situation in the light of day, and I imagine that he'll attempt to prove that, despite this isolated lapse, he's the best man to represent Thurmarsh in Parliament.'

But the Conservative candidate, Mr Nigel Pilkington-Brick (aged 47), urged his opponent to resign. 'He's clearly not a fit person to represent the wonderful people of Thurmarsh,' he said. 'He should do the honourable thing.'

Henry's anger at Tosser's statement made his temples throb. He put the paper down slowly. He could hardly bear to look up and meet Diana's eyes.

'I'm so terribly sorry, my darling,' he said.

'So am I,' said Diana.

A small army of reporters and photographers was waiting outside the front door.

'I suggest I make a short statement and we pose for photographs, if you're game,' said Henry.

'Do you really think we should?' asked Diana.

'Yes. There's absolutely no future in skulking.'

Henry had taken a double dose of pills and drunk five pints of water. He had dressed very slowly.

Magnus phoned. Henry took the phone as if it was a hand-grenade.

'Hello, Magnus,' he said. 'Sorry.'

'What a pitifully inadequate word,' said his agent.

'Yes. Sorry. There's an army of pressmen here, Magnus.'

'Don't say *anything*. Not *anything*. Come to the club straight away, and we'll thrash out a statement. Understood?'

'Absolutely,' said Henry. 'Perfectly understood. I go out and talk to them, short statement, pose for photographs with Diana.'

'No, Henry!'

'Yes, Magnus! I've lost my dignity, my reputation and very possibly my wife. I'll do this my way, thank you.'

Magnus groaned.

Henry took a last glass of icy water, and said, 'Come on. Let's go.'

He tried to smile at Diana. There was no answering attempt.

He took a deep breath and opened the door. Sunshine and cloud, a horse running friskily in a paddock, a green van with dirty windows rattling towards the village. These things filled Henry with a breathtaking yearning for their unattainable normality.

The moment the door was open Diana took his arm and smiled.

There was a barrage of questions. Cameras flashed on all sides.

Henry held up his hand, and at last silence fell.

'I can't answer questions now,' he said, 'but I will make a statement. I don't remember anything about last night. I was drunk. I've read the morning paper, and I can only assume that I did what I'm reported to have done. I'm very, very sorry. I've let myself down, my party down, my family down, my supporters down, and above all my wife down. We've had a happy marriage for eleven years and during that time I've never looked at another woman. My wife is a wonderful woman. I hope that in time she'll forgive me. I don't intend to resign. Our policies haven't changed because of what I did. Thurmarsh's needs haven't changed because of what I did. The nation's needs haven't changed because of what I did. Has anyone got an Alka-seltzer?'

There was laughter, and even a smattering of applause.

Henry hadn't expected Diana to make a statement, but she began to speak in a firm, assured voice.

'This was an isolated lapse, completely out of character,' she said. 'My husband's a good man. Thurmarsh is lucky to have him. I'll be standing by him.'

They held hands, clutched waists, gave smiles of undying affection and love, and the cameras clicked busily.

The early edition of Henry's old paper, the *Thurmarsh Evening Argus*, carried the headline, IS THE CUCUMBER MAN'S CAMPAIGN SNOOKERED?

After the journalists had dispersed, Henry got a taxi to the Liberal Club.

'I'm fighting on,' he told Magnus, 'and I'm not going to ignore what's happened. I'm the one who has to face the world, knowing that every single person is talking about me and laughing about me. I do it my way.'

'Oh my oh my,' sighed Magnus. 'I age before your eyes.'

'Have you checked up on Pilkington-Brick and his exotic brothel?'

'It's a bit late for that now. We've vacated the moral high ground.'

'Then let's win it back. Pursue the matter, Magnus. Hound the bastard. That's an order.'

The first Asian Conservative candidate since 1895 said in Greenwich that 'bounders and cads should be flogged'.

Mrs Thatcher promised 'a barrier of steel' against the breakdown of law and order.

Mr Callaghan said that the reduction of 61,659 in the unemployment figures, to a total of 1,340,595, was 'no fluke'.

Henry told hecklers, 'I'm not perfect. Who is?'

He canvassed bravely. He met anger and disgust, but also sympathy and even a little admiration. He spoke about the incident frankly and promised never to repeat it.

He telephoned Helen at home from a call box in the pedestrianised Malmesbury Street, in the Fish Hill Shopping Complex. Asda stood now on the site of Uncle Teddy's old nightclub, the Cap Ferrat.

'Has it struck you that my line may be bugged?' said Helen.

'Can't be helped,' said Henry. 'I have a question I need to ask you. Did you set me up?'

'Henry! The anonymous caller was male.'

'Could have been Ted. Could be one of the obscure ways you two get your thrills.'

'Henry! That's awful!'

But he suspected that her anger was simulated, and he pursued the matter.

'Henry!' she said. 'I've been made to look ridiculous as well as you. On the green baize, for God's sake. Every grotty little sex-starved man in Thurmarsh is asking me to pocket his balls. It's appalling. And the editor's absolutely livid.'

He admitted that she had a point.

'Well, if not you, who did?'

'I'll try and find out.'

Henry and Magnus conferred at the end of the day's activities.

'I get the impression that all is not lost,' said Henry bravely.

'I've found that it may not be the total cataclysm I'd feared,' admitted Magnus. 'Oh, and Yorkshire Television want a live three-way debate between the Thurmarsh candidates. Suddenly Thurmarsh is big news. You shouldn't touch it with a barge-pole. You've too much to lose.'

'I've nothing to lose. I've lost already. My only chance is to fight back as publicly as possible. I'll do it.'

Magnus groaned.

'No luck with my enquiries, incidentally,' he said.

'What?'

'I tackled Pilkington-Brick head on. I said, "What were you doing in a male brothel?" He said he knew of no brothel. I said you'd seen him coming out of the premises of "World-Wide Religious Literature Inc." He said he was buying a Bible. He reads it every night for guidance and strength, and his old one is getting so well thumbed that it's falling to pieces.'

'I don't believe it!'

'Oh nor do I. I saw his face. I know he's guilty. To prove it we'd have to bust the place wide open.'

'Why don't you?'

'I spoke to Derek Rectory.'

'Parsonage.'

'Parsonage. He says he knows you. He says you deliver him regular consignments of forged paintings and carry fake jewellery to Suffolk for him.'

Henry groaned.

'It's true, is it?'

'I did carry packages for my uncle. I didn't get anything out of it.'

'Well, we can't do anything.'

'No. Bastard.'

This news jolted Henry badly. He got home at half past eleven, worn out. Diana was still up, and her mood was icy.

'In public I support you,' she said. 'In private we have separate rooms. I didn't want any of this.'

Next day it was raining, Henry's shame was as great as ever, he felt at a low ebb, and he faced two ordeals, one public, one private.

He dreaded the private one more.

He was pleased that Cousin Hilda was in. He could get it over with straight away.

He sat opposite her at the table where so many meals had been eaten. There was no smell of cooking now, and no fire burning in the blue stove.

Cousin Hilda sat with her severe spectacles and her pale pink bloomers – did they still make them or had she bought in bulk or was she wearing the same ones for ever? – and looked at him sadly and with great pain.

'You've read the papers, then,' he said.

She nodded grimly.

'I'm sorry.'

'Words are cheap.'

'Yes. But I really am. I know how you must feel.'

'It's not so bad for me. I have nobody to be ashamed in front of any more. I'm just grateful for one thing.' Henry knew what she was going to say before she said it. 'I'm just glad Mrs Wedderburn didn't live to see this day. It would have broken her heart.'

'Anyway, I felt I had to come and apologise to you personally.'

'Thank you for that.'

'I'm extremely grateful for all you've done for me.'

'Oh stuff and nonsense.'

'I'm going on television tonight.'

Cousin Hilda sniffed.

'Well, I know,' said Henry, 'but I think it's an opportunity to mend some fences. I hope you'll watch.'

'I might. You never know.' She paused. 'I don't usually watch ITV. I don't like the advertisements. But there's not much on our side tonight, to say we pay for a licence.'

He longed to leave. It was painful to feel so guilty. It was painful to have so many memories of this room. It was painful to think how unlikely it would have seemed, in all the years of the gentlemen, if someone had said that these were the vintage years.

'Well, I'd better be off,' he said. 'The campaign goes on.'

'If this were a sensible world, not a soul would vote for you. Not a soul.' Cousin Hilda looked at him severely, over her glasses. 'But it isn't a sensible world. It hasn't been for years. And I'll tell you this. I wouldn't give the other two house room.'

Henry felt that he had got off more lightly than he deserved.

Tosser Pilkington-Brick needed more time in Make-Up than Henry did! So Henry was already feeling quite good before the television debate began.

The three candidates sat in tubular, slightly futuristic chairs, facing the four cameras. The sound recordist fitted them with microphones, and the portly presenter, Dickie Blackleg, star of the hilarious quiz show *Whoops – I've Boobed*, entered and lowered himself carefully into a chair.

'Some people say they find the election campaign boring,' began Dickie Blackleg, 'but they aren't saying that in Thurmarsh. Henry Pratt, whatever else you've done, the fact that you've been liberal with your favours on a snooker table has galvanised this particular campaign. How do you feel about it?'

'I feel absolutely awful,' said Henry. 'How would any human being, who hopes he's decent, feel when he lets down his wife, his family, his party workers, his party and the voters?'

'Nigel Pilkington-Brick is the Tory candidate,' said Dickie Blackleg. 'You've suggested that Mr Pratt should resign. Why?'

'He's behaved in a deeply immoral fashion,' said Tosser. 'Who does he think he's representing? Sodom and Gomorrah? I'll tell you what. I think even the Sodom and Gomorrah Liberal Party would wash their hands of him.'

'Martin Hammond? Does the Labour Party think he should resign?' asked Dickie Blackleg.

'Yes, but not because of his sex life,' said Martin Hammond. 'Because he's a political charlatan.'

'We'll come to that later.' Dickie Blackleg didn't want politics rearing its ugly head and spoiling the sex. 'You've been caught "at it" naked on a snooker table. Have you a leg to stand on?'

'If people are disgusted with what I've done,' said Henry, 'they can tell me on polling day.'

During Tosser's next answer, he made a disparaging remark about Henry as 'the cucumber man'.

'I'd rather be a cucumber man than a financial adviser,' said Henry. 'I led the fight against pests at the Cucumber Marketing Board. I can recognise a parasite when I see one.'

'On the question of policy,' began Martin.

'Wait a moment,' said Tosser. 'I'm sorry, but I've been insulted. I have the right to defend myself.'

'Absolutely,' said Dickie Blackleg, who preferred an argument to policy any day.

'Financial advisers are not parasites,' said Tosser. 'I aim to enable people to use their money more wisely. I certainly aim to save them more than I am paid. I wouldn't sleep if I didn't. And I happen to regard standing for Thurmarsh as a privilege. You wouldn't catch me having it off on a snooker table.'

No, thought Henry, but you did go to a male brothel. Maybe Tosser expected some crack about that, because when Henry said, 'You told me you never expected to be sent to this God-forsaken hole,' Tosser said, 'That was a private conversation,' and Henry was able to say, 'So you admit you did say it? A God-forsaken hole,' and Tosser had no option but to admit it, but even Henry had to admit that his reply was a brave and effective damage limitation exercise. 'Yes, but that's before I came up here. I've never been so wrong in my life. I too can make mistakes.'

'You've been a Socialist all your life, Henry,' said Martin Hammond. 'You've turned Liberal purely in order to get selected.'

'I turned Liberal *before* I was selected,' said Henry. 'Yes, I believe in many of the Socialist aims – much greater social justice et cetera. I respect you. I don't respect Tosser. That's what we called Nigel at school.'

'Is this relevant?' protested Tosser.

'No,' said Henry, 'but we're on the telly purely because I've made an awful fool of myself, so I'm ruddy well going to say what I like.' He looked straight into the camera, pretending it was Cousin Hilda. 'I want to tell you what sort of man I am. Not tall, a bit fat, not brilliant, cocked up two marriages, sometimes drink too much, often feel useless, haven't achieved a great deal, *but* . . . *but* I am deeply sincere, I love my country, for all its faults, I love this God-forsaken hole called Thurmarsh, I care about people and the world and I would love, just love, the chance to serve the community and my party and redeem my life.'

When he got back to Thurmarsh, Henry expected a ticking-off from Magnus.

'I could hear you groaning,' he said.

'No, no,' said Magnus. 'No, no. You were right and I was wrong. You're a one-off.'

Gallup gave the Tories a 2 per cent lead across the nation, with the Liberal vote up to 13½ per cent.

Polling day was cold and bright, with occasional blustery showers. Henry cast his vote early. He voted for Martin Hammond, believing this to be the honourable thing to do. He spent the rest of the day touring the polling stations, encouraging the party workers. Everyone was in good spirits. Their vote was much higher than expected.

The Conservatives and the Socialists were also in good spirits. Their vote was much higher than expected as well.

If everybody who'd promised to vote for the three major parties had actually voted for them, the turn out would have been 167 per cent.

The count was held in the Town Hall, at long trestle tables. It was done at breakneck speed. Thurmarsh had secret hopes of being the first constituency to declare. It would be one in the eye for Torquay and Billericay.

Rumours began to sweep the hall. It was unexpectedly close. The Tories and the Socialists were neck and neck. The Liberals had done astonishingly well. Excitement grew. Martin Hammond looked sick at the unimagined possibility that he might lose. Tosser Pilkington-Brick looked sick at the unimagined possibility that he might win.

The candidates were informed that the Conservatives had won by five votes.

'I don't believe it,' said Tosser, going ashen. 'I demand a recount.'

'But you've won,' said the returning officer.

'I demand a recount too,' said Martin, who was shaking.

'I'm sorry,' said Tosser, recovering rapidly. 'It's the shock. This is beyond my wildest dreams. But I think it's only right to have a recount. I must be sure of my mandate. That's what I meant.'

As the recount began, Helen walked across the hall towards Henry. The conversational level dropped dramatically. All eyes were upon them. Henry could feel the blood rushing to his cheeks. He glanced uneasily at Diana. Helen's eyes looked feverish, as if she had a temperature, but he knew that it was the result of excitement.

'Is this wise?' he said.

'I was never wise,' she said.

The conversation level in the hall rose again, and to new heights, as everybody discussed Henry and Helen.

'It looks as though you may be doing all right,' she said.

'Yes. Not too bad, I think. You haven't lost your job, I gather.'

'No. No harm done, eh?'

Henry glanced at Diana again.

'I wouldn't say that,' he said. 'No, Helen, I wouldn't say that.'

He could see Ted watching them from the middle of a knot of journalists at the far side of the hall. He could see the gleam in Ted's eyes.

'Well at least you got to appreciate my legs at last,' said Helen.

'I don't remember them.'

'What? You said they were the most beautiful legs you'd ever seen. You said they were the most beautiful things you'd ever seen in the whole world. I hoped you'd feel that had made it all worthwhile.'

'Unfortunately, no. There's no value in an experience you can't remember. I'd like you to go now.'

'Perhaps we'd better do it again some time when you're sober, in that case.'

'No, Helen. Now everybody's looking at us out of the corners of their eyes so I suggest we shake hands and look as if we're parting amicably. Otherwise I'll turn away abruptly and it'll look as if I'm snubbing you.'

'Do you think I give a damn what people think of me?' said

Helen, and she turned away abruptly, leaving everyone in the hall to think that she was snubbing him.

The conversational level rose again.

Results were pouring in. It was clear that the Conservatives would win nationally. In Thurmarsh, the first recount gave Tosser a majority of one.

'I demand another count,' said Martin.

'Absolutely. You must have one,' said Tosser.

The second recount produced a dead heat. So far from being the first to declare, Thurmarsh looked as though it might have to carry on all night. Faces were ashen and drawn. The poor folk counting the votes were hollow with fatigue.

Martin looked devastated. So did Mandy. Tosser tried to look happy, but Felicity didn't even make the effort. Diana was bored and tired and angry. Only Henry didn't look devastated by the counting, and the rumour swept the hall that he had won.

The result was finally announced, after five recounts, at ten past five.

It was:

Tanya Elizabeth Bell (Ecology)	383
Martin Neil Hammond (Labour)	19,808
Terence Ingrams (British Hermit Party)	1
Nigel Timothy Anthony Pilkington-Brick (Conservative)	19,811
Henry Ezra Pratt (Liberal)	10,001
Ron 'Hardcase' Trellis (National Front)	1,404

There were loud cheers for Henry, who actually felt disappointed by the result, but even louder cheers, mixed with some booing, for Tosser, who managed, somehow, to smile and smile and smile. Felicity burst into tears at the result. 'It's the surprise,' Tosser explained. 'She's overcome with joy at the privilege of helping to serve this town.'

Henry could hardly bring himself to smile. Tosser had won. Martin had lost. It was a disaster.

Still, he must follow the protocol. He dragged himself across to Tosser, smiling broadly, and holding out his hand.

'Congratulations,' he said. 'Well done.'

'Don't be so bloody stupid,' growled Tosser. 'I'm going to have to buy a house in this disgusting town now. I'm going to have to visit it at weekends and hold surgeries. You bastard!'

'What's it got to do with me?' asked Henry, bewildered.

'You attacked me viciously, so all my supporters closed ranks behind me. You attacked Labour much more mildly, so their waverers all came over to you. Just don't expect a Christmas card.'

'I could cheerfully strangle you with my bare hands,' said Felicity.

Henry walked less confidently towards Martin and Mandy. They couldn't have looked more hostile if they'd been a couple of turkeys and he'd been Jesus Christ.

'Well, you've really done it, haven't you?' said Martin. 'You took our right wing *en masse*. You took nothing off him. Mrs Thatcher should give you a gong.'

'Judas!' said Mandy.

Tosser's agent approached Henry.

'Well done,' he said, 'and thank you. It was your success that saw us home.'

Henry smiled a sickly smile.

'May I ask you a personal question?' asked Tosser's agent.

'Go ahead,' said Henry wearily.

'They say that your wife, your very attractive wife if I may say so . . .'

'Thank you.'

'Was my candidate's first wife.'

'Yes. She was.'

'Has she ever been in a mental institution of any kind?'

'Good Lord, no.'

'The bastard!'

'I beg your pardon?'

'That was off the record. No, Nigel's story has always been that he nursed his first wife through a long mental illness and eventually had to put her in a home, where she died.'

'The bastard!'

'But a winner.'

'Not if I'd known that before today.'

'Don't worry. Our leader will be told what sort of man he is.'

'Oh, please, no. It'll get him promoted.'

Henry walked slowly towards the exhausted Diana.

Magnus bounced forward to intercept him.

'Why so glum?' he cried. 'Ten thousand votes in South Yorkshire. This is an amazing, incredible, unprecedented triumph.'

Somehow, Henry couldn't agree.

15 An Offer He Can't Refuse

One Saturday morning in 1981, almost two years after the General Election, as Henry was writing out his shopping list, the telephone rang.

'Hello. Is that Henry Pratt?' said a well-educated English establishment voice with not entirely successful pretensions to the fruitiness of eccentricity.

'Yes,' admitted Henry reluctantly.

'Excellent. I've caught you. I *do* hope this isn't an inconvenient time.'

'What for?'

Almost Fruity laughed. 'Very good! You're everything I've been told.'

'I don't think I've said anything amusing and just what have you been told and what is this all about?' said Henry drily.

'Right. Sorry. Anthony Snaithe. Overseas Aid. You've been suggested to me as a possible manager of one of our aid schemes. It would involve spending at least two years in Peru. Are you thunderstruck?'

'Well, yes. Yes, I am.'

'What do you say?'

'Well, good Lord, I . . . er . . . I mean, here I am . . . and suddenly to think of going to Peru, I . . . er . . . I mean there are so many things to take into account. I couldn't just say "yes" straight away.'

'No. Quite. Quite. But the significant thing to me is that you haven't said "no" straight away. You are prepared to entertain the prospect as a possibility, then?'

Henry looked round his bare, bachelor flat. He thought of the coming day – making his shopping list, going to Safeway's, going to the pub for a couple, watching the rugby, maybe nodding off, having a shower, going to the pub for a couple, cooking himself something from the stuff he bought at Safeway's, eating it, switching the television on and nodding off in the chair.

'Yes, I am,' he said.

'Good. We should meet for lunch. When can you come down to town?'

'Well, I haven't my work diary with me, but I should think I could come down to town any day the week after next.'

'Shall we say Tuesday week?'

'Fine.'

'Good. Do you know the Reliance Club?'

'Er . . . no.'

'Oh! Well, the food's only passable, but they do a legendary spotted dick.'

As the train slid slowly towards London, Henry's excitement grew. Peru. 'Manager of our aid scheme.'

Here at last was something to fill the yawning gap left by the collapse of his political ambitions. The Liberals had begged him to continue, but his electioneering memories had become inextricably bound up with the scandal on the green baize, his loss of Diana, and Tosser's victory, and he hadn't the heart to continue.

Here at last was something to free him from the emptiness that he'd felt ever since that morning, the day after the General Election, when Diana had packed all her things for the removal men, had denuded the house of its charm and vitality, had kissed him on the cheek and said, 'It hasn't really worked for some years, has it? Goodbye, my darling,' and he had stood there with the tears streaming down his face but hadn't called her back.

He opened his *Guardian* and there was an article about Peru in it. A good omen, even if the unfortunate misprint in the headline, which read, THE LAND OF THE SOARING CONDOM, seemed an echo of his own past disasters.

He read about condors and pan pipes, Inca ruins and pelicans, the mighty Amazon and the stupendous Andes, and realised how deeply, how terminally bored with cucumbers he had become.

Excitement beckoned. He began to feel nervous. As he passed

through the double doors of the grimy stone fortress that housed the Reliance Club, he wished he was taller than his measly five foot seven.

'I've an appointment with Mr Snaithe,' he told the porter, hoping he sounded confident.

'He's not here yet. He'll meet you in the reading room. First floor. Top of the stairs. Straight ahead.'

He walked up the long, broad, shallow staircase, between innumerable pictures of past members, most of whom were no oil paintings and should have been allowed to remain so.

At the top of the stairs there was a large mirror. The forty-six-year-old Henry Pratt who walked towards him out of the mirror had receding, greying hair, a distinct paunch and a suit that looked cheap and crumpled in these distinguished surroundings. Henry wondered, uneasily, whether he would give this man a job.

He entered the Reading Room. There were two other occupants, both holding copies of *The Times*. He didn't know what the form was. Should he say anything? He ventured a hesitant 'good morning'. One man, who looked about ninety, lowered his paper, gave a strangled grunt that might have been 'good morning' and raised his paper again. The other man, who looked somewhat older, didn't move a muscle. Henry assumed that he was deaf, or possibly dead.

He picked up the *Spectator* and looked through it, seeing nothing.

At last Mr Snaithe entered. He was tall – why was everybody so tall? – and slim and had a distinguished streak of grey in his jet-black hair.

'Henry Pratt?' he said.

'Yes.'

'Splendid.'

They shook hands.

'Let's repair to the bar.'

'Terrific.'

Henry chose a dry sherry.

'An excellent choice. I'll join you,' said Mr Snaithe.

The bar began to fill up. All the members were men and none of them were under forty. Mr Snaithe chatted about cricket and London restaurants and France. Henry longed to get down to business, but it wasn't for him to broach the subject.

A man whom he vaguely recognised detached himself from the throng and approached their corner.

'It's Henry Pratt, isn't it?' he ventured.

Henry stood up, thrilled to know somebody, but wishing that he knew who it was that he knew.

'Roger Wilton. We lived next door to you in Thurmarsh.'

'Oh! Yes! How are you?'

'Fine. Fine. And you?'

'Fine.'

'Good. I'll never forget that night when you'd been pushed in the Rundle and came home covered in sewage. What a sight.' He laughed.

'Absolutely. Huh! Most amusing.' Henry laughed mirthlessly, and glanced uneasily at Mr Snaithe.

'I'm sorry. I think I'm embarrassing you,' said Mr Wilton.

'No, no. No, no,' said Henry, but he didn't introduce the two men, and Mr Wilton returned to his friends in some confusion.

Henry gave Mr Snaithe a rather sickly smile. He didn't feel that the encounter had done wonders for his status in his prospective employer's eyes, and suddenly he wanted to go to Peru with a desperation that frightened him.

'Let's go and eat,' said Mr Snaithe.

'Terrific.'

He must stop saying 'terrific'. He'd caught a bad dose of the word.

The dining room was huge and high-ceilinged. Portraits of long-gone judges, cabinet ministers and explorers adorned the walls.

Henry chose oxtail soup and boiled lamb with white caper sauce.

'Make sure you leave room for the spotted dick,' said Anthony Snaithe. 'It's formidable.'

'Terrific.' Damn.

'How do you like the club?' asked Anthony Snaithe.

'It's very impressive. I can understand the appeal of tradition. But I personally would miss the presence of women.'

'Ah. You still have an appetite for them, despite all the problems you've had with them?'

'How do you know about my problems?'

'Everything's on file. Privacy is an outdated concept. The computer tells me there's nobody to detain you in England at the moment.'

'Unfortunately, no.'

'Though that may be fortunate for me?'

'I hope so.'

Henry hoped that they were about to get down to business, but the soup arrived and Mr Snaithe veered off the subject.

'A lot of men like to get away from women,' he said. 'Some are homosexual. Some are frightened of women. Some are frightened of their wives, who'll be much happier about their wasting their afternoon in a place where women aren't permitted than outside in the real world. And you know, Henry, the conversation of women can be really rather boring. Only last week I had a three-hour chat in this very room about Gloucestershire cricket. Impossible with a woman.'

The room hummed with the vicious gossip that men only feel free to indulge in when there are no women around to point out what an illusion it is that only women gossip. Throughout the boiled lamb with white caper sauce Mr Snaithe talked about life and literature and travel and painting and gardening and the art of relaxation, and Henry couldn't relax because he was convinced that his every word was being examined under Mr Snaithe's social microscope.

When the waiter brought them the dessert menu, Mr Snaithe waved it away. 'No need for that. We're looking no further than the spotted dick.'

Henry would never know how he managed to finish what would surely be his last spotted dick ever, especially if he went to Peru, but he felt that it was a condition of the job that he did finish it.

At last, over a glass of madeira, Mr Snaithe turned to business.

'Right,' he said. 'Now this little job. You'll have a team of six people, whom you'll help to appoint. When you get to Peru you'll recruit six Peruvians in preparation for the day when you withdraw and leave them to run the whole caboosh themselves. We've got twelve Range Rovers lined up, which will be shipped out to you. You'll be based in the Cajamarca Valley, which is a delightful corner of northern Peru. We're offering you a salary of £17,000, and after two years there's an option on both sides. How does that strike you?'

'Well, it's amazing,' said Henry. 'Absolutely terrific.' Damn! 'Er . . . the only thing is . . . what exactly is the scheme?'

'Cucumbers. We plan to cover the Andes with cucumbers. Why do you think we've picked on you?'

He took Jack for a meal at La Bonne Étoile, Thurmarsh's first French restaurant, and broke the news to him over the *moules marinières*.

Jack looked quite shaken, to Henry's surprise. He seemed such an independent soul.

'You'll be all right,' Henry said. 'We hardly see each other, anyway.'

'I know, but . . . I'm used to knowing you're there, if I need you.'

'You won't need me.'

'No. By the time you get back I'll have set up on my own.'

'Terrific.'

'We should see more of each other.'

'Yes. It's my fault.'

'It's a two-way process, Dad.'

'True.'

'We only appreciate things in life when we haven't got them, don't we?'

'My word. You're quite the philosopher.'

'Sometimes I think you think I'm as thick as two short planks, just because I'm not arty.'

'Jack! I don't! Did I sound like that just then? Perhaps I did. If so, I'm sorry. This sauce is too creamy.'

'I do them without cream.'

'You cook *moules marinières*?'

'Yes. Your builder son is not entirely uncivilised. Surprise surprise.'

'Sorry.'

'I'm a very good cook. Tell you what, Dad, come to dinner before you leave.'

'Terrific. We don't know enough about each other, do we?'

'No.'

'Jack? I go and see Cousin Hilda regularly, though not as often as I should. She's going to miss me very much.'

'I always mean to. I mean, I like her. I'm always going next week. Next week never comes.'

'Everything all right, sir?' enquired the waiter.

'Very nice, thank you,' said Henry.

'Why didn't you say the sauce was too creamy?' said Jack.

'Because I'm English. Maybe Peru will change all that.'

'Oh, Dad! Peru's so far away!'

'Jack!'

Their main course arrived. Henry had chosen *coq au vin*, Jack steak *au poivre*.

'Will you promise to go and visit Cousin Hilda while I'm away?' said Henry. 'Regularly. You don't need to stay more than an hour, but she'll appreciate it.'

'I promise. Have you told her yet?'

Henry made a face.

The waiter saw and hurried over.

'Is something wrong, sir?' he asked.

'Yes,' said Henry. 'I've got to go and tell Cousin Hilda tomorrow that I'm going to Peru.'

'I could get you something else, sir,' said the waiter.

Jack grinned.

Henry realised how much he was going to miss him, and how big a thing it was to be going to Peru.

'I'm leaving Thurmarsh, Cousin Hilda.'

298

'Leaving Thurmarsh?' She sounded appalled at such geographical recklessness.

'Yes. I've . . . got another job.'

'I see.' Cousin Hilda's lips were working with anxiety. 'Is it far away?'

'Er . . . quite far.' There are moments when death doesn't seem such a bad option. 'It's . . . er . . . well . . . Peru.'

'Peru??'

'Peru.'

'But that's abroad.'

'South America. But not for several months yet, and it may only be for two years and I'll get holidays.'

Cousin Hilda's hand flapped towards the coal skuttle, but the stove was out, so her favourite displacement activity in times of stress wasn't possible.

'Who'll bury me if I die when you're away?' she said.

'Oh, Cousin Hilda. Don't be so morbid.'

'It's not morbid. I'm seventy-five.'

'I'm sure you won't die, Cousin Hilda. But if you do, I'll fly back. I wouldn't let them bury you without me.'

She nodded, as if this was some slight reassurance.

'What does tha want to go to Peru for, anyroad?' she said in a disparaging tone.

'It's a fine country.'

'I'm sure it is, if you're Peruvian. You aren't Peruvian.'

'No. It's a British government scheme.'

Cousin Hilda sniffed.

'Governments!' she said disparagingly.

'I'm . . . er . . . I'll have twelve people under me. And twelve Range Rovers. And it's all in aid of the Third World. We're going to grow cucumbers all over the Andes.'

'How's that going to help the Third World?' asked Cousin Hilda. 'Do they like cucumbers? Don't they have their own cucumbers? They have potatoes. Potatoes came from Peru.'

Henry didn't dare tell her that he hadn't asked these questions, that he'd been so relieved to be asked to do something important that he'd taken it all for granted. He was astounded by her sharpness.

'They'll have researched all that,' he said feebly.

'You'd think they'd have learnt their lesson with groundnuts,' said Cousin Hilda.

Henry sold his flat and rented a bed-sitter in West Hampstead. Almost every day he saw Anthony Snaithe or his assistant. They held interviews, and sent the first two appointees to Peru to find accommodation and generally set things up.

Prince Charles married Lady Diana Spencer in St Paul's Cathedral, South Africa invaded Angola, Voyager 2 found that Saturn's rings were numbered in thousands, and in Chile, which was disturbingly close to Peru, President Pinochet banned all political activities for eight more years.

As the date for his departure drew near, Henry had a series of moving farewells.

His heart was heavy as he drove down to Monks Eleigh. It was quite likely that this would be the last time he saw Auntie Doris.

As usual, on his arrival, Uncle Teddy rushed out to meet him.

'It's one of her better days,' he said. 'She knows you're coming. She knows who you are. But, Henry, I suggest you don't mention Peru. Best she never discovers that you're away.'

Auntie Doris came down the path towards them, tottering slightly. There was a staring look in her eyes, and she was slowly losing weight. One side of her hair appeared to have been severely hacked.

'Hello, Auntie Doris. How are you?' he said.

'Oh, not so bad, Henry. Not so bad.'

'She cut her own hair yesterday, didn't you, Doris?' said Uncle Teddy.

'It's very nice,' said Henry.

'Oh, do you think so?' said Auntie Doris. 'I wasn't sure. It's not easy.'

'You're a clever girl,' said Uncle Teddy.

'Get him some tea,' said Auntie Doris.

'Right.'

Henry sat with Auntie Doris in the garden. It had been raining, but the sun was shining now, and steam was rising from the ground all around them. There were very few plants left in the garden, as Auntie Doris kept picking them all.

'How's Hilary?' she said.

'Fine,' said Henry. 'We've split up.'

'Oh dear,' said Auntie Doris. 'That is sad. Do you really like my hair?'

'Well, I think it's very nice, but I think next time you ought to have it done by the hairdresser.'

'So do I. I think I've made a right mess of it, to be honest, but Teddy says it's fine. He tells lies, you know. Maybe his mind's going.'

'I don't think so.'

'I remember now. Of course you split up with Hilary. I meant Diana. How's Diana?'

'Fine,' said Henry. 'I've split up with her too.'

'Naughty boy. You really are a naughty boy. Is Ollie going to open up tonight or do I need to?'

'Ollie'll do it,' said Uncle Teddy, bringing the tea things. 'Leave it all to Ollie.'

When Henry and Uncle Teddy went for their usual walk, past the green that led to the church, past the fairy-tale cottages, and round the corner to gaze over the bridge onto the little reed-shivering river, Henry said, 'I don't want to criticise, I think you do brilliantly, but don't you think it'd be better to correct her when she's wrong, tell her she isn't at the White Hart any more? Otherwise she'll spend all weekend thinking she is.'

'It doesn't work like that. She'll have forgotten all about the White Hart when we get back,' said Uncle Teddy.

'I mean I agree about Peru.'

'She'll forget how long it's been since you've last been. If she says, "We haven't seen Henry lately," I'll say, "Yes, we have. We saw him last month." '

'Will you let me know if she . . . if anything . . . well, you know. Obviously I'll fly back.'

'I will. Oh, Henry, I just hope I don't go first.'

They had a very pleasant weekend. Uncle Teddy warmed up some meals which proved highly palatable when washed down with smuggled wine and brandy. They played two games of Scrabble. Auntie Doris won them both.

As he was leaving, Henry couldn't resist teasing Uncle Teddy just a bit.

'Er . . . it may be quite a while before I get down again, Auntie Doris,' he said.

Uncle Teddy glowered at him.

'Oh dear, that's a shame,' said Auntie Doris.

'It may be towards the end of next month.'

Uncle Teddy relaxed.

'Oh well, that's not too bad,' said Auntie Doris.

It wasn't the wittiest bit of fooling in the history of the world, but it was better than crying.

Henry was appalled, on arrival at Lampo and Denzil's, to find that Tosser and Felicity had been invited.

'Why?' he said.

'Two reasons,' said Lampo. 'One – we're both so emotional. We'd cry buckets if we didn't have that greedy ape here. Two – you're angry with him still. Anger is so corrosive.'

'We love you,' said Denzil. 'We want you to be at peace in Peru.' He wasn't far short of eighty, but age suited him. He had turned into a distinguished old gentleman.

'I hope you'll come to visit,' said Henry.

'I couldn't bear it,' said Lampo. 'If your behaviour in Siena was anything to go by. You'll sit there, staring at the Andes in all their majesty, trying to work out how many street lights weren't working in Thurmarsh last time you went through it.'

'Of course we'll come,' said Denzil.

Tosser and Felicity were twenty minutes late.

'I couldn't find anywhere to park,' said Tosser. 'Sorry it had to be

302

mid-week, but we have to spend every weekend in bloody Thurmarsh. I went into politics to make my name, not meet a lot of wretched little people with breathing problems and defective damp courses and dogs with diarrhoea. And I'll be re-adopted there, and I'll probably lose next time, and that'll be the end of a glorious career, thanks to you.'

'You might not have won,' said Henry, 'if you hadn't got out of it – rather brilliantly for you – when I accused you of calling Thurmarsh a God-forsaken hole.'

'I know,' said Tosser. 'I go over it time and again to try and work out where I went right.'

Over Denzil's walnut and celery pâté, Felicity said, 'We were sorry to hear about you and Diana.'

'Yes, we were,' said Tosser.

'A difficult woman,' said Henry. 'Mental problems. Nigel knows.'

'I never knew that,' said Denzil. 'She always seemed fine to us.'

'*Hidden* mental problems,' said Henry. 'They're the worst.' He managed to convey to Denzil and Lampo that this was part of a game against Tosser. 'Still, Nigel, you have your bible to comfort you.'

'Bible?' said Felicity. 'Since when did you have a bible, Nigel?'

'Don't you remember?' said Tosser. 'I said in Thurmarsh that I'd bought a bible because my old one was so thumbed.'

'I never believed that,' said Henry. 'What were you really doing in "World-Wide Religious Literature Inc."?'

Tosser's eyes met his across the table and he could see the hatred in them.

'Canvassing, of course,' said Tosser.

'So why tell that whopper about the bible?'

'To win votes.'

'And in the end you won too many.' Then Henry changed tack abruptly, hoping to catch Tosser off-balance. 'Was it you who informed on me and Helen?' he asked.

'So what if it was?'

'So it was! Who told you?'

'The landlord. He'd spent fifteen years putting up with leftie jazz fans. He'd had enough.'

'I think you may have done me a favour,' said Henry. 'You enabled me to present myself as human.'

'I think I may have done.'

Suddenly baiting Tosser didn't seem any fun at all. Henry felt humiliated by the hatred he'd seen in the man's eyes. It was awful to hate, but it was even worse to be hated, because that was outside one's control. He knew that Lampo and Denzil had been right to invite him. He no longer cared what Tosser had been doing in Derek Parsonage's exotic brothel. If he couldn't get the satisfaction he needed with Felicity, it was sad.

Denzil had made a beautiful, uncompromising *daube* of beef. It was altogether too uncompromising for Felicity, who struggled from the start. Henry thought of how most of the women in his life would have risen to the challenge of dining with four men. Felicity seemed over-awed, and he felt sad for her and for Tosser.

He called Tosser Nigel several times, and praised Buckinghamshire, where Tosser now lived, in order to be nearer the M1 and Thurmarsh. He spoke of their early days at Dalton College, and how Tosser had seen off the bully J. C. R. Tubman-Edwards, and how he had worshipped Tosser for his athletic prowess. He made his peace, and Felicity was pleased and maybe one day the anger would depart from Tosser's eyes.

Over the orange syllabub they talked of France and Italy and Felicity continued to perk up. She even had a second helping of syllabub. She said how lovely the house was with all its knick-knacks and 'those divine biscuit tins'.

'Worth quite a packet, I should think,' said Tosser. 'Quite shrewd investments.'

'I don't buy them as investments.' Denzil was shocked. 'I buy them because it's fun.'

'Maybe Henry'll pick up some interesting biscuit tins in Peru,' said Felicity.

'Now there's a thought,' said Henry.

Tosser was saddened that none of them could see the true glory of art for investment's sake, and quite soon he said they had to leave.

'I've had a lovely time,' said Felicity. 'I don't know when I've enjoyed myself so much.'

When Tosser and Felicity had gone, Henry said, 'Thank you. You were right.'

Henry had been delighted to receive a letter from Camilla, saying that she'd like to see him before he went to Peru, so for his very last day, he arranged a farewell lunch with her and Kate. It had to be lunch, because Kate was working every evening as stage manager at the Unicycle Theatre in Willesden.

They met in a pub in Soho and went on to an ornate and fairly expensive Italian restaurant round the corner.

Camilla had developed into quite an extrovert. Her face, which had once been so horsey, had filled out and become cheerfully sexy in a way that reminded him of Diana.

Kate's pale, rather private beauty, illuminated when she smiled like a dark valley that is suddenly bathed in sunshine, reminded him painfully of Hilary. Now, when he was on the verge of departure, Henry realised how they had all said too little to each other over the years. Today, under what suddenly began to seem like the shadow of his absence, was a time for frank talk, no Anglo-Saxon evasions.

'How's your mother, Camilla?' he asked, as he attempted to eat his spaghetti *alla vongole* with fork only.

'Very well.'

'Is there . . . er . . . anybody in her life?'

'I rather think there is. I was awfully upset with you, you know, for a time.'

'I'm not surprised.'

Camilla was having no trouble with her spaghetti, but Henry splattered sauce down his shirt front.

'But I realise now that she was much happier with you than with Daddy. And that's something to be thankful for, isn't it?'

'We were very happy for a while,' said Henry. 'I'll never forget

305

those happy years. Then it began to go wrong, very slowly. It wasn't anybody's fault. That awful snooker table business . . .' His heart was pounding. His cheeks were red. He couldn't meet their eyes. But at least he was talking about these things, which he'd never before mentioned to his children or step-children, '. . . was a symptom, not a cause.'

Camilla and Kate were both embarrassed, but Henry knew that they were pleased.

Over their main courses – Henry and Camilla had sea bass, Kate a vegetarian pasta – they talked about Camilla's love life. There was somebody, a first-generation British Jamaican trumpeter called Leroy, and he was quite special, but not especially special.

'Terrific,' said Henry.

She was working in graphic design and drawing horses for fun.

'They're brilliant,' said Kate. 'Leroy says she's better than Stubbs.'

'She's prettier than Stubbs, anyway,' said Henry.

They laughed, and then they turned their attention to Kate.

She told Henry that she wanted to be a theatre director, and the job at the Unicycle, though poorly paid and very hard work, was part of the learning process.

'There are so many arty-farty people who think they know what they're doing,' she said. 'I want my work to be securely based. How's Jack?'

They talked briefly about how lovely Jack was, and this led to Benedict and general gloom. Henry told them about the fruitless search for him.

'Dad's done nothing,' said Camilla. 'You know, knowing Ben, I bet Malaga was a smokescreen. I bet he was somewhere at the other end of Spain.'

'Kate?' said Henry. 'We haven't really finished with you.'

'Oh Lord. That sounds ominous,' said Kate, laughing defensively.

'I've never really asked you about Edward. Don't tell me if you don't want to but I'd really like to know.'

'He was so mixed up. So guilty about his good looks and his

306

privilege and yet so ambitious for overnight success. When the chips were down the guilt all rolled away and he was just another ruthless upper-middle-class bastard. I loved him. I didn't like him. I think you need to like as well as love. I ditched him.'

'Well . . . right . . . gosh. So . . . er . . . is there anybody new?'

'Semi. I'm semi-detached. He's called Peter and we'll see. If it develops I'll write to you about him. Promise.'

Zabaglione wasn't on the menu, but they explained about Henry's going to Peru, and the chef agreed to make it. That was what Henry liked about the Italians. They were so sentimental.

Over the *zabaglione* Henry at last jumped off the cliff. He broached the subject that he longed and yet dreaded to hear about.

'And how . . . er . . . how is your mother, Kate? Have you seen her recently?'

'I saw her in the summer. She's all right. She still isn't writing, though, and it's such a shame.'

'Oh dear. And . . . er . . . this feller that she's got, what's he like?'

'What?'

'Her feller. This *zabaglione*'s absolutely delicious. I wonder what the food'll be like in Peru. What's he like?'

'What feller? She hasn't got a feller.'

'She hasn't got a feller? She told me she had. She told me it was a very satisfactory relationship.'

'You know Mum. She was trying to make you feel free to be happy with Diana. There's never ever been anyone but you.'

Mixed emotions number 127 – disbelief, joy, horror, regret, pride, shame and frustration.

'Oh my God,' he said.

'What? What, Dad?'

'Why the hell . . . why the bloody ridiculous stupid ironic unbelievable miserable soddish hell . . . am I going to Peru for two years tomorrow?'

16 A Dip into the Postbag

Apartado 823
Cajamarca
Peru
Nov 26th, 1981

Dear Hilary,

I know you'll be surprised to get a letter from me after all this time, and above all from Peru! I arrived here last week, to head an overseas aid project to save the Peruvian economy single-handed by planting cucumbers all over the Andes! But the point of my writing is to tell you that on the night before I left, Kate told me that there was nobody else in your life, and never had been, and that you'd told me there was so that I'd feel free to be happy with Diana.

I thought it extraordinary that you could be so self-sacrificial and then I realised how conceited that was and how probably it's no sacrifice for you after what I did to give up all further chance of a relationship with me.

Anyway, I discovered with extraordinary force how deeply I love you, and here I am stuck in Peru for two years. It's awful to feel stuck here because from the little I've seen so far it's a breathtaking country. I flew here from Lima over the Andes, feeling very safe in my first Third World plane, perhaps because of the free *pisco* sours, the delicious national drink of Peru, made of brandy, egg white and lemon.

Cajamarca is a flat, predominantly Spanish town, full of Quechua Indians. It gleams white in the mountain sun. It's set in a beautiful, broad valley, studded with irrigation channels and rich in eucalyptus trees. Indians in plaits and sombreros lead donkeys along the roads, and the majesty of the high sierras is all about. There's great poverty by English standards, but it's not a hopeless place, and the street scenes are very lively. I have a lovely shady apartment built around a patio in a beautiful old Spanish villa in the best part of town. As a British government official I'm important at last, which I find hilarious. Everything in the apartment is lovely, except for a picture of a rather fat Madonna, who looks as though she has wind, holding a rather fat baby, who definitely has wind.

This could be the most amazing experience of my life, yet all I can think of is that I'm not with you. Every crowd has an empty space at its centre, where you would have been. At every meal – and the food's good – there's an imaginary chair for you, my darling. I love you and would like to marry you again. I believe that I'm a better person now and that I could make you happy this time. Writing these words has given me an erection. Henry Pratt's libido is alive and well and living in Cajamarca.

Tomorrow work begins in earnest. I'll have my six English staff under me for the first time. 'Under me'! I'm a boss for the first time!

I hope you and your father are well. Please send him my best wishes and to you I send my deepest love,

Henry

XXXXXXXXXXXXXXXXX (One for every year that we have been apart)

Apartado 823
Cajamarca
Peru
December 5th, 1981

Dear Cousin Hilda,

This is to wish you a very happy Christmas and New Year. It'll be strange to be so far from Thurmarsh at the festive time and you'll be very much in my thoughts, and I'll have lots of memories of Christmases past, and all the fun we had with the crackers and paper hats and jokes and of course the delicious food. I hope you won't feel lonely and will be comforted by the memory of all the merry times and also by the fact that I'll be thinking of you.

Well, I'm busy setting up the project, and Peru will soon be covered in English cucumbers. Peru does have quite a lot of cucumbers already, which is a bit disturbing, and they don't rate them very highly. In fact there's a Peruvian saying, '*Me importa un pepino*' – 'I couldn't care a cucumber.' However, their cucumbers are short and stumpy, so maybe they'll like our long, firm English ones.

We're busy trying to find land. The Cajamarca valley is very fertile, but the best land is already in use. Still, we won't need the best land, as we'll be growing our cucumbers under glass. We've begun interviewing Peruvians for jobs, and have met some very interesting people of high calibre.

Our office is in Baños Del Inca, a village a few miles away. It has hot springs, and is the place where the Inca leader Atahualpa was having a nice hot bath when the Spanish invader Pizarro called on him the day before the Spaniards slaughtered his army in the main square of Cajamarca. I saw these events described once in a play called *The Royal Hunt of the Sun* by Peter Shaffer in London, so that is very interesting.

I look forward to hearing from you and will write again soon.
Happy Christmas and much love,
Henry

> Sarajevo
> Rua de Matelos
> Altea
> Costa Blanca
> Spain
> 14th December 1981

Dear Henry,

I was astonished to get your letter and even more astonished that it came from Peru! My heart raced terrifyingly when I read that you love me, and it races now, as I sit on the terrace on a sunny, but rather windy December afternoon.

Yes, it's true that I made up about there being somebody else. There has never been anybody else and never will be.

I love you still, Henry darling, and feel no anger towards you after all these years, and I certainly won't accept that all the blame was yours. If only I'd not been such a brittle reed and so hopelessly perfectionist. If I could have accepted that love is irrational and nobody is perfect, and tried to help you through your jealousy, how different things might have been.

I'm quite happy here, although I suppose my life isn't exciting. I look after Daddy, who is slowly growing old, and is missing England and all his political life dreadfully. We never found anywhere at the right price, prices have leapt in England, and we've left it too late. We're trapped in exile, and neither of us like it. This is not a criticism of Spain. I would love it if we were *of* Spain, we are only *in* Spain, and that's a horse of a very different complexion, as Mr O'Reilly might have said if he'd been a more loquacious kind of Irishman!

We're in the middle of doing a big jigsaw, and Daddy loves to do them together as he's really very lonely, so I must stop now.

Write soon.

With love,

Hilary

PS I nearly forgot. Happy Christmas!

Apartado 823
Cajamarca
Peru
Jan 2nd, 1982

Dearest Hilary,

I was delighted to get your letter, which didn't actually arrive till after Christmas. I'm absolutely thrilled to hear from your own pen that you still love me and always will. In fact reading your letter led to a solitary activity which has to be indulged in not too violently at this altitude! But your letter also puzzles me and worries me. You talk about our relationship as if it was all in the past. Surely, as we both love each other, we should be thinking of the future?

I want to ask you two simple questions. I've gone on bended knees to write the first one, so my writing may not be very clear.

311

Will you marry me? And the second question is equally simple. Will you come and live with me in Cajamarca? Please say 'yes', my darling.

You'll love it here, the landscape is on a grand scale. The valley throbs with vitality and fertility. The great hills are arid but steeped in melancholy beauty.

You'd get on well with the team. They're a fine bunch of blokes. I can hear you laughing at me. Yes, maybe in this far-off spot the public school ethos has got to me at last. We had a good Christmas. I even got a turkey and made my own crackers, which is what my lovely maid Juanita (sixty-six years old – no rival!) thinks I am. I thought of you constantly, and could only half enjoy myself, so thirsty was I for your reply. I'd promised Cousin Hilda to lay aside a moment to think of her, but I forgot. I did think of our dear, dear Kate and Jack and lovely Camilla and poor Benedict. I wish I believed in God, so that I could pray for him.

Other countries have aid schemes here. There are Belgians trying to plant trees everywhere, and a German is making German sausages. We all know him as Bratwurst Bernhardt, and I understand I'm known as Cucumber Henry!

Only two shadows darken my life. The Range Rovers haven't arrived and, more importantly, I don't have my beloved with me.

I should have said earlier that, if you can come, it will be fine for you to bring your father. I'm sure we can get you both on the payroll somewhere. Baños Del Inca is a long way from Whitehall.

With deepest love,

Henry

X (One kiss from you is worth a thousand from anyone else)

66, Park View Road
Thurmarsh
South Yorkshire
4th January, 1982

Dear Henry,

Thank you very much for your letter. Thank you for your good

312

wishes for Christmas and the New Year. I had a very enjoyable Christmas, if solitary. I did myself very well, but I avoided 'over-indulgence'. I were a bit badly over the New Year, but then I don't see the New Year in, believing that one year is very much like another. So did Mrs Wedderburn, incidentally.

Your news is very interesting. I have never had experience of 'foreign parts', finding the North York Moors a very satisfying run, so I cannot imagine the Andes. Are they at all like the North York Moors?

I were right touched to hear that you would be thinking of me on Christmas Day. I must admit I do feel a bit quiet at times, now that the Good Lord has taken Mrs Wedderburn and Mr O'Reilly, and the gay days of my gentlemen are gone for ever.

I were interested to hear that you are busy setting up your project, and that Peru will soon be covered in English cucumbers. I'm sorry the Peruvians have lots of cucumbers already, but interested to hear that theirs are short and stumpy, and pleased that you think you can do well with long, firm English ones. It were interesting to me that the Cajamarca valley is very fertile. Parts of the North York Moors are very bare. It's funny the way places differ. It was interesting that you had met some interesting Peruvians of high calibre. I were brought up to believe that there were very few foreigners of high calibre, and now it seems that the reverse is true. I pray to God for guidance.

It was interesting about the play by Peter Shaffer. I saw *The Desert Song* with you at the Temperance Hall in Haddock Lane, but I don't think it was by him. Mr Frost were in it and you went to the pub afterwards with that journalist and milk bottles were later knocked over. I don't hold with the theatre. It leads to bad behaviour. Mrs Wedderburn did take me twice to the Playhouse, but neither play was by Peter Shaffer. They were both by Agatha Christie, and they were both very good, and I didn't guess who had done it. Nor did Mrs Wedderburn, incidentally.

A lorry delivering electrical goods swerved to avoid a dog and completely demolished the bus shelter at Thurmarsh Lane Bottom yesterday, but otherwise we have had no excitements to match yours, so I will close now, hoping you are well and not catching any of those foreign diseases which those poor foreigners have to contend with.

　　With love,
　　Cousin Hilda

Sarajevo
Rua de Matelos
Altea
Costa Blanca
Spain
19th January 1982

Dear Henry,

　　Thank you very much for your letter, and I must say straight away that my answer to your first question is 'not at the moment' and to your second question, 'no'.

　　I didn't mention the future because I've learnt to live in the present, it's the way I get by, and I talked about our relationship as if it was in the past, because it is. Of course we may have a relationship in the future, but I'll only find that out a step at a time. I'd like to meet you on your return to England, and see if we can cope with a return to normality together. I lived for a very long time in a world more sombre than you are capable of imagining. Nobody knew. Not my father, my psychiatrist or, above all, my mother. I feel now that I'm sitting on a green lawn, but the lawn juts out over that sombre chasm and it would be all too easy to fall back into it. I couldn't cope with seeing you again in somewhere exotic like Peru. It'd be make or break, and I'm not brave enough for that.

　　Please treat me as a pen-pal and send me lovely descriptions of your times in Peru. Then, when you return, and you will return, we'll meet like pen-pals. It'll be exciting and terrifying, but if you're truly patient and loving I believe we may have a chance.

　　Sam made a flying visit last week. He's a cheery bachelor. He lives in Luton and devises recipes for tinned soups. 'Well, somebody's got to,' he says.

　　Dad and I are off to our local English bar now. I'd prefer a tapas bar but the English bar has fish and chips on a Friday, and once a Yorkshireman . . .

I think of Benedict often and with despair.

With love and hope,

Hilary

Apartado 823
Cajamarca
Peru
Feb 2nd, 1982

Darling Hilary,

Do other people feel conflicting emotions about seven hundred times a day, or is it just me? I'm so depressed at knowing that I won't see you for almost two years. (I won't stay here when my option comes up. Without you, I feel as though I'm doing my National Service all over again.) But I'm thrilled that you want to see if we can make a go of things and that you love me still, and believe we may have a chance. (I sound like Cousin Hilda, who went through my letter paragraph by paragraph.)

Progress on the project is a bit slow. The really good Peruvians don't seem interested. Two or three accepted posts and simply didn't turn up. Apparently, they hate to disappoint you, so they tell you what they think you want to hear: 'I will start next Monday.' Lots of big smiles, lots of bad teeth, nobody starts next Monday!

The Range Rovers are another problem. They've arrived, and we don't know what to do with them! Only three of the English staff drive anything, let alone Range Rovers, and I wouldn't dare give them to the Peruvians, because they'd simply get too excited at the prospect of driving something so magnificent.

Peru is a smiling, rickety land, full of humour. The main newspaper has a photographic feature on its front page called 'Pothole of the Day'. An elderly lorry bears the legend, 'Apollo 2½'. On the frequent, teeming, breast-feeding, sombrero-shaking buses between Cajamarca and Baños Del Inca, the conductor calls out the stops by name. 'Sausages,' he cries as we approach Bratwurst Bernhardt's. I turn to smile at you. You aren't there.

I flew to Lima last week, on business. I can't begin to describe Lima and its contrasts, the rich suburbs, the endless shanty towns, it would depress you. I came back on the night bus – a fifteen-hour trip! All along the Pan-American Highway the great lorries roared through the night, lit up with fairy lights, liners of the road! I turned to share the romance with you. You weren't there.

At every stop, in the dusty, single-storey villages, small boys came on the bus to sell limes and pancakes. Even at four in the morning the boys came. To sell a few limes is worth losing a night's sleep if your family is really poor. Yet they smile and look bright and well. We stopped every now and then at roadside stalls, rich with sizzling meats and pancakes, the Little Chefs (!) of Peru.

The bus began to growl up into the Andes. The headlights picked out the rocky hills. Dawn came quickly. We were winding through a narrow, astonishingly green valley. White storks were feeding in their hundreds in paddy fields that made me think of China. High above us the road wound ever upward through the sierras, pale yellow and green, dry but covered in plants except for a few rocky outcrops, briefly turned red as the sun rose. It took us two hours and forty minutes from sea level to the summit. As I saw the Cajamarca Valley laid out before us like a smiling woman, I turned to share the moment with you. You weren't there.

To have this amazing continent to experience, and yet not to be able to share it with you, it's the story of my life.

One day I'll share everything with you, my incredible darling,

With ever deepening love,

Your pen-pal!

Apartado 823
Cajamarca
Peru
March 28th, 1982

Dear Martin,

I've been meaning for a long while to tell you how sorry I was about the way the election turned out and about my part in it. I'm in

Peru now (!) running a Government Overseas Aid project, and getting a very different slant on life.

The people here migrate from the poverty-stricken countryside to the teeming towns, squat on the outskirts, build primitive shanty towns, skimp and scrape and slave and eventually turn them into houses. It may take thirty years to create a respectable neighbourhood, but they do it, and in the end the State conveniently forgets that they've done it all illegally, and gives them electricity, water and sewage as they can afford them. To see the patience, determination and good nature of these people makes one ashamed of Western assumptions. To regard dishwashers, video machines and microwaves as essentials seems to me to be deeply obscene.

I don't suddenly have renewed faith in the Labour Party or any less disgust at its feuding and pettiness. I don't believe in grand designs and great schemes, or centralised planning. I still have a lot of sympathy for the Liberals' approach. But I now believe that only socialism can possibly solve the world's problems, because at least some of its supporters care enough even if its leaders don't.

I have no more party ambitions. I don't believe the world will ever change for the better from the top downwards. It can only change for the better from the bottom upwards, through the actions of millions of good individuals. It's unlikely, but it's the only hope.

Nevertheless I'd like to canvass for you in the next election, if I'm home. We're the only two members of the Paradise Lane Gang who're still in touch. Can we be friends again?

All best wishes to you and Mandy,
Henry

Apartado 823
Cajamarca
Peru
May 8th, 1982

Dear Cousin Hilda,

Thank you very much for your letter, and I'm really sorry I never replied to your Christmas letter. My only excuse is I've been really busy. If I tell you that our twelve Range Rovers haven't moved since they were parked on some waste ground outside Baños Del Inca, you'll realise how busy we've been. Getting greenhouses built is a major problem. The greenhouse is a foreign concept here, like the garden shed, probably because they don't have a *Radio Times* to advertise them in!

Some of our staff have left, partly because they don't see us getting quick results, and partly because it's not very good to be British here during the Falklands War! Yet again my timing's bad. Peruvians believe that in withdrawing our survey ship we signalled to Argentina that we weren't interested in the islands, they believe our huge fleet to knock the conscript troops off the island is a colonial fantasy, they believe the sinking of the *General Belgrano* was murder on the high seas. The play *No Sex, Please, We're British*, which ran in Lima under the somewhat less catchy title of *Nada de Sexo, Por Favor, Somos Británicos* would stand no chance now. I can hear you saying that that would be a good thing!

I was moved to hear how moved you were to know that I was thinking of you on Christmas Day.

I was interested in all your news in your letters. I'm glad Jack's been visiting you. He's very fond of you. I hope the bus shelter in Thurmarsh Lane Bottom has been repaired, and fancy Macfisheries closing. It's the end of an era.

This will have to be the end of this letter, as I have a budget meeting to attend and I want to catch the post.

With much love as always,

Henry

PS You ask if Apartado is a nice street. It isn't the street name. It's actually the equivalent of PO Box 823.

Honeysuckle Cottage
Monks Eleigh
Suffolk
May 19th, 1982

Dear Henry,

I'm sending this to your friend Lampo Davey for forwarding, as agreed, just in case Doris sees the address on the envelope and worries about your being in Peru.

We're as well as can be expected. I have some arthritis, and Doris continues to slip an inch at a time towards a world of her own. My job is to make sure that it's a happy world. Of course she can never remember when she last saw people, and will fret that it's ages since she saw someone who called that very morning, but in your case I think she has a genuine feeling that it's been a very long time. She does have moments of comparative lucidity. So perhaps you could drop us a line, not mentioning Peru, saying you had a nice visit.

I hope everything's going swimmingly for you, and that the Peruvians will soon be enjoying cucumber sandwiches for tea. I wish you could find some way of sending me your news.

With much love,
Uncle Teddy

9, Bromyard Mews
London SW3
June 4th 1982

Dear Uncle Teddy and Auntie Doris,

Thank you very much for having me last weekend. It was a very enjoyable visit, as always. It was good to see you both looking so well and it was nice to have good weather for once. I was disappointed that I didn't win any of the games of Scrabble, but *c'est la vie*, and at least they were hard-fought scraps.

I had a good journey back and when I got home I found a letter from a friend who's living in Peru. It was full of good news, he's doing well with his government project, loves the country and is in friendly correspondence with his ex-wife, so that cheered me up no end and prevented my return home being an anti-climax, as these things sometimes can be after a weekend of your hospitality.

Well, I won't bother too much with my news, as I hope to see you the weekend after next and will tell you it all then.

Have that Scrabble board ready. I think my luck's about to change.

With much love as always,
Henry

Apartado 823
Cajamarca
Peru
Sept 6th, 1982

Dearest Hilary,

I'm writing this as the train rumbles through a land halfway between mountain and jungle, beside the Urabamba, a tributary of the Amazon. Lampo and Denzil are sitting opposite me. They send their love. I send more than love. I send a shriek of desire.

When we meet I'll tell you of the sights we have seen on this almost memorable holiday. We travelled on the second highest railway in the world. Our beautiful train, so beautiful that the excited station staff at Arequipa kept it for two hours before letting it go, wound across the desert, up over the arid mountains, past rare oases and shy, gentle vicuña, past lakes seething with bird life, down to Puno on the shore of Lake Titicaca, the world's highest navigable lake.

I'll tell you of Puno, where the restaurants are full of strolling bands who play the haunting music of the *zampona* (pan-pipes), the little pipes of the *antara*, the cane flutes called *quena*, the twelve-stringed *charango* with body made of armadillo shells. They even make music with a comb stroked against the side of a gourd. They play music fervent with lyrical sadness, sometimes hauntingly yearning, sometimes ferociously triumphant. Every note sings to me of love and absence.

I'll tell you of the long train journey from Puno to Cuzco, through the *altiplano*, the great upland plain of the Andes, empty save for isolated thatched stockades and adobe villages. Waiters set tablecloths throughout our third-world train, and without leaving our seats we ate stuffed avocado, beef casserole and a banana. Eat your heart out, InterCity Catering. A lone Indian on horseback watched gravely as a whole trainload ate their bananas. What did he think?

I'll tell you of the almost memorable town of Cuzco, Spanish elegance built upon foundations of massive Inca stonework that has stood undamaged for five hundred years although no mortar was used, such was the perfection of the masons.

I'll tell you of the almost memorable four-hour train journey from Cuzco to the foot of the great mountain on which the almost memorable Inca city of Machu Picchu was built, of the climb round hairpin bends on buses brought by train to this road that connects with no other road, built of materials brought by train, to the immaculately terraced, deserted city of the sky, high on its narrow rock several thousand feet above the curving Urabamba, mortarless stonework unflinching before four hundred years of winds.

Why were these great sights only almost memorable? Because you are not here, my impossibly wonderful love.

Henry

PS You'll never guess who we met in Lima. Neil Mallet, who tried to destroy my journalistic career with deliberate misprints. He went white at the sight of Denzil and me. He's working on an English-speaking paper in Lima. Hardly a glittering career, and I found I couldn't hate him any more. Not all of us have to cope with the sackfuls of envy and inadequacy that were dealt to him. We all had a drink together, but he had to leave early to do his laundry. *Plus ça change* . . .

Sarajevo
Rua de Matelos
Altea
Costa Blanca
Spain
30th September 1982

Dear Henry,

I'm glad you enjoyed your holiday. I enjoyed living it through your letter.

Yes, I too am looking forward to our meeting. It'll be nice to see my pen-pal. I wonder if you'll look the way I imagine you!

I won't look the way you imagine me. I'm quite a shadow of the person I was, Henry, and I don't think you should be using phrases like 'my impossibly wonderful love'. Even if I ever was wonderful, which I doubt, I'm not now. When I look at myself in the mirror, I see a kind of emptiness, a sense of there being nobody there. I doubt if I'll ever again be able to cope with the great rousing excitements of life. Please, please, please don't expect too much of me.

Kate and Jack both managed to get over for a few days. We're blessed in our children, and that at least gives me hope that there was and is something worthwhile between us. Camilla sends her love via them, which is nice. I know that you write to them all and are disappointed that they aren't managing to get to Peru, but they're all very involved in building their own lives.

With a heavy heart, I have to report that Benedict has been sighted in Portugal – in Albufeira, in fact. My informant – that makes me sound like a policewoman – saw him in a restaurant in unsavoury company and looking as if he might be drugged up. The informant is reliable. He's none other than my own dear Daddy. The Mathesons have a villa there and invited us both. I didn't go as I thought Daddy needed a break from me.

I feel depressed by my country. It's strange that we're both among Spanish peoples at this time. The Spaniards here feel that the Falklands War was the last dingy death-twitch of our imperialist illusions. (Not that Spain wasn't imperialist!)

I despair over Benedict. Should I go to Portugal? Do Nigel and

Diana really care? I've never before been so sad that you are so far away.

    With love,
    Hilary

Apartado 823
Cajamarca
Peru
Oct 14th, 1982

Dear Nigel,

    I'm writing this from Peru, where I'm running a government aid programme which will eventually cover the Andes with cucumbers. I'm writing because I've just heard from Hilary that Benedict has been sighted in Albufeira and I wonder what you're planning to do about it. I gather he looked as if he was on drugs. I feel so helpless here, as I won't be back in Europe till November next year. We're all responsible for the boy, Nigel, and we're all in some way to blame. We've got to try to save him.

    Lampo came over recently and we chatted over late-night glasses of rum about the old days at Dalton. If he knew I was writing, I'm sure he'd join in sending best wishes and hoping that you're getting real satisfaction out of serving your wonderful constituents in Thurmarsh! I'd love to be a fly on the wall at one of your 'surgeries'.

    I suppose you were very bullish over the Falklands and spoke proudly of our troops. We know our troops are good. We don't need wars to prove it. Would that our politicians were as good as our troops.

    With all best wishes,
    Henry

Dear Henry,

Thank you for your letter. Yes, I heard that Benedict had been 'sighted' in Albufeira. You say we're all responsible. Well, as his father I accept my share, but I have responsibility for all sorts of people, especially Felicity, who doesn't enjoy the most robust of health. The very mention of the boy is liable to give her 'an attack'. I'm responsible to my partners, and this is a very busy time. I'm responsible to my government in Parliament. I believe in our policies (including the defence of the Falklands. How twisted you are). I can't let the side down through sudden trips to Albufeira to chase my son, who may well be there on holiday and gone before I arrive. Above all, Henry, I am, as you rightly point out, responsible to the great British electorate, to my constituents, the people of Thurmarsh. And yes, I do try to serve them well. I'm a good constituency MP. I'm not by inclination a kisser of babies, but now I kiss some horrendous specimens. You'd hardly recognise me.

I simply cannot chase the boy every time there's a sighting. He's an adult, he can choose his own life, and nobody, frankly, can force me to like him just because he's my son.

In any case, I believe Diana has gone over to Portugal to hunt for him.

When you get back to England, it will be time for you to think very seriously about pensions, if you have not done so already, and, knowing you, I will be surprised if you have. Do get in touch. I can suggest all sorts of ways of providing that 'nest-egg' that we all need. You will not do better elsewhere.

I hope your Peruvian venture continues to prosper.

Yours et cetera,

Nigel

Flat 5
36, Nantwich Crescent
London NW1
17th November 1982

Dear Henry,

I haven't written earlier as I decided to pop over to Portugal as soon as I could. I've been into every bar and restaurant around Albufeira and have found no sign of Benedict. I've also tried most of the other resorts on the Algarve. No joy. Probably he was just on holiday there.

I've got an exciting bit of news. Well, it's exciting for me. There's no reason why it should be exciting for you. I'm engaged. I'm marrying a Swiss dentist with three teenage children living with him! My parents are *not* pleased. In retrospect, you seem to them to belong to a golden age! But Gunter and I are very much in love and we are going to be very happy in his tidy little house above Interlaken.

I hope your project is going well. You didn't tell me much about it. Now that I'm happy, I wish you nothing but good. You were a good man to me for most of our life together.

With love,
Diana

Apartado 823
Cajamarca
Peru
Jan 5th, 1983

Dear Diana,

I'm actually writing this in our project office in Baños Del Inca, a village outside Cajamarca. It's summer here, and women are washing clothes in the hot streams and leaving them to dry on the grass beside the streams. Steam is rising everywhere.

I was very pleased – and excited – to hear your news, not least because it amuses me no end to hear that I'm now part of a golden age. It's nice to be appreciated, even in retrospect. I'm truly delighted and hope you'll be very happy. I've nothing but feelings of great warmth for you, darling Diana, and I hope your life with Gunter will be utterly delightful. May you have happy sex, tinkling cow-bells and perfect teeth for many years to come.

Our project proceeds very slowly. We've only managed to build six greenhouses. People keep trying to live in them, and then the glass was broken in one of the first terrorist attacks in this area for many years. Sendero Luminoso, the Maoist terrorists, are becoming more active and threatening the fragile stability of this lovely land. At the moment I'm busy giving our staff driving lessons so that we can start to use our Range Rovers, which are sitting in a field. This summer we'll swing into action.

I do hope you make proper contact with Benedict soon and will do anything I can to help at any time.

From my window I've just seen a group of women in jeans and tee-shirts going into the parish church, and one of them looks very like Anna, Hilary's friend, who once pretended to be a nun. I can't remember if you ever met her.

Outside the church a man is playing beautiful but mournful music on an instrument called the *clarin*. It's ten foot long and can't go on public transport so it's never travelled beyond Baños Del Inca and Cajamarca. Yet another reason for coming to this fascinating spot.

With love and all best wishes,
Henry Pratt,
Unpaid publicist,
Baños Del Inca Tourist Board

> Apartado 823
> Cajamarca
> Peru
> Jan 6th, 1983

Dearest Hilary,

Just a quick one. The most incredible thing happened yesterday. I met Anna, and she's a nun! I know I like irony, but this is ridiculous!

I saw this group of women in jeans entering the church and one of them looked very like Anna. I went across and, lo and behold, it *was* her. The whole group were Canadian worker nuns, very cheery, very casual. I was invited to join them and we had a very jolly time in the priest's house next door, a very friendly place where we (including the nuns) drank very strong gin and tonics. We all repaired to a little booth-like restaurant in a row of such restaurants, simple wooden tables and seats, and had the national speciality, which I regret to say is guinea pig, and which I regret to say is delicious cooked with saffron.

There we sat, as darkness fell over the high sierras and the pretty village with its steaming streams, and we laughed, ate, shared left-wing political assumptions, and I felt so full of memories, of our first meeting in Siena, of my disastrous date with Anna, of my early evenings out with you, and I was overwhelmed with love.

Anna says that she turned to God in selfishness and cowardice, in retreat from emotional chaos, found peace first and then strength and decided to devote her life to service. She's utterly happy and looks beautiful now that the slight smugness and coarseness that marred her beauty have gone.

Is it possible that there is a God for Anna but there isn't for me, and that that is what God is – a relative reality?

It's interesting to reflect on how much Anna's pretence of being a nun reflected a need that she hadn't yet acknowledged.

It's wonderful to think that we are now in the year in which you and I will meet. Oh blessed 1983.

With deepest love,
Henry

Crete, March
Grabbing an early break in the sun. *Many thanks* for your letter. Glad to hear Anna looks well and is enjoying G and T! It makes her seem not quite so lost to us. That other order was just too religious for us to stomach.

With love, Peter and Olivia

327

My darling Hilary,

It is night. It is dark. I sit behind my mosquito nets in my simple hut in a travel lodge on the banks of the Amazon, about thirty miles from Iquitos. I listen to the cruel pageant of nature's fertile night. Grunts, croaks, hoots, squeaks and screams. I can't sleep. I have to write to my beloved. I have to confess.

The Amazon, though mighty, strikes me as a dull river, slow, brown and straight. I came to this lodge in a thatched boat with sixty seats. There was only one other occupant, a German travel agent with a haircut that made him look thatched. The business, mainly British, has slumped since the Falklands War and now, as the memory of that recedes, the increasing violence of Sendero Luminoso may stop any revival in its tracks.

We were taken on a jungle walk, the German travel agent and I. We saw no animals. There's plenty of jungle. Why should they go where we are? I thought only of you, and the confession I must make.

We dined together, the only two customers in a restaurant designed for one hundred and twenty. After dinner it was cabaret time. The cabaret consisted of our waiters playing guitars. Darkness fell. The macaws went to sleep. The jungle awoke.

Tomorrow we visit an Indian village. They don't use money, so we must barter. It was suggested that we buy cigarettes. I did. The German travel agent refused. 'I will not spread this noxious weed,' he said. 'I will deal in fish-hooks. I have many fish-hooks.'

To what am I going to confess? A sultry affair with a laundress in Baños Del Inca? A mad hour of buggery with the German travel agent? No. To failure. Stark, utter, total failure. I haven't fooled you, have I? The cucumber scheme has been a fiasco. A staff of six Britons and six Peruvians, owners of twelve Range Rovers that have never moved, has produced a total of 1,673 cucumbers, of which 884 were destroyed by South American diseases that I couldn't identify, 211 were too small to sell and 176 were so grievously bent that it was kindest to give them a decent burial. 420 healthy cucumbers, and the Peruvians didn't want even those. They have enough of their own, and don't like them much anyway!

Another fiasco for Henry Pratt. I think it's probably best that we don't meet after all. I can give you nothing. Nothing. You'll be better off free of me.

Iquitos
The next day

Forget what I wrote yesterday, my darling. Perhaps I shouldn't be sending it, but I am, because I want you to know the real me in all my moods.

This morning we went to the Indian village, the German travel agent and I. Our guide, Basil, rang a gong twice before we left. He told us that it was an Indian gong, used for signals. I later realised what his signal meant. 'Only two of them today, chaps. Take it easy, eh?'

An hour's jungle walk took us to a village of thatched huts on stilts, where three people in grass skirts, two men and a woman, met us. She was the first topless seventy-year-old Indian I'd ever seen. They had goods to sell, crocodile-teeth bracelets, poisoned darts without the poison, just the things for Cousin Hilda. For payment they wanted full packets of cigarettes. 'Why do they want this noxious weed?' asked the German travel agent. 'Why do they not want my fish-hooks?' He couldn't even give the fish-hooks away. The answers to his naïve questions were: 1) They use nets; 2) Their children sell the cigarettes in Iquitos, which is why they need full packets, because of course they use money, how else do they buy the jeans we saw drying on the line? The grass skirts are for tourists only.

How tourism corrupts. How it destroys the world it wants to see.

We had lunch on the thatched balcony of the thatched lodge. The thatched boat arrived with no tourists. My trip was over, but the thatched travel agent had a two-day booking and was to be taken on a jungle expedition that afternoon.

He came to the boat to wave goodbye. As we set off up the slow muddy river, he shouted, 'I will insist they give me the full expedition. I will not take short measure.' We waved to each other, the German travel agent and I. I will never see him again. I don't even know his name, nor he mine.

And I thought, I will not give in. I will not be defeated by this absurd and corrupting world. There will be no self-pity.

So tonight I write to say, I don't feel so useless after all. My report will state that the whole scheme was absurdly unrealistic and badly conceived. I am not to blame. That will not be accepted, of course. Only my head will roll. Anthony Snaithe will admit to an unwise appointment, caused by falsely glowing reports about me from other people. But I know . . . I really do know . . . this one was not my fault.

Hilary darling, I am going to fight on. I am going to do something good, I don't know what, but IT WON'T BE TO DO WITH CUCUMBERS. And, my darling, I WILL MAKE YOU HAPPY.

Less than three months till we meet. I cannot be sad for long.

With deepest love,

Cucumber Henry (Retired)

17 We'll Meet Again

On Wednesday, November 16th, 1983, it was revealed that under a scheme to get rid of thousands of senior bureaucrats the National Health Service had ended up with 600 more than before, at a cost of £45 million. Ken Livingstone banned the giving of goldfish as prizes at fairs in Greater London. The main Brighton to Portsmouth railway line was closed for four hours when a six-foot-two signalman fled from his box after seeing a field mouse. And Henry Ezra Pratt met Hilary Nadežda Lewthwaite for only the second time since she'd walked out of their house nineteen years ago.

The venue was the foyer of the Midland Hotel, the appointed time six thirty, but Henry was there ten minutes early.

The claret-coloured carpet had threadbare patches. Some of the leather armchairs had burst arms. The photographs of the halcyon days of steam had not been adequately dusted. The hotel was closing its doors for ever on January 1st.

Henry sat in a quiet corner, with a view of the swing doors. Above him, number 46231 *Duchess of Argyll* was still steaming through Crewe Station past knots of train-spotting schoolboys in baggy, knee-length trousers. His heart was thumping.

For all the three days that he'd been in England it had thumped. England seemed so small, so impossibly genteel after Peru, but it was Hilary's birthplace, so he was glad to be back, in the land of the thumping heart. He was staying at Cousin Hilda's, in his old room, in that cold house. No amount of airing could remove the aura of emptiness, the accumulated dampness of the gentlemenless years. Last night he'd dined off roast lamb and spotted dick, because it was a Tuesday, and in the stifling basement room he'd told Cousin Hilda about Peru, and she'd said, 'Ee!' and, 'Well I never!' and, 'I've never been able to see the point of deserts, me. I mean, where's the sense of them, if nothing grows?' and, 'I just wish Mrs Wedderburn was here. She had an ear for foreign parts, did Mrs

Wedderburn. I haven't. I can't imagine them in me mind's eye,' and the evening, which Henry had dreaded, had passed swiftly, pleasantly and affectionately, and Henry had felt strangely touched, after all his adventures, to be back with spotted dick on a Tuesday. At the end of the evening he'd said, 'I'll be out tomorrow night, Cousin Hilda,' and her face had fallen, and her lips had worked anxiously, and she'd said, 'Out??' as if she couldn't believe that a man of forty-eight could be so irresponsible, and she'd said, 'But I've bought the sausage for the toad-in-the-hole. I've got the sponge for the sponge pudding,' and he'd said, 'I'm sorry. I didn't realise. I should have told you. I'm seeing Hilary,' and she'd gone pink and said, 'Hilary! You're seeing Hilary?' and he'd said, 'We've been corresponding like pen-pals,' and Cousin Hilda had said, 'Well, I daresay the toad-in-the-hole can wait till Thursday. There's no need to be hidebound now it's just the two of us.'

And now a woman entered through the swing doors and Henry's heart almost stopped, but this was an elderly lady, and Hilary would not have been flattered.

And then there she was, pale, tall, not looking her forty-eight years, tense, shy, subdued, yet so beautiful.

'Hello, darling,' he said, as he kissed her on her cold, cold cheek.

'Hello, Henry,' she said. He noted that she hadn't said, 'Darling.' It was going to be a long job.

In the dusty, quiet vastness of the exhausted, ghostly bar, Henry ordered a pint of Tetley's, and his companion plumped for mineral water. 'I don't drink much these days,' she said.

They sat in the alcove in which, almost twenty-eight years ago, Henry had introduced Lorna Arrow to his journalist friends. The stuffing was bursting out of the seats. Above them, a Patriot-class engine was still pulling a mixed freight out of Carlisle Upperby Yard in light snow.

'It's lovely to see you,' said Henry, wondering if even this was too bold and forward. Suddenly it all seemed desperately difficult.

'How was your flight?'

'Very punctual.'

'Good. Cheers.'

332

'Cheers.'

'How's your father?'

'Very well.'

'Good.'

'How's Cousin Hilda?'

Ah! At least she had volunteered a question.

'Very well.'

'Good.'

'Slightly smaller.'

'Smaller?'

'Shrinking slowly. We all do.'

'Oh.'

'We had spotted dick.'

Her first laugh. Oh, the unbelievable beauty of that first laugh.

His throat was dry. He drank the beer quickly and bought himself another one.

'Thank you for all your letters,' she said.

'Oh, Hilary,' he said. 'I wish you'd seen Peru.'

'Missing it already?' she said wryly. Oh, the incredible loveliness of that returning wryness.

'Oh yes. Two years spent largely missing you, and now I'm missing Peru.'

A tactical error! Not saying that he'd miss Peru. Saying that he'd spent two years missing her. She couldn't cope with that.

'The Range Rovers are still there,' he said. 'There is a corner of some foreign field that is for ever England.'

She smiled. Oh, the gentle splendour of that shy smile.

'Where do you fancy eating?' he asked. He expected her to say, 'I don't mind.' Imagine his joy when she said, 'Is the Taj Mahal still there? I rather fancy that. There aren't any Indian restaurants in Spain.'

Never mind Indian restaurants in Spain. She wanted to go back to their old haunts. Henry began to dare to believe that it was going to be all right.

Hilary stayed with the Mathesons for a week. That first night they had a pleasant meal at the Taj Mahal, where Count Your Blessings was delighted to see them and they were delighted to see him, and pleased that the worrying pain in his left testicle hadn't been the harbinger of a fatal disease, though disappointed that he'd never qualified as a doctor or given public concerts on the sitar or married Petula Clark.

Afterwards, Henry kissed Hilary demurely on the cheek.

The next day, they had a bar lunch at the Pigeon and Two Cushions, which was a mistake, because they missed Oscar dreadfully. That evening Henry had the extraordinary experience of eating toad-in-the-hole and sponge pudding with chocolate sauce on a Thursday instead of a Wednesday, and Cousin Hilda astonished him by suggesting he bring Hilary on the next evening.

So on the Friday evening Henry and Hilary had battered cod and jam roly-poly at Cousin Hilda's, and Cousin Hilda went slightly pink and said, 'Ee! That were grand, though I say it as shouldn't,' and they invited her out for Sunday lunch, and she said, 'Sunday lunch! Whatever next?'

On the Saturday night they ate at the Mathesons', and talked about Anna, and nuns, and Anna, and gin and tonic, and Anna. Olivia Matheson, who had a bruise on her left cheek, drank too much and fell over, and Peter Matheson said, 'I've never ever known her do that before.'

For their Sunday lunch they went to the Midland Hotel. The restaurant seemed to Henry much changed, but he realised that they must be sitting in exactly the spot where he and Lorna had endured a disastrous meal, because behind them Royal Scot number 46164 *The Artist's Rifleman* was still passing through Bushey troughs with the up Mid-Day Scot.

This meal was not disastrous, just very predictable. Henry had tomato soup, Hilary egg mayonnaise, Cousin Hilda pineapple juice, and they all had the beef. Cousin Hilda ate every scrap. To their surprise, she ordered sherry trifle. 'Sherry's alcohol, Cousin Hilda,' Henry pointed out. 'Aye, well, I don't expect they put much in,' said Cousin Hilda. 'It's all profit with these hotels, isn't it?' She took coffee and an after-dinner mint, saying, 'I don't know. Will it never end?' and as they stood up to leave she said, 'Thank you. I wish Mrs Wedderburn could have seen me today. What a time I've had.'

The next day, at Cousin Hilda's insistence, they dined with her off liver and bacon and rhubarb crumble, and on Hilary's last night they went to the Taj Mahal again and Count Your Blessings said, 'So! Maybe you marry each other again!' and roared with laughter.

But at the end of each day, and at the airport, Hilary's demeanour was such that Henry felt able to give her no more than a gentle kiss on her cold, cold cheek.

Henry and Hilary were married for the second time on the day that Ian Macgregor, Chairman of the Coal Board, announced that he would write to every miner in Britain appealing for a return to work, Jeffrey Archer told Lynda Lee-Potter that he wasn't afraid to cry, and police warned children that thousands of Superman transfers might be impregnated with LSD. It was Thursday, June 14, 1984.

Hilary was staying with the Mathesons again. She hadn't yet been to bed with Henry. It was strange to reflect that they had already spent several years married to each other, and had slept together before that marriage, at a time when the permissive society was but a gleam in a pop-festival promoter's eye. Now, when it was respectable to have sex before marriage, and living together for a trial period was regarded as sensible (if hardly romantic), Henry and Hilary sensed a need to be formal and dignified and correct.

As he shaved, Henry thought how incredibly lucky he was. Even when he'd visited Spain for the New Year, and when Hilary had come to Thurmarsh again in February, it had seemed by no means certain that they'd ever manage to find the old intimacy. Then, on his next visit, in March, they'd slipped into it. They'd kissed long and hard on the terrace of her father's little villa, beside the slatted table with the huge, half-finished jigsaw of the *Mauretania*. 'Darling,' he'd said the following morning, 'will you marry me?' 'Yes, please,' she had said.

So here he was, butterflies in his stomach, ploughing through bacon and egg in Cousin Hilda's basement. 'Eat up,' she commanded. 'Excitement needs a solid foundation.'

Henry couldn't wait to see how Cousin Hilda handled the Indian food. Wishing the day to be entirely different from their first wedding, Henry and Hilary had hit upon the happy idea of a wedding feast at the Taj Mahal.

Apart from Cousin Hilda, they'd invited Hilary's father; her brother Sam and his Danish girlfriend Greta; Kate and her theatre director boyfriend Adam; Jack and his girlfriend with the strange name of Flick; Camilla and her beautiful Italian lover Giuseppe; Martin and Mandy Hammond; Lampo and Denzil; Joe and Molly Enwright; Peter and Olivia Matheson (reluctantly, because Hilary and Howard were staying with them); Nigel Clinton (as a symbol of the renunciation of jealousy, did he but know it) with his attractive wife Rebecca; Paul and Christobel Hargreaves; and, from the old *Argus* days, Colin Edgeley with Glenda; Ben Watkinson with Cynthia; and Ginny Fenwick with nobody, because there was nobody.

They had not invited Tosser and Felicity Pilkington-Brick (because Henry didn't want to discuss his pension plans); Princess Michael of Kent (because they didn't know her); Ted and Helen Plunkett (because of a surfeit of embarrassing moments); Diana and Gunter Axelburger (because it seemed inappropriate to invite an ex-wife); Mr and Mrs Hargreaves (because it seemed inappropriate to invite an ex-wife's parents); Petula Clark (because fantasy withers if it touches reality); or Auntie Doris and Uncle Teddy (because Uncle Teddy still didn't dare be seen in the town where he had supposedly been burnt to death, and Auntie Doris wouldn't have been up to it, anyway).

As they arrived at the Taj Mahal from the Register Office the staff were lined up and smiling broadly.

'Congratulations,' said Count Your Blessings. 'You have brought honour on our establishment by choosing it as venue for your nuptial celebrations.'

Henry caught a half-smile on the face of Paul Hargreaves, and wished that he hadn't invited him.

But Paul saw Henry's reaction, and hurried over, and said, 'I wasn't laughing at him, Henry. I was laughing for joy at the delightful sentiments and charming expression of them. So much better than a strangled "I hope everything will be to your satisfaction, sir," squeezed out of some dry Anglo-Saxon lips.' Henry looked at him in astonishment, and Paul said, 'We're thrilled to be invited. We bear you no ill-will over Diana.'

'Whose Swiss dentist is gorgeous,' interrupted Christobel.

'Whose Swiss dentist is very nice,' said Paul. 'As we're lifelong friends, shall we make a vow to like each other more, Henry? Or is your puritan heart still shocked by our easy money?'

'Are you making easy money?'

'We hope to,' said Christobel. 'We're opening a private HRT clinic.' She saw Henry's blank expression. 'Hormone replacement therapy. It's the coming thing, and not just for women. You don't want to age, do you?'

'Actually I think I'm odd,' said Henry. 'I rather like the idea of being old.'

The waiters brought champagne and served it very professionally. Henry offered them a glass, and Count Your Blessings said, 'Oh no, sir. We have a saying in India. "Intoxication is the thief of service." '

'Really?' said Henry.

'No, but I thought it sounded good.' Count Your Blessings roared with laughter.

Henry hurried over to Cousin Hilda and said, 'What would you like, Cousin Hilda?'

Cousin Hilda looked embarrassed, even coy.

'I thought I might try a glass of champagne,' she said. 'I've always wondered what it's like.'

Henry looked at her in astonishment.

'Tha's given me some worries, Henry Pratt,' she said. 'Tha's done some right foolish things.' She sniffed. 'Today tha's not doing a foolish thing.' She went pink. 'I always said it. I said it to poor Mr O'Reilly. "Henry and Hilary go together like two shakes of a lamb's tail." "Oh, you're right there," he said. I can't do the accent.

"You're not wrong there." ' Cousin Hilda went very pink and raised her glass. 'I believe the word is "Cheers".' She took a cautious sip of her champagne, rolled it round her tongue, swallowed it, and nodded. 'Well, I don't know what all the fuss is about, to say it's supposed to be so special,' she said, 'but I'd not say it were unpalatable.'

Howard Lewthwaite joined them and said, 'Oh, Henry. If only you two hadn't wasted so many years.'

'I can't look at it like that,' said Henry. 'I love your daughter dearly, and this time I will make her happy, but Diana was a lovely person and I can't call that a waste of time. Do you know Cousin Hilda? Cousin Hilda, Howard Lewthwaite, Hilary's father.'

'How do you do? Nice to meet you,' said Howard Lewthwaite.

'We met last time your daughter married my . . . married Henry,' said Cousin Hilda.

Henry moved on, making a beeline for Nigel Clinton, who was now managing director of a relatively new publishing house, Clinton and Burngreave.

'I think she'll start writing again before long,' he said.

'Do you really want that?' said Nigel Clinton, who'd lost most of his hair, thus looking more intellectual but less handsome.

'Oh yes,' said Henry. 'I want the complete Hilary Pratt this time.'

He moved on and took Hilary's arm, and they moved through the crowd at the bar of the flock-wallpapered provincial restaurant like royalty at a garden party.

'Where are you going to live?' asked Ben Watkinson's wife Cynthia, who had once been shy and petite.

'We've bought a little terrace house in the best part of Rawlaston,' said Henry.

'I didn't know there was a best part of Rawlaston,' said Cynthia.

'How many tennis players of either sex have won all four grand slams in a calendar year?' asked Ben.

'Do shut up, Ben,' said Cynthia.

'Where are you going for your second honeymoon?' asked Ginny Fenwick, blushing.

'Even at purely social events it's the press asking all the questions,' said Henry.

'Force of habit,' said Ben Watkinson.

'Genuine interest,' said Ginny.

'Answer the question,' said Colin Edgeley. 'Where *is* the bonking marathon to be held?'

'Colin!' said Glenda, who looked pale and exhausted.

'Please, Colin!' said Henry, looking at Hilary anxiously.

'We aren't going anywhere,' said Hilary. 'We're going home. My father's going on our honeymoon.'

The journalists gawped.

'We're so excited about setting up home again,' said Hilary. 'We can't afford much, but to us it's a palace, because it's ours. Daddy's coming to live with us, but we'd like to be on our own at first, so he's going to Majorca for a fortnight. He's tickled pink, and we'll have a lovely fortnight on our own.'

'Bonking like rabbits,' said Jack, passing by.

Jack could get away with such things. Nobody ever took offence at Jack. Henry and Hilary grinned, and Hilary said, 'Well, I can hope,' and Henry said, 'I'm not a young man any more,' in a mock-elderly voice, and as they walked on Henry looked at Hilary with such love that he thought for an awful moment that he was going to faint as he'd fainted on seeing Kate for the first time, and Kate, almost twenty-six now, passionately radical, with no make-up and a long shapeless sack of a dress but lovely because it suited her, said, 'I'm *so* happy for you both. This is the best day of my life,' and Camilla nodded her agreement with tears in her eyes, and Giuseppe said, 'She weeping a little bit. She mostly a wonderful girl,' and Camilla laughed and said, 'I hope you mean, "She's a most wonderful girl",' and Giuseppe laughed and said, 'Oh yes. I am magnified by my mistake,' and Camilla said, 'mortified,' and Giuseppe said, 'Oh yes,' and laughed again.

Count Your Blessings announced that luncheon was ready, and they all took their places at the long table under the huge lurid photograph of the eponymous edifice.

Count Your Blessings had told Henry that there would be

magnificent food, 'not from the menu. Menu is standard Indian restaurant. Real Indian food.' There were chats and doshis and all kinds of bhagia, and spicy dumplings and whole marinated trout and quail, and beautiful stuffed marrow and delicately stuffed ladies' fingers and banana methi and coconut rice and lemon rice and lovely breads. Cousin Hilda tried the food cautiously, and said, 'Well, it's not tasteless. I'll give it that.' Kate's boyfriend Adam ate with his fingers. 'I hope nobody minds,' he said, 'but I like to eat as the common people do.' None of them minded, but the waiters giggled.

Howard Lewthwaite, sitting beside Henry, turned to him and said, 'I asked Hilda out.'

'You did what??'

'For a meal. For companionship. I said to her, "Just for companionship. No hanky panky." She went pink and said, "Mr Lewthwaite! I should hope there wouldn't be." I said, "Well, come on, then," and she said something strange. She said, "Mr Lewthwaite, you're fifty years too late." '

'That isn't strange,' said Henry. 'That's poignant.'

Henry and Hilary kept touching each other under the table, wine and beer and lassi flowed, and it was all the most tremendous success.

Peter Matheson leant across and said, 'Is it really true you're working as a waiter, Henry?'

'Yes, Peter,' said Henry. 'At the Post House.'

'Good God!'

'And proud of it. An honourable profession. Only the British think it's demeaning to wait on your fellow men.'

'Really hard work, though, badly paid and rarely appreciated,' said Joe Enwright.

'Rather like teaching,' said Henry.

'Touché,' said Joe Enwright with feeling.

'I tried going back to the market garden,' said Henry. 'I just couldn't face it.'

'Have some raita. It's delicious,' said Nigel Clinton.

'I can't even eat them,' said Henry. 'Forty-nine years old,

receding hair line, expanding stomach line, doesn't know anything except cucumbers, absolutely fed up with cucumbers, Hilary's got herself a real prize catch.'

'I think I have,' said Hilary lovingly.

'I wonder how much these people send back to India,' said Martin Hammond.

'Lots,' said Howard Lewthwaite. 'They're wonderfully non-materialistic.'

'Unlike the Thurmarsh Socialists,' said Peter Matheson.

'Oh shut up about politics, Peter,' said Olivia.

Henry stood up.

Silence fell slowly.

'This is not a formal wedding,' he said. 'We aren't having speeches.'

'Hooray!' shouted Jack.

'But I would like to call on my best man, Martin Hammond, who I believe has some telegrams.'

Martin Hammond stood up.

'I know you're supposed to make jokes at weddings,' he said, 'but I can't make jokes, so I won't.'

'Hooray!' shouted Jack.

'Henry and I met when we were four. We joined the Paradise Lane Gang. We thought we were right little tearaways too. Tearaways? We were boy scouts compared to today's lot. Law and order? Now there is a joke. Oops, sorry, I promised not to be political.'

'Quite right, too,' said Peter Matheson.

'Shut up, Peter,' hissed Olivia Matheson.

'We had our well-publicised disagreements over the 1979 election,' continued Martin. 'But it was all taken in good part, and we remained friends, as witnessed by my having the honour to be best man today. Politicians always speak too much . . . '

'Hear hear,' said Olivia Matheson.

'Shut up, Olivia,' hissed Peter Matheson.

'So I'll get straight on with my main job, the reading of the telegrams,' continued Martin. 'This one's from Switzerland: "We wish you happiness for the rest of your days – Diana and Gunter." '

There was a murmur of approval. Camilla's eyes filled with tears and Giuseppe held her hand.

'That is very nice,' said Martin. 'An ex-wife saying that. That is highly delightful. The next one is from Suffolk: "We wish we were with you – Auntie Doris and Uncle Miles." That's nice. And one from London: "Many congratulations – James and Celia." '

'Diana's parents. Very nice,' said Henry.

'Oh, and here's one from Thurmarsh,' said Martin Hammond. ' "Congratulations. Don't do anything we wouldn't do. That leaves you quite a lot – Ted and Helen." '

Ginny Fenwick gave a loud derisive snort, and everyone looked at her, and she blushed.

'Ah!' said Martin. 'Now this is definitely a case of last, but not least, because this one has come all the way from Peru.'

'It'll be from our daughter,' said Olivia Matheson. 'She's a nun.'

'Let the man speak, dear,' said Peter Matheson.

'I'm sorry to have to disappoint you,' said Martin, 'but somehow I don't think this one's from a nun. It says, "Get stuck in – Anna." '

There was laughter. Cousin Hilda frowned. Olivia Matheson looked embarrassed. Peter Matheson gave a smile so fixed that it was impossible to tell what he was thinking.

'That concludes the telegrams,' said Martin. He sat down, and there was applause.

Henry stood up.

'Ladies and gentlemen,' he said. 'I find I must say a few words. First, a huge thank-you to the staff of the Taj Mahal for the wonderful food and service.'

Everybody clapped and cheered. Count Your Blessings couldn't have smiled more widely if Petula Clark herself had walked in.

'In a minute I'm going to propose just one toast,' said Henry. 'To absent friends. Before I do, I'd like to mention four absent friends briefly. My Auntie Doris, who can't be here due to illness, and her companion, Miles Cricklewood, who can't be here because he's looking after Auntie Doris. I've known them both all my . . . well,

I've known Auntie Doris all my life and Miles ever since he came on the scene. I do wish they could have been here. Also, our friend Anna Matheson, who is a nun in Peru – yes, that telegram was from her and as you'll have gathered she's no ordinary nun, she's a worker nun, a nun of the world. Last, but definitely not least, my step-son, Benedict. He's an unhappy soul, a lost soul. I just wish he'd come back and give us another chance. We might not fail him so badly next time. Ladies and gentlemen, thank you for coming, and I give you the toast of "absent friends".'

They all said 'absent friends' fervently, and then they drank, and then they applauded Henry heartily.

Soon the guests began to leave.

First to go was Howard Lewthwaite. He had to catch the plane for his honeymoon. He left to a chorus of good wishes.

Next were Sam and Greta. 'Lovely do. Hope you're incredibly happy,' said Sam. 'Sorry to rush off, but I've an idea and I've got to work on it.' 'He's always like this when he feels a soup coming on,' said Greta in her charming Danish accent.

Lampo and Denzil kissed Hilary but, in deference to being in Yorkshire, they only shook hands with Henry. Denzil said, 'This is a great day. Lampo cried,' and Lampo said, 'You cried too,' and Denzil said, 'I'm allowed to be sentimental. I'm old,' and Lampo said, 'You are, aren't you? What am I doing living with a disgusting old man?' Henry smiled. He'd suddenly realised that there had never been the slightest risk that Lampo and Denzil, for all their quarrelling, would ever split up.

Ginny kissed Henry and Hilary and blushed, Joe and Molly Enwright invited them to dinner, Colin Edgeley said, 'Keep in touch, kid. You're my mate,' Paul said, 'Don't forget we have the secret of eternal youth,' Nigel Clinton said, 'Get her writing,' Cousin Hilda said, 'If my gentlemen could see me today! Indian food! Whatever next? Thank you, and I wish you so much happiness this time,' and they gazed at her in astonishment; Jack said, 'I'm very pissed. Sorry. But I'm right chuffed. It's grand to have you two together again'; Olivia Matheson stumbled and fell, and Peter Matheson said, 'She's never ever done that before';

343

Giuseppe said, 'You very happy, I make your step-daughter very delirious'; and Kate just shook her head and cried.

Last to leave were Ben Watkinson and Cynthia. Ben had never known how to leave a room except by saying, 'Well, I'm off to give the wife one.' He couldn't say that when she was there, so it was Cynthia who said, 'Come on, Ben. We're outstaying our welcome,' at which neither Henry nor Hilary demurred.

The happy couple got into their hired car and were driven to their new home.

The house wasn't large, it wasn't luxurious, it wasn't beautiful, but it was theirs, and they had a lovely, gentle fortnight, getting to remember each other's rhythms, exploring each other's bodies, finding happiness. Howard, meanwhile, enjoyed their honeymoon, the concept of which had really amused him, and he sent a card saying, 'You're having a wonderful time. Wish I was here.'

As soon as Howard's honeymoon was over, Henry and Hilary enacted what they saw as the final part of their wedding. They went to see Uncle Teddy and Auntie Doris.

Auntie Doris's eyes were sunk deep into her face now, and her face had become pinched and hollow. Uncle Teddy had lost weight, was moving rather stiffly, and was slightly round-shouldered, but he'd worn better than her, and in fact they both thought that he'd worn incredibly well, considering the strain he'd been under.

After lunch, Uncle Teddy said he fancied a walk. Henry went with him. They walked past May Cottage, Old Cottage, the Old Thatcher's Cottage, Christmas Tree Cottage, April Cottage, High Cottage, Jane Farthing Cottage, Oak Cottage and Little Pond Cottage to the river, and back up the green past a cottage called The Cottage, as if there were no other cottages, and Uncle Teddy breathed in the air and said nothing until, as they passed the church, he said, 'Beautiful. All this air, Henry. I've been cooped up, you see. I can't leave her.'

They walked for two hours. Soon after they got home, the sun went down over the yard-arm, and after their drinks Uncle Teddy heated up some tinned soup and Marks and Spencer's cannelloni, and after their meal they settled down in the rustic little living room with its floral suite, and Uncle Teddy said, 'I hope you weren't expecting a game of Scrabble. Doris doesn't like that any more.'

They assured him that they weren't expecting a game of Scrabble.

'What she likes best is the story of our life,' said Uncle Teddy.

'Oh yes,' said Auntie Doris. 'Tell me the story of our life.'

'Do you mind?' said Uncle Teddy. 'Only I tell her it every night, and she likes it.'

'Of course we don't mind,' said Hilary.

'We met in 1927,' said Uncle Teddy.

'1927!' exclaimed Auntie Doris.

'At the Mecca.'

'Don't you have to stand in a certain direction at the Mecca?' said Auntie Doris. 'Facing the South Pole or something?'

'No, no. This was a dance hall,' said Uncle Teddy. He leant across to Henry and Hilary and whispered, 'Surprising what the old girl remembers sometimes. Quite surprises me.'

'Can't do much dancing if you're all facing the South Pole,' said Auntie Doris. 'Bit inhibiting.'

'No, no,' said Uncle Teddy. 'Mecca is a holy city, and Muslims face it when they pray. *The* Mecca is a dance hall.'

'Oh, I see.'

'Reginald Lichfield and his Boulevardiers used to play. It was packed Saturday nights in them days. Packed. Cigarette smoke everywhere. Through the smoke I saw this vision. Know what it was?'

'Was it me?' mouthed Auntie Doris.

'Well done! It was you. Prettiest girl in all the hall.'

'Was I?'

'Curves in all the right places. Lovely legs. Beautiful lips. Bright red.'

'Ee!'

Henry gave Hilary a wry grin. Auntie Doris hadn't said 'Ee!' for over fifty years. It wasn't posh.

345

'I asked you to dance. You said, "I don't mind." All casual and offhand.'

'Oh dear! Was I a little minx?'

'You were a vixen! We danced. I asked you out. Within five weeks we were engaged.'

'No! You were a quick worker, then?'

'I'd say. Never met anyone like you. Had to be. Too many rivals to hang about!'

'O'oh! Really? And then?'

'We got married in St Matthew's Church. A hundred and twenty guests.'

'Ee! A hundred and twenty!'

'Grand wedding. The Sniffer sniffing like mad. Face like a cupboard full of brooms.'

'The Sniffer?'

'Cousin Hilda. Mellowed now from what Henry tells me. Amazing what fear of the grim reaper can do. We bought a house in Dronfield. I went into import–export.'

'We had children.'

'No, Doris. We decided not to. We were good-time people.'

'I've always liked a good time.'

'Right. I did well.'

'Did you, Teddy?'

'Oh yes. Very well. Bought a big house. Called it Cap Ferrat.'

'That's a place.'

'Absolutely spot on. A very nice place where we had our holidays. Then war came. Then after the war . . .'

'Don't you usually tell me more about the war? Summat brave that you did somewhere.'

'Absolutely right, Doris. You're in good form today.' He looked at Henry and Hilary uneasily. 'I'm shortening it tonight. We have guests. Our Henry, our nephew, and his wife Hilary. Henry's mother died, you see.'

'Oh no!'

'And his father hanged himself.'

'Oh no!! What a tragic boy.'

'Yes. So we took him in as our son.'

'Oh! Lovely!'

'Yes, he was.'

Henry smiled sheepishly.

'He was,' continued Uncle Teddy. 'But I was a naughty boy. I went to prison.'

'Teddy! What for?'

'Oh, just technical offences. Tax evasion. Evading currency restrictions. Fraud. Nothing criminal.'

'Good. That's good. How long did you get?'

'Three years.'

'Three years! That's hard.'

'It was hard. It was hard for you, too. You were lonely. You couldn't manage without a man. You took up with a business friend of mine. Geoffrey Porringer.'

'I didn't! Naughty me.'

'Well! Partly my fault.'

'Was he nice?'

'He had blackheads.'

'Oh dear. I don't like the sound of him one bit.'

'I came out of prison. You were with Geoffrey. I was . . . upset. I took up with a . . . slightly younger woman.'

'You rogue!'

'Yes. I pretended to be burnt in a big fire, and you had a funeral for me.'

'No! Teddy!'

'And I lived in the South of France and married this . . . slightly younger woman, and you married Geoffrey.'

'Teddy! We were both rogues then?'

' 'Fraid so.'

'Well!'

'Anyway, Anna . . . the slightly younger woman . . . we parted, and I realised that I'd loved you all the time.'

'Teddy! All the time?'

'All the time. And you didn't love Geoffrey Porringer. So, you left Geoffrey and I came back to England and we bought this cottage.'

347

'Well!'

'But because I'm supposed to be dead, I have to live as Miles Cricklewood, a retired vet, in Suffolk, where nobody knows me.'

'And we lived happily ever after.'

'Well, no, nobody does that. But almost.'

'And all this happened to us?'

'Yes.'

'Well, we've lived a bit, Teddy.'

'We certainly have.'

'We've given them a run for their money.'

'We've cut the mustard.'

'We certainly have. Well, thank you, Teddy, that was lovely. I remembered bits of it, of course.'

'Of course. But not all.'

'No. Not all. I think you're very kind to me, Teddy.'

'I think I probably am, now.'

They said goodbye to the bottle of port and went to bed and they all slept like tops.

18 They Also Serve

His employers at the Post House were pleased with Henry's performance as a waiter. At last there's something I definitely do well, he thought wryly. He even invented a character for himself. He'd been on the ocean liners. 'When I was on the ocean liners . . . ,' he'd begin. It wasn't truly a fantasy. He hadn't lost touch with reality, and he said it even to people who knew it wasn't true. But he enjoyed the performance, and avoiding being caught out in contradictions kept his mind sharp. 'I'll never forget – sixty miles off the Azores – a force six easterly – I slopped mulligatawny soup all over the dress tunic of a colonel in the New Zealand army . . . Ructions? I'll say there were ructions!'

One day, towards the end of 1984, Henry came home to find Hilary somewhat tense and her father watching television.

'Henry?' she said.

'I'll go,' said Howard Lewthwaite. 'My room isn't really terribly cold.'

'What?' said Hilary.

'You're going to say something serious,' said Howard Lewthwaite. 'I don't want to be in the way.'

'You aren't in the way. I think you should hear this.'

'Oh. Because I don't want to be a nuisance.'

'You're only a nuisance when you keep saying you are.'

'Well I am. I'm stopping you saying what you want to say.'

'Well shut up, then.'

'You see. I am a nuisance.'

'You aren't! Please stay!'

'You're angry now.'

'Daddy! Shut up!'

Howard Lewthwaite sat solemnly, looking hurt.

'Henry?' said Hilary. 'I've something to tell you.'

'Oh?'

Henry could feel his heart thudding.

'I started a novel today.'

'Darling! Oh, I *am* glad!'

He hugged her and kissed her.

'Are you really?' she said.

'Utterly,' he said. 'Totally.' Hilary was smiling and Howard was smiling and Henry couldn't bear being the recipient of so much warmth, so he said, 'Well, I'm fed up with living off my tips.'

All through 1985, Hilary wrote; Howard said, 'I'm in the way, I'm under your feet'; and Henry proved how right the Director (Operations) had been all those years ago, when he said, 'They also serve who only stand and wait.'

The miners' strike ended after almost a year, French security agents set off two explosions on the Greenpeace ship, *Rainbow Warrior*, which was aiming to disrupt French nuclear tests in the South Pacific, the wreck of the *Titanic* was found in the North Atlantic, and Ronald Reagan and Mikhail Gorbachev achieved very little in Geneva in the first US–Soviet summit for six years.

Nearer home, a Leeds art dealer was gaoled for selling forged paintings. His crime came to light when Timothy Whitehouse's successor at the Cucumber Marketing Board realised that his office was full of reproductions of non-existent old masters. To the relief of Derek Parsonage, Henry, Uncle Teddy and the forger, the art dealer refused to reveal his sources. He might need their help again.

One night Henry arrived home full of excitement: 'I've served eleven lobster thermidors. Eleven in one night!' to be comprehensively upstaged by Hilary: 'I've finished my novel.'

Howard Lewthwaite said, 'This is a great moment for you. You'll want to be alone,' but didn't move.

Henry read Hilary's book. It was called *Towards the Light* and was a story about the conquering of depression. He found it deeply moving, but with a caustic wit. Nigel Clinton loved it and scheduled publication for October 1986, and Hilary met him for rewrites, and Henry went to the Post House and said, 'The *Mauretania* was a bugger for serving *zabaglione*. Something about the stabilisers, I suppose,' and came home tired and made himself a light supper, and didn't mind about Nigel Clinton or about Howard Lewthwaite saying, 'You want a quiet snack, a moment to yourself, you're tired, it's natural, you don't want to listen to an old man rabbiting on, I understand,' and not going.

The book was an instant success. Henry opened a bottle of champagne to celebrate the good reviews, and said how thrilled he was, and meant it, and Howard Lewthwaite said, 'No, no. I'll go to my room. You share the bottle. I don't want to be in the way,' and Henry said, 'Have some champagne, Howard, and enjoy your daughter's success. That's an order,' and they all laughed, and another summit meeting between Ronald Reagan and Mikhail Gorbachev, this time in Iceland, ended in bitter disappointment after seeming to promise so much, and a chemical spill in Switzerland threatened to destroy all life in the River Rhine, and one evening, early in 1987, on Henry's night off, as the three of them were watching television, Howard Lewthwaite suddenly gave a gasp of pain.

'What is it?' said Hilary.

'Nothing,' said Howard Lewthwaite in a strangled voice. 'I don't want to spoil your programme.'

His face was contorted with pain. He tried to stand. Hilary rushed over to him. Henry switched the programme off with the remote control. Howard Lewthwaite died in his daughter's arms.

Councillors and council officials and Labour Party workers and his new-found cronies from the Mulberry Inn, Rawlaston turned up in force for Howard Lewthwaite's cremation. Peter Matheson flew back, leaving Olivia in Albufeira. Sam discovered that the world wouldn't end if he didn't think up any new soups for three days, and came to support his sister. After the brief, impersonal service, Henry and Hilary and Sam and his girlfriend Greta stood among ageing men and women with watery eyes, and there was much talk about the end of an era, and there not being many of us left, and they don't make them like that any more. The landlord of the Mulberry told Hilary, 'The moment he walked in I knew he were a gentleman. He stood out.' Hilary had as many as she could back to the house, and after they'd all gone she flopped exhausted into a chair and let Sam and Greta make a fish pie for supper.

Over supper they talked about anything but death. They laughed about how obnoxious Sam had been as a child and told Greta all the awful things he'd said. Sam grew broody. He could feel a soup coming on. Almonds. Something to do with almonds, possibly. He went for a walk. While he was gone, Greta talked about the differences between Aalborg and Luton. They were many. Sam returned, suffering from soup creator's block. They were all tired, and went to bed early.

In bed, cuddled deep against Henry's soft body, Hilary said, 'I'm so glad we got together again. You know why?'

'No,' said Henry, 'but tell me.' It had been a long, exhausting day. A compliment would come in nicely.

'Because if I hadn't, Daddy would have died in exile, and he'd have hated that,' sobbed Hilary.

A few days after Howard Lewthwaite's cremation, Henry got home tired at a quarter to twelve, having had an amazing run on apple strudel – 'Funnily enough, on the old *Queen Mary* the apple strudel always went like hot cakes, whereas on the *Queen Elizabeth*, the old *Queen* not the QE2, it could be decidedly sticky. No explanation for it. One of the mysteries of the deep.'

Hilary was standing with her back to the grate, as if she was the squire and there was a roaring log fire, rather than the battered coal-effect electric one they'd picked up second-hand.

'Sit down,' she commanded.

Henry realised that she was going to broach a difficult subject. She was never bossy otherwise.

He sat down. His heart was thumping.

'You're the person I love most in all the world,' she said. 'I loved Daddy, too, and I'd never have suggested it while he was alive, but now that he's dead I think it's possible. But if you decide you don't want to, we won't, and I won't mention it again, and that'll be the end of the matter.'

'That'll be the end of what?' said Henry. 'What won't you mention again? What are you talking about?'

'Moving to London,' said Hilary.

There was a moment's silence in the little terrace house.

'Actually I'd like to move to London,' said Henry. 'It'd be perfect for what I have in mind.'

'I didn't know you had anything in mind,' said Hilary.

'I didn't,' said Henry. 'I've only just thought of it.'

'Only just thought of what?' said Hilary.

'The Café Henry,' said Henry.

On March 18, 1987, treasure worth £20 million was found by Danish divers aboard the wreck of the P and O liner *Medina*, torpedoed by a German U-boat off Start Point in 1917, a pizza-parlour manager and a hotel barmaid became the first couple in Church of England history to be married by a woman, and Henry and Hilary set off for another cremation. They found Uncle Teddy dazed and lost.

Jack and Flick came down the night before, and an Adamless Kate arrived on the day. A smattering of old drinking cronies from Monks Eleigh's two pubs also attended. The small gathering, barely filling two rows of the chapel of Ipswich Crematorium, hung their heads as Auntie Doris's coffin slid slowly away, much as her mental faculties had done.

They went for lunch at the Swan in Lavenham. At the bar, Jack told Henry, 'I don't want to upset Great-Uncle Teddy by giving good news, but you're going to be a grandfather.' Henry flinched at the thought of the potential size of any child produced by burly Jack and earth-mother Flick. 'That's wonderful, Jack,' he said. 'I think you should tell everyone. Life must go on.' So Jack made his announcement, and Hilary cried, and Uncle Teddy smiled bravely and said, 'Well, that's good news. That's really cheered me up.'

After lunch Jack and Flick set off in their BMW, and Kate left in her Deux Chevaux. As they stood outside the old hostelry, in the venomous March wind, Henry said, 'Not interfering, darling, but you haven't mentioned Adam recently.' 'No,' said Kate. 'We've split. I may find somebody perfect one day, Dad. I may not. I'm twenty-eight. I'm happy. I love you both. Goodbye.'

Henry drove Hilary and Uncle Teddy very slowly back to

Honeysuckle Cottage, dreading the silence of the house. Hilary made tea.

'Fancy a spot of Scrabble?' said Uncle Teddy.

'Do you?' said Henry.

Uncle Teddy reflected.

'No,' he said at last. 'No. I think it might seem a bit tame without the cheating.'

At six o'clock Uncle Teddy said, 'They're open. We've nobody to look after. What say we have a couple or three?'

They had a couple or three, and then Hilary made a light supper.

After supper, over a whisky, Uncle Teddy said, 'It's been very difficult, you know.'

'I can imagine,' said Hilary.

'Can you? Yes, I suppose you can. You're a novelist,' said Uncle Teddy. 'No, it has been extremely difficult. I haven't been able to let her out of my sight. I've had to do everything for her. I've had to tell her the story of our life every night. *Every* night. I've been a prisoner and a warder. It's almost driven me crazy.'

Even Hilary couldn't find a reply.

'I didn't go to the pub for over two years. I saw mirages of beer in my dreams. I haven't even been able to go for walks. Henry knows how much that's meant. But do you know what I've really longed for? Not a juicy steak in a posh restaurant. Not a well-pulled pint of Adnam's in a low-beamed pub. The sea. That cold old North Sea. Wind in my hair, ozone in my lungs, salt on my lips, gulls mewing in my ears.'

'Well now you can go to the sea any time you like,' said Henry.

'Exactly!' said Uncle Teddy. 'Exactly! And I will. Oh yes. I will.'

He poured Henry another whisky. Hilary declined.

'Cheers,' said Uncle Teddy.

'Cheers,' said Henry.

'Oh God!' said Uncle Teddy. 'I don't care if I never see the bloody sea again. Great big stupid thing sitting there full of salt. Who cares? I just wish she was here now, to tell our life story to.'

19 The End of an Era

It was a really good day at the Café Henry until the phone call came.

Henry had arrived early, as usual. He helped lay out the splendid array of excellent cakes and salads, for which the café was justly famous, and chalked up on the blackboard the three hot dishes of the day – spinach and red-pepper cannelloni, lemon chicken (free-range) and plaice *dieppoise*.

Trade was brisk. There were happy actors on their way to rehearsals, unhappy actors on their way to auditions, the odd writer (one of them very odd), a sex-shop proprietor, a head waiter, some artists, a group of Japanese tourists who took photos of the Henrygraph and giggled, even a yuppie or two.

For which the café was justly famous? Yes, gentle reader, Henry's establishment in Frith Street had become well-known. As he looked round his little kingdom, the marble floor, the attractive wooden tables, the clever use of mirrors, the jumble of notices and slogans which breathed life into the elegance without quite destroying it, as he forced himself to look at all this as if he'd never seen it before, so that he would never for a moment forget how fortunate he was, Henry smiled as he recalled Hilary's initial doubts.

'Will it lose us lots of money?' she'd asked. 'I mean, I'm all for it, but I don't want to lose *lots* of money.'

'It'll make money,' he'd said.

'How can you be so sure?' she'd asked.

'Because I'm not doing it for the money.'

She'd nodded and accepted that, but he knew that she hadn't really been convinced. He might be her lovely Henry, but she couldn't believe that he could also be successful.

And now they were both successful! Hilary's third and fourth novels had been best-sllers, and the first two had been reissued.

There's nothing like a long creative silence for arousing interest in an artist.

There was a congenial group seated at the bar stools that morning. Behind the bar hung three prominent notices: '*You are in a no-privacy area. If you don't wish to talk to your fellow human beings, please sit at a table,*' '*No minimum charge at any time. No maximum charge either!*' and '*If you look miserable you'll be asked to leave unless you have a good reason. The state of the world is not acceptable. That's a reason for having one place where nobody looks miserable.*'

The phone rang, a gentle noise like a happy frog, carefully chosen by Henry to avoid creating tension.

It was a journalist.

'No,' said Henry. 'I don't give interviews. Neither does Hilary about her private life. We've turned down "Relative Values", "How We Met", "A Typical Day", "A Month in the Life of", "My Favourite Childhood Memory", "What We Like About Each Other", "What We Hate About Each Other", "Twenty-Five Things You Didn't Want to Know About Our Sex Lives", *and* "Our Favourite TV Supper" . . . Well, we want people to come here because they've been told about it, not read about it. So sorry.'

He beamed round the bar, and said, 'The press again. How I'm hounded.'

Took photos of the Henrygraph and giggled? What on earth is the Henrygraph? the puzzled reader cries. The Henrygraph is a sculpture, a rather unflattering caricature of our hero, with a large screen where his large stomach should be. It was made by Giuseppe, Camilla's husband, who is a caricaturist. Henry no longer minded being short and podgy, with thin strands of white hair. Adverts, films and magazines poured forth the obscene message that you weren't worth anything unless you were tall, slim and beautiful. The Henrygraph, standing at the back of the café, redressed the balance. Every week Henry held a competition, and the results were shown on the screen. That week in April 1994, the results were 23 per cent John Selwyn Gummer, 17 per cent Cliff Richard, 15 per cent Nancy Reagan, 12 per cent Wet Sileage, 10 per cent Anneka Rice, 9 per cent Dry Sileage, 8 per cent A Pregnant Ferret, 6 per cent Other. Above the Henrygraph there was a notice – Henry loved his notices – which read, *'There are no prizes in our competitions, because a) there are no answers, only results, and b) we don't like greedy bastards.'*

'Have you done the competition?' he asked the group at the bar. 'I rather like this week's.'

That week's competition was, 'Which of the following do you think is "The English Disease"? 1) Hypocrisy 2) Arthritis 3) Self-consciousness 4) Strikes 5) Bronchitis 6) Shyness 7) Snobbery 8) Buggery 9) Neuralgia 10) Nostalgia 11) All ten.'

So that he would never forget for a moment how fortunate he was? It was almost ten years now since Henry had married Hilary for the second time, and they had never had a single argument in all that time. The atmosphere in their large, rambling house over-looking Clapham Common was always cheery and welcoming. Kate was always popping in, Camilla and Giuseppe came when they could, even Jack and Flick had been known to overcome their fear of London and bring little Henry to see his grandparents.

The morning proceeded peacefully. A party of young German trainee undertakers, having a day off from their study of British burial, proved polite, humorous and warm, destroying several preconceptions at a stroke, but also providing an intimation that Henry didn't recognise. They even seemed to understand some of his slogans.

There were slogans everywhere. Sometimes Henry thought that they were pathetic, his feeble attempt to compete with Hilary, but they'd become a tradition and he was the prisoner of that tradition. They included, *'Nothing that cannot stand mockery of itself is to be trusted,' 'Fish don't farm us, so let's not farm fish,' 'Double negatives aren't necessarily unconstructive,' 'Everyone has a role in life. Mine is to show that it isn't important to be good-looking,' 'I've just taken my sex test. Failed the written, passed the oral,' 'Everything goes in cycles. One day it won't be politically correct to be politically correct,'* and *'I have no doubt that the really frightening people in this world are those who have no doubt.'*

Does anything smell better than really good coffee? Could anything taste better at eleven o'clock than a slice of lemon cake, as light as a feather and pleasantly sharp? How delightful it is, if one is on one's own, to read the leading British and world newspapers in peace, with nobody hurrying you.

So why was the man at the corner table looking so miserable? Under the rules of the establishment, Henry was forced to approach him.

'Excuse me?' he said. 'I don't want to be rude, but I have to say that you're as miserable-looking a man as I've clapped eyes on in many a month of wet Sundays. I'm afraid I'll have to ask you to leave, unless you can provide an adequate reason.'

'I'm the only writer of detective fiction in the whole country who hasn't got a series on television,' said the miserable-looking man miserably.

'Best excuse so far this week,' said Henry. 'Have a glass of wine on the house.'

The gentle frog croaked pleasantly. Henry answered it happily.

'A Mrs Langridge has rung from Thurmarsh,' said Hilary. 'Bad news, I'm afraid. Cousin Hilda is sinking fast.'

On Thursday, April 14th, 1994, two American F.15 fighters shot down two United Nations helicopters over Iraq, killing twenty-six allied officers. There was a furious row in the House of Commons over allegations that NHS hospitals were refusing treatment to people because they were too old, the Bosnian Serbs drew close to a full-scale confrontation with Nato and the United Nations, and Hilary, travelling with Henry from St Pancras to Thurmarsh, said how glad she was that her Croatian mother hadn't lived to see the terrible destruction of her beloved Yugoslavia.

How Henry hoped that Cousin Hilda would live to see him that evening. He loved her. He hadn't seen her for several weeks. She was the last of her generation. He was going to feel very exposed. It was the end of an era. Each time the train slowed down he grew anxious. His legs became exhausted as they pushed forward to will the train on faster.

The last of her generation? Oh yes. Uncle Teddy had died almost two years ago. But don't be sad, gentle reader. He died a perfect death. He simply didn't wake up one morning. He'd come to live with them in 1989, a fortnight after they'd bought the five-bedroomed house overlooking Clapham Common. Gradually he'd learnt to live again, to sniff the ozone, to tell old codgers in pubs about his exotic past. Once a week he'd come with Henry to the Café Henry, 'had a fruitcake among the fruitcakes', as he'd put it, wandered the dirty streets of Soho, visited several pubs, glanced at the photographs of the strippers outside the sleazy clubs and sighed more for the human race than for himself, and slept noisily in the car home after his raffish afternoon. They'd been astounded to find that he was eighty-seven, and he'd died before he lost his faculties. Happy Uncle Teddy, not to wake up one morning. Sad Henry, to whom he hadn't said goodbye.

Henry hoped that Cousin Hilda wouldn't go without saying goodbye. Oh hurry up, lazy train.

They'd invited Cousin Hilda to live with them too. They'd taken her to the Post House for dinner in the restaurant where Henry had been a waiter. 'Oh no,' she'd said. 'I couldn't. I couldn't live in London. I just don't see the sense of its being so huge. No, it may be all right for the *hoi polloi*, but I'm the common herd.' When Henry'd pointed out that *hoi polloi* meant the common herd, Cousin Hilda said, 'Well there you are. That settles it. That's what I'd get in London. Ridicule.' She'd come close to panic, as if they were forcing her to go. 'I don't want to go. I want to die in my own bed,' she'd said. And then, as if suddenly realising that she was being ungracious, she'd said, 'Not that I'm not grateful for being asked. And for the meal. It were quite palatable, to say it were so messed about.'

And now she was getting her wish. She was dying in her own bed at the age of eighty-eight. Oh hurry, hurry, indolent train.

Everything on the train irritated Henry as it nosed past Kettering and Wellingborough and Leicester.

Middle-aged men with mobile phones irritated him. 'Everything all right in the office, Carol? . . . Good. Sent that stuff off to Mr

Harkness, have you? . . . Good.' Unnecessary messages, given so that all the coach knew that they had mobile phones, when everybody knew that the truly powerful didn't need mobile phones because the world waited on them.

Young people with Walkmans irritated him. They played them just loud enough for the underlying beat, if you could call it by so musical a word, to come crashing out in its endless monotony without any of the colour and detail that might have made it worth hearing.

The smoke from the cooling towers irritated him. Some people must be having to live under perpetual cloud in this brave land of ours.

The smell of hot bacon and tomato rolls and chicken tikka sandwiches irritated him. This nation of animal lovers was awash with chicken tikka, all made from chickens kept in disgusting conditions. He got out his slogan notebook, and wrote another slogan for the café. *'We can't call ourselves a nation of animal lovers until all battery farming is outlawed.'*

The endless messages from the senior conductor irritated him. 'Customers are reminded, on leaving the train, to take all your personal possessions with you.' Yes, and why don't you tell us to try walking by putting one foot in front of the other? Not his fault, of course, poor bastard. Instructions from on high. It irritated him that it had taken an interview with Tony Benn MP to reveal to him why passengers were now called 'customers'. It was to get home yet again the message that if you haven't any money, you don't count.

Money, money, money, said the wheels of the train, and they said it with such a loud and increasing clank that at Derby engineers had to examine the train. 'Welcome to customers boarding the train at Derby. This is your late-running 7.07 service to Chester-field, Sheffield, Rotherham, Thurmarsh, Wakefield and Leeds. We apologise for the delay. This is due to technical problems with a carriage.'

Oh, please, engineers, please mend the carriage quickly. Cousin Hilda is dying.

Off they clanked again, money, money, money, not noticeably

less noisily. Hilary slid her right hand into his left hand and entwined her long fingers round his chubby ones.

'Relax,' she said. 'You can do nothing about it.'

He kissed her lovely mouth, felt for her lovely tongue, drew his tongue across her lovely teeth, and relaxed. Dusk lent enchantment to the rich countryside north of Derby and drew a tactful veil over the derelict areas where once the drama of the great steelworks had lit the skies. Now the genteel tracery of the lights around the Meadowhall Centre, an ocean cruiser going nowhere, were the only bright spot in the gathering sodium gloom.

At last the train was jerking towards its ignoble halt at Thurmarsh. It was thirty-seven minutes late. A fine drizzle was falling. You will be proud to learn, gentle reader, that Henry 'Your Obedient Customer' Pratt and his lovely wife Hilary remembered to take all their personal possessions with them *and*, for their own safety as well as that of other customers, did not open the door until the train had come to a complete stand.

There weren't any taxis. There never are when you need them, except in films.

At last a taxi came. Past the gleaming Holiday Inn, which had once been the Midland Hotel, they went. Oh, why had they got such a polite driver? He stopped at a pedestrian crossing for a teenage girl, who pouted slowly across the road. Please, please, hurry.

They met two sets of roadworks. The fabric of Britain's roads was crumbling under the weight of ever bigger lorries and increasing car ownership. One day, the whole nation would grind to a halt.

At last the taxi crunched gently to a stop outside 66, Park View Road. The house looked dark and gloomy, as if its owner was already dead.

Mrs Langridge opened the door before they'd even knocked, a bent little woman with bow legs and a floral headscarf.

'She's been asking for you,' she said.

Relief took all the strength from Henry's legs. Hilary took his arm and supported him.

They sped through the dark hall. 'Wet and windy,' threatened the barometer. As they descended the narrow stairs to the basement where Henry had so often been wet and windy, Mrs Langridge stopped, turned to them, and whispered, 'The doctor wanted her moved to hospital. She were adamant. Adamant. "I want to die in my own bed, doctor." She could be right adamant when she wanted, but I've never seen her as adamant as that. "Will she get better if she goes to hospital, doctor?" I asked. "No," he said. "She's had enough. Her body's had enough." "Then leave her here, doctor," I said. I hope I did right.'

'You did absolutely right, Mrs Langridge,' whispered Henry.

Cousin Hilda was lying in bed, breathing heavily. She opened her eyes when they entered and gave them a faint smile, the sort of smile you might have attributed to wind if a baby had given it.

'Hello, Henry. Hello, Hilary. Well, this is a rum do,' she said in a weak voice.

They both kissed her on the cheek. Her cheek was very cold.

'You're doing fine,' said Henry. 'You'll be up and about in a few days.'

Cousin Hilda sniffed.

'I suppose it's habit,' she said.

'What is?' said Henry.

'Lying,' said Cousin Hilda. 'You've told me so many. Drinking, girls, Miles Cricklewood, liking spotted dick. Lies.'

'I do like spotted dick.'

'There's no point in lying now,' said Cousin Hilda. 'Does he like spotted dick, Hilary?'

'Not very much,' said Hilary. 'And we're so glad we got here in time.'

They sat very close to Cousin Hilda, in two hard chairs. Her breathing was laboured and her voice was faint. They leant forward.

'I want Mrs Langridge to have my barometer,' said Cousin Hilda. 'Mrs Wedderburn herself couldn't have done more.'

'That's quite a tribute,' said Henry. 'She shall have it.'

Cousin Hilda closed her eyes and for a moment they thought that she had gone. Then she opened them wide.

'I'd like my bloomers to go to Bosnia,' she said. 'Not that I usually believe in helping foreigners till we've helped our own. But what man has done to man in that benighted land is unbelievable. And it snows a lot.'

'Your bloomers will be sent to Bosnia, post-haste,' promised Henry.

'Hilary?' said Cousin Hilda. 'Henry lies, so I'm asking you. Are you both happy?'

'Very happy,' said Hilary. 'Very happy indeed.'

Cousin Hilda put one thin, veined, wizened hand on Hilary's hand and the other on Henry's, and tried to squeeze, but she had no power left.

'Then I shall die happy,' she said. 'So don't be sad about my dying. Hilary won't be, she's sensible, but you, Henry, don't grieve. I've lived long enough, and it isn't the end of the world, isn't dying.' She paused, breathing heavily, exhausted. 'I'll be joining Mrs Wedderburn in a better place. She always had a soft spot for you, did Mrs Wedderburn. I could list the number of people she'd have lent her camp-bed to on the fingers of one hand.'

She closed her eyes again. Again they wondered if she had gone, but she was merely getting her strength back after her long speech.

Suddenly her eyes were quite bright and she gave a curious little smile.

'And if I'm wrong, and if there is no heaven, I'll never know owt about it, will I?' she said.

She closed her eyes. They looked at each other. This time they were certain that she had gone.

But then her eyes opened and she looked straight at Hilary, who had always been her favourite, perhaps even more than Mrs Wedderburn.

'Hilary?' she said. 'I never gave myself to a man. Did I miss the best thing in life? Or was I lucky?'

Cousin Hilda closed her eyes again, and Hilary thought long and hard about her answer. She needn't have worried. This time, Cousin Hilda's eyes did not reopen.

Next day, Hilary aired and cleaned the house, and Henry began to sort out what it would be an exaggeration to call Cousin Hilda's estate.

In the evening, they went to the Lord Nelson and met Henry's old journalist colleagues for what might well be the last time.

The Lord Nelson had been knocked into one big bar and managed, somehow, to be both garish and gloomy. It no longer felt like a cosy watering hole.

Colin Edgeley, aged sixty-two, was white-haired and retired, living in his little house with Glenda and not knowing what to do with the rest of his life. He reminded Henry of a fine old cart-horse that has pulled the brewery dray with pride and is now in a home for elderly horses.

Ginny Fenwick, aged sixty-three, was soldiering on. She'd sought to become a Kate Adie, but had found only local battlefields on which to report.

Helen Plunkett, aged sixty, who had dreamt more of becoming a Lynda Lee-Potter, had also found her star shining only over a very small pond. Ted, aged sixty-five, was almost entirely bald now, and working on the subs' desk. He would retire in September. Helen remained glamorous, if lined. Ted had become the oldest swinger in town, and rumour had it that they were still trying to persuade people to 'have a bit of fun'.

Seventy-eight-year-old Ben Watkinson had left Cynthia for a retired florist who had represented Lancashire at hockey and lacrosse, and who knew the answers to some obscure sporting questions. He still toddled down to the pub on the occasional Friday night.

'Have we another glittering novel ready for our delectation, Hilary?' Ted asked.

'Careful, Ted, your jealousy's showing,' said Helen, thus ensuring that Ted's spleen was vented on her for the rest of what turned out to be a very short evening.

Colin punched Henry vigorously on the arm and said, 'Great to see you again, kid. What times we had, eh?'

But nobody took him up on his invitation to nostalgia. The

events they were invited to recall had happened too long ago. Time is a great healer, but also a great destroyer. Nobody took up Ben's challenge either. Perhaps naming the runners up in the last thirty years of the Currie Cup cricket tournament in South Africa was just too difficult, or perhaps they were just growing old.

The pub began to fill up with noisy young people who drank their beer from the bottle. The jukebox played loudly. But it was still a surprise when Ted said, 'Well, we ought to be pushing on. Must get to Sainsbury's before they close.' Helen said, 'I thought we were all going to have something to eat,' and Ted said very firmly, 'You know we always do the weekend shopping on a Friday night, Helen,' and Helen sighed and said, 'So exciting, my husband. Shopping Friday night, swapping Saturday night, yawn yawn,' and Colin said, 'Well, I must be off soon too. Glenda comes first now. We all grow up, don't we?' Quite soon Ben said, 'Well, it's time to go home and give the mistress one,' and Henry and Hilda were left alone with Ginny. Henry said, 'You'll come and eat with us, won't you, anyway, Ginny?' and she said, 'Honestly, no, it's very kind of you, but I get very tired by the end of the week nowadays,' and Henry and Hilary went to the Yang Sing, and Henry sighed, and Hilary said, 'Depressed?' and Henry said, 'A bit,' and Hilary said, 'They're almost old now, and I suppose that brought home to us that we are too,' and Henry said, 'I don't mind too much about that. I'm going to enjoy being old. It's just that our little group on the paper seemed like real friends, but it was more habit than true affection,' and Hilary said, 'It's because I was there tonight, not only an outsider but a successful outsider. You should have gone on your own,' and Henry said, 'I didn't want to. I love you,' and Hilary said, 'I'm glad you do, but you must learn to expect a reduction in warmth from the rest of the world because you do,' and Henry said, 'No! I don't and I won't,' so fervently that several people looked round.

On the Saturday night they went to the Taj Mahal with Martin and Mandy Hammond. Count Your Blessings had gone home to India. One or two people whispered, 'That's our MP.' Martin, uncharacteristically, tore into pints of lager and became maudlin.

'I've discovered something terrible about myself,' he confessed over the kulfi. 'I think I have perverted tastes.'

He had his audience on the edge of their seats in a way that he hadn't managed on the three greatest opportunities of his not-so-glittering career in Parliament – his one appearance on *Question Time* and his two phoned interviews with Jimmy Young.

Henry realised that Mandy didn't know what was coming next, and he felt the hairs on the back of his neck standing on end.

'I'm speaking of political tastes,' said Martin.

Was it Henry's fancy, or was there a touch of disppointment mingled with the relief on Mandy's face?

'I've become addicted to opposition,' said Martin Hammond. 'I've enjoyed fifteen years of Tory cock-ups. I've relished every moment. I'm not sure if I want power any more. It'd be so much more difficult.'

Mandy shook her head sadly. You aren't the man I thought you were, her weary gesture said.

The hearse was waiting in the street, the funeral limousine sat behind it, and still none of the family had arrived. For an awful moment Henry feared that they'd all let him down on this important day.

Then Giuseppe's red Lamborghini slid into the drive. Giuseppe pulled up with an Italian flourish, stepped out of the car, beamed at Henry and Hilary, suddenly remembered that it was a sad occasion and looked comically grave.

He hurried round to the passenger door and held it open for Camilla. Dressed in black, seven months pregnant, and given a dignified self-possession by the success of the exhibition of her drawings of horses and by the happiness of her marriage, Camilla at thirty-five was almost unrecognisable as the gawky schoolgirl who had once resented Henry. She kissed him warmly and said, quietly, 'Nothing?'

'Nothing.'

She grimaced. Her first words with Henry were always about Benedict.

Kate's rusting white Renault stuttered towards them next, and pulled up behind Giuseppe's car.

'You made it,' said Henry gratefully.

'I decided my assistant could manage. It'll do him good,' said Kate, who was in the throes of directing *The Caretaker* for the new Lewis Casson Theatre in Milton Keynes. 'I had to see Cousin Hilda off.'

She was wearing red.

At the last moment, as usual, Jack drove up in his blue BMW. If his reputation as a builder was anything to go by, he'd probably promised to be at four cremations at the same time. His ruddy outdoor face and heavy body didn't go with the tight, old-fashioned striped suit that he wore only at funerals. Flick had plumped for navy, also too tight. She'd not got back to her old, never-inconsiderable, weight after the pregnancy.

'I've left Henry with Mum,' she said.

Henry had been flattered that Jack and Flick had called their son Henry, but had been slightly mortified that the first-born of the cheerful burly builder and his cheerful burly earth-mother wife was a pallid little lad with eczema, asthma, a weak digestion and a low pain threshold. 'He'll grow out of it all,' everybody had said. He hadn't yet, but then he was only six years old.

Henry, Hilary, Camilla and Kate went in the hired limousine. Jack and Giuseppe followed in the BMW and behind them came Mr and Mrs Langridge in their Metro.

Mrs Langridge had called, the day after Cousin Hilda's death, with an offer of help and an embarrassed expression. 'We'll just come to the cremation and then leave the family to it,' she'd said. 'It'll suit us. Len's very shy with strangers.' Henry hadn't attempted to persuade her to change her mind, and had booked a quiet family lunch at the Post House.

As they slid smoothly up the drive to the crematorium, between banks of rhododendrons and hydrangeas, they passed an elderly man wearing a trilby, with a stick, who was standing to regain his breath.

The mourners from the previous cremation were still pouring

out. There must have been more than a hundred of them. Henry wished there could have been more to see Cousin Hilda off. It wasn't much to show for a long life.

They got out of the cars and stretched their legs in the lamb-numbing April easterly.

The elderly man approached them slowly. He was wearing a smart green overcoat. The creases in his trousers were razor sharp. His shoes shone.

'Don't you recognise me, Henry?' he said.

'Norman Pettifer!' said Henry.

Norman Pettifer smiled shyly.

'Couldn't let the old girl go with none of her gentlemen here,' he said. 'Most of the others are dead.'

'It's wonderful of you to come,' said Henry. 'And good to see you. I didn't even realise you were . . .' He stopped, embarrassed.

'Still alive?' Norman Pettifer finished his sentence for him. 'Oh yes. Just. I'm living in the Yorkshire Retired Grocers' Benevolent Home.'

So there were just ten mourners in the over-polished crematorium chapel, to see Cousin Hilda move sedately to her last resting place.

Afterwards, they stood around, feeling sad and inadequate. Quite soon, the Langridges took their leave. Shy Len Langridge blushed at the warmth of Henry's praise of his wife.

Henry didn't know what to do about Norman Pettifer.

'I'm so glad you could come, Norman,' he said. 'We're having a little family lunch party at the Post House. We'd be very pleased if you joined us.'

'Oh no,' said Norman Pettifer. 'No, no. It's a family do, fair play. I wouldn't intrude. No, no. I were glad to pay my last respects. That's enough.' He turned to smile at them all. 'She were a fine landlady, of the old school. I ate three hundred and eighty-two portions of her toad-in-the-hole. Three hundred and eighty-one portions of her spotted dick. That sort of thing makes folk close.'

A combination of shyness, respect for privacy, lack of interest and sheer awe at these monumental statistics prevented any of the

English mourners from raising the question. Giuseppe, being Italian, had no such scruples.

'Why one less spotted dick than toad-in-the-hole?' he asked.

Norman Pettifer blushed.

'One Tuesday I went to dinner with my ex-lover,' he said.

They all hid their astonishment politely, and again it was Giuseppe who asked the question that was in all their minds.

'Only once?' he said gently. 'Was it not a success?'

'You should never try to relive the past,' said Norman Pettifer.

Henry and Hilary gave Norman Pettifer a lift home. On the way, he said, 'We get our last meal at five thirty. It makes for a long evening. There's always the telly. We play chess and cards, those of us who still have our marbles. We talk. We discuss the changing face of grocery. Supermarkets at all four corners of the town. Shopping for motorists when we're supposed to be fighting pollution. The huge Fish Hill development sucking the lifeblood out of the town. Boarded up shops in all the old streets. Banks and building societies and charity shops and second-hand shops everywhere. Old folk with no neighbourhood shops, long bus journeys and then no small portions of everything and having to queue at check-outs, where once we delivered groceries to their door. There's not one of us that isn't glad to be in a home, the way grocery's going.'

He was silent after that, until Henry had pulled up outside the old Regency mansion that housed the Retired Grocers' Benevolent Home. After he'd got out of the car he turned and said, 'One funeral I'd have given my eye-teeth to be at was old Ralphie Richardson's. Thank you for the lift.'

After their funeral lunch, the family went their several ways.

As she kissed Henry goodbye, Camilla said, 'Mummy's really happy with Gunter, and you're really happy with Hilary, and you're both pleased the other's happy, and I love you both, and Giuseppe and I are really happy. If only . . . ' She stopped. She could no longer bring herself to mention Benedict by name.

As she kissed Henry goodbye, Kate said, 'You will come to the

369

play, won't you?' and Henry said, 'Of course. We love your work. You're good, but then you know that.' 'Yes, I do, actually, isn't that awful?' said Kate. 'No,' said Henry. 'You're entitled to enjoy the fact. You've given up a lot for it.' 'Given up a lot? Given up what?' said Kate. 'Marriage, children,' said Henry. 'And sex,' said Kate. 'Really? Oh dear,' said Henry. 'How hopelessly old-fashioned you are, Dad,' said Kate.

As he gave Henry an embarrassed bear-hug, because kissing fathers wasn't possible in Thurmarsh, Jack said, 'Come up again soon,' and Henry said, 'You come to London,' and Jack said, 'Oh no. Not again. I hate it.' Flick said, 'Let's take a cottage by the sea for a fortnight. That's what Jack would really like,' and Henry and Hilary agreed, and Flick said, 'I didn't say anything, because I'm not absolutely sure, but I'm almost certain I'm pregnant again at last,' and Henry said, 'That's the second time you've given us good news after a cremation,' and Flick said, 'Sorry,' and Henry said, 'No, it's as it should be. Life goes on.'

That night, in Cousin Hilda's house, Henry said, 'We've all the time in the world to make love here now. Poor old Cousin Hilda won't be coming back with any more shopping,' and Hilary said, 'I'd really rather not. Not here. Not tonight. It'd seem like taking advantage. It'd seem disrespectful. I didn't think I believed in life after death, but I get the feeling that she'd know.'

In the morning, Hilary set off for London and her unfinished novel, while Henry stayed behind to deal with lawyers and estate agents. As the London train groaned wearily out of Thurmarsh (Midland Road) Station, Hilary leant out and yelled, 'If I'd married Nigel I'd have been known as Hilary Clinton.'

They exchanged deeply fond grins, they waved, the train rounded a bend, Hilary was gone, and Henry shivered.

All day, as he tied knots on the parcel of Cousin Hilda's life, Henry felt uneasy.

That evening he neglected Norman Pettifer's advice. He tried to relive the past. He went back, to Paradise Lane, to the little back-to-back terraces where he'd been born. The house wasn't there any more. The streets weren't there any more. Paradise Lane,

Back Paradise Lane, Paradise Hill, Back Paradise Hill, Paradise Court, Back Paradise Court. All gone. Boxy little houses with horrible brown window surrounds were rising in their place, and in the far distance there were tower blocks, back-to-back terraces turned on their end, with all the inconveniences and none of the neighbourliness.

At first he felt wry. Bang goes my chance of a blue plaque, saying, 'Henry Pratt, founder of the Café Henry, was born here.'

The great steelworks of Crapp, Hawser and Kettlewell had gone too. In its place were huge, ugly, prefabricated stores – Texas, Homebase, Do-It-All.

Henry would never be banned from the Navigation Inn again. There was no Navigation Inn to be banned from.

Anger began to replace wryness.

Between the Rundle and the Rundle and Gadd Navigation, on the waste ground where the Paradise Lane Gang had played and fought, there was a gleaming new brick building, an old warehouse in modern dress. A huge sign announced, in ironically antique lettering, 'Rundle Heritage Centre'.

Henry walked slowly over to it, across the hump-backed canal bridge, now dwarfed. Two brightly painted old working boats were tied up against the Heritage Centre.

The Heritage Centre had closed for the day. Henry looked through the ground floor windows and saw . . . a reconstruction of the Navigation Inn – gleaming, glistening, dead.

His fury took hold of him. He banged on the window and shouted, 'What about my heritage, you bastards? You've taken it all away.'

The east wind snatched his words and sent them floating towards the Pennines, to the mystification of those passing curlews and plovers that had avoided being shot on their journey across Europe.

Henry walked slowly up the hill, past Brunswick Road School, through the almost deserted town centre. Paper bags soared like gulls, plastic bottles bounced across roads, tins lurked among the beautiful daffodils that the council had planted all around the town. On trees not yet quite in leaf, in the Alderman Chandler Memorial Park, black refuse bags shuddered like skewered rooks.

Suddenly Henry felt a dreadful premonition. Town planners and developers had taken his past. Something equally dreadful would take away his future. He knew now why he had shivered at the station. He had a sudden certainty that 'If I'd married Nigel, I'd have been known as Hilary Clinton' would be the last words he ever heard from his darling Hilary. It seemed entirely appropriate to his life that his marriage should end in a meaningless remark about the soon-to-be-forgotten wife of a soon-to-be-forgotten American president.

The next day, after a sleepless night and a morning spent tying up loose ends, he hurried to the station as if his life depended on it.

As the train pulled out, he looked at his home town for the last time – the backs of grimy houses, the unlovely tower blocks, the waste ground that had once been marshalling yards, the trim outer suburbs, a used car dump, a sad farm, and the golf courses, where people took refuge from the breakdown of law and order. Soon it would be possible to play golf from Lands End to John o' Groats, and somebody, probably Ian Botham, would.

As they approached London, the knot in his stomach tightened. He was almost paralysed with fear.

He gathered his belongings together slowly, and left the train reluctantly. Above him, the huge majesty of St Pancras station was shrouded in scaffolding.

He walked slowly along the platform, trying to calm himself, and entered a tunnel that led down to the underground station. He didn't know why he was entering the tunnel, but he knew that he must.

A tattered figure was walking towards him. He saw a flicker of recognition in the tramp's bloodshot eyes, and a gleam of anger. Henry's blood ran cold even before he saw the knife.

Benedict advanced on him with the knife held high. Henry grabbed his arm and tried to bend the wrist to release the knife, but Benedict was astonishingly strong considering his unkempt, emaciated condition.

Henry missed his footing, fell against the wall of the tunnel, and crashed to the ground on his back. Benedict loomed over him and raised the knife. Henry wondered where the rescuing crowds were, but there was nobody there at all. Maybe they'd all melted away in fear. He'd read about that being a common occurrence in 1990s Britain.

It is said that at the moment of death one's whole life flashes before one. Luckily for you, horrified reader, since you've been right through his life already, this did not happen to Henry. Instead, images of the future that was being snatched from him flashed through his mind – English spring mornings, Hilary bent over her latest book, gentle mornings at the Café Henry, Hilary kissing him, grandchildren playing happily.

Suddenly he felt no fear of dying. His last wry thought, as Benedict made to lunge at him, gripping the knife fiercely in both hands, was that at least he was being killed by a member of the privileged classes, whose rich father had sent him to public school. He might not have led a good humanist's life, but he was achieving a politically correct death.

He stared bravely at Benedict, showing no sign of pleading for mercy. Benedict raised the knife above his head, gave a wild cry of despairing aggression, and lunged forward as he began to bring the knife down. Suddenly he slipped sideways, overbalanced and crashed into the side of the tunnel. The knife slid from his grasp.

Henry was up in a flash, and he grabbed and pocketed the knife before Benedict could get up.

But Benedict didn't get up. He lay concussed, glassy-eyed, his brief mad strength gone. Henry, who had once dreamt of a career as a stand-up comedian called Henry 'Ee by gum I am daft' Pratt, had been saved by a joke even older than the ones he had made at school. At the crucial moment, Benedict had slipped on a banana skin.

I should have remembered that my premonitions are always unfounded, thought Henry.

He took a photocopy of a recipe for sea bass on a bed of green lentils out of his wallet, crossed through the recipe, and wrote

'PTO' in large letters. On the back he wrote his home address and phone number and the message, 'There'll always be a place for you at our table, son.'

He kissed Benedict's filthy forehead. The glassy eyes blinked.

Henry felt an overwhelming urge to get away, but he couldn't just abandon Benedict. He went back into the station concourse, and told a member of the transport police about the tramp lying in the subway. He asked for a contact number, so that he could find out what happened to the tramp. The transport policeman gave him an odd look, and the number.

Henry waited until he was sure that Benedict was being seen to, and then he hurried off into the late spring sunshine of a London afternoon. He felt a deep joy that was probably entirely selfish, because Benedict was still in terrible trouble and there was no knowing whether he could be saved.

When he got back to the café, Henry would stick another motto on the crowded walls. *'Until you are no longer frightened of dying, you cannot enjoy life.'*

He would enjoy life. Maybe he would remain content to dispense happiness in his café. Maybe even at fifty-nine he would find some useful role in the battle to save radical and humane ideas from the humourless arrogance of political correctness.

As Henry walked along Marchmont Street, he saw a man carrying an ice-cream cornet mount his bicycle, and set off, holding the handlebars with one hand. The bicycle wobbled, the man grabbed the handlebars with his other hand, and all the pistachio ice-cream fell out of the cone onto the road. He gave Henry a rueful smile and said, quite cheerfully, 'Worse things happen at sea.'

Thank you, unknown cyclist, thought Henry. I shall always console myself with that. I shall become Henry 'Worse Things Happen at Sea' Pratt.

He turned right into Tavistock Place, and set off, in tranquillity at last, in maturity at last, to relish the astonishing richness of everyday life.

A List of David Nobbs Titles Available from Mandarin

☐	7493 0379 4	**The Fall and Rise of Reginald Perrin**	£4.99
☐	7493 0469 3	**The Return of Reginald Perrin**	£4.99
☐	7493 0468 5	**The Better World of Reginald Perrin**	£4.99
☐	7493 1015 4	**A Bit of a Do**	£4.99
☐	7493 0966 0	**Fair Do's**	£3.99
☐	7493 0097 3	**Second From Last in the Sack Race**	£4.99
☐	7493 0020 5	**Pratt of the Argus**	£4.99
☐	7493 2267 5	**The Cucumber Man**	£4.99